Jacqui Rose is a novelist who hails from South Yorkshire. She first came to appreciate the power of the written word when as a child she charged her classmates a packet of sherbet dips to write their essays for them. Adopted at a young age and always a daydreamer, she felt isolated growing up in a small mining village and it was her writing which kept her company. Jacqui has always written for pleasure, whether it be screenplays or stand-up, and she is the author of eight bestselling novels as well as the author of two political thrillers written under a male pseudonym. She is a keen equestrian and the owner of two horses and spends most days riding.

Also by Jacqui Rose

Poison
Jacqui Rose

Published by AVON
A division of HarperCollins*Publishers* Ltd
1 London Bridge Street
London SE1 9GF

www.harpercollins.co.uk

HarperCollins*Publishers*
1st Floor, Watermarque Building, Ringsend Road
Dublin 4, Ireland

A Paperback Original 2020
4

First published in Great Britain by HarperCollins*Publishers* 2020

A catalogue copy of this book is available from the British Library.

ISBN: 978-0-00-836696-4

Typeset in Minion Pro by
Palimpsest Book Production Limited, Falkirk, Stirlingshire
Printed and bound in UK by CPI Group (UK) Ltd, Croydon CR0 4YY

MIX
Paper from
responsible sources
FSC™ C007454

To my Family.

'It is easier to forgive an enemy than to forgive a friend.'

William Blake

1

Alfie Jennings opened his eyes and groaned. His head was pounding and his mouth was dry, which he thought was pretty ironic considering how much he'd drunk at the club. Though in truth, he'd lost count after he'd knocked back the tenth double whiskey.

Not that he cared. He was done with caring. The only place caring had ever got him was up shit creek, which was exactly where he was now. Swimming in it, sinking in it and certainly wallowing in it . . . *Fuck.*

Rubbing his temples in annoyance, Alfie sighed and turned his head slowly to the side. Next to him, with her head on the pillow, sleeping soundly and letting out the tiniest of snores, was the brass he'd picked up sometime between entering the club and leaving it.

Though for the life of him he couldn't remember bringing her back to the flat in Soho. In fact, apart from the argument he'd had with Vaughn Sadler, one of his closest friends, he couldn't remember much, which was exactly what he'd wanted. His motto now was going to be: drink, fuck and forget.

Irritated, he yawned and roughly pushed the naked woman's leg off him. Then, growling and wincing at the loudness of his own voice, he snapped, 'Oi! Sleepin'-fucking-beauty, wake the frig up, will ya? I want you out of here, *pronto*. This ain't no bed and breakfast.'

The prostitute, who Alfie thought looked no older than twenty-five, stretched and broke wind at the same time. She pushed back her dyed, dried blonde hair and pouted sulkily.

'Well if I'm sleeping beauty, that would make you the prince, and I'm damn sure you ain't supposed to wake me up like that. That's not how the story went, mate.'

Alfie sat up. He picked up his boxers from the floor and pulled them on. His blue eyes darkened as he stared at her. 'No, darlin', that's exactly how it went. I just reckon you must've missed that line, like the other line you missed. The one that said . . . get your fucking clothes on and get the fuck out of here before I throw you out and then we can all live happily ever after.'

Before the woman had a chance to reply there was a loud banging on the front door, followed by a man's voice calling Alfie's name. It was Vaughn.

'*Open up, mate. Come on, I ain't playing with you. We need to talk. You were well out of order last night. I know things have been fucked up lately but you got to sort your shit out.*'

Alfie slumped on the bed, lighting up a cigarette. He inhaled the smoke deeply and ran his hand through his thick black hair. The last thing he wanted to do was speak to Vaughn. His head was pounding and he didn't need the grief.

'Alf, I know you're in there, so do yourself a favour and open up . . . Alf! Alf! Come on, I ain't got all day . . . Fine. If that's the way you're going to be.'

The next moment Alfie heard a louder banging and then a crash as Vaughn booted open the door, swiftly and easily.

Alfie stood up quickly but the minute he had done he regretted it as a sharp pain rushed through his head. 'Why the fuck did you do that? I'll have to get that repaired now.'

Standing in the doorway, Vaughn Sadler shrugged, a smile on his handsome face. 'What am I supposed to do if you won't answer?'

'What most people do, go the fuck away . . .?'

'As much as you'd like that, it ain't going to happen. So how about you make us both a nice cup of Rosie Lee and whilst you're doing that, you could work on making your face look less like a slapped arse.'

Incensed but too hungover to show it, Alfie snarled, 'If you've just come to take the piss, do yourself a favour and turn back round. I don't need this.'

Vaughn looked at Alfie, seeing the stress lines etched into his face. He was worried about him. Really worried. He'd seen Alfie spiral before, but this was different. It was clear Alfie had given up caring about everything and anything. He was on a path of self-destruction, which seemed to be lined with drugs, drink and women.

Letting out a sigh, Vaughn glanced at the hooker who was busily getting dressed in a pair of pink flimsy hot pants and a gold crop top, which barely hid her ginormous fake breasts. He nodded to her in recognition.

She was one of the women who worked in the club that he and his friend Johnny Taylor owned and ran.

Knowing that Alfie had been in a bad way last night and after the row they'd had about Alf taking it easy with how much coke he was shoving up his nose, he'd ended up paying her to keep an eye on Alfie, and not to let him out of her sight. And if that meant her sleeping with him, so be it. She could do worse than go to bed with Alfie, though, looking at him now, he was hardly anybody's Prince Charming.

'None of us need this,' Vaughn said, by way of response to Alfie's sarcastic comment. 'And by the way, you look like shit, Alf.'

Not wanting to make any sudden movements, Alfie stepped in closer to Vaughn. He was hit by the smell of Vaughn's expensive aftershave. Then without warning, he promptly vomited all over the black silk shirt Vaughn was wearing.

Like an electric shock, Vaughn jumped backwards, fighting against the urge to vomit too. He grabbed the nearest thing next to him – which happened to be a cushion – and began to wipe the vomit off with it as he marched into the en-suite bathroom to get a towel, calling back over his shoulder as he went, 'Jesus Christ, Alf, what's wrong with you? You're like a fucking animal. I don't know why I bo—'

4

'Vaughn? Sorry I was so long – I had to change her nappy again.' A teenage girl with bright red hair and bright green eyes appeared in the doorway carrying a baby. She grinned an almost toothless smile. 'I don't think I'll ever get used to changing them things. I thought weaning meself off crack was difficult, but facing Mia's nappies is something else.' She giggled, stretching out her arms to give the baby to Alfie. 'Here you go, sweetie, go to Daddy. He looks like he could do with a cuddle from you.'

Alfie's eyes flashed with anger as Shannon Mulligan held the baby in mid-air. He backed away, pushing himself against the wall, knocking an expensive glass vase off the silver shelf.

As Vaughn came back into the room, Alfie spoke, his voice almost inaudible. 'I don't want to see her. Get her out of here. Get her out!'

Not knowing what to do, Shannon glanced at Vaughn then stepped nearer to Alfie. She spoke firmly. 'She's your baby. She needs to see her daddy.'

Alfie's bellow echoed through the flat, giving Mia a fright and causing her to scream loudly.

'I said get her out of here! Fucking get her out of here *now*!'

With the prostitute watching with interest, Vaughn's face hardened, then he gently took Mia from Shannon and rocked her before placing her on the thick, cream carpet, which matched the matt cream walls. Not unkindly, he said, 'She's your daughter, Alf, and I reckon it's time you and her did some bonding. We'll be back to pick her up in a couple of hours.' He turned to Shannon, taking the nappy bag off her shoulder as he continued to talk. 'It's got everything you need in there: her milk, her dummy, her nappies, her cuddly toy. You'll be fine.'

'I don't know why you're doing this, Vaughn, but in case it escaped your notice, I ain't Mary fucking Poppins. So you need to take her.'

'Sorry Alf, no can do. You might surprise yourself – the other night I found myself singing "Twinkle, Twinkle, Little Star". Though in fairness it does get a bit repetitive, but who'd have fucking thought it, eh? Point is, you've got to make an effort – she's your kid.'

Alfie licked his lips, trying to get some salvia onto his parched, chapped lips. He shook as he spoke. 'I told you, I don't want her here.'

'Alf—'

'You're not getting it are you? I can't even look at her. I don't *want* to look at her.'

Vaughn shook his head sadly. 'Then you'll just have to learn to.'

Alf stared coldly at Vaughn. 'I don't have to do anything. Just take her. You ain't going to leave her here with me.'

Vaughn gestured to the others to follow him. 'That's exactly what I'm going to do because it seems that's the only way I'm going to get you to spend some time with her . . . She won't bite, Alf. Get over yourself. Unfortunately for her, she needs you.'

Alfie ran to the doorway, blocking the entrance. He pushed his face into Vaughn's and hissed angrily, his voice cracking as he fought back the tears. 'Don't you fucking do this to me. You are *not* going to do this.'

With not much of an effort, Vaughn pushed Alfie out of the way. 'Looks like I've already done it.'

And with that Vaughn and the women walked away, leaving Alfie alone with his screaming daughter.

2

Franny Doyle glanced around the small interview room of the prison, looking at the peeling grey paint and the bars across the windows.

She sat back in the uncomfortable orange chair, feeling the hard, cracked plastic digging into her back. Not that she minded. It was a distraction from the anger, which ran through her veins as she brought her gaze back to stare at the person sitting across the table from her.

'So come on, Francesca. Let's go over it again, shall we? Because so far the only part of your story that seems anywhere near the truth was the part where you got up in the morning and went for a piss.'

Franny sat forward, leaning her body on the table. Her face contorted with hatred. 'Is that how you get your kicks, Detective, imagining me with me knickers around me ankles . . . Go fuck yourself!'

'Temper, temper, Francesca.'

Even though Franny knew she shouldn't, she seethed openly, snarling out her words as she pushed back her long chestnut brown hair. 'First off, my name's Franny – as well you know – and secondly, don't push me, Detective. Don't play games because that would be a *really* stupid thing for you to do. I won't be in here forever.'

Detective Balantyne roared with laughter, his round, acne-scarred face lighting up. He stared at her, his hazel eyes twinkling with delight. 'There you are. That's the Francesca I know and love – full of threats and anger. Is that why you killed Bree Dwyer? Did she say something you didn't like? Did she wind you up the wrong way? Is that what happened, *Francesca*?'

The light touch on Franny's arm from her solicitor was all that was needed for Franny to get herself back under control. She took a deep breath and a small smile appeared at the corners of her lips. 'No. As much as you'd like that, that's not what happened, Detective – not even close, darlin'. We've already been over this a hundred times.'

Detective Balantyne glared at her. Over the years he'd always been struck by three things when it came to Franny Doyle. Her brains. Her beauty. But, above all else, her ruthlessness. Her father – a notorious Irish gangster – had been the same and, by God, that man had certainly taught her well. Franny Doyle was a hard bastard. No more. No less.

Breaking his own thoughts, Balantyne opened the thin grey file in front of him. 'Then explain to me why forensics found some of your DNA on the plastic sheeting Bree's body was wrapped up in?'

9

'Is that the best you can do? It's obvious, ain't it? Like I already told you, I'd visited her plenty of times. I always gave her a hug when I saw her—' Franny answered, matter-of-factly.

Balantyne interrupted. 'Out of everything I've heard, that's the hardest thing to get my head around.'

For a moment, Franny looked puzzled. She spoke suspiciously. 'What are you talking about?'

'That the ice queen shows affection. I can't picture it myself, can't quite see you giving anyone a *hug* . . . But anyway, carry on.'

Franny had to take another deep breath; she could feel her temper rising *again*. What she wouldn't do to take down this man.

For as long as she could remember, Balantyne had been sniffing around – wanting to bang first her father up then her – and now, after all these years, he might've finally got her, and God wasn't he just delighting in it.

She spoke snootily. 'The point is, Detective: what that bunch of muppets down at forensics found on Bree's clothes had obviously been transferred from me. You know, from me to her clothes then onto the plastic sheet. It's a no-brainer that one.'

Balantyne pulled some photos out of his file and slid them across to Franny. She glanced down at them then looked up. She shrugged, not giving anything away of her emotions.

'What? What about them?'

Balantyne shook his head. Even he had recoiled at the sight of Bree's body – decomposing and broken – yet here was Franny Doyle not even taking an extra blink when she looked at the graphic photographs.

He snatched up one of the photos and pushed it into Franny's eye line. '*What?* Is that all you can say? She was found in a shallow grave, wrapped up in plastic. Most of the bones in her legs were broken. Snapped. Like she was a stick of wood. Her shoulders were dislocated; her neck was twisted around the wrong way. What sort of an animal does that to another human being?'

Franny continued to stare coldly. 'You tell me, you're the detective.'

'You know what I think? I think I'm looking at the animal right now, and I'm going to prove it. And then, *Francesca*, you are going to spend the rest of your days looking at four walls, with nothing else to do than think about what you've done.'

Franny sneered then smiled. 'In your dreams, Detective. You haven't got a chance in hell of pinning Bree's death on me. Both you and I know you'll have to prove it beyond a reasonable doubt to get a conviction, and let's face it, under scrutiny, your evidence will never stand up.'

Detective Balantyne nodded his head slowly. This time it was his turn to smile. 'Perhaps if it was this evidence alone you might have a point, but unfortunately for you, I've got a little bit of help . . .'

'What are you talking about?'

Balantyne laughed. 'Oh nothing, I just like to see you sweat and it's been a long time coming.'

'This won't stick, however much you want it to.'

Balantyne leant across the table and smirked. 'Then let the games begin.'

'There ain't no games. You've got it wrong. I never killed her.'

As Detective Balantyne collected his things and stood up from the chair, he smirked before leaning down and whispering in her ear. 'To tell you the truth, I don't care if you did or not. The point is . . . I've finally got you, Doyle!'

Then pulling his navy anorak on and heading for the door, Balantyne stopped and turned to look at Franny. 'You've been laughing at us all too long, Ms Doyle, but you won't be laughing soon. The jury will be happy to convict scum like you . . . and if you want my advice, I'd confess – the courts always like someone who pleads guilty. Saves a lot of time and they look at that favourably when it comes to sentencing. Who knows, you could be out before you turn ninety. Think on, Ms Doyle, think on.'

3

After Detective Balantyne and her solicitor had left the room, Franny put her head in her hands. She fought back the tears of anger and frustration, determined not to show or even feel anything because, after all, where would that get her? But she knew that was going to be hard. The situation she was in, if she was being honest with herself, she didn't know if she was ever going to get out of it.

Her solicitor – who'd been her father's solicitor and had acted for most other men in the firm when they'd been in trouble – frowned as he came back into the room. 'I've just been on the phone to one of my sources in the police. I've got some bad news for you, Fran.'

Franny's face darkened. 'Do I need to hear this now, Ed?'

'I think you do.'

Taking a sip of water, Franny braced herself. 'Go on then, hit me with it.'

Ed Romano spoke with the faintest of Italian accents. 'I think – and my source is good, they're reliable – I think Balantyne has got some witness statements.'

Franny sat up. 'What? That's impossible.'

'I wish it were, Franny.'

'Who? For fuck's sake, Ed, just tell me?'

'It's Vaughn. You've certainly made an enemy there. My source didn't know exactly what was in the statement but Vaughn's told them he saw what happened. He's basically saying he witnessed you killing Bree.'

Franny blanched. She knew that Vaughn was gunning for her, but even she didn't think that he'd be cooperating with the Old Bill. In their world, what Vaughn was doing went against all the rulebooks. She shook her head. 'No, that's bullshit. Your source must be wrong; I would've known if he'd given a statement.'

Ed, playing with his gold ink pen, shrugged. 'That's where you're wrong. It's a wonderful thing, anonymity.'

'You can't give a statement anonymously.'

'I'm afraid you can, under sections 74 to 85 of the *Coroners and Justice Act 2009*, orders known as "investigation anonymity orders" can be requested at the very start of an investigation – especially in a murder case. They can also apply to the court for a "witness anonymity order" during trial. Shall we say, it provides certainty to people who may have relevant information that their identities will not be disclosed.'

'So not only is Vaughn a snake, but he's also a coward, hiding behind anonymity,' sneered Franny.

'I suppose he needed to keep it quiet. Vaughn talking to the police . . . well, that's the ultimate betrayal, isn't it?'

This time Franny didn't answer. He was right though – Vaughn giving a statement was so far removed from what they were and what they stood for, it was hard to even believe. And she was certainly going to make him pay . . . however long that took.

Taking a deep breath, Franny said, 'Anyway, his word won't stand up for much. What jury is going to believe a face? Who's going to believe a man who's spent his days in a life of crime?'

Absentmindedly, the solicitor touched the small bald spot on the back of his head.

'I don't know, but it seems they're willing to put it to the test. And there's one more thing . . .' Franny's whole body slumped as the solicitor continued to say, 'You're not going to like it but there's another statement as well.'

Franny looked puzzled. 'Who?'

'Shannon Mulligan. Apparently her statement is almost identical to Vaughn's.'

This time, in the privacy of the prison's interview room, Franny did lose her cool. She slammed her hand on the table and shouted, 'They're lying! They're both lying! Shannon's always been nothing but a lying bitch!'

Calmly Ed said, 'Look, try not to let this rattle you. We'll sort it.'

Franny's eyes widened. 'How? How the fuck are you going to get me out of here?'

'I don't know yet, but, Franny, you've got to stay positive.'

Hating feeling emotionally vulnerable, Franny pulled herself together. She bit her lip, trying to control the panic. Then she shrugged and did her best to look and sound

15

casual – but the feeling of anxiety still sat heavy on her chest.

Her eyes narrowed and a steely look crossed her face as she said, 'Vaughn was beginning to lose his control with Alfie.'

'In what sense?'

'Well, Alfie had stopped listening to him. He'd started to ask me advice, take my opinion over Vaughn's – whether it be in business or money matters. And of course, Vaughn didn't like that and now he's doing all he can to get rid of me once and for all. I was a threat to him before, but believe me, I'm going to be a threat to him again. Not only that, I'm going to be his worst nightmare.'

She stopped speaking for a moment and gripped her fists together before adding, 'I have to get out of here, you understand? And I want you to get Alfie to come and see me. I *need* to see Alfie.'

4

Alfie sat with his back to Mia, his hands covering his ears as she screamed. He wasn't sure how long he had sat there or she had cried, but it seemed like an eternity. He couldn't bring himself to look at her. And yes, fucking yes, he hated himself for it, but he certainly hated Franny more for it.

She was to blame for it. She was to blame for all of this but the thing he hated more about it – the thing that ate away at him – was that, as much as he hated her, he loved her. And God almighty, above anything else *that* was the most fucked-up thing about it all.

'*Shit!*' He lashed out, kicking a small glass table, sending it flying across the room, causing Mia to scream more.

The whole situation was so fucked up; his girlfriend was behind bars for killing the mother of his child, and on top of that he now had a banging headache. How it had all come to this, he couldn't even begin to get his head around.

A voice interrupted his thoughts. 'Hello, Mr Jennings. You should really get that door fixed – you never know who might come by when you're least expecting them.'

At the sound of the voice, Alfie jumped and turned around. Standing there with a machete in his hand was Mr Huang, the head of a notorious South East Asian triad gang, and a man who spelt trouble. Big, big trouble.

As Alfie watched, his heart beginning to race, Mr Huang – slender and immaculately dressed in a three-piece grey-striped suit – nodded to his men, who made a human wall behind him. Staring at the baby and sounding younger than his sixty-plus years, Huang asked, 'Yours, Mr Jennings?'

Alfie cautiously nodded but said nothing as he kept his eyes on the large blade Mr Huang spun in his hands. 'How old is she? Seven, eight months?'

Again, Alfie nodded and again he said nothing.

Huang's tone danced between icy and amusement. 'Parenting isn't easy at the best of times, but especially at this age. You have to watch them all the time; they're always having accidents when you least expect it. You can't be too careful.'

Smiling, but without it reaching his eyes, Huang looked around the small but expensive flat, decorated in matching silver and purple furniture. Then casually, he walked over to Mia, picking her up. Immediately she stopped crying and began gurgling happily, her nose running as her tiny fingers played with Huang's red bow tie.

'They like to be rocked, Mr Jennings; it's something about the motion that soothes them. But then I'm not here to swap baby notes with you, I'm here to talk about the money you owe me and *show* you the kind of penalties I charge for late payments.'

'Look . . .' Alfie tried to say something, but as he did, Mr Huang, who was still holding Mia, drew back his leg and kicked Alfie hard in the side of his head, sending him crashing into the wall.

Alfie felt the pain shoot through his head to his jaw to his chin and tasted the blood in his mouth as he watched Huang put Mia back down on the floor next to him.

Through the pain Alfie stared up at Huang. He could feel his right eye closing and a burning agony at the back of it. He listened as Huang spoke in a whisper.

'Mr Jennings, if I were you I'd watch your tone. One thing I can't abide is rudeness, it's certainly no example to give your daughter . . . So, come on, Mr Jennings, let's try again shall we? Where's my money?'

'You're going to get it,' Alfie snarled roughly.

Huang chuckled. He glanced at his men then ruffled Mia's soft, blonde curly hair. 'Oh, I know I am, that isn't in question. What I want to know is *when*?'

Watching Mia become fascinated by Mr Huang's grey, leather shoe, her tiny fingers playing with the tassel on it, Alfie shrugged, more aware than ever of his tone. He needed to stay calm and at least *try* to sound respectful. 'I'm working on it, okay? I ain't taking the piss. You just need to give me a bit more time.'

Mr Huang crouched; his knees cracking as he did so. Staring at Alfie directly, he tilted his head to one side and grinned as he put the tip of the machete blade on Alfie's cheek. His small, beady eyes were dancing with amusement

19

behind his thick, round glasses. 'I think I've given you enough time, don't you? If it weren't for the fact that I quite like you, Mr Jennings, you would be dead by now. But that isn't to say you won't be dead by next week if you don't give me my money, and what's your little girl supposed to do then? Little girls need their daddies you know.'

Then without warning Huang slashed the blade across Alfie's face. Alfie yelled out in agony as the blood spurted out of the three-inch wound, flowing through his fingers as he pressed his hand against his cheek, hoping to stem the rush.

Every part of him wanted to fight, wanted to beat Huang senseless, but he knew better than to try to attack; for a start he was outnumbered and Mr Huang and his men wouldn't think twice about chopping him up into tiny bits if he retaliated.

Trying to hold together the thick flaps of skin on his cheek, Alfie grimaced and groaned in pain.

'Mr Jennings, don't be such a baby, it's only a little cut. I don't think even your daughter would make such a fuss.'

Huang spun round and placed the blade on Mia's cheek. She gurgled and laughed as Huang said, 'Shall we see?'

With no hesitation, Alfie leapt at Huang, knocking the blade out of his hand. 'Don't you fucking touch her, you bastard. You fucking animal. You hear me! Get the fuck away from her.'

Immediately Huang's men charged forward. They leapt on Alfie, pinning him down on the floor as Mia started to scream again.

Getting up, Huang straightened and dusted down his

expensive hand-made suit. He turned and glared at Alfie, pressing his foot into Alfie's throat whilst watching the blood pooling onto the thick, cream carpet.

A mixture of pain and fury raced through Alfie. He tried to say something but he struggled to breathe under the pressure as Huang's foot continued to press down on his throat.

'That was very foolish of you, Mr Jennings, and I'm also somewhat surprised. What do you take me for? Do you really think that I'm capable of hurting your daughter? Or rather it would be more truthful to say that's really not my style at all. Whatever happened to the British having a sense of humour? And look what's happened now; you've ruined my shoes. These were my favourite pair you know.'

Huang took his foot off Alfie's throat then proceeded to wipe the blood from his shoe using Alfie's face as a cloth, causing Alfie to scream in agony as the steel-toe-capped loafer ground into the wound on his cheek.

Huang cleared his throat. 'I'll be back soon, but in the meantime, I want you to think on. Next time I might not be so kind . . . oh and, Mr Jennings? Don't forget what I said: babies like to be rocked. You should really try it.'

And with that, Huang nodded to his men who set about Alfie, knocking him unconscious. The last thing Alfie Jennings heard was the sound of Mia screaming.

5

Franny lay back on her bed staring up at the empty top bunk's rusting springs. Unlike a lot of the other women, she hadn't bothered to make the magnolia-walled cell anything like homely. It was bare and uninviting, cold and bleak. No photos, no posters, certainly not a calendar – Jesus, she already knew exactly how long she'd been on remand and the last thing she needed was a reminder.

No, she didn't want anything up on the walls – to her it was like saying she was staying, that this would now be her home for the next twenty years. It was almost like admitting defeat, and as her father had told her on a number of occasions, death was her only defeat.

Sighing, she glanced around. The whole place stunk. The prison had a constant smell of shit, sweat and Spice – a nasty, synthetic drug that either turned the women into zombies or psychotic animals. Only last week some Spice had been smuggled into the prison inside the bodies of three dead rats, thrown over the prison walls. And now the smoking ban had come into play, it seemed the intake of Spice had gone up tenfold.

Although there was supposed to be a flushing toilet in the corner of her cell it hadn't actually worked since the second day she'd been here, so she was forced to use the bucket in the corner.

The whole place seemed to be ingrained with dirt that just couldn't be washed out. The bed sheets – which were supposed to be fresh each week – looked like they'd just been swapped from one dirty set to another and the cold air whirled in through the prison window bars as if looking for some sanctuary.

Absentmindedly playing with her hair, she sighed again, forcing herself not to think of Mia and how much she missed her. From the time Mia had been born she'd loved and treated her like she was her own, which had come as a surprise; she'd never seen herself as maternal, and certainly no one in her life had ever accused her of it.

That was the main reason she needed to get out . . . That and having her day of reckoning with Vaughn. She could taste that. She was hungry for it and it was what was keeping her going. Vaughn and Mia were her motivation and, of course, Mia needed her . . . *Her* Mia. None of them deserved such a beautiful little girl, not even Bree, her mother, had deserved her.

To her, Bree had been weak, and when it had mattered, Bree just hadn't been able to cut it. Even before Bree had died, the whole situation had been a mess. Franny thought about the fact that when Alfie had thought that she'd run off with his money and left him – which hadn't actually been the case – he had drowned his sorrows in the bottom of a bottle and in the arms of Bree, who he'd known since childhood.

When eventually she'd reappeared and discovered that Alfie had taken up with Bree, as usual she'd hidden her hurt and just got on with it. Though that hadn't been the end of the story – far from it, *that* had just been the beginning.

Alfie had still been in love with her but he'd also fallen in love with Bree and that's when things had become really complicated.

Bree had been like a fish out of water in the life she and Alfie lived. She'd found it frightening and hated every part of the life of crime. So, when Bree had discovered she was pregnant that had been it; Bree had wanted out. She'd wanted to run, but she knew that if and *when* Alfie found out about her pregnancy, she would never escape Alfie or the life he lived. Because, to Alfie, family was everything.

Although it was the last thing Bree had wanted to do, she had decided to have an abortion; however, strange as it was, by then Franny had actually become friends with Bree, so instead of standing by and just watching Bree go through with it, she'd decided to help her by putting a plan into place.

She had felt sorry for Bree – at first – and even though she knew it was dangerous for her, she had helped Bree get away from Alfie, though of course he'd known nothing about the pregnancy. So behind Alfie's back Bree had settled into a new life and a few months later had given birth to Mia.

But the overall pressure of living a secret life had gotten to Bree and as a consequence Bree had put them both in danger by thinking she could come out of hiding or, even worse, tell Alfie what she had done, believing he would just forgive and forget. Which was a joke in itself; Franny knew Alfie well enough to realise that the betrayal alone would've meant a bullet in her head and, though she doubted Alfie would've actually hurt Bree, he would've taken Mia and not let Bree see her ever again.

But Bree hadn't wanted to listen and in the following months not only had Bree become a loose cannon with her continual threat to confess all to Alfie, but in Franny's opinion, Bree had also become a useless mother. So, not having anyone else around, it had fallen on *her* to look after Mia. Surprisingly Franny had relished the challenge, and even more surprisingly, she had come to love the little girl like she was her own.

Looking back, she supposed Bree was probably jealous of her bond with Mia or perhaps Bree was just one of life's parasites; unable to live without having someone to latch on to. In any case, Bree had certainly pushed her to the limits: needy and neurotic, crying all the time and generally being emotionally unstable. Something Franny had no patience for; traits she despised in people, especially in women. She and Mia had certainly had enough of Bree on the day in question. The day Bree had died . . .

Before Franny's thoughts had time to move on, she felt someone sit on the corner of her bed, and quickly she slipped the prohibited phone her solicitor had smuggled in for her into the hole she'd made on the bottom side of the top bunk mattress.

Bringing her eyes up, she saw Christine Lucas sitting there with two of her cronies standing at the cell door.

Christine spoke in a reassuring tone, her Geordie accent apparent. 'Hello, Franny, sorry I've taken so long to make your acquaintance, but I was down in "seg". But now I'm back, I like to come and welcome the new women to my wing. I'm Christine.'

Franny stared coolly at Christine Lucas, noticing the huge roll of fat that hung down like an apron onto Christine's lap. She knew exactly who this woman was. She was the 'Daddy' of the wing, the top dog, serving a triple life sentence for the violent murder of her three children.

Franny also knew why Christine had been in 'seg' – segregation; Christine had got a group of women to pounce on one of the new girls who had shot her mouth off about not being afraid of Christine. They had jumped on her in the showers – one of the few places in the prison where there was no CCTV – and had not only given her a good beating, but had also sexually assaulted her, damaging her insides.

Wanting to be on an equal level with Christine, Franny sat up, her eyes narrowing. She spoke icily. 'I appreciate the visit, Christine, but if you don't mind I'm a little bit busy.'

Christine looked around at the empty cell and then at the two other women who looked like a pair of club bouncers standing by the door. She laughed, showing off her ill-fitted false teeth. The sagging skin on her fat face fell into folds as she spoke to the women guarding the door. 'We've got a right one here. It's always the same; all the girls on remand think they can come in here and do what they like . . . but you all soon learn who's in charge.' She paused a minute before adding: 'I reckon she owes me an apology.'

Showing no emotion Franny blinked. 'As I told you, I'm busy, so if you wouldn't mind . . .' Franny gestured with her head to the door at which point Christine lunged at her, gripping Franny's chin between her pudgy hands. 'Maybe the memo didn't get to you, but I rule this place and I say what goes on, do you understand me?'

Franny's eyes darkened. 'If I were you, I'd take your hands off my fucking face.'

About to pull the hidden razor blade out of the clip in her hair, Christine stopped as she heard a familiar voice behind her.

'What's going on here?' Officer Jessie Ford, who'd worked in the prison for the past five years, stared at the women.

Christine grinned and sniffed loudly. 'Oh you know how it is, miss, I just like to give all the new girls a welcome. That's right, isn't it, pet?'

Christine stared at Franny.

Jessie Ford clearly knew only too well how it was, as she said, 'I just hope you're not causing any trouble because I'm sure the governor would be happy to see you put back in seg, Lucas.'

Christine stood up, her obese six-foot-one frame towering over the diminutive prison guard, and this time when Christine spoke, her tone was colder. 'Howay, man!

I don't like threats especially when I haven't done anything wrong.'

Officer Ford refused to back down but the flicker of unease as Christine continued to loom over her didn't go unnoticed by any of the women in the cell. 'I'll be the judge of that. Now go on, get back to your cell, Lucas, and take your buddies with you.'

Christine smirked, her green eyes void of any emotion as she turned to Franny.

'How about you and I pick up this conversation another time?'

Franny held Christine's stare. Her voice was as steely as Christine's had been. 'Let's do that, *anytime* you want, darlin' . . . you know where I am.'

Christine leant down to Franny, whispering her next words, her Geordie accent strong and sharp. 'You must have a death wish, pet – either that or you're stupid.'

At which point, Christine and the other women barged past Officer Ford, who followed them out, leaving Franny sitting in her cell wondering once again just how the hell she was going to get out of this mess.

6

'Are you sure we did the right thing? You heard what Alfie said. He ain't bothered about her. He don't give a flying fuck about Mia.'

Worried, Shannon chewed on her tasteless gum as she sucked on her vape. Her bitten-down nails were painted a pearly pink.

In the past few months not only had her life done a three-sixty, but for the first time in her life she had actually experienced happiness that hadn't been brought on from sucking on a crack pipe.

It had been pure and natural, brought on from Vaughn's kindness, from his care, from his trust, from him not wanting anything from her, and for that, she would do anything for him. *Anything*. And she certainly wasn't going to allow anyone to get in the way of it. Now she knew how intoxicating happiness was, the buzz from it better and higher than any rock of crack, she wasn't about to let it go.

After her mother had died in an alleyway from a heroin overdose, Shannon had been taken in by Uncle Charlie and her aunt. But rather than it having been a loving environment, most of her life she'd worked for Uncle Charlie, being forced to give blow jobs and have sex with whoever he put in front of her. On occasion, her uncle had wanted the odd blow job from her as well, though thankfully he'd never wanted full sex with her; he'd just groped and rubbed himself and his flaccid penis all over her. The thought of it made her sick. But then, when all hope had gone out of life, she'd met Alfie, and through Alfie, she'd met Vaughn – and he had saved her.

And whilst Alfie was spinning, drinking and sniffing as much coke as he could lay his hands on, Vaughn had trusted her enough to help look after Mia, which she had done with pleasure. The distraction of Mia had helped her not to focus on her crack habit. Having another human being needing and relying on her was something else she'd never experienced.

But now the problem was if Alfie decided to take on Mia, to look after her like a father should, then what use would she be to Vaughn? The thought of it terrified her. She loved Vaughn, not that he knew it, not that he probably loved her back . . . *yet* . . . but maybe one day he would, one day he would make her his wife. Mrs Sadler – now that would be something special. That was what dreams were made of.

So she needed to make sure not only that that nasty bitch, Franny Doyle – who'd always looked at her like she was a piece of dirt – stayed in prison, but also that Alfie stayed in his stupor, stayed spiralling . . . Yes, yes, that was it, all she needed to do was make sure that Alfie continued to be an unfit father, and then she would become completely indispensable to Vaughn and then – perhaps, just perhaps – Vaughn would see her in a different light and fall in love with her as she loved him.

And with a renewed sense of relief, Shannon sighed and pushed her bright red hair back behind her sticky-out ears and smiled a crack-ravaged, toothless smile.

Vaughn stared at Shannon. She was a good kid and by Christ she'd had the worst start in life, used and abused and passed around by her uncle. She was only sixteen and she had seen and been through stuff that no one, least of all a kid, should go through.

He was surprised at how fond of her he was; after all, she was a scrawny teenager, and an ex-crack addict at that. But she was sweet and he was happy to put a roof over her head. She seemed a bit lost. After all she had no friends or family that she could count on.

If anyone had told him this time last year that he'd be looking after a kid and a baby, he would have thought they'd been smoking crack. But funny thing was, he was actually enjoying it. Though of course when the time was right, when she'd got herself together a bit, he'd talk to her about moving on; not that he would see her on the streets again. Far from it . . . Who knew, perhaps, he could set her up in a shared house with other girls her age. Maybe she could go to college. Shit, he didn't know what he was supposed to do with a teenager.

31

Anyway, he could worry about all this later. For now he was grateful to her for not only backing up his story about Bree, but also for looking after Mia. And once Alfie saw that he needed his daughter as much as she needed him, Vaughn expected that Shannon would be more than happy to get on with her own life. But for now having her about worked – because he did care; Shannon felt like the wayward kid sister he never had.

With a renewed sense of relief, Vaughn sipped on the now cold cup of coffee, turning his thoughts back to Alfie.

He'd chosen to have a drink in the Italian deli across the road from Alfie's flat. He had thought about going home to his flat, which he was renting from Johnny Taylor – above the club in Greek Street – but he'd thought better of it. He wanted to stay in striking distance of Alfie in case he really couldn't cope with looking after Mia.

He checked his phone again just in case Alfie had rung and he'd missed it. Nothing. And he guessed nothing was a good sign. So why did he feel nervous in the pit of his stomach? It was stupid – almost as stupid as how much he'd been smitten by Mia.

'I reckon Alfie is up there right now sticking the whole of Colombia up his nose.'

Irritated by Shannon making him feel more stressed than he wanted to feel, Vaughn snapped, 'Do you have to chew that gum like that? You sound like a bleedin' cement mixer and it's getting on me nerves. And for the record, no, I don't think he's doing that, and yes, I think we've done the right thing.'

32

Shannon pulled a face. 'I don't know how you make that one out.'

'The point is Alfie has always been stubborn, and sometimes you have to be tough with him to be kind. At the end of the day it's his daughter and family means everything to him. Everything. It's just been a rough couple of months. You'll see; he'll be fine. He's probably up there now singing "Three Little Pigs".'

Shannon pulled on her vape. 'Then why do you look so worried?'

Vaughn banged down the coffee cup, spilling the milk over the table. 'Because you keep going on about it. So do us a favour and stop. We're here, he's just over there, so it's not like much can go wrong is it? He only . . . Fuck. Fuck. Fuck.'

'What? Vaughn, what is it?'

Vaughn's handsome face paled and he began to stand up, scraping back his chair as he stared out of the window.

'What's wrong?'

Still not answering, Vaughn watched a group of men coming out of the block of flats in Old Compton Street where Alfie's flat was. He recognised most of them, and he certainly recognised the person who was walking down the street. It was Mr Huang. Ruthless, violent and someone he'd heard Alfie mention recently – not that he knew what business they had together. But what he did know was anything that spelt Huang spelt trouble. *Big, big trouble.*

And without waiting to explain to Shannon, Vaughn Sadler ran towards Alfie's flat.

7

Detective Balantyne slammed through his front door, throwing his bag to the side. He didn't know what it was about Franny Doyle but she always got under his skin. She was a smart-mouthed bitch, smarter than a lot of people he knew, but finally, *hopefully*, she would get her comeuppance. And God, wouldn't it be a long time coming.

Stalking through to the grey and silver wallpapered lounge of the mid-terraced house in East Grinstead, which was located in the north-eastern corner of Sussex – a place he'd moved to last year – Balantyne kicked the tabby cat out of the way.

He sighed heavily as he sunk into the putrid coral-coloured chair and gritted his teeth – too hard – immediately feeling a throbbing pain run through his jaw, making his current mood even worse.

He would much rather be at work, busy and not having

time to think about anything else but the job at hand. Being at home meant all the distractions disappeared and he was left with his own thoughts, something he'd rather run from.

Reaching over to finish off the half glass of whiskey that had been sat on the walnut coffee table since last night, Balantyne stared gloomily into the glass before dipping his finger in, to flick out the midge that had landed in it. Then knocking back the whiskey, he felt the welcoming burn in his throat, hoping that the drink would not only lighten his mood but would lessen the dull ache from his tooth as well.

His thoughts drifted back to Franny and her father, as well as Alfie and Vaughn. The faces of Soho, old and new, who as far back as he could remember he'd played a cat and mouse game with – though frustratingly, and he hated to admit it, they were always one move ahead of him.

To try to catch them out, he'd even stepped over to the wrong side of the law at times: getting information by bribing or blackmailing terrified witnesses, planting evidence to try to get some kind of confession, or even strong-arming the suspects when they were in custody. *Anything* just to bring them down.

He knew that if they'd known some of the things he'd resorted to over the years, a lot of people he worked with would wrongly label him as a bent copper. And of course, that would be a joke; he was far from that. He did what was needed to try to get results, to try to get the lowlife scum put away. It was as simple as that.

He wasn't the criminal, they were. And when it came

down to the likes of Franny Doyle and Alfie Jennings and his sidekick, Vaughn Sadler, the *only* option was to play dirty, to play the game at their level. So if walking the wrong side of the line occasionally would keep the streets clean of them, he was more than happy to do that.

'I suppose you've been with her again?'

Balantyne's thoughts were abruptly broken as he looked towards the sound of the voice. Standing in her dressing gown in the doorway was his wife, Emma. Tall and thin, her long blonde hair falling messily out of the high pony-tail and yesterday's mascara sitting smudged under her eyes.

Quietly, Balantyne shook his head as he placed his glass down on the floor. 'Emma, *please*, I've been working. I'm tired, and I just wanted to unwind.'

'Then why don't I believe you . . .? And if you haven't been with her, I know you've been with some other cheap slag.'

'Em, I've just told you. I've been working. That's it. So I'd appreciate it, sweetheart, if we didn't have to go through the same thing again,' Balantyne said quietly, staring into the glass of whiskey.

Without warning, Emma shrieked, her expression screwed up with anger. She rushed into the room, pushing her face inches away from Balantyne's. 'Liar! Liar! You're a liar! I know it! I can smell her on you.'

A mix of anger and despair rushed through Balantyne. 'The only thing you can smell is the booze you've been necking back all day.'

Emma's eyes blazed with anger. 'Do you blame me, Tone? Are you surprised that I drink? Wouldn't you in my position?' She paused then her gaze searched Balantyne's face and with her voice full of resentment, she hissed, 'It's all your fault, Tone. I will *never* forgive you for what you did to me. You owe me.'

Balantyne, wanting Emma just to stop, nodded and said, almost inaudibly, 'I know. I know, sweetheart.'

'Then come on, tell me. Tell me the truth, have you been with *her*?'

Staring straight into Emma's eyes, Balantyne shook his head. 'No, Em, of course not. It's all in your head. There is no *her*.'

It was like a red rag to a bull. Emma leapt at her husband, scratching his face as she tugged on his hair. 'Don't lie to me! I know you're screwing around on me!'

Flinching from the pain in his scalp, Balantyne raged, 'Well if you know that, Em, why bother asking me then?'

Emma's shriek filled the room again. 'You bastard! You fucking bastard! You think this is all a big joke, don't you?'

Balantyne grabbed her arms, pulling them off him. He bellowed back, 'Are you kidding me? Does any of this look like a joke? I'm just sick of it. Every day it's the same thing, Em . . . I just want to know why you're doing this? Why do you *always* have to do this, Em?'

Emma's eyes filled with tears. Her voice danced on the edge of hysteria. 'Don't you dare turn this round! You know why I'm like this; *you* made me like this. I can't trust you, and it's all I think about. I know you're seeing someone. I know it. I can smell her on you.'

Balantyne looked at Emma despairingly. 'That's just not true.'

Again, Emma lunged at him but this time she clawed at his eyes, screaming at the top of her voice.

Scrambling up from the chair, Balantyne knocked Emma backwards, forcing her against the wall where he grabbed her by the throat, banging her head against the tall wooden sideboard.

Balantyne's face flushed red. 'Is this what you want, Em? Are you happy now? Happy that you've pushed me to do this again? So now you can say I'm the bad guy, can't you? That's what you want isn't it? Now you can go around telling everyone I knock you about, can't you?'

Emma yelled in Balantyne's face. 'Who is there to tell? I haven't got any friends because you won't let me. I've got no one because of you.'

Enraged, Balantyne dropped his hand from her throat and punched the wall next to the side of her head. 'Stop lying. Just fucking stop! The truth is you pushed them all away because no one wants to be around you. No one can cope with it. No one can put up with your drinking. You're toxic, Em.'

'And whose fault is that? Whose fault is it that I drink?'

Balantyne pushed his body close to Emma's. He hissed his words: 'I told you if you want to blame me then go ahead, blame it all on me.'

Again, Emma's gaze darted over Balantyne's face, which was only centimetres away. 'Is she better than me?'

'What? What are you talking about now?'

'*Her*. Does she make you feel something that I don't?'

Feeling the blood run down his face from the scratch on his head, Balantyne spoke softly. 'Em, I've already told you, it's just you and me.'

'Then prove it . . . Prove that you love me. Let's have a baby, Tony . . . You know how much I want a baby. Our own little family.'

'Em, please . . . You can't even look after yourself let alone a child at the moment—' Balantyne felt the sting from the slap. His cheek turned red and the mark of Emma's hand left a welt.

'How dare you! How fucking dare you? Who do you think you are?'

'I'm sorry okay. I didn't mean that,' Balantyne muttered.

'But you did . . . Look at me, *Tone*, look at me!'

Desperate and unable to hold Emma's gaze, Balantyne dropped his stare.

'You can't can you? You can't even look at me. Do I repulse you that much?' She looked him up and down. 'I *said*, do I repulse you that much?'

Balantyne shook his head. He spoke quietly. 'No . . . no, it's just difficult . . . It's all such a mess. And I'd be lying if I said that when I look at you, it doesn't remind me of what happened . . . what I did, but that's not to say you repulse me.'

The screech from Emma startled the cat who leapt away out of the room as Emma's eyes flashed with anger and her hands moved down to Tony's trousers. She began to unbutton his jeans. 'Then why don't you want me? I can tell you're lying, you're hiding something . . . and you can't tell me I wouldn't be a good mother – you know I would.'

Balantyne thought it wise not to say what he was actually thinking, so instead he mumbled, 'For Christ's sake . . . can't you see, we just aren't in a great place right now . . . Maybe in time—' He stopped talking to grab hold of her hand before adding, 'Em, stop, *please*, you're not listening to me . . . I don't want this.'

'Well I do, and you owe me Tony, after what you did. You owe me.'

And as Balantyne – fighting back his emotions – stared at his wife and let her undo his trousers, the one thing that he couldn't deny, whether he liked it or not, was that he did indeed owe her . . . Big time.

8

Not bothering to wait for the lift, Vaughn rushed up the thick, grey carpeted stairs to the second landing. *Shit*. He was annoyed with himself. It was a stupid mistake. He must've missed seeing Huang and his men walk into the block of flats when he'd gone to the counter to order the drinks. *Fuck*.

Rushing onto Alfie's landing, he raced down the corridor, knocking over the large potted plant in the corner. He could feel his heart racing and sweat dripped down the back of his shirt. He knew from personal experience that Huang was vicious and inhumane, getting his kicks out of violence. He just hoped that he wasn't too late.

Hearing Shannon run up behind him, Vaughn's thoughts suddenly came to an abrupt halt as he saw Mia crawling happily along the corridor in his direction.

'What's she doing out here?' Shannon said, her voice

filled with worry. As she went to scoop up Mia, Vaughn held her back, his eyes darting up and down the corridor as he listened out for any noise.

'Wait. There could still be somebody inside the flat.'

Shaking Vaughn's grip off her arm, Shannon moved forward towards Mia. 'I don't care who's about. I ain't leaving her there, and if you ask me, the only person in that flat is Alfie, pissed out of his head.'

Vaughn hissed as his temper rose. 'For fuck's sake, turn it in and just do as you're told.'

Ignoring him, Shannon picked up Mia who gurgled in delight, though her chubby little face was stained with dry tears.

Fuming, Vaughn growled. 'Don't you ever listen to anyone anymore?'

'When it comes to her I don't and I told you we shouldn't do this. *I told you* leaving Mia with him was a bad idea.'

'Will you just shut the hell up? For fuck's sake, Shan, this ain't about his parenting skills, is it? You just don't get it, do you?'

Bouncing Mia in her arms, Shannon – having no clue about Huang and no idea why Vaughn was so upset – wiped her nose with her sleeve. 'Say what you want, it was always going to end tits up when it came to Alfie.'

'Keep your voice down, will ya, and your mouth shut. If it wasn't for Alfie, you would still be working for your uncle Charlie. After all, he was the one who took you in and helped you in the first place. So think on before you slag him off,' Vaughn whispered angrily as he pulled out his gun from his jacket pocket. He glared at Shannon. 'Take her back to my flat.'

Shannon stared at the gun, suddenly appreciating that whatever was happening was serious. Worried, she shook her head. 'I ain't leaving you here. You might need me.'

Incensed and on high alert Vaughn spoke through gritted teeth. 'And what are you going to do, hey? Fight them off with Mia's dummy? Now stop being so frigging stupid and *go*.'

A flash of hurt ran through Shannon's eyes. 'I'm just saying that . . .'

Vaughn interrupted. 'Well, don't. I ain't got fucking time for this. It's a big enough worry knowing Alfie's just been paid a visit from a man who makes Hannibal Lecter look sane, and I don't want to worry about you as well. Now just go home, will ya?'

In the long, cream, quiet corridor Shannon tilted her head as she stared at Vaughn. Shyly she asked, 'You . . . you *worry* about me?'

'Shan, will you just piss off home?'

As Shannon turned to go, a small smile appeared on her lips. She knew it. She just knew she'd been right about Vaughn. He did care. He did worry about her and maybe he was even beginning to fall in love with her . . .

None the wiser to Shannon's feelings, Vaughn raced down the hallway to Alfie's flat, where only a couple of hours ago he'd kicked down the front door.

He paused, readying himself. In the back of his mind he couldn't help thinking that the most sensible course of action would be to call some of his men, but that would mean waiting, and maybe Alfie just didn't have time.

Feeling the prickle of sweat at the back of his neck, Vaughn pushed himself against the wall. Then after a mental countdown he craned his head around the doorway, his heart thumping. Immediately he froze at the scene in front of him. There on the floor in a pool of his own blood was Alfie.

'Jesus Christ.' Checking left and right, Vaughn quickly tucked away his gun as he ran forward. He bent down to take Alfie's pulse . . . Yeah, yeah, he could feel it. Relief washed over him. He let out a long sigh then spoke warmly. 'Alf, Alf, can you hear me mate?'

There was no sound from Alfie, and Vaughn, staring at the slice across Alfie's cheek, shook him gently. 'Alfie, it's me . . . It's me, Vaughn.'

A small groan came from Alfie, and encouraged by the noise, Vaughn continued to speak. 'Do you want me to help you sit up?'

Struggling to speak, let alone open his eyes, and with his whole body hurting, Alfie murmured, 'I just don't think I can. My head's banging and my face feels like it's been through a shredder.'

'I know, mate, and it certainly looks that way . . . You'll need to get that cut seen to – it'll need some stitches. I can take you up to A & E.'

Alfie tried to shake his head as he felt the thumping pressure behind his right swollen eye. He grimaced, unable to remember the last time he felt so much pain. 'No, no way, I ain't going. There'll be too many questions. I'll sort it, I'll get Davey to do it.'

Vaughn nodded. Davey was an old-timer – once an East End face to be reckoned with – and someone who could give any surgeon or doctor a run for his money when it came to pulling out bullets or sewing up knife wounds. He was a handy guy to have about, because as Alfie said, it stopped any unwanted questions.

'Don't worry, I can give him a call . . . Look, let me help you up.'

Vaughn scooped his arm under Alfie's shoulders, carefully helping his friend to sit upright. Alfie yelped in pain; his body ached and his face was a rainbow of red and blue bruises. The slash on his face wept and oozed blood, and his eye was so swollen that he couldn't see out of it. His nose ran with blood, and a gash on his forehead sat under his hairline. His lip was torn and engorged.

'Fucking hell, Alf, do yourself a favour and don't look in any mirrors.'

'I ain't planning to.'

Popping a cigarette carefully in Alfie's mouth for him and giving him a light, Vaughn looked at him hard, not letting on how shocked he was to see him in such a state.

He'd known Alfie for as long as he could remember, though in truth, it'd had been Alfie's brother, Connor, who he'd first been friends with. They'd been the best of mates, totally inseparable and to this day he missed him.

Even back in the early days – whilst he and Connor were closer than a lot of blood brothers were – he'd had a love-hate relationship with Alfie. And over the years there were many times he'd wanted to walk away from him. But he couldn't; not even when Alfie had ripped him off, nor when

Alfie had tried to get off with his missus, or when Alfie had put their lives at risk – and that was all because Vaughn had made a promise to Connor.

When Connor had died in his arms after a robbery had gone wrong, the last thing Connor had asked him was to look after Alfie, no matter what. And through a mixture of both guilt and love for Connor, that's exactly what he'd been doing for all these years. But it'd been hard, really hard, and he wasn't sure how long he could keep on doing it, especially as he and Alfie had been clashing so much recently – and not over little things either. In particular he'd always hated the way Franny had such a hold over Alfie – so it was about time that she had her comeuppance.

Sighing and irritated now, he turned his attention back to the present.

'So as you're still alive, I guess you can start talking . . . Go on then, Alf, tell me about it.'

Propping himself up against the wall, Alfie, grateful for the cigarette, took a deep drag before slowly turning to Vaughn. 'I don't want to talk about Mia. I already told you, I didn't want to see her.'

Annoyed at his attitude towards Mia, Vaughn said roughly, 'I ain't fucking talking about her. Though fuck knows I don't know what your problem is with your own daughter. We can talk about that later.'

His face still seeping with pus and blood, Alfie mumbled out of his torn mouth, wincing at the incessant pain in his lips, 'Then what? What the fuck are you going on about?'

'Huang. What the fuck was Huang doing here?'

'I don't know what you're talking about.'

Vaughn leant forward, speaking in a quiet hush. 'Don't treat me like a mug, Alf, you know *exactly* what I'm talking about, and if you don't start spilling the beans, I'm going to finish off what Huang started.'

9

Shannon hurried along Lexington Street, holding on to Mia who wasn't exactly light. She cut through to Beak Street, passing the Chinese herbal wellness centre and the old coffee house, pushing through the afternoon office crowds and negotiating her way around the groups of chatting visitors and people who'd ground to a dead halt to stare down at their phones.

She knew these streets and roads well; after all she'd spent most of her teenage years soliciting on them or searching for crack cocaine from the various drug dens that were hidden from the milling tourists. And truthfully, the whole place made her feel uncomfortable. It was a constant reminder of what she had been, what she had seen, and what she was afraid she still was.

She'd lost count of the number of blow jobs she'd given and how many times she'd laid on her back letting some overweight sweaty punter ride her hard as if she was a piece of meat, or the times her uncle had made her dance naked for a crowd of men who were old enough to be her great-granddad, let alone her granddad.

She shivered at the memories, feeling sick, the knot in her stomach always triggered when she thought back.

She glanced down at Mia who was looking up at her curiously and she smiled, her grin almost as gummy and toothless as the baby's. 'And none of that is going to happen to you, is it, Mia? You're going to have a good life, ain't you? You're not going to let any frigging—'

'Hello, Shannon. Fancy seeing you here.'

The voice coming from behind her made sixteen-year-old Shannon almost vomit. The nausea rose and she tasted the bile at the back of her throat. Swallowing it back down, she trembled and began to turn around. There in front of her was Uncle Charlie. The same Uncle Charlie who'd always talked in bust lips, black eyes, broken ribs and knocked-out teeth.

Seeing his niece, Charlie Eton licked his lips. He surveyed her hungrily. The last time he'd seen her she'd been a scrawny drug addict without an ounce of fat on her; her skin had been sallow and spotty and her face often unwashed. But now, she looked like a turkey that had been fattened up for Christmas. 'Now look at you, all done up like a dog's fucking dinner. You must be sucking the bollocks off Vaughn and Alfie to get them to look after you so well. Finally you've got a bit of weight on that skeleton of yours.'

Shannon's big green eyes filled up with tears as she looked down at Charlie who sat in a wheelchair, a result of Alfie doing what she wished she'd done a long time ago – taking a gun and shooting off one of his kneecaps.

Charlie's bald head shone in the May sun, his nose and face a ruddy red map of veins.

Eventually trusting herself enough to speak, Shannon glared at her uncle from under her fringe of red curly hair, her bottom lip quivering. 'It ain't like that.'

'Oh come on, Shan. I know you and I know men and there's no way Alfie and Vaughn would be looking after the likes of you if you weren't shoving them huge tits in their faces and nibbling on their dicks like there was no tomorrow.'

Shannon covered Mia's ears. 'Not everyone wants what you wanted. Not everyone's as sick as you.'

Charlie's hand flew up, his face screwed up in anger, as he grabbed Shannon's arm. 'I never heard you complain when you were with me.'

Even though she hated herself for it, Shannon was crying now. 'No, and you know why? Cos if I did you'd just batter me, so you get to learn that complaining ain't gonna get you nowhere.'

Charlie smirked nastily then changed tack. 'Why don't you just come home, Shan? You belong there. We all miss you.'

Shannon snorted in derision, ignoring the odd looks she was getting from passers-by. 'The only thing you miss is the money I earned you.'

Charlie's beady eyes stared at her hard. 'That's not true.'

Distraught, Shannon buried her face against Mia's head, seeking comfort, seeking to find strength to stand up to Charlie.

Taking a deep breath and inhaling the smell of Mia's freshly washed baby hair, Shannon lifted up her head. She glared at her uncle. 'It is true, and I never did anything other than be on me back or on my knees . . . You know something, I'd never been to a restaurant or to the cinema until Vaughn took me. Can you believe that? I never walked inside one, *ever*.'

Charlie shrugged. 'I never said me name was Pearl & Dean, did I? Oh come on, Shan, if that's what it takes for you to be happy, I'll take you to the bleedin' cinema. I'll even get you some popcorn.' He stopped and a twinkle appeared in his eyes before he continued with, 'And in return, whilst you're watching *Dumbo*, you can wank me off in the back row.' He burst into laughter before it turned into a nasty cough. He wiped away the thick lump of yellow spit from his chin and grinned. 'That was a joke, it was a joke! Jesus, Shan, you don't have to look like that, do you?'

Verging on hysterical, Shannon shook her head furiously, tears rolling down her cheeks. 'But it ain't a joke, is it? Well, is it? How many times have I done that to you . . . *How many*? And how young was I when it first happened?'

Nonplussed, Charlie gave an exaggerated yawn. 'How the hell do I know?'

'I'll tell you, shall I? I was eight. That's what you gave me for my eighth birthday. What was it . . . what did you say to me? *Here you go, Shan, get your lips round that. Happy birthday.* Most kids get a fucking Barbie or . . . or a Matchbox car. Not me, I got my uncle's dick.'

'Oh drop me out, you wanted it. It was mutual.'

Shannon wanted to scream, and if it wasn't for the fact she was holding Mia she would've done, but instead she bit down on her lip, drawing blood as her body was racked with sobs. The pain in her voice cut through the air. 'I was eight! Eight, Uncle Charlie, *eight*.'

'Look, for the life of me I don't know why you're crying, but you've obviously got a problem. Like I say, you need to come home . . . You know what I think? I think you're missing us, Shan – or at least this.' Charlie went into his pocket, pulled something out, then had a quick look around before he opened his fist. Lying in the middle of his palm was a rock of crack.

On seeing what it was Shannon jumped backwards as if she'd had an electric shock. She shook her head and she could feel the beads of sweat prick at her forehead.

Charlie cackled. 'I thought you might like that. Go on, take it. You can have that on me.'

'I don't want it.'

'That's not what your eyes are saying. Look at them, they're lighting up like it's the frigging Blackpool Illuminations.'

Shannon stared at the tiny off-white rock of crack, lying on Uncle Charlie's palm. That tiny piece of cooked-up cocaine had nearly killed her and it had changed her into someone she didn't want to be.

She would've done anything, sold anything, just for a hit on the pipe. And the worst thing about it, when she was high, she had actually liked it. It had made her forget; it had helped her to cope with the pain of her life. Pain was something she didn't like and wasn't very good at handling.

So she knew she needed to stay far away from it because if she ever went there again, she would lose everything. And losing everything when she'd only just found life was something she didn't even want to contemplate . . . Because, above all else, she would lose Vaughn.

'I'm not interested – that's all in the past for me.'

Charlie rubbed his tongue over his teeth, tasting the remains of the breakfast he'd had a few hours ago. 'Don't kid yourself, Shan. You were born a smack baby and you've lived your life as a crack baby, so whether you like it or not, this will always be in your DNA. It's a part of you. Face it, Shan, there's no escape, so you might as well take it, because sooner rather than later you'll be banging down my door begging for it,' he said nastily.

Crying hard now – which set Mia off – Shannon blubbered out her words as she tried to stand up to the man she'd always been terrified of. 'Stop it! Just stop, I ain't interested. I don't want it anymore, I've got something better now.'

Charlie roared with laughter, giving the passing traffic warden a fright. 'Better? Better? You're trying to tell me looking after that little sprog is better than the life you had?'

'Yeah I am. For your information, I enjoy looking after Mia – and Vaughn treats me well. He's a gentleman.'

There was something in the way Shannon said it that made Charlie stop and stare at her for a number of seconds before he said, 'Oh my God, you stupid, stupid fucking bitch.'

Wiping her tears away, Shannon looked at her uncle in puzzlement. 'What?'

'You've fallen for him, ain't you? You've got a tingle in your pussy for Vaughn, haven't you? You stupid cow.'

Not sounding very convincing, Shannon shouted, 'No of course I ain't – what do you take me for?'

Charlie pointed at Shannon, his eyes a mixture of anger and amusement. 'Let me tell you something: he would never look at you twice. Look at the state of you, you're nothing but a little scrubber and soon, Shan, soon, he's going to get fed up of you – especially if you ain't even sucking his dick. He'll get someone else to look after Mia and then you'll be back in the gutter.'

'That's not true! That's not true.'

Feeling the chill wind pick up, Charlie zipped up his navy tracksuit jacket. 'But it is true, Shan. The problem is you just don't want it to be true.'

'Leave me alone, leave me alone!' Shannon turned and started to run down Broadwick Street, holding Mia tightly against her. She pushed past the group of tourists again, hearing her uncle shout after her.

'Mark my words, Shan, you're nothing to him. Nothing.'

And as Shannon continued to run, something deep inside her began to believe her uncle's words.

10

Vaughn stared at Alfie, who was sat on the high leather stool in the kitchen. From where he stood, he could see the whole of Old Compton Street out the wide, tinted panoramic window. It was busy; the theatregoers had come out in their droves and crowds of tourists and Londoners had descended on Soho to enjoy the sunny May day.

But as Vaughn continued to stand and watch Davey sew up Alfie's cheek, his thoughts were slightly distracted . . . He'd texted *and* called Shannon, but so far, he hadn't heard anything back. And maybe it was nothing and he was just winding himself up. After all she was street-savvy, more than she should be . . . *But*, and it was a big but, she was just a kid. A kid who not so long ago was on crack cocaine and anything else she could get her hands on.

He rubbed his head, massaging his temples. Fuck, he had to stop this. He was just being paranoid. He trusted her – or at least he thought he did – and besides Shannon seemed to be thriving looking after Mia. Plus, he'd already read her the riot act about even *speaking* to people from her old life, and that if she ever went near the pipe again, she could wave goodbye to him and Alfie looking out for her. Hopefully that was a big enough incentive as anything else, better than any expensive rehab treatment.

He'd seen it too many times before. He'd seen people think they could still acquaint themselves with their old life, thinking what harm would it do. But only too quickly and too easily they were spiralling back down the dark, drug-fuelled rabbit hole.

'For fuck's sake, do you have to jab me like that? What happened to a bit of TLC?'

Davey Stevens laughed, his slim face crinkling up in a mass of wrinkles as his grey eyes watered. 'Stop being such a drama queen.'

Alfie glared at Davey, looking at the long, sharp suture needle he was using. 'It fucking hurts, and you ain't exactly Florence Nightingale. I think you need to work on your gentle touch a bit.'

Again, Davey laughed as Alfie took a swig from the bottle of whiskey next to him. He felt sick from the pain but sicker from the fact that Huang and his men thought that it was okay to come to his flat and give him a pasting. And the worse thing was: he knew it wasn't over; it had only just begun.

Wincing at the whiskey as well as the pain of Davey sewing up his face, Alfie tried to distract himself from his thoughts. He glanced around the expensive white and silver kitchen before his gaze came to rest on Vaughn, noticing the worry on his face.

Still in acute agony, and through gritted teeth, Alfie said, 'What's up with you? You look like you've walked in on someone fucking your missus.'

Vaughn, irritated by Alfie's comment but also not wanting to tell him the truth about his concerns about Shannon, snarled, 'Turn it in, Alf, and as if you have to ask what the matter is.'

'Well it seems like I do,' Alfie snapped back, just as irritated.

'What the fuck do you think's wrong with me? I leave your daughter with you for a couple of hours then when I come back, you've been sliced up. Are you really surprised I ain't happy?'

Bitterness poured from Alfie's mouth, his thick black hair falling over the gash on his forehead. 'Oh, so it's my fault is it? I'm to blame for cutting up my face, am I? Well thanks for the sympathy.'

Knowing that he could trust Davey, who no doubt was a keeper of a lot more secrets than just theirs, Vaughn felt comfortable to continue to speak in front of him. 'Do me a favour will you, Davey? Stab that fucking needle into him, will ya? Stick some sense in him, cos he's starting to do my head in.'

Pushing Davey out of the way, Alfie – with the thread still attached to the needle hanging down from his cheek – jumped up from his seat, marching across to where Vaughn was leaning. He held his ribs, feeling the throb in them from where Huang's men had kicked him senseless.

'What is your problem? I already told you not to bring her. I ain't interested, so if anyone's to blame, it's *you*, because as usual *you* wouldn't listen.'

Vaughn moved away from Alfie to grab hold of the packet of cigarettes on the side. He lit one up, inhaling deeply, staring at Alfie in anger. 'Alf, you're not getting it. Look at the state of you: you can hardly see through one eye, your mouth looks like it's been put through the mincer and your cheek is half hanging off. This ain't anything to do with me bringing Mia to you, but whilst we're on that subject, I ain't happy you never told me about Huang, cos I certainly would've thought twice about leaving her here if you had.'

'Well I told you not to.'

Vaughn prodded Alfie in his chest. 'Don't give me that, you weren't concerned about her – you've already said as much. You're just pissed off that I found out . . . So go on then, what have you done, Alf? How did you fuck him over . . . Why is Huang after the great Alfie Jennings?'

Feeling ill again from the pain, Alfie slumped down on the stool once more. The last thing he wanted was for Vaughn to chew off his ear, and besides, thinking about what happened – talking about it – opened too many boxes for him, stuff he just didn't want to deal with.

'Leave it, Vaughn, will you? Anyway, you're just presuming that it was Huang. You're the only one who's mentioned his name.'

Taking another drag of the cigarette, Vaughn stared contemptuously at Alfie before laughing bitterly. 'Oh, do me a favour, don't try to mug me off. I saw Huang come out of these flats. You're not trying to tell me that it was a coincidence and the person who did that to your face was someone entirely different.'

Getting almost to the end of the whiskey, Alfie took another slug then spoke wearily. 'I ain't trying to tell you nothing. Can we just do this another day?'

'No, mate, we can't cos right now, I've got the upper hand. You're in a hell of a lot of pain, crippled with agony no doubt, and the last thing you want me to do is to keep at you. So that's exactly what I'm going to do: keep at you. I'm not going anywhere until I find out exactly what's going on. And both you and I know, by tonight you'll be gagging to tell me the truth, just to shut me the fuck up.'

11

Deep in thought, Franny walked along the prison corridor to the showers, passing a group of women who were chatting outside one of the cells. They gave her hostile stares, but rather than turn away she stared back; cold and steely, narrowing her eyes to give a threatening glare, until the taller of the women, suddenly seeming less assured, dropped her gaze to the floor.

In this place it was dog eat dog, and the first sign of weakness . . . well, she knew only too well that not only would the vultures begin to circle, that's when the nightmare would really begin.

Bullying and violence were big problems in most prisons and certainly the one she was in. And although it was mainly the men's prisons that were written about in the media, the women's jails had their fair share of trouble. Whatever the men did, the women could do it just as well.

The wing she was on was a mixed bag; unlike some prisons where they kept them separate, the long-termers and the women on remand were held together. Apparently it was supposed to help the remand prisoners integrate to prison life by having the long-termers support and mentor them. To her, that was a joke – it was prison, not Girl Guides, and the simple fact was that everyone was out for themselves. It was the only way to survive.

Yawning, and feeling a sharp tension in her shoulders and back, Franny continued down the noisy corridor, carrying a towel and a prison washbag. The sound alone was difficult to get used to. Day or night, the whole prison was a constant racket of women shouting and calling, banging and clattering, peals of laughter and screams of terror. But the sound she found most difficult was the wailing from the psychiatric wing. Unremitting howls that sent a chill down even her spine. And not for the first time it struck Franny that, of all the things she hadn't appreciated before she'd arrived, the biggest was the simple pleasure of silence.

Turning the corner to the showers, Franny hoped that this time they wouldn't be filthy. Yesterday when she'd gone in there, the whole place looked like it had been used as a pig shed. Shit and vomit had been wiped all over the cracked beige and green tiled floor and walls and it had taken all her willpower to stop herself vomiting from the smell alone. So she was praying that, today, there wouldn't be any nasty surprises in store.

Pushing open the large swing door, Franny was relieved to see it was not only pretty clean but also empty. Grateful, she made her way to the far-end cubicle; entering and leaning on the cool of the tiles, she sighed.

She felt tired, drained of all energy, and it hadn't helped that last night she'd slept heavily and dreamt of Spain, a place she had fond memories of. So when she'd woken, it had taken her a few seconds to get her bearings and realise where she was – and when she *had*, the reality had come crashing down on her like a crowbar.

Placing her washbag and towel on the floor, Franny put her head in her hands, knowing that no one was watching – there was no CCTV – and for the first time in longer than she could remember, she felt the tears well up and begin to fall.

Immediately angry with herself for being weak, she took a deep breath, wiped the tears away with her sleeve and felt the simmering hatred in her soul for Vaughn rise up once again. And she welcomed that, because *that* feeling would keep her strong.

Wrapping her long chestnut hair in a bun, Franny took off her grey marl sweater and sweat pants and clicked on the shower, straight away letting out a groan. It was freezing cold; yet again, it seemed the prison boilers weren't working. But having no other choice, she gritted her teeth and began to wash herself quickly, trying to scrub the smell of prison out from her skin.

Shivering and with her body now covered in goose pimples from the cold, Franny washed the last of the soap away before clicking off the shower. Hearing voices coming from down the other end, she grabbed her clothes, pulling them on without bothering to dry herself.

Slipping her elasticated pump shoes on – the lace-up ones having being confiscated due to the prison's suicide risk policy – Franny stepped out of the shower to see Christine Lucas and her cronies huddled up in the far corner, laughing like a bunch of hyenas.

Not wanting to get involved in whatever they were up to, she took another quick glance at them, picked up her washbag and started to make her way out.

Christine, having not spotted Franny until that moment, turned her head and grinned as she stopped what she was doing to block Franny's way. Her neck fat jiggled as she chuckled at Franny. Her Geordie accent as strong as ever as she said, 'Well hello, pet, this is a nice surprise. It's a shame I wasn't here a few minutes ago, I could've helped you soap yourself down. Help you get into all those tricky places.' She licked her lips, flicking off the dry piece of food stuck to her mouth.

From the corner of her eye, Franny could see there was someone on the floor hidden behind where the other women were standing. Not only that, she could see a trickle of blood making its way from whoever it was lying there to one of the drains in the centre of the shower area.

Franny nodded towards the blood. She spoke as coldly as she felt. 'Someone had an accident?'

Christine stepped nearer to Franny. Her eyes blazed with hatred. 'It depends on your definition of an accident, pet.'

Franny shook her head. She glanced down at the ground before looking back up at Christine. 'Anyway, it ain't nothing to do with me, so if you don't mind, I've got things to do.'

But as Franny went to step around Christine, her path

was blocked once more. 'I think you must've forgotten what I told you, love. I run this place. So I say what people do and don't do. I say when they piss, I say when they shit and I say when they sleep, and I also say you're not going anywhere until we finish that *chat* we were having before.'

Even though Franny was more than used to violent confrontation, her heart still began to beat faster and she could feel her mouth becoming dry. 'I ain't got anything to say to you, Christine. So how about we keep out of each other's way? It'll do us both a favour.'

Christine burst out into laughter, her beady eyes disappearing under the fat on her cheekbones. 'In another life perhaps you and I would've been friends. I like a woman who can hold her own.'

'Let's just get this clear from the start: I would never be friends with the likes of you, no matter what life we were in.'

The tension between the women was palpable as Christine spoke. 'So I take it you've heard what I did?'

'Yeah, Christine, I know exactly what you did. We all know how you took a hammer to your kids and battered them to death, and you wear that fact like you're wearing a frigging rosette.'

Christine shrugged. Again she smiled. 'Well, what can I say? I'm famous.'

With as much hatred as she could muster, Franny whispered, 'No, Christine. You're evil. Make no mistake about that, and everyone around here knows it; it's just that they don't say it.'

Christine's face darkened. She turned to the other women. 'Is that what you all think?'

64

The women chuckled but didn't answer, as Christine added, 'Shall we show her what happens to smart-mouthed bitches?'

The circle of women opened up and there on the floor, her face sliced to ribbons and the word *dead* carved into her forehead, was a young woman, probably no older than twenty.

Franny ran her tongue along the back of her teeth and stared coolly without blinking, making sure she gave no reaction to Christine.

'Why aye, pet, you're a hardened bitch, aren't you? Not even a flinch. You play the game nearly as good as I do. Not that it makes much difference – like I say, I'm the one who calls the shots around here.'

Christine stopped talking to nod to a tall, skinny blonde woman with tattoos and self-harm markings covering both her arms. 'Keep watch for me will you, pet?' Not having to be asked twice, the woman grinned and sauntered to the door. Then turning back to Franny, Christine winked. 'That's better, we won't be disturbed now.' And with those words Christine Lucas slammed her elbow viciously into Franny's nose.

Blood spurted out and across Franny's cheeks like a fountain, and for a moment she felt light-headed. The whole room spun around. She staggered backwards as Christine – to the roar of the rest of the gathered women – lunged at her again. But, being faster and more agile, Franny ducked just in time, avoiding Christine's clenched fist.

Managing to grasp Christine around her waist, Franny pushed and slammed her into the tiled walls with a loud thud, but not before Christine gripped hold of Franny's hair, pulling it so hard that it felt to Franny like it was being ripped right out of her scalp.

The impact of being barged against the wall made Christine lose her balance. She fell sideways, taking Franny down with her like a ton of bricks.

Her teeth bit down on her tongue and with her mouth full of blood, Franny tried to clamber off Christine, stretching out for her washbag. She grabbed hold of it but immediately she felt Christine's grip on her ankle.

To the baying sound of the women, Franny frantically kicked at her, twisting her body to shake herself free as she quickly scrambled to open her washbag, pulling out the sharpened-ended toothbrush to use as a weapon.

Breaking free of Christine's grip, Franny was able to jump up, holding the makeshift shank in her hand, the end of the toothbrush razor sharp and pointed, ready if needed to do some damage.

Her voice was hard and dangerous as she glared at Christine. 'Come near me, and I won't think twice about using this. Do you understand me?'

Christine's face broke into a smile. She pulled up her trouser leg – which exposed a huge, faded fist tattoo on her calf – and grabbed something out from her sock. 'Oh I understand, but you're not the only one who enjoys a fight.'

Franny stared at what Christine held in her hand. Like her own weapon – which, if they were sensible, most of the women carried and hid on their persons for protection – Christine's shank was made out of a toothbrush, but unlike hers, Christine had melted the end of it and inserted razor blades into the plastic. 'Come on then, Franny, what are you waiting for, love?'

With her heart pounding, and her eyes fixed on the shank, Franny stood working out what she was going to do. She was outnumbered and right now she wouldn't have placed her money on getting out unscathed.

She glanced over to the small group of women who gazed back at her curiously and seeing Franny on the back foot, Christine cackled again, spinning the shank in her hand. 'Seems like our Franny's going to lose that pretty face of hers. Howay, man, never mind!'

'Screws are coming, screws are coming!' Suddenly, the blonde-haired woman who'd been keeping guard rushed in, shouting out her warning.

There was an immediate scramble as the women darted out of the shower room but not before Christine, with the quickest of flicks, nicked Franny on her neck with the razor blade.

Flinching, Franny's hand shot to her neck. She could feel it was only superficial but the pain was still sharp and she felt the warmth of her blood beginning to flow through her fingers.

Christine hurried towards the door. As she was about to exit, she turned back and said, 'Take that as a warning. Next time, pet, you'll look more like her.'

She laughed as she nodded towards where the young woman was lying in a pool of her own blood, her face torn and carved up, and with that Christine disappeared out of the room.

12

Rushing over to the woman on the floor, Franny bent down. She spoke quietly to her. 'Hey, you're okay now. They've gone. Can you get up at all?'

Through half-closed eyes the woman – barely being able to move her head – looked at Franny, who stared curiously back at her. Or rather who stared curiously at what was in her mouth. She had something stuffed into it. Carefully, Franny opened the woman's mouth, prising her fingers between her teeth to pull out the soggy mess. The minute she did so, the woman began to cough and splutter.

'Take a deep breath, that's it.' Fearfully, the woman glanced at Franny and even though she didn't say anything, Franny could see the gratitude in her eyes.

Chucking the paper on the floor, Franny suddenly saw that it had something written on it. Intrigued, she picked it up, but immediately her attention was drawn back to the woman, who started to vomit violently. Shoving the paper in her pocket for later, Franny gently rubbed the woman's back whilst she retched noisily.

Wincing slightly as she watched, Franny spoke warmly, 'That's it, doll. Get it all out, sweetheart.'

It was after a couple of minutes – and after Franny herself began to feel sick – that the woman actually did get it all out. She turned to Franny, her voice trembling and so quiet that Franny had to crane forward to hear what she was saying.

'Thank you, I dunno what I would've done if you hadn't come along. I think she would've killed me . . .'

Franny had no doubt that's exactly what would've happened. She really wanted to ask the woman a lot of questions but it was clear she was in no fit state, so instead she simply asked, 'What's your name?'

'Jessie.'

Giving a small smile, Franny nodded. 'Well it's good to meet you. I'm Franny by the way. Look, let's get you under the shower shall we? And then you need to get looked at. The cuts are deep, but I reckon they'll be able to fix you up.'

Before Franny had time to say anything else, the door of the shower room was abruptly opened. Standing in the doorway were four prison officers and on seeing them Franny muttered under her breath, *'Shit.'*

The stockier, more masculine-looking screw stared at Franny. She spoke in a Scottish accent. 'What's happened here, Doyle?'

Standing up, Franny said nothing as the prison officers walked over to her and Jessie.

'I asked you a question, *what happened here*?'

Again, Franny didn't answer. There was an unwritten rule in prison. It was simple: never say anything. Not unless you wanted the whole prison on your back. Even when the governor would promise the women a safe transfer to another prison to grass someone up, word would travel to the place you were going and life would be a living hell. Franny knew only too well that there was no room in prison for a grass: no matter what, it was still a question of the screws on one side, and the women on another.

'The cat got your tongue? Because if it hasn't you better have a good reason for not answering me. Not that I can't see for myself.'

Franny spoke evenly. 'Then why ask?'

Realising she wasn't going to get anything from Franny, Officer Brown crouched down to give Jessie an icy glare. 'So who did this to you? Come on, Jessie, look at the state of you. Even when they fix you up, your face is going to look like a game of criss-cross. You need to tell me the name of whoever it was so I can deal with them . . . Come on, Jess, you can't go around protecting the scum that did this.'

Jessie's eyes glanced up to Franny who gave a quick, small shake of her head, warning Jessie not to say a word. If Christine got one sniff that Jessie had said anything – which she would, *especially* as some of the prison officers liked to wind up and cause trouble amongst the women – it was doubtful Jess would make it back home alive.

Frustrated by both Franny and Jess, Officer Brown pushed slightly harder. 'You better tell me, Jess, because I don't like the fact that someone around here thinks they can do this and get away with it. Is that what you want? You want someone to slice you up and not answer for it? Just say the name for God's sake and we can get you transferred out of here, or at least to another wing.'

Without saying anything, Jessie put her head down and stared at the floor as Officer Brown gave a rueful smile. She stood back up, brushing down her prison uniform and absentmindedly playing with the chain fixed to her security belt. She glared at Franny. 'You bitches don't do yourself any favours do you? You're a bunch of animals and deserve . . .'

Suddenly, Officer Brown stopped what she was saying as her gaze came to rest on Franny's washbag. Thrown by the side of it was her homemade shank.

Franny's heart sank as she listened to Brown say, 'Well, well, well, is that yours, Doyle?'

Feeling the dried blood on her nose and cheeks, Franny shook her head. She spoke ruefully. 'If I say no, will you believe me?'

'Not a chance and if you or Jessie won't give me a name, whether you did this to Jessie or not – which just between you and I – I don't think you did, I'm going to hold you responsible.'

'Now why doesn't that surprise me?' said Franny, laughing bitterly.

The officer shrugged. 'It's your call, Doyle. Are you going to tell me who did this?'

Franny leant towards Officer Brown. 'Go to hell.'

'Fine, have it your way, Doyle . . . So here's how it's going to work: I'm going to tell the governor that I've got the culprit and that we found the weapon. Easy really. Job done. I can get off home early. I mean, if you lot don't want to help yourselves, why should I care what happens to you?'

Full of hostility, Franny stared back. Knowing what was coming she listened as Officer Brown spoke to the other members of staff. 'Take Jessie down to the medical wing and I'll take Doyle to seg, give her some time to think about the error of her ways.'

And as Franny was dragged off to segregation by Officer Brown, the only feeling she had was of revenge, but it wasn't Christine Lucas she was out for. She had two other people on her mind: Vaughn Sadler and Detective Balantyne.

13

On the other side of London, Detective Balantyne gazed in the mirror of his office bathroom. He felt terrible and looked even worse. After the argument with Emma, he'd wanted to get out of the house – away from her and away from her drinking – so he'd pulled up in a lay-by near work on the north side of Woolwich and made his car his bed for the night.

It wasn't the first time he'd done that, and he knew it certainly wouldn't be the last. He wanted out so badly; he wanted to get as far away from Emma as it was physically possible. But how the hell could he get out when the guilt over what had happened always ate him up, and the memory of that day was literally burnt on her face?

On the odd occasions he'd packed his bags to go, when the situation had become too intolerable to take any more, she'd screamed and cried, threatening to take her own life if he left. And every part of him had wanted to keep on walking and not turn around, but the problem was he knew that it wasn't an empty promise. Emma would be prepared to die just so she could punish him – and God, how he fucking despised her for it.

He despised *every* part of her but especially her drinking, which had been a problem *even* before the day in question. From the beginning of their marriage she'd been drinking but she'd hidden it well. And then as time went by he'd either turned a blind eye to it or he'd been too busy with work to notice or to care. Then by the time he *had* realised, it was too late.

Emma was difficult at the best of times, but her drinking – which seemed to start almost from the moment she woke up – made her completely impossible to deal with. And it made an already difficult situation a whole lot worse, a whole lot nastier.

And as much as he hated to admit it, over the last few months he'd found himself putting his hands on her more and more. Slapping her around a bit . . . Only a bit . . . Not hard, not like some of the men he used to arrest when he was a bobby on the beat, the ones who would knock their wives so senseless they'd look like they'd been in a road traffic accident . . . No, he wasn't like that. Okay, he'd left a few marks, a few bruises, a few cuts . . . But Jesus, what did she expect if she was always pushing him, always pouncing on him the minute he walked through the door, always accusing him of sleeping with anything that moved? Testing him, pushing him to the limits – and the fact was the drinking, the accusations and her obsession with having a baby had turned his life into a living nightmare.

So no, he didn't want to be the kind of man who knocked his wife about, but she didn't give him any choice.

'Sir, the Chief's waiting for you.' A young officer – who for the life of him, Balantyne couldn't remember the name of – popped his head around the men's bathroom door. 'She's not very happy by the way . . . But when is she?'

He nodded and answered half-heartedly as he continued to adjust his tie in the mirror.

'Thanks, I'll be there in a few minutes.'

'I think she wants you now, sir. She was very adamant about that.'

Balantyne swivelled around to stare at the young officer. His tone was as hard as his steely gaze. 'I *said*, I'll be there in a few minutes. Now if that isn't fucking good enough for the Chief or you, then there's nothing much I can do.'

'It's just that—'

Before the officer could finish, Balantyne jumped at him, dragging and pulling him up against the wall. He pushed his forearm into the man's neck, his eyes bulging. 'What is it that you didn't understand about what I just said? Didn't I say I was coming? Didn't I say that I'd be with her in a few minutes?'

Spluttering and in shock, the officer nodded, unable to get his words out. Then suddenly, Balantyne dropped his hold, realising what he was doing. He shook his head at himself as he mumbled a half apology whilst attempting to straighten the startled officer's uniform. 'Jesus, I'm sorry, I'm sorry . . . I . . . I . . . Look, I'm just a bit tired. It's no excuse I know, but . . . but . . . listen, can we just keep this between ourselves. No harm done, hey?'

Flustered, the young officer nodded. When he spoke, his voice was quiet and strained. 'No harm done, sir.' And without saying anything else he disappeared quickly out of the bathroom, leaving Balantyne to stare at himself once again in the mirror. He thought about Franny Doyle and he thought about Emma. Two bitches that he could do without.

As he continued to stare, rage surged through him and he smashed his fist against the glass. He watched the broken mirror fall into the sink before he took a deep breath, closed his eyes and felt the pricking of tears at the back of his throat. And not for the first time he realised how much he hated his life; it seemed he was going to be stuck with Emma forever if he didn't think of a way out . . .

14

Half an hour later, Balantyne sat slumped, brooding and summoned, trying to keep his composure as he fought the temptation to give the Chief a piece of his mind. He wondered quite how it had come to this, and why it wasn't him whose name was on the door of the office after he'd given his life to the service.

So now he had to sit opposite the newly promoted Chief Inspector Claire Martin, being admonished like he was a school kid.

He sighed as he gazed past her and out through the window, which looked over the River Thames.

'Why am I getting the feeling I'm the only one in the room?' Claire Martin's voice cut through the air, jolting Balantyne out of the daze he found himself in.

Irritated, Tony stared at the Chief. She was young for the position she held and apart from the tiniest of crow's feet beginning to show around her blue eyes – no doubt from the strain of the job – her petite features, smooth pale skin and blonde pixie bob gave her a youthful, and attractive, appearance. Balantyne suspected that, dressed in civilian clothes, no one would guess she held the position she did.

Suddenly needing a cigarette, Balantyne's face looked like thunder. 'I don't know, *ma'am*, because I'm doing exactly what you want me to do. I'm sitting here listening. Anything else, I can't help you with.'

Chief Inspector Martin came around from behind her desk to perch herself on the edge of the table. She stared at Balantyne as she sat opposite him, tapping her pen against her leg. 'I don't like your attitude, Detective, and I know I'm not the only one around here who doesn't.'

Balantyne gave her a cutting stare and his voice dripped with bitterness. 'I thought this conversation was about Franny Doyle, not about who does or doesn't like me.'

It was Claire's turn to feel irritated. She pursed her lips before she spoke, keeping her tone even. 'I'll make this conversation about what the hell I like, do you understand that? In case you've forgotten, it's my name on the door and you need to get over that fact, otherwise I suggest you put in for a transfer to another division.'

Balantyne leant forward. 'Don't worry, ma'am, I haven't forgotten. I can't forget your name's on the door *especially* as you seem to remind me at every opportunity you can.'

The room fell silent and tension sat in the air before Claire said, 'Anyway, tell me what's happening with the Doyle case. Are you any further forward? The CPS have been on my back because they've been reviewing the evidence and they need more. If we're going to get a conviction – which as you know everyone's desperate for – you need to bring more to the table . . . But no shortcuts. Play by the book. That's the only way we'll be able to nail her, by you playing it *straight*. The last thing we want is the case collapsing before it's begun.'

'You need to trust me on this. I'll get Doyle, but I have to be able to do it my way.'

Chief Martin shook her head. Her voice verged on hostility. 'No, and it's not up for negotiation either. Play it by the book, Detective, or I'll take you off the case.'

Furiously, Balantyne pointed his finger, emphasising each word he uttered with a jab in the air.

'Doyle's mine. I've spent years trying to pin the likes of her and Alfie Jennings down, and you have no right to threaten to take me off this case.'

'Then don't give me a reason to.'

Balantyne glared at Martin. He couldn't understand her. She knew as well as anyone that to get Doyle, he had to play by *their* rules, which meant bending them. How the hell could she say that she wanted a conviction if he wasn't allowed to do what was needed? But then again, what did he expect? She was a woman after all, and he'd never been able to understand women at the best of times, let alone in the male-dominated world of the police force – though even that balance was being challenged.

He thought about the influx of women who were coming through the doors, full of hormones and shouting out about having equal rights. But when you did treat them as an equal, Tony thought, with locker-room jokes and the traditional light-hearted initiations and innuendos, before you knew it they'd start making official complaints.

Over the years he'd been told he was a chauvinist, a bigot and even a sexist, but he just liked to think of himself as a real man – and real men had real women around them, who knew their place. And their place certainly *wasn't* in charge of a few hundred men, making their decisions based on what time of the month it was.

Tony sighed. He knew it wasn't the politically correct way to think but he also knew the truth; women's decisions were first and foremost emotionally driven and he would be damned if he was going to listen and take orders from a woman whose idea of detective work was to find her lipstick in her oversized handbag.

Not that he'd always thought that way about Detective Martin . . . At one point he'd respected her, but things happen. *Shit* happened; it felt like there was more shit raining down on him than he'd like – and in his opinion, it all started and ended with the women he had around him.

'Detective, I haven't had your answer . . . Do I have your word or not? Am I going to have to take you off *now* or . . .' She paused and her voice dropped to a softer tone as she rubbed her temples, feeling the first signs of a headache coming on. 'Why do you have to make this so damn difficult? I'm not the enemy here. I want to see Doyle put away as much as you do but I need you to do it the right way. And I don't want anyone knowing about Vaughn Sadler giving a statement. If they did, it would put the cat amongst the pigeons; someone could get hurt. There'd be a lot of trouble.'

'Well, they won't hear it from me.'

'I'm not saying they would . . . *Please*, Tony, I'm not having a go at you.'

Detective Balantyne stood up. He straightened up his jacket and spoke coolly. 'Will that be all, *ma'am*?'

Chief Martin stepped towards Balantyne; she put her hand lightly on his arm. 'Tony . . . wait. Are you okay? You don't look so good . . . Is everything all right at home?'

Shaking her hand off him, Balantyne nodded. 'I'm fine, everything's fine. And now if you don't mind . . .'

As Balantyne went to leave, she grabbed him. Her voice was gentle and quiet. 'Don't shut me out, Tony. Just tell me what's happening. Talk to me. *Please*.'

It wasn't Claire's imagination that she could hear the pain and bitterness in his voice. 'I can't talk to you. Strictly work, remember? We agreed . . . or rather *you* did.'

'What was I supposed to do, Tony? Emma needed you.'

Balantyne grabbed hold of Chief Martin's arm. 'Well, I needed *you* . . . I *needed* you.'

'I know, but we couldn't have carried on . . . Look, Emma was a mess.'

'She's always been a mess and . . . what happened, she did that to herself,' growled Balantyne, shaking his head.

Chief Martin's blue eyes filled with tears. 'You don't believe that. If you did, then why are you always blaming yourself and . . . and why did you end up in my bed again?'

Balantyne's gaze darted over Claire Martin's face. 'Because

I made a mistake . . . It happens . . . Now if you don't mind, *ma'am*, I've got work to do.'

'Fine, but don't forget what I said. By the book, Tony – or you're off the case.'

Claire Martin took a deep breath and pushed her personal feelings aside, watching out of her window as Balantyne marched over to his car. She'd known him for the past ten years and instead of mellowing over time, the man had become more unpredictable, though she suspected it might have less to do with the job and more to do with Emma and what had happened the night of the accident.

The thought of the accident made Claire feel the same familiar rising sense of guilt that had plagued her over the last two years. At the time, she'd seriously thought about quitting the force. But she hadn't; instead she'd quit the relationship with Balantyne. Though it hadn't brought closure – far from it: she'd been miserable and Emma's drinking had got worse and Balantyne had hated her for it.

They'd hardly spoken since, working on different cases and generally avoiding each other. Until about three months ago, that was, when they'd found themselves working on the night shift together. Then unsurprisingly, one thing had led to another . . .

At the time she hadn't regretted it. She'd missed him. He was a different person when he was with her: funny, warm, caring – a world away from his behaviour most of the time. And looking back, she didn't think he'd regretted it either. But then, a couple of weeks after it'd happened, before they'd even had a chance to talk about where they were going to go from there, she'd got promoted to the job he'd been overlooked for, and he'd hated her all over again.

She sighed loudly as she continued to watch Balantyne's car drive out of the station car park. The problem was, he was a stubborn man, always had been, and from what she could see, he always would be. A man who didn't want to bend an inch to the inevitable changes that were filtering their way through the force and who resented where he was in life. Though she couldn't blame him – his life had taken a turn that he couldn't have possibly predicted.

As much as he was infuriating to work with, and not many of the other officers liked him, she had to admit that he was a bloody good detective. In fact, if it hadn't been for the accident, it might've been his name on the door and not hers . . . *Crap*. There she went again, thinking about something she didn't want to.

She was angry with herself now; every time she'd anything to do with him, the same old thoughts and feelings would shoot back around. But she'd be damned if she'd let her emotions rule her head when it came to her job. Detective Balantyne would abide by her orders over the Doyle case, or he would face the consequences.

A couple of hours later, Franny – who still had Balantyne and Vaughn firmly on her mind – lay on the hard mattress in the segregation wing. The cell was sparser than her own; it didn't even have a window, only a flickering fluorescent light, which gave the whole place a sinister glow. The walls were a faded cream, and although they'd been scrubbed,

83

Franny could see the remains of where a prisoner had smeared her name in blood.

She sighed as she stared at the ceiling, but suddenly a thought came to her. She sat up, swinging her legs off the bed before going into her pocket and pulling out the piece of paper that had been stuffed in Jessie's mouth.

Looking up to make sure that none of the screws were peering in through the safety flap, Franny flattened out the crumpled-up paper. On it was written a set of numbers. It read like a sort code and what seemed to be a bank account number. She frowned, wondering quite why Christine and her cronies would stuff this into Jessie's mouth. But then, there was only one way to find out . . .

15

Alfie didn't know how long Vaughn had been sat there staring at him, but he knew it was long enough for a couple of his men to have come and fixed the front door, and it was long enough for the painkiller that Davey had roughly injected into his thigh to wear off. Not to mention, long enough for him to finally say, 'All right, all right. For fuck's sake, I'll tell you what happened, I'll tell you everything – but you got to promise me you'll drop it after that. The last thing I need is you chewing me ear off.'

Vaughn pulled deeply on his cigarette as he sat on the velvet couch opposite Alfie. Speaking with smoke coming out from his mouth, he shrugged. 'I ain't promising you anything, I just want to know the truth, Alf. I wanna know what you did for him to be so pissed off . . . And don't bullshit me.'

'I said I'd tell you, didn't I?' Weary and still in excruciating pain, Alfie paused as he gazed through his lounge window. He could see the rooftops of Soho from where he sat. It was one of his favourite sights and had always seemed so uplifting, but now he felt a sense of melancholy, like a dark cloud had come over him. Opening the box about all that had happened felt raw and painful and the memories of his own childhood abuse came flooding in whenever he thought about it.

Taking a deep breath, Alfie began to speak again, though this time he was hesitant. 'Do you remember when Charlie Eton's dad, Barry, came out of prison, and Franny and I thought that he'd kidnapped Mia for his own sick fantasies?'

Vaughn nodded but didn't say anything as he let Alfie continue to talk.

'Well as you know, at the time, I didn't realise that Mia was my daughter. Franny was still keeping it a secret, and of course Bree was . . .' He trailed off. It still hadn't sunk in that Bree was dead and that Franny had killed her. It was hard for him to get his head around. The last few months seemed like a pack of lies, a twilight zone, and he couldn't work out the truth.

Impatiently, Vaughn said, 'Dead. Bree was dead and your missus killed her.'

'Oh that's right, thanks very much for that, Mr Fucking Sensitive. For a moment there I thought I was talking to someone that actually gave a fuck.'

'Look, Alf, if it hasn't escaped your notice, neither of us are in this business to be sentimental.'

Alfie shook his head and answered bitterly, 'Says the man who seems to have taken over the role of looking after my . . . well, looking after Mia.'

It was Vaughn's turn to shake his head. 'You can't even say it, can you? You can't even say she's your daughter.'

Taking a swig of a bottle of beer he'd found at the back of his fridge, Alfie leant forward on his chair, staring hard at Vaughn. 'What I do or don't say, ain't got anything to do with you. And I ain't too hard to admit that I'm cut up about Bree. I'm a bit gutted.' Alfie stopped talking again, knowing that it was more than a bit gutting. Although he hated what Bree had done – run away and not tell him that she'd been pregnant – Bree *had* been someone he'd loved, fallen for when Franny had disappeared out of his life.

Of course he hadn't intended on falling for Bree. He wouldn't have bothered putting his feelings into her if he'd known Franny was coming back. But he hadn't known. Franny hadn't told him anything; she'd just picked up one day and disappeared.

That was the problem with Franny: she was always full of secrets and lies. Even now he didn't know the truth of what happened. He hadn't even been to see her to find out, because what would be the point? She would only lie to him. So all he knew was that, somewhere between Bree leaving him and Bree having his baby in secret, unbeknownst to him, Franny had been in the thick of it.

How and why, was something else he didn't know. And he definitely couldn't work out why Bree had kept the pregnancy from him, because he would've looked after her. He would've cared for her like there was no tomorrow. She would've wanted for nothing. And he would've loved Mia and made sure that nothing, and no one, ever hurt her.

But now . . . Now, it was all fucked up. Mia didn't feel

like his. She was a stranger to him – and Bree and *especially* Franny were to blame for that. And it hurt. Christ, it hurt like no other pain he'd experienced before. The betrayal cut so deep it felt raw . . . And no matter what Vaughn thought, it *did* bother him. It bothered him that he couldn't feel the way he wanted to about Mia.

And if he were facing cold, hard facts, the truth was he couldn't even look at Mia because she reminded him of what Bree had done, of what *Franny* had done; everything he was trying to run away from. So no, he didn't want to be reminded of it all, he didn't want to think. He just wanted to blot out the pain with a whole heap of drink and a shitload of drugs.

'I'm waiting . . . Come on, Alfie, I haven't got all day. I ain't got time for you to sit there in a daze. I want to know about Huang.'

With no other option, Alfie snapped, 'Fine . . . But it ain't pretty . . . When Franny and I went looking for Mia, it took us down a dark road. As you know we thought that Mia had been taken by a paedophile ring, but what you don't know is when we were looking for her we came across a little boy who was being auctioned off by Charlie Eton's dad.'

'How, where, when? Jesus Christ, Alf. What about the kid's parents though?' said Vaughn, feeling sick.

'The mum was nowhere to be seen, and can you believe, it was actually the kid's *own* father who'd sold him to Charlie's dad for a percentage of the profits so he could feed his crack habit.'

Vaughn paled. He knew both Charlie Eton and his dad,

Barry, had been a sick pair, but he hadn't known how sick or that they'd been directly involved in selling kids. Alfie had spoken so very little to him since the day Franny was arrested and held on remand . . . In fact, most of the time Alfie had been in a stupor, so this was the first time he'd really had a sit-down chat since it'd all kicked off.

'I never knew, mate. Shit, I'm sorry. And I had no idea that Charlie was involved in something so fucking evil.'

'Actually he wasn't, not really, but Barry and the whole situation was part of the reason I put a bullet in Charlie's leg. Everything got out of hand and at one point, Charlie was covering for Barry, so you can imagine how things got very messy. Anyway, the point is there was no way I could leave the kid. I couldn't have it on my conscience that a little boy was going to be auctioned off by some sick fucker to another even sicker fucker . . . Anyway, to cut a long story short, it's sorted now. The kid's safe and he's doing well.'

Vaughn shook his head. 'But why didn't you tell me any of this?'

Alfie shrugged. 'The fewer people knew the better. Anyway, I had Franny. She held her own and she had my back . . .' Alfie paused then added bitterly, 'Well I thought she did . . . Turns out she had her own agenda because the whole time I was trying to help her find Mia, she never once told me the truth about Mia or Bree.'

Viciously, Vaughn growled, 'Well she wouldn't, would she? This is Franny we're talking about . . . But how does this have anything to do with Huang?'

Alfie stared down at the floor as he continued to recall

what happened. 'The bid for the kid was going to be a high one. He was young and innocent. *Fresh* . . . He was exactly what those sick monsters were looking for.'

'So how much are we talking?'

'It turned out to be nearly half a million, and I never had that kind of money to lay me hands on, not after those bad deals last year – and certainly not after Franny decided to take it upon herself to give her uncle two million quid behind our backs.'

Vaughn clenched his teeth. The thought of what Franny did last year with the money – *their* money – was certainly a sore point for him, and another reason he was pleased to see Franny rot. She'd clearly thought she could do what she liked without consequences, but now things had finally caught up with her. 'You should've come to me, Alf. I could've sorted something if you'd said.'

Alfie shook his head, and lit another cigarette. 'I needed it straight away. I didn't have time to wait and I know most of your money is tied up with the clubs.'

'So what I don't get is why you didn't ask Franny – she could've lent you that money.'

'Apparently not. Apparently most of her money – and the house – is tied and knotted up in some complicated trust fund that her father set up in case she ever got nicked. He wanted to make sure the Old Bill couldn't touch a penny if she was collared, wanted her to have something to come back to. But that meant she couldn't even get a loan against the house to help.'

Vaughn frowned. 'But she owns it outright and it's worth a hell of a lot more than half a mill.'

'I know, but that's just the way it is.' Alfie shrugged.

Vaughn sat silently for a moment, mulling over what Alfie had said. Eventually he spoke. 'So let me get this right. You went to Huang, even though you knew what would happen if you didn't pay him back?'

Irritated and in chronic pain, Alfie nodded. 'Well what fucking choice did I have? Should I have left the kid with those perverts?'

'No, Jesus, of course not. I just think it's odd that Franny couldn't put her hands on any readies.'

Alfie was beginning to get even more agitated. 'What can I tell you? Her father thought the sun shone out of her fucking arse. He just wanted her to be secure in this fucked-up business we're in.'

Again, Vaughn didn't say anything straight away, but after a minute or so he stared at Alfie. 'So why aren't you dead, Alf?'

'Why aren't I fucking dead? Oh sorry about that, Vaughnie. Am I inconveniencing you being around? Fuck me, I'll put a gun to me head right now, should I?'

Vaughn took a large drink from the glass of vodka he'd been nursing. 'Don't be such a prick. All I'm saying is, if you owe Huang all that money *plus* the interest – which will be going up by the day – I don't understand why you ain't at the bottom of the Thames or buried in Epping Forest, like all the other mugs who borrowed money from him.'

Alfie glared at Vaughn. 'I dunno, perhaps it's because we go back a long way.'

'Bullshit. Look what he's done to your boat race. He don't

care. And we both know Huang hasn't got one sentimental bone in his body. This is the same man who tied his wife up in the house before he burnt it down with her and his sister still inside it.'

Throwing the now empty bottle of beer on the floor, Alfie shrugged. 'At least he sorted it out himself.'

'What the fuck are you talking about? You saying it's okay for him to deep-fry his missus just cos she cheated on him and took a bit of his money?'

'I never said that. What I meant is, at least he didn't involve the Old Bill.'

Vaughn stood up and grabbed his jacket. 'If this is about Franny, I don't want to hear it. It was only a couple of months ago or so that she left me for dead, remember? I've still got the scar to prove it. So just save your breath when it comes to her. I never want to hear her name again.'

Alfie went to get up himself but decided against it after a sharp shooting pain rushed through his body. He snarled, 'Maybe you don't, but the problem is, I ain't got my head around a lot of things, and one of those things is that you called the Old Bill instead of letting me deal with Franny. You went against everything we stand for, every rule we've ever lived by. We don't grass on our own, no matter what.'

Heading for the door, Vaughn stared at Alfie, full of hostility. 'I did what needed to be done. And at the end of the day all I did was call the Old Bill; it was their choice to arrest her. I only made one call. Nothing more, nothing less.' He paused before saying, 'I ain't spoken to them since.'

Alfie looked at him coolly. 'That better be the truth, Vaughn, cos it ain't your place to go around stirring shit, and no one in our business likes a snake. And if I find out—'

Vaughn sniffed and his eyes darkened. 'Don't start threatening me, Alfie. That wouldn't be very wise. And if I were you, I'd stop worrying about Franny and start worrying about the fact that Huang is out for you. I'd also ask yourself why you ain't dead yet, because if you ain't dead by now, it means he's got other plans for you. And if that's the case, Alf, you'll probably end up wishing you *were* dead.'

16

'Where the fuck have you been, Shan? I was calling you.' Three hours later Vaughn stared hard at Shannon as she walked into his opulent flat off Tottenham Court Road.

Bouncing Mia in her arms, Shannon shrugged. 'I just went for a walk.'

Dressed in jeans and a grey Ralph Lauren shirt, Vaughn looked at her suspiciously, knowing that some of his anger was partly relief on knowing that she was safe, and partly from being pissed off with Alfie. 'I told you just to come back here, didn't I? How fucking hard was that to understand? You need to sort yourself out, cos I ain't going stand for you not listening.'

'I'm sorry . . . I was going to bring her straight back like you asked, I swear, but I saw . . . I . . . I . . . I saw . .' Shannon fought back the tears, though both she and Mia were exhausted from crying. She glanced timidly at Vaughn.

The only thing she wanted was a hug from him, and perhaps she was feeling sorry for herself, but she couldn't remember the last time she had one that hadn't led to her having to give someone sex or a blow job.

'Who? What are you talking about? Shannon, who did you see?'

Shannon's face paled. She really wanted to tell Vaughn about Charlie and how much he'd upset her, but something in his eyes told her that she was probably better off leaving it. 'I . . . I . . . just . . . saw someone I knew from my past and I was worried that they might follow me here . . . That's why I didn't come back straight away.'

Vaughn continued to stare at her. She looked terrible. It was clear that she'd been crying and she did sound genuine. 'You better not be lying to me, Shannon, because I've had it up to here with people lying right to my face, and if you and me are going to make this work, then we have to have nothing but honesty between us. Do you understand?'

Shannon swallowed and nodded as she passed Mia to Vaughn. Apart from making sure Mia was safe, the only thing that did matter to her was making sure that Vaughn trusted her.

'Yeah, of course, but I wouldn't risk it, I wouldn't do anything to mess this up. I'm happy here and I appreciate what you've done for me. The last thing I'm going to do is screw this up. It's the best thing that's happened to me.'

Shannon smiled and in that moment Vaughn felt terrible. He had no right to take it out on her. She was a good kid and had basically done everything that he'd asked of her, *including* giving a statement to Detective Balantyne behind Alfie's back.

She hadn't questioned it. She hadn't asked him for anything in return and she certainly hadn't mentioned it to Alfie. She'd just listened to what she had to do and backed up his story about Franny and what had happened to Bree. So who cared? Who cared that she took Mia for a walk, instead of letting some scummy lowlife follow her to the flat? In fact, it was a pretty smart thing she'd done.

Backing down, he smiled at her. 'Look, Shan, I'm sorry, okay? I didn't mean to snap at you. I'm a bit wound up. I had no right to have a pop at you. What do you say I go and get a curry for us both? And then we can watch a bit of telly later. You up for it?'

Shannon's smile lit up her entire face. She nodded enthusiastically. 'Yeah, that would be great. I'll put Mia to bed now if you like.'

'Sounds like a plan.'

Vaughn leant over and kissed Mia on the head before impulsively kissing Shannon on the head as well. She really was like a crazy kid sister. 'That's my girl.'

And with that, Vaughn turned and left, leaving Shannon to whisper back at him, 'Yeah, I am your girl, I am.'

Twenty minutes later, Shannon had given Mia a quick bath and put her in her cot where she was now sound asleep.

She stood watching Mia for a moment, her thoughts fleeting from Alfie to Franny and then to Vaughn before she quietly closed the door.

She could feel butterflies in her tummy at the idea of

spending the evening watching a movie on the couch with Vaughn. Just her and him with no one else about. It was perfect.

Looking about and realising she'd left the flat in a bit of a mess, she rushed around to tidy up the magazines, nail polish, make-up and the numerous different cuddly toys Mia had.

Sticking most of the stuff underneath the expensive leather couch, she smiled to herself in anticipation. Any minute now Vaughn would be home. Then, hearing a tap at the front door, Shannon rushed over to it. No doubt Vaughn was weighed down with takeaway food, having never been very good at making a choice between the various dishes on offer. She took a deep breath and smoothed down her clothes before taking a quick look in the mirror.

And with a huge grin, she threw open the big, cream front door. 'I don't know why you get so much. We chucked most of it away last time, and anyway—' Shannon's words and smile froze. Standing opposite her on a pair of crutches was Uncle Charlie. 'What the fuck are you doing here?'

Charlie roared with laughter as he leant his weight on one of his crutches to enable him to wipe his nose on his hand. 'I take it you ain't exactly pleased to see me. You could hurt a fella's feelings with talk like that. Look, I just thought our conversation didn't end very well, and you seemed upset.'

Shannon glanced nervously down the marbled corridor. She hissed at her uncle, 'You need to get out of here. If Vaughn finds you . . .'

She trailed off as Charlie's obese body heaved with laughter. 'He'll what? I didn't know there were any rules about me visiting me niece . . . I know I said this already but you're looking good by the way – Vaughnie is certainly looking after you well.' He stared at her large breasts, licking his lips.

With her voice full of worry, and a sense of weight pressing down on her chest, Shannon pleaded with her uncle. 'I'm begging you, he'll go mad if he finds you here. You'll ruin it. You'll ruin everything . . . He doesn't want me speaking to you.'

Charlie feigned hurt. 'Well that's not a way to treat family, is it? I tell you what, why don't you invite me in and let me take the weight off me feet, well, foot.' He chuckled unkindly and stopped to look down at his legs, one of which was clearly a prosthetic limb from the knee down. A consequence from the 'run-in' he'd had with Alfie.

Desperate, Shannon's face was drawn. 'Uncle Charlie, he'll chuck me out if he thinks I'm having anything to do with you . . .'

Shannon recoiled as Charlie leant forward. 'And we can't have that can we, not now you've got the hots for him.'

Wide-eyed, Shannon said, 'Why are you doing this? Why do you want to spoil this for me? I ain't ever done anything to you. Please, please, this is the best thing that has happened to me and . . .'

'Shan, is that you? Come and help me with this. I've got me arms full.'

From down at the bottom of the corridor, Shannon heard Vaughn calling from the stairwell. She felt sick and began to tremble. The only way out was the same way as Vaughn was coming up, and there was no way that he could see Charlie.

Charlie winked at Shannon as he stood opposite her. He could see the sweat beginning to form on her forehead. 'It'll be nice to reacquaint myself with him. Long time and all that. I can tell him what a good job I think he's doing with my niece and see if his intentions are pure.'

'Shan. Get off that phone and come on. There's a tikka masala with your name on it and I'm about to become worse off with a poppadum.'

Shannon leapt forward grabbing hold of her uncle's top. 'He can't see you here, he just can't. He can't!' She paused, her eyes darting around wildly, then pulling her uncle into the flat, she nodded. 'Second door on the left. Go on . . . go on . . . That's my room. Wait in there for me . . . But whatever you do, don't make a sound.'

And just as Charlie went into her bedroom, Vaughn appeared at the end of the plush corridor, laden down with Waitrose bags and several takeaway bags. 'Christ almighty, girl, didn't you hear me calling? What were you doing anyway, smuggling your boyfriend in?' Vaughn laughed as he struggled down the corridor.

In response, Shannon shouted angrily, her eyes filled with tears. 'Of course not! What do you fucking take me for? I ain't that sort of girl! Just because I sold myself don't mean I'm easy. I had no choice and you know that. You know I never wanted to do that. I never wanted some old fella sweating and spunking all over me.'

'Whoa, whoa, whoa! It was a joke, darlin'.'

'Why does everyone think it's okay to tell shit jokes at my expense?'

Vaughn placed the bags on the floor, then bent down to Shannon's eye level. 'Hey, hey, hey. I never meant anything by it.'

Wiping away her tears and shaking, Shannon's voice trembled. 'But why would you say stuff like that, anyway? I wouldn't do that to you. I wouldn't have a boyfriend.'

Vaughn spoke gently and warmly. 'You know you're allowed boyfriends or, I dunno, girlfriends. Whatever, just as long as they're not some waster . . . Shan, it's okay, it's what teenagers do. They go on dates, they enjoy themselves.'

Coldly, she stared at him. The idea that Vaughn wouldn't mind if she had a boyfriend cut through her, and the hurt of it made her fill with anger. 'Well it's not what I do, and anyway, it's hardly like I've got fucking time for all that, is it, when I'm looking after Mia. Some chance of getting a frigging boyfriend.'

Vaughn looked at her hard. 'Sorry, Shan, I didn't mean any harm . . . Listen, let's go inside and munch on this – fuck knows I think I got a bit carried away again. Next time I'm sending you, but for now, how about we have that nice evening, hey?'

Shannon nodded but didn't say anything. As she followed Vaughn down the long hallway, she glanced at her bedroom door, trying to stop the sense of nausea, knowing that Uncle Charlie was a matter of only a few feet away.

17

It was the early hours of the morning and Alfie still hadn't been able to sleep. Partly due to the fact that his face felt on fire, and partly due to the fact that he was ruminating about what Vaughn had said, and the thought that he'd grassed on Franny – no matter what they thought of her – was winding him up. He still didn't know what he was going to do about it, and if he found out that Vaughn had even so much as looked at the Old Bill again, he would be a dead man. The third reason why he couldn't sleep was that he'd snorted over three grams of coke and he was wired to the hills.

Sighing, he sat up in bed and, dressed in only his joggers, Alfie dragged on his grey marl T-shirt, carefully pulling it over his bruised torso. He winced and ground his teeth, a side effect from the copious amounts of cocaine he'd taken.

Not that it had made him feel any better. After the first

hit he'd been chasing the high and then after that he'd spun into a spiral of agitation and anger, thoughts of Franny and Vaughn rushing through his mind.

From the corner of his eye he saw his phone screen light up: two missed calls. Frowning, he pressed voicemail, putting it on loudspeaker as he stood up and grabbed the bottle of vodka from the side.

'Mr Jennings, it's Ed Romano, Ms Doyle's solicitor. She's requested that I get in contact with you. She's hoping that you might pay her a visit, so perhaps you can contact me. There's a—'

Not wanting to hear any more of the message, Alfie rushed back across to the phone and clicked it off. The pain from the sudden movement shot through him and just for a moment he closed his eyes, picturing Franny. Then with a loud roar of anger he threw the phone across the bedroom.

Breathing heavily, with his whole body aching, Alfie took a large swig of vodka. If that bitch thought for just one second he was going to go and see her, then she had another thing coming. Hell would freeze over first.

He always knew that women could be dangerous and calculating, but Franny was something else. She had surpassed everything he thought she was capable of, with a ruthlessness and a coldness that would surprise some of the hardest men he knew.

She had lied. Pretended. Befriended, before she went on to kill Bree. He didn't understand what had happened. What had Bree done so wrong for Franny to have murdered her in cold blood?

No one had answers for him; when he'd asked Vaughn

all he'd said was that he'd been trailing Franny because he suspected she was stealing from them again and he'd wanted to know exactly what she was up to.

So, with Shannon in tow, Vaughn had tracked her down and apparently seen Franny and Bree together having a huge row. He'd then followed them into Bree's flat, and he'd watched Franny – too late to do anything about it – deliberately push Bree down the stairs. When Franny had seen Vaughn and Shannon, she'd run off into the night . . . That had been Vaughn's version of events.

But something just didn't feel right, or add up about it. Alfie felt like there were too many unanswered questions. Or perhaps it was just he didn't *want* to believe that Franny had done that . . . Yes, yes, he knew she was ruthless and tough – after all she'd been brought up by one of the hardest, toughest faces around – but to kill Bree who she'd genuinely come to like? It seemed inconceivable.

To kill someone like Bree, who was to all intents and purposes harmless . . . well, it just didn't sound like Franny. But then, Franny had fooled him before; lied to him *and* betrayed him by keeping the fact that he had a daughter from him.

Even when Mia had gone missing and when they'd thought Barry had taken her, Franny hadn't *actually* told him who Mia was. She'd told him Mia belonged to a friend of hers. And because he'd been too fucked up at the time, too high on coke, he'd believed her. And God, didn't he feel a mug.

Maybe all along Franny hadn't even cared in the first place about Bree. Maybe it had just been an act, and perhaps it came down to the fact that Franny wasn't capable of loving or caring . . . and that thought cut deep, because as much as he'd never say it to Vaughn or anyone, the idea that Franny might not have cared about *him* either, bothered him more than he wanted to admit. *Shit*.

God, she must've been laughing at him. So when he actually put it all together, maybe it wasn't so much of a stretch to believe Franny had killed Bree in cold blood. And now the bitch wanted him to go and see her. Well, he had news for her: she could rot in hell.

Suddenly a noise coming from the hallway disturbed his thoughts. He turned quickly to look, and instinctively reached for the gun he kept hidden under the bed.

Quietly he moved, creeping around the room, reaching for and switching off the light.

In the darkness Alfie edged forward, listening out all the time for noise. But he couldn't hear anything now – only his heart racing as he gripped the gun, feeling the sweat beginning to run down his back.

Trying to steady himself, he breathed out. It wasn't helping he was still high and he wasn't sure if it was paranoia kicking in, but he was certain there was someone in the corridor on the other side of his newly fitted front door.

Carefully and as silently as he could, Alfie crouched down, staring at the bottom of the door, trying to see if he could spot a shadow moving underneath it. But after a few moments, he stood back up, unable to see or hear anything else.

Still being cautious, Alfie stepped over to the door, leaning in to look through the door's peephole. There was no one there. Or no one he could see. So, taking another deep breath, he reached for the handle, opening the door slowly at the same time as flicking the safety off the gun.

His heart pounded as he pointed his gun left and right into the hallway, but seeing the corridor was empty, he began to relax. He put the safety catch back on the gun and sighed. He was tired and clearly paranoid and needed some sleep.

Annoyed with himself for being so jumpy, Alfie went to go back inside his flat, but he stopped and frowned. On the floor there was what looked like a small present, gift-wrapped in baby pink and silver paper.

Picking it up, Alfie took it into the flat. He walked through to the kitchen and placed the gun on the side alongside the parcel. No doubt it was for Mia. Probably left earlier by Vaughn on his way out; this thought pissed him off no end.

He shook his head. It was clearly Vaughn's fucked-up way of trying to encourage him to take an interest in Mia. Well, the next time he saw him, he'd give him a piece of his mind. In fact, why wait for the next time when he could do it right now.

Stomping through to get his phone from the bedroom, he grabbed it off the floor from where he'd thrown it at the wall earlier. Then marching back through to the kitchen he pressed dial. It went to voicemail, but undeterred and full of anger, Alfie decided to leave a message as he started to unwrap the present.

'Vaughn, it's me, Alf. I don't know what the fuck you were thinking, but if you reckon leaving presents for Mia is going to make me want to look after her, then you can think again, mate, cos—' He suddenly stopped talking and in shock he threw the package down on the counter. Inside the paper was a jewellery box and inside the jewellery box was a severed ear.

Breathing hard, he stared at it in horror. It was a freshly cut human ear sitting in a pool of blood.

Suddenly realising that he was still on the call to Vaughn, Alfie muttered into the phone.

'Listen . . . forget about it . . . I'll speak to you later . . . okay . . .' He clicked it off and as he did so he saw a card in the box.

Not wanting to touch the ear, he shook the contents out onto his kitchen counter. The card was covered in blood but Alfie was just about able to make out the words. It read.

Mr Jennings, this is what happened to the last person who didn't listen. I thought this might be useful to you because it seems to me like you're a bit hard of hearing when it comes to giving me my money back. So think on, Mr Jennings, neither of us would want anything to happen to your daughter, would we?

Alfie bellowed an incoherent noise and with trembling hands he screwed up the card and threw it into the sink. Huang was enjoying playing games with him and he couldn't see any way out of this. One way or another he needed to come up with the money as soon as possible. And as much as he hated the thought of it, perhaps he'd need to pay Franny a visit after all . . .

18

Shannon woke up and stared at the ceiling. Last night had been ruined. She'd thought she was going to spend a fun evening with Vaughn watching a movie. Instead she'd spent most of the evening thinking about Uncle Charlie waiting in her bedroom. Then to make matters worse, Vaughn had taken an important phone call and the night they'd originally planned together had turned into a disaster.

Wiping away the tears that rolled from the corners of her eyes, Shannon continued to stare at the ceiling. Mia would be waking up in a minute and as much as she enjoyed caring for her she wasn't certain that she could concentrate enough to do a good job today.

She sighed heavily and felt more tears begin to run down her face.

'Good morning, sweetheart, I hope you slept as well as me.' Her uncle Charlie lay in the bed next to her. He snuggled up and she shuddered as his obese body rubbed up against hers.

Shannon whispered even though she had locked the door – something that she never usually did. She had always left it open, hoping, in the back of her mind, that Vaughn might come in, but now she was locking it hoping to keep him out. 'I didn't sleep at all. How the hell do you expect me to sleep with you here?'

'This bed is the best I've slept in. I'll give it to Vaughn, he certainly knows how to choose a mattress.'

Shannon's eyes were wide open with fear. 'Just keep your voice down.'

Charlie rolled over towards Shannon. 'I could get used to this.'

'You have to leave. You hear me, you've got to get out. If Vaughn finds you . . .'

Charlie put his finger over her mouth and Shannon winced in disgust as he grinned at her, his stale breath warm on her face. 'Sshhhh, Shan, what's all the drama for? It's like home from home. And to tell you the truth I could do with some TLC from you.'

Shannon sat up, staring down at her uncle. Her voice shook. 'Uncle Charlie, I'm begging you, please just go.'

'You've been doing a lot of begging recently, Shan. Anyone would think you didn't care about me.'

With her eyes full of worry, Shannon grabbed hold of Charlie's fat hairy shoulders and shook him, desperate for him to listen. 'You can't do this to me, you can't!'

'That's where you're wrong, darlin', I can do anything I want. And I'm going to start with this.' He pushed down the covers to expose himself, his fat stomach lying on top of his half-erect penis. He cackled as he began to caress himself. 'Get your lips around that.'

Backing away off the bed, Shannon shook her head, her whole body trembling. 'I don't want to . . . I don't want to.'

Nastily, Charlie stared at his niece. 'I don't care if you want to or not. But if you don't want to, I could always call Vaughn in, tell him how you invited me to stay.'

'You wouldn't do that to me.'

'Oh but Shan, you know I would. Do you want to put it to the test?'

Shannon shook her head violently. She put her hands over her face, speaking through her fingers, which were wet with her tears. 'He wouldn't believe you anyway. He would know that you're lying.'

Again Charlie cackled. 'Don't kid yourself, Shan. For starters how are you going to explain me being naked in your bed, and secondly but more importantly, underneath it all he knows the truth about you.'

Taking her hands away from her face, Shannon whimpered. 'What are you talking about?'

'Well he knows you're a dirty little skank. A whore through and through.'

Unable to stop herself, Shannon shrieked. 'Don't say that, don't say that!' The minute her words came out she slammed her hands over her mouth. And a second later, there was a knock on her bedroom door.

'Shannon, are you all right in there? What's going on?'

It was Vaughn.

'Shannon!'

110

Trembling, her eyes darted to Charlie who lay on the bed, pleasuring himself. He winked at her and whispered, 'One word from me, Shan, and your perfect little life here is over. You'll be back on the streets, back in the gutter. Is that what you want?'

Shannon shook her head as Vaughn banged again on the door. *'Shannon, answer me! What the fuck's going on?'*

With her heart racing she opened her mouth to speak but stopped as Uncle Charlie whispered again, 'If you don't want that, tell him everything's fine. Go on . . .'

Shaking and trying to keep her voice sounding normal, Shannon spoke through the door. 'Sorry about that, Vaughn, I was just having a row with one of my mates on the phone. I forgot how loud I can be.'

Vaughn answered suspiciously. *'Who? I told you, Shan, I don't want you mixing with your old crowd.'*

Glancing again at Charlie, Shannon said, 'Don't worry, she's not anyone from my past. Just someone I met in the park when I was with Mia . . . I got upset because she was saying mean things.'

'Like what?'

Shannon thought quickly; she began to stutter as she struggled to come up with an answer. 'That . . . that . . . that Mia didn't look as well cared for as she should do. Making out like I wasn't doing my job properly. I know I shouldn't get so upset, but I'm doing me best.'

'I know you are, honey. I think you're doing a great job. And if it makes you feel any better, that would piss me off too. Maybe you should find yourself another friend, one that doesn't go about saying shit like that . . . But are you okay, otherwise?'

Shannon leant her head against the wooden door; she breathed deeply and closed her eyes, feeling Vaughn's presence on the other side. She wanted to scream and cry. She wanted Vaughn to break the door down and protect her. To care for her. To love her. To help her get away from Uncle Charlie. But she couldn't. She couldn't risk Vaughn not believing her. She couldn't risk a life without him, so instead she just said, 'I'm fine, thanks for asking . . . I'm just getting ready. I'll be out in a bit.'

She listened to Vaughn's footsteps disappear down the corridor before she slowly turned to Uncle Charlie, who grinned. 'That wasn't difficult, was it, Shan? Simple really. Now this is the way it's going to go. I'll keep quiet, I won't break your cover and Vaughnie will never even know I'm here, *but* that's as long as you do *exactly* what I say. Do we have a deal, Shan?'

Trembling, with tears running down her face and her nose streaming, Shannon was so distraught she couldn't speak; she could only nod her head.

'Good, Shan, good, that's what I like to see . . . So now that's all decided, how about we start as we mean to go on . . .' He stopped to laugh and he winked again before grabbing his penis.

'And then do you promise you'll go?'

He winked at her then nodded. 'Cross my heart . . . So come on then, what are you waiting for, Shan? Get your lips around this.'

19

Two days later, on Thursday afternoon, Alfie sat in the visitors' room of Hartwood prison. The walls were painted a dull grey and the barred windows were thick with a film of dirt. The rusty-coloured threadbare carpet had dark stains dotted all over it, and a box of broken children's toys sat in a grubby cream plastic box in the corner.

He looked around at the women and their visitors; some with children, some sitting there as if they'd rather be anywhere else, and some looking like it was the mother's union tea party. The whole place was a buzz of noise, and a rancid smell sat alongside the tension in the air.

Chewing the same piece of gum he had been for the last half hour, he glanced over at the screws, giving them a dirty look. Most of them looked like they could rugby tackle him to the floor and most of them didn't look like they'd need much excuse to do so.

Jesus, he felt uncomfortable. It was the very last place he wanted to be, visiting the very last person he wanted to come and see. And if it wasn't for Huang, well, he wouldn't even be within ten foot of the place.

He sighed and touched his face. It still hurt, though not as much as it had a couple of days ago, but then he guessed it also helped that Davey had given him some extra pills, which he didn't know the name of but which took away most of the pain.

'Hello, Alfie. Thanks for coming.'

He gazed up and standing there in front of him was Franny.

He held his breath. He hadn't seen her for a couple of months or so and looking at her now seemed so surreal.

'You're looking . . .' Franny paused. She couldn't bring herself to say the word 'well', he was looking anything but well. His face was a rainbow of coloured bruises and cuts, his eye was a swollen mess and his lips looked so painful she could almost feel it herself.

Alfie, irritated by the fact he felt something other than hatred towards Franny, answered gruffly. 'What? What am I looking? Because hopefully the only thing I do look like is a man who would rather be any-fucking-where but here.'

Franny sat down slowly, sliding into the seat to sit opposite Alfie across the small prison table. She was surprised at how good it felt to see him. But then, she'd be pleased to see anyone who reminded her of the outside world at the moment.

So, maybe it was just a case of being stuck inside, with her feelings ranging from a sense of despair to a sense of anger – and God knows, certainly a sense of betrayal – that she was pleased to see Alfie.

Oh God, she didn't know. Because she could feel the familiar tightness in her stomach when she looked at him. The excitement she'd mostly felt towards him. And if she really thought about it, she'd missed him. Because when had she *actually* stopped loving him? Well she hadn't, had she?

The truth was over the past few months she'd had to put her walls up to help Bree and to keep everything a secret from Alfie. Then when she'd been arrested, she'd gone into survival mode because she had to. So, when it came down to it, underneath everything, there was a good chance, a really good chance, that what she was feeling was love . . . That was it. That was the point. She still loved him . . . not that it would do her any good at all. It would only make her weak, make her stupid, make her make wrong decisions.

So whether she did or not, it was really beside the point and, as such, without letting her feelings be known, she simply said, 'I'm just shocked to see you looking like that.'

Alfie grabbed hold of her hands across the table, squeezing them tightly. Too tightly.

She winced but she didn't say anything as he hissed through his teeth. 'What were you expecting, Fran? To see me looking like I've just come back from the Costa? Because whether me face is battered or not, I ain't ever going to be looking good after what you did.'

He let go of her hands and sat back, trying to keep his surging anger under control. 'Anyway, you don't look so pretty yourself. What happened?'

Automatically, Franny's hand shot up to her nose – it was still sore from where Christine had smashed it with her elbow, and the impact had caused bruising under her eyes. 'Let's just say I had a run-in with a door.'

Trying not to feel instinctively protective over her, Alfie shrugged. 'So, who did you turn over this time, Fran?'

Franny blinked and stared at Alfie coolly. 'Like I say, I walked into a door. Anyway, tell me what happened with you?'

'You're a fucking ice queen, you know that? My head has been well and truly fucked up because of you and you're sitting here like we're old mates on a catch-up,' Alfie raged, unable to hold his anger down anymore.

Franny's expression didn't change. 'What do you want me to say, Alf?'

Alfie smashed his fist down on the table causing the prison officer to give him a warning stare. He lowered his voice but the rage inside him didn't quieten down. 'Are you for fucking real, Fran? Or maybe you've just lost it, maybe you just ain't right in the head.'

Again, Franny's demeanour was cool. 'Look, Alf, I appreciate you coming to see me. I thought you wouldn't come.'

Alfie's face was red with rage. 'Oh, believe me, darlin', I never wanted to.'

A small smile appeared at the corner of Franny's mouth. 'Then why did you?'

At this point, Alfie didn't know whether to laugh or cry, but he certainly wanted to scream, to grab her by her throat and shake some sense – some *feeling* – into her. His voice shook with anger as he spoke. 'Desperate people have to sometimes do desperate things.'

'What are you talking about?'

Alfie pointed at her. 'Before we get into that, I just want to make it clear that I ain't here because I want to be. You understand?'

Franny nodded, her face void of emotion. 'I understand, Alf. You've made it quite clear.'

Rubbing his chin then instantly regretting it as the pain shot through his body, Alfie shook his head. 'What happened to you, Fran? When did you become so hard? What happened to the woman I fell in love with?'

'You make me sound like I was a Disney princess before. I was never that, Alf. You know that. We are who we are. I haven't changed.'

Alfie's eyes darted all over her face as if he was trying to work out a puzzle. 'Fran, for fuck's sake, have you forgotten what you did?'

Ignoring what he had said, Franny's reply was detached. 'Why are you here, Alf? What do you want?'

'Don't turn this around on me. You called me remember, Fran, or rather that prick of a solicitor did.'

'Yes, but you came, which means *you* want something.'

Alfie's reply wasn't forthcoming. As much as he wanted to hate every part of her, he couldn't, which in turn just made him angrier. As much as he wanted to believe that he'd like her to rot in this place, he actually wanted her home – back in his life, back in his bed, back together. And just knowing he felt like that incensed him.

He whispered, and Franny had to bend across to hear him and he hated how good it felt to be close to her, 'You are a fucking cold-hearted bitch.'

She whispered back, 'If it makes it easier for you to think like that, then that's fine.'

Alfie stared at her, his blue eyes penetrating hers. 'I don't think it. I know it. You lied to me, over and over again. You kept my . . . my . . . you kept Mia from me and then you killed Bree. How else could I possibly see you?'

Franny sat up. She regarded Alfie for a moment before saying, 'You're right, I did lie to you, but you've lied to me on *many* occasions. And I did keep Mia from you, but at the time it was for the best.'

'Says who?' Alfie said, incredulously.

For the first time in the conversation, Franny's tone and the look in her eyes softened. 'The life we're in, it ain't a life for a little girl. It ain't really a life for anyone. I was born into it, you fell into it – but neither of us would choose it.'

'How fucking dare you play judge and jury! I was her father.'

'You still are.'

Alfie shook his head. 'No, sweetheart, you put paid to that. I don't want anything to do with her.'

Franny blinked slowly. Her voice was tense. 'Who's looking after her, then?'

'Shannon.'

It was Franny's turn to raise her voice. 'Shannon? Are you being serious? How could you leave that crackhead looking after Mia? Anything might happen to her. You will not leave her there another day. You need to go and pick her up, do you hear me, Alf?'

'The days of me listening to you are well and truly gone.'

Franny's face darkened but she didn't say what she was thinking. Instead she stared at him coolly, took a deep breath and said, 'You're wrong about one thing. I didn't kill Bree. I didn't touch her. It was an accident and Vaughn knows that, but he and Shannon are trying to set me up.'

20

Claire Martin drove along the high street. She was deep in thought and the presenter's voice on Radio Four was a distant murmur as her mind raced from the Doyle case to the house repairs she needed doing in her front lounge to the non-existent holidays she was supposed to book – and finally to Tony Balantyne.

She hit the wheel with her fist, not wanting to think about him. She wasn't sure what it was about that man, but he bothered her like no one she'd ever met. And it certainly didn't help that in less than five minutes, she was going to pick him up for one of the management task meetings the Chief Super insisted she attend.

When she'd heard that the Super had roped in Balantyne she'd tried to get out of going, but even though he knew about her past relationship with Balantyne, he'd ignored all her appeals to be excused from attending.

To make matters worse, the Super hadn't just insisted she go, but he insisted that she and Balantyne travel down to Dorset together, in what he called a *bonding session*. It was a complete joke. The last thing she needed was any kind of bonding session with anyone, least of all Tony.

As if her thoughts had conjured him up, Balantyne appeared on the corner of Newell Street. She beeped her horn, then indicated and pulled over.

Sighing, she watched him saunter up to the car, and reaching over the passenger seat, she opened the door for him.

On edge and cursing the Chief Super for the hundredth time that day, Balantyne slid into the cream leather passenger seat. Without turning to look at Claire, he stayed staring ahead and simply said, 'Ma'am.'

About to drive off, Claire gripped the wheel and with emotion getting the better of her, she spoke. 'Look, Tony, I don't like this any more than you do. I tried to get out of it but the Super was having none of it, so why don't we try to make the most of a really shit situation?'

'Whatever you say, ma'am. You're the boss.'

Infuriated, Claire stared at the side of Tony's head. 'For Christ's sake look at me, Tony.'

'No, I'm good, thanks.'

Trying to think of something else to say, Claire asked, 'So how's the Doyle case coming along?'

'Slowly, but then it would be, wouldn't it?'

'What, because you have to play it by the book? That's the only way, Tony.'

'If you say so, but the CPS aren't happy that the case is based on pretty circumstantial evidence.'

'You've got the statements though.'

Balantyne shook his head. 'If they stick. They're hardly ideal witnesses, are they? A gangster and a crackhead.'

'That doesn't mean they're not telling the truth though, does it?'

Balantyne stayed tight-lipped and eventually Claire filled the silence again. 'Why are you being like this with me? I won't let any officer of mine cut corners. Or is this about the fact that I got the job and you didn't?'

Tony, against his better judgement, turned to look at Claire. 'No, ma'am, it's not. I won't say it didn't bother me because it did, at first. To be looked over for a job because of . . .' He stopped, not wishing to go into it any more than he had already. The truth was if it wasn't for what happened with Emma at the party a couple of years ago and then what had happened afterwards, he probably would've got the promotion. No question. And it did get to him, but it wasn't *all* there was to it. The fact was he resented Claire for ending it with him. He resented her taking away the one piece of happiness he had in his life, and because of that, he resented Emma even more and his hatred for her grew each day.

'Ma'am, I'd appreciate it if we didn't go there.'

'Well I'm sorry, Tony, but I'm not going anywhere until we sort this out or at least talk about it.'

Snapping at her and angry he was finding himself drawn into the conversation, Balantyne growled as he looked around the street, 'Fine, if we have to but I'd rather we didn't do it here . . . Drive to the top of the road, there's a quiet lane off to the right.'

Ten minutes later, Claire put on her hand brake and turned to look at Tony, refusing to acknowledge how much she felt towards him. 'So, go on then, Tony. No one's around, so you've got no excuse. Talk to me. Tell me why every time I speak to you, you make me feel *this big*.' She held her thumb and forefinger a few centimetres apart. 'You make me feel like shit.'

'Well, the solution to that is simple really: we *don't* talk. We *don't* speak. And after the Doyle case, I'll put in for a transfer. Until then, we'll avoid each other as much as we can. And as for the journey down today, I'm happy to sit in silence if you are.'

Claire bit on her lip, once again fighting back the emotions she tried so hard to hide. 'No, I'm not happy, Tony. How could I be? How could I be happy after everything that's happened? Tony, for God's sake, don't ignore me. Talk to me, please.'

'Okay you want to hear it, here goes . . . You've been the one who's called all the shots. It's been your choice all the way and I've just had to sit back and accept it, so to tell you the truth, *ma'am*, I don't give a fuck whether you're happy or not.'

Exploding with a mix of anger and hurt, Claire yelled, brushing her tears away, 'Well, I'm not, and you know I didn't have any choice *but* to end it! I'm miserable without you and that night we spent together a couple of months ago—'

Balantyne interrupted with words he didn't quite mean. 'It was a mistake.'

With her emotions running away with her, Claire

continued to yell, 'Well, mistake or not, it reminded me of what we once had. So, there you go, Tony, you can delight in the fact I'm not happy without you – or about anything in fact. About the accident, about what happened to Emma or . . . or having to pick you up ten minutes' walk away from your house in case she sees us. And I'm certainly not happy that I'm pregnant . . .'

She trailed off and silence fell between them. It was a minute before Tony said, 'Pregnant?'

Claire nodded, already regretting blurting it out and at the same time waiting for the inevitable question from Tony.

'Is it mine?'

She nodded again and her voice was a small whisper. 'Yes, it's yours, Tony, and I have no idea what I'm going to do.'

21

Emma Balantyne staggered along the road, dressed in an old pair of joggers and one of her husband's white police shirts. For the life of her she'd thought that she had another bottle of vodka tucked behind one of the kitchen cabinets but when she'd looked all she'd found was empty bottles.

She'd then gone into the bottom of the wash basket to see if she still had some gin hidden there. It had been the same story – she'd already drunk it. And when she checked her last resort – the back of her wardrobe – she found that it again only held empty miniature whiskey bottles.

It had aggravated her, mainly because she knew she only had a small amount of cheap, bad supermarket vodka left, and as the off-licence didn't open until later, it meant a twenty-minute walk to Sainsbury's seeing as Tony always hid the car keys.

The thought of it made her seethe with anger. Here she

was without a car, having to walk to the shops to get a drink, and being treated like a criminal, when she had done nothing wrong. It was him. Tony. He was the villain of it all.

The thought of what he'd done to her and done to her face made her want to drink. It was all because of *him* that she drank in the first place, and it was certainly because of him that she had to hide the bottles. For some reason he thought she drank too much. It was total crap, but if she did – and she certainly didn't think she did – then the only person to blame was Tony.

He played games with her. Made her feel like she was going mad when she knew he was playing around. She knew that he was chasing women like a whippet after a rabbit. Sniffing around them, getting his leg over anything that moved and screwing them like there was no tomorrow.

He was doing all that but he wouldn't touch her, he wouldn't come near her, even though he *knew* how much she wanted to have a baby, start a family of her own – but he refused to even contemplate the idea. No wonder she drank.

At the thought of it, Emma quickly looked around and unscrewed the half bottle of vodka in her handbag.

Not wanting to take the bottle out of the bag, she lifted it up to her lips with the vodka still inside.

Gulping it back and feeling it quench her agitation, she put the lid back on and continued to walk unsteadily along the pavement, thinking about Tony . . . Tony and that bitch.

Of all the women he'd been with, it was Claire Martin who'd caused the most trouble, the most pain. She'd been the one who'd nearly destroyed them, getting her claws into Tony and getting into his head.

Claire had been with him the night of the accident. And, even though it was now over two years ago, she could remember the night like it was only yesterday . . .

The party had been in full swing by the time they'd arrived and as usual they'd had a row in the car on the way over.

Tony had turned to Emma in the car and snapped, 'Just make sure you behave yourself, Em. I've a got a lot of work colleagues here. I don't want to be embarrassed. No more drinking – look at the state of you already.'

He'd slammed out of the car before she'd had the chance to answer and marched into the party, which was being held to celebrate the retirement of a long-serving officer in the force.

Sighing, and quickly taking the miniature bottle of whiskey she'd hidden at the side of the passenger seat, Emma gulped it back in one before she followed Tony inside.

The hallway of the country house where the party was being held had been adorned with draped white silk offset with red roses – it seemed each room had been themed around winter, tastefully decorated in gold and rich berry reds.

It had taken Emma over twenty minutes to find Tony again and in that time she'd knocked back several glasses of Champagne. She was beginning to feel better until she'd seen who was standing in the group chatting to Tony. Claire Martin.

She stood watching them for a moment, grabbing another glass of Champagne from the passing waiter.

She'd never met Claire, she'd only seen her in passing when she'd picked up Tony after work, but for the past few months she'd had a suspicion that there was something going on between them. Of course he'd denied it, but she'd heard him on the phone with her. The way he'd whisper quietly, the way he'd laugh, and then shut the door when he thought she was listening. It wasn't just colleagues discussing work; there was so much more to it.

Continuing to watch them, Emma noticed Tony's hand lightly brush down Claire's back. She also saw her give him the quickest but most intimate of looks, almost as if they were the only two in the room.

And in that moment, that touch, that glance, was all the proof she needed.

She marched up to the group and perhaps it was the look on her face that made Tony's own face drain of colour as she approached them.

She stood unsteadily, her voice slurred as she spoke. 'You must be Claire. Tony's told me all about you. In fact, he doesn't do anything but talk about you. My husband always says any friend of mine is a friend of his, but I'm afraid I'm not so fucking generous.' And with that, Emma Balantyne threw the drink she was holding in Claire's face.

Grabbing Emma, Tony shook her. 'What the hell are you doing? You're drunk.'

'Yeah, and you're fucking her. Touché.'

Clearly unsure what to say, Tony glanced at Claire who stood frozen by humiliation, her clothes dripping with Champagne.

Eventually, Tony said, 'You . . . you don't know what you're talking about. You need to drink some water and sober up.'

'Why? Why the fuck should I?'

Tony's voice was full of anger though he kept it down. 'Because you're embarrassing yourself.'

Emma shook her head. Her voice danced on the verge of hysterical. 'You mean I'm embarrassing you.'

With his grip still on Emma's arm, Tony growled, 'I think we better leave this conversation where it is.'

'You'd like that wouldn't you? For me not to make a fuss so you and Claire can cosy up and enjoy your evening together? Mustn't humiliate the mighty Tony Balantyne, must we? Well I'm sorry, Detective, but I'm not one of your officers and I'm not one of your whores, I'm your wife.'

Heads were turning in the room to look at them as the other guests sensed the argument over the beat of the music, and – not wanting to make a spectacle of himself – Tony proceeded to drag Emma towards a side room off the main reception hall.

Enraged, Tony slammed the door behind him and – now away from prying eyes – pushed Emma into the middle of the room, raising his voice in fury. 'Let me tell you something, Emma: you're my wife in name only. In my head I left you a long time ago. Now, just go away, Em, go and do what you do best; go get a drink.'

The slap from Emma probably hurt Tony's ego more than it did his face and the slight sting on his cheek melted into total insignificance compared to his temper. 'You bitch! Just go home.'

Emma stared at him. 'If you think you can get rid of me that easily, think again. Let's have it out here once and for all.'

Tony shook Emma hard, her head flicking back and forth. 'Why the fuck are you doing this, Em? Happy now? Are you happy that you've embarrassed me? That all my colleagues out there know that you're nothing but a drunk? Is this what you wanted?'

'Tony, enough! Stop it! Don't do that!' Claire Martin said as she walked into the room. She looked at Emma and said, not unkindly, 'Perhaps you'd better leave? Let everything calm down?'

The comment from Claire made Emma shriek with anger and like an alley cat, she launched herself, clawing and scratching, at Claire's face.

'Go to hell, Claire, who the fuck do you think you are? There's a word for women like you; I know you're sleeping with my husband, just admit it. Admit it!'

Tony Balantyne had had enough. He yelled at the top of his voice as he dragged Emma off Claire, 'Fine, okay, I'm fucking her. I'm fucking her hard. I'm fucking her every day, every hour, every moment, and you know something, Em, I like it. I like fucking her. So there you go, there you have it. Are you happy now?'

Staggering back without saying anything, Emma felt pained. Suddenly, she leapt for the door, pulling it open and revealing, to Tony's humiliation, a number of his friends, work colleagues and superiors – including the Chief Superintendent – watching in horror as Emma screamed at them.

'What are you all looking at? Listened to everything that was said, have you? I bet this is funny to you, isn't it? This is just one big joke? Did you all know that my husband was shagging that whore? Did you . . .' But before Emma could say another word, she started to vomit, retching up the expensive bottle of red she'd consumed earlier.

With her hair covered in sick, she stood frozen for a moment then, shaking, turned to her husband and said quietly, 'I want to go home now, Tony. We need to go home.'

He shook his head and pulled her back into the room, hurriedly closing the door. Tony snarled, 'Look at the state of you. I'm not going anywhere. I'm staying until the end of the party, then afterwards, I'm never coming home. I'm leaving you, Em . . . That's right, I've had enough – and fuck knows why I stayed this long. I felt sorry for you, and that's the joke because you're nothing but a drunk.'

Wiping away the vomit from her mouth Emma, humiliated, muttered, 'Give me the car keys.'

As Tony went into his pocket to give them her, Claire held on to his arm. 'Don't, Tony. She's been drinking.'

Emma stared daggers. 'Give me the keys, unless you're going to take me home yourself.'

Tony shook off Claire's hand as he gave Emma the keys. 'Take them, Em. Just get the fuck out of here. I hate you. Do you hear that? I hate you.'

Claire's eyes flashed with worry. 'Tony, think about what you're doing. This is crazy. I'll take her home, if you won't.'

Losing patience with the whole situation, Tony glared at Claire. 'For fuck sake she's a grown woman. I'm not her keeper.'

'No, you're not, but I know if anything happens, you'll have regrets for the rest of your life.'

131

Tony didn't move as Emma raced out of the room. As she reached the car she saw that he'd had second thoughts and followed her outside. But it was too late; as Tony called after Emma, she jumped into the car and sped away.

22

Shaking the memories away as she took the short cut across the field to the supermarket, Emma sighed and touched her face. She couldn't remember anything else about that night, but they'd told her that she'd driven the car into a ditch and it was there the police had found her unconscious in the upside-down vehicle, which had burst into flames.

They'd rushed her into surgery but the burns from the accident had left a huge, angry scar taking up most of the left side of her face. Though she supposed she'd been lucky, she'd been told she very nearly died – sometimes she wished she had done, because that would've shown Tony, would've made him realise that he couldn't go around hurting people. He would've suffered like she did . . . like she still did every day.

At times, when she didn't know where Tony was – the times she lay in bed on her own – she often thought about ending it all. Killing herself. Not because she wanted to die; she didn't. But because she wanted Tony to be punished, and she knew that would be her ultimate way to do it.

At the thought of Tony suffering, a small smile appeared on the corner of Emma's lips – but as quickly as it had appeared, it vanished as she stood, frozen, staring in horror at the grey Land Rover parked on the corner of the street.

Emma's heart pounded so hard she had to take a deep breath and beads of cold sweat broke out on her forehead. The ringing in her ears blocked out all the surrounding noise. She felt light-headed and she squeezed her eyes closed and opened them again, wondering if what she was seeing was caused by her drinking. But no, they were there. Him and Her. Together.

Suddenly she screamed in rage, and looked around, her eyes darting from one side of the lane to another. Her gaze rested on a large stone underneath the bushes and she ran to pick it up.

Wielding it in the air, Emma continued to scream as Balantyne and Claire, shocked and surprised and not quite certain what was going on, got out of the car.

On seeing his wife, Balantyne's face drained of colour. His gaze glanced towards the stone she was holding. 'Put it down, Emma.'

Emma's eyes flashed with hatred and anger as she yelled at the top of her voice. 'I knew it, I knew you were fucking her again, I knew it. You made me feel like I was going crazy but all the time I was right.'

'It's not like that, Emma. Tony and I were just talking. I promise.'

Emma swung her attention towards Claire. She hissed through gritted teeth, 'How dare you! How dare you! Look at my face. You did this to me. It's because of you that I look like this!'

Claire, who hadn't seen Emma since the party, stared at the angry, disfiguring red scar. Her eyes filled with tears. Guilt-stricken at the extent of her injuries, she muttered her words. 'I'm so sorry! I'm so sorry, Emma.'

Again Emma screamed. 'No you're not, and you know why I know? Because even after everything that's happened you're still down a country lane with my husband. You don't care who gets hurt, you don't care about anything but your sordid little affair.'

Claire shook her head. 'Emma, please listen—'

'Listen, why should I?' Emma demanded, incensed.

'Because I'm telling you the truth.'

'Liar!' And with a yell that startled the birds, Emma threw the stone into the back window of the car. She swivelled around and lunged at Claire, pulling her hair and scratching at her face with her nails. She swung her bag, then pushed her towards the bushes where Claire staggered backwards.

'Stop it, Emma! Stop it!' Balantyne boomed out, gripping Emma's arm, but she leant down and bit his hand, drawing blood. The sharp pain made him let go and as he did, Emma took the opportunity to swing her fists at Claire.

Balantyne scrabbled quickly towards Emma, yelling at her. 'Stop, Em, stop! She's pregnant!'

Emma stopped in her tracks. She blinked once, then twice, then stared from Balantyne to Claire, then back to

Balantyne. She could hardly get the words out. 'Is . . . is . . . is it yours?'

Slowly he nodded, glancing at Claire as he did so. 'Yeah, it is.'

Once again, Emma, feeling the effects of alcohol rushing around her body, suddenly lunged at her husband. 'I'm going to kill you, I'm going to fucking kill you!'

Balantyne put up his hands as Emma's fists flailed towards him. He gripped her by her neck, putting her in a chokehold as she struggled. He dragged her along the lane as she kicked and hit at him but he didn't let go, he only held her tighter. 'I'm taking you home.'

As he threw Emma into Claire's already open car, he slammed the door closed and nodded towards Claire. 'I'll be back soon. Are you okay? Will you be all right?'

'I'm fine, just make sure she's okay . . .'

Without answering, Balantyne ran around to the driver's seat.

Inside the car, Emma was screaming. He could smell the booze on her breath as he reversed down the lane. She began to hit him and with one hand he fought her off.

'For fuck's sake, Em, stop! Stop!'

'I hate you! I hate you! How could you do this to me?'

She grabbed his hair and he winced from the pain as he screamed back, 'I said get off me! For fuck's sake, you crazy bitch!'

Tears of anger and frustration ran down Emma's face. 'Well if I am, it's you who's made me like this!'

Balantyne shouted back, just as loud, just as frustrated. 'Oh yeah, it's so easy to blame isn't it, Em? Because if you do that then you don't have to look at yourself – and let me tell you it isn't a pretty sight. You're nothing but a drunk. Do you wonder why I ended up in bed with her? Do you wonder why I thought it was such a joke you wanted to start a family? Who wants a drunk for a mother?'

'Stop the car, Tony, stop the car! I want to get out. Let me out!' With those words Emma grabbed the steering wheel at the same time as Balantyne put his foot on the accelerator. Immediately the Land Rover spun out of control, careering towards the bushes. Balantyne heard a scream then a sickening thud as the car hit Claire.

She was thrown into the air and a second later she hit the ground. Balantyne slammed on the brakes and Emma shot forward. She smashed against the dashboard, banging her head hard, the impact knocking her unconscious.

'Oh my God, Claire! Claire!' Panicked, Balantyne leapt out of the car, racing around to Claire. He knelt down, picking up her head gently. A warm trickle of blood pooled into his hands. His voice trembled as he spoke. 'Claire, Claire! Wake up, honey. Claire?'

There was no response, but he could see she was breathing, and Balantyne gently rested her head back onto the ground before racing back to the car.

He opened the passenger-seat door, speaking quietly. 'Em? Em? Em, are you okay?'

Like with Claire, there was no response. He gently sat her back, putting her in an upright position, placing his fingers on her neck, checking for a pulse. It was strong, which was good, but he knew he needed to call for help.

Quickly Balantyne pulled out his phone to call the ambulance, his heart racing as he glanced again at Claire lying on the ground. As he went to press the emergency call button on his mobile he suddenly stopped. A thought came into his head.

Balantyne looked around then shoved the phone back into his pocket. He ran around to the other side of the car and leant across the seat to the still-unconscious Emma.

Taking a deep breath, he dragged her across to the driver's seat, carefully adjusting her, getting her into the correct position. Satisfied, he nodded to himself and pulled out his mobile once again, then pressed dial.

'Hello, which service do you require?'

'Ambulance . . . and police . . . My name's Detective Tony Balantyne. There's been an accident. My . . . my wife was driving . . . She's also been drinking. It's not the first time she's done it. She's knocked someone over, and I'm afraid to say, I think it may have been on purpose.'

23

Bringing Franny a watery coffee from the drinks machine, Alfie – deep in thought and not only still struggling with his temper but also with his desire to reach across the small visitors' table and throttle her – sat down hard in his chair.

He didn't think it was possible for his head to be more messed up now than when he'd first entered the prison, but it was, and, growling, he said, 'Why would Vaughn be setting you up, and why would Shannon? It don't make sense, but it wouldn't, would it, cos you're lying.'

Franny's eyes hardened. 'I'm saying it because it's true. Come on, Alfie, you've got to believe me.'

Alfie's embittered laugh was so loud it caused the baby across the other side of the visitors' room to become startled and it began to cry.

Alfie's face screwed up in anger. 'Are you kidding me? Are you for real? I don't know if you'd know what the truth was if you stumbled over it. Your nine lives are up, Fran. Face it, I ain't going to believe anything you say again.'

It was Franny's turn to hiss out her words. Her eyes narrowed. 'Then you're stupid because you need to believe this; Vaughn is working with Balantyne and so is Shannon.'

Alfie tried hard not to sound shocked, though he knew he did and that he probably looked it too. 'What are you talking about?'

'Vaughn and Shannon have given statements to the Old Bill.'

Alfie took a sip of the watery coffee and immediately regretted it. 'That's crazy, he'd never do that. Not a statement. I know he was bang out of order to call them in the first place – more than out of order in fact – but there's no way he'd do that. No way. And anyway, he told me himself the call was all he did, and he knows even that crossed the line.'

'Of course he'd say that to you. But the fact is, he did, he just didn't want anyone to find out. My solicitor got the intel through a source he's got.'

For a moment Alfie didn't say anything. In truth, he couldn't really get his head around it. Of all the people to grass, Vaughn wasn't one of them. Their entire life they'd known the rules: no one grasses, no one talks, and if they did, they were soon six foot under. 'Are you absolutely sure, Fran, cos he knows that no matter how much you try to hide something, sooner or later you'll be found out . . . You only have to look at what happened to you.'

Ignoring the dig from Alfie, Franny kept her voice to a whisper. 'I'm one hundred per cent sure. And it's obvious why Vaughn's doing this; he wants to get me out of the way. He's always wanted to take me down. You know that's true – and perhaps to Vaughn it's worth it.'

Not really wanting to get into conversation but not being strong enough to stop himself, Alfie asked, 'In what sense?'

'Perhaps seeing me banged up is worth mugging you off. Who knows what deal he's got with the Old Bill? For all we know he might be planning on doing a midnight flit with Shannon . . . and your daughter.'

'Don't call her that.' Alfie's voice was full of hostility.

Franny's voice softened again. 'But that's what she is . . . Look, Alf, I know this sounds crazy but . . . but if I ever get out of this mess, we could give it another go . . . be a family. Me, you and Mia.'

Alfie leant back in his chair and looking like he'd tasted something rotten he said, 'You're having a laugh, ain't you? Vaughn's already told me about the unhealthy relationship you had with Mia.'

'What?'

'He told me, you were acting like she was yours. Like you were one those sickos who nicks kids and passes them off as their own.'

Franny's face twisted with anger and she spat out her words. 'Go to hell, Alf. Who else was supposed to look after her? Who else was going to be strong enough for her? Who else was going to love her the way I did?'

Alfie looked at her strangely. 'Have you heard yourself, Fran? It ain't right.'

'I'll tell you what ain't right. For Mia to have parents like she does. Bree was weak and you're not much better. You're pathetic.'

Alfie's hand shot out under the table, he gripped Franny's leg hard. Squeezing it so she winced. 'Is that why you killed her? Is that why you pushed her down the stairs – because you were jealous that she was a mother and you weren't? Was that it, Fran? Because you can't have kids and you wanted hers.'

With her face still distorted with anger but now mixed with pain, Franny kicked Alfie under the table, immediately causing him to let go.

He yelped and rubbed his shin. 'Ah fuck! Jesus Christ! I really don't need any more bruises on my body after Huang.'

Franny stared at him. 'Huang? What has Huang got to do with anything?'

'He's got everything to do with it. He's the reason why I'm here . . . And yeah, in case you're wondering, it was Huang who did this to my face, and soon he's going to come back and do worse if I don't come up with the money I borrowed. And yes, yes, before you say it, I *know* you told me at the time that I shouldn't borrow it from him, but I did. And now I'm a dead man if I don't come up with a fuck of a lot of money. And I'm so fucking desperate I came here to see if . . . oh fuck knows why I came, because you already told me that you couldn't help me. But then it would probably suit you, wouldn't it? Me being dead?' He fell silent and Franny shook her head.

'No, Alf, I don't want you dead, I don't. But then no matter what I say you won't believe me, will you?'

'How can I? Nothing that comes out of your mouth is the truth.'

'I know why you'd say that, I get it, but, *please*, you've got to believe what I'm saying about Vaughn. He's setting me up, and I'm worried you could be next.'

Alfie looked at Franny curiously. 'He wouldn't do that.'

'Wouldn't he? All of us would turn someone over if we needed to, in one way or another. That's how we got to the top, isn't it?'

Alfie snorted. 'Speak for yourself.'

Franny gave a small smile. 'Don't kid yourself, Alf. Just think about it. Look back on what you've done in the past, then tell me you ain't turned anyone close to you over.'

Alfie stayed silent knowing what Franny was saying was true. She continued, 'We don't really have friends in this business. And when we do, we've got to keep them close. Like you and me. Even after everything that's happened in the past, we've still managed to find our way back together.'

'Not this time, Fran. This time you fucked it. You went too far. Give me Vaughn over you any day.'

'What, Vaughn? The same Vaughn who called the Old Bill in the first place? The same Vaughn who's working with Detective Balantyne? And I know you keep saying you don't believe it, but if he'd call them, then why wouldn't he give a statement? I mean what's the difference? A snake is a snake,' sneered Franny.

'The difference is . . .' Alfie stopped to think. Franny was right – in their world a grass was a grass. A snitch was a snitch. So, in one way there wasn't any difference. Not that he was going to say that to Franny. No way was he going to admit that, rather than not believing what she was saying about Vaughn, it was more the fact he didn't *want* to believe

143

it. No way was he going to admit *anything* to her, so instead he just said, 'Well, the difference is . . . Look he was just upset when he called the police. After all you did try to kill him, and you *had* killed Bree, and you *had* lied to me and you *had* . . .' Having wound himself up, Alfie slammed his hands on the table, making the plastic cup of coffee jump in the air before it landed on its side, spilling its contents all over Alfie's lap.

'For fuck's sake, for fuck's sake!' Alfie leapt up, trying to wipe the coffee off his now saturated trousers.

'Keep it down over there, else the visit comes to an end.' One of the prison officers called across the room to Alfie. He nodded, though it took everything in him to do so.

Sitting back down on the chair, Alfie put his head in his hands and suddenly, to his embarrassment, he felt the prick of tears in his eyes, and before he knew it, his whole body was racked with sobs.

Rubbing his back and leaning into him, Franny spoke gently. 'Alf, hey Alfie, it's okay, it's okay.'

'Don't touch me. Just don't fucking touch me!' He pushed Franny's hand off him and sat up as he wiped the tears angrily away. 'Well done, Fran. Once again you have successfully fucked my head up. Anytime you're near me, you do this. You're twisted, Fran. And all the lies, all the betrayal . . . that's what hurts the most because – stupid me – I thought we had something special.'

'We did . . . *we do* have something special.'

'Yeah, so special you were quite happy to fuck it up. Don't treat me like I'm stupid, Fran. You say one thing then it turns out the opposite is true. I'm watching my back from

144

all angles. With you, with Huang and now you're telling me I have to watch my back with Vaughn. All those fucking lies you told me about Mia, about Bree . . . you must enjoy mugging me off.'

Franny's gaze darted across Alfie's face. 'I don't and that's not what I was doing . . . Look, you know I was helping Bree. Looking back, I can see it was wrong; I can see I should've told you that she was pregnant. It was just that everything felt such a mess at the time.'

'That don't excuse you lying about Mia or explain why you just coldly went ahead and murdered Bree. And to be honest with you, it's fucked me up and I'll never know why you did it.'

'But I didn't, Alfie. I *never* killed her . . . Look, I'll tell you what happened, and I swear it'll be the truth . . .'

24

A few months ago . . .

Turning her back on the door, Bree ran across to Franny's car keys lying on the side. She immediately grabbed them before rushing across to the small kitchen off the lounge to grab Mia's tin of formula milk. Quickly turning around, Bree froze.

'Who did you think you were messing with, Bree? You should've known better than that.'

Bree could hardly breathe as she stared into Franny's cold and angry face.

'How . . . how did you get out?'

Franny laughed, harsh and bitterly. 'Didn't you listen to anything I said about my childhood, about my father? I was turning locks before you could even ride a bike.'

'Stay away from me, Franny.'

Franny tilted her head to one side. 'Why does it have to be like this? We were friends, Bree, and now look, you're telling me to keep away.'

'Just let me go, okay? Let me walk away with Mia and whatever happens, I'll take responsibility. No one will ever know you've been involved.'

Franny's tone was disconcerting. 'It's not as simple as that though, is it?'

'It can be. It can be whatever we want it to be.'

Franny's eyes narrowed. 'And what about Mia? Are you just going to walk away and take her out of my life forever?'

Bree shook her head. 'No, no of course not. You can see her anytime you want.'

'The minute you leave this flat, both you and I know you'll change your mind.'

Clearly uncomfortable, Bree, still holding Franny's car keys, went to walk out of the tiny kitchen, pushing past Franny. 'I wouldn't do that to you, but believe what you like. I'm not going to live like this any longer.'

Following her through to the lounge where Mia was still happily lying on the changing mat, Franny snapped angrily, 'You're going to ruin everything. All you have to do is wait a bit longer.'

With renewed strength, Bree spoke firmly. 'No, I'm sorry, Franny, but I ain't listening to you anymore. This has to stop, now. So here's how it's going to go: I'm going to take your car, but I'll let you know where I'm going to leave it, and I promise I'll be in touch.'

'Look, just stop being stupid. You haven't got anywhere to go. You can't just go out in the middle of the night with Mia.'

'Anywhere is better than here.'

'You're being ridiculous, Bree. You sound like a spoilt child. Just give me my keys back!' Franny snatched towards Bree, who pulled away her hand and raised her arm, dangling the keys high in the air. Franny lunged towards them, and as she did so, Bree took a step back, but she stumbled. Her arms began to flail, her face paling as she tried but failed to reach for the bannister, unable to stop herself from falling backwards down the open staircase. She screamed Franny's name as she fell, but Franny was frozen to the spot. In shock she couldn't move, let alone answer.

There was a loud thump and a bang, then nothing but silence.

Horrified, Franny stared down the stairs at Bree's body lying sprawled and broken, her arms twisted, her legs bent, her eyes staring wide open. Then snapping herself out of the trance, Franny ran down the stairs, kneeling by Bree, speaking quietly. 'Bree? Bree, honey? Bree, wake up, darlin'. It's okay, you've just had a nasty fall. Bree?' There was no response and desperately, Franny put her ear against Bree's chest before feeling for a pulse. Nothing. Gently, she lifted Bree's head up, but it lolled back like a broken doll's. 'Bree, come on! Come on! Don't do this to me. Please, baby, wake up.'

As Franny spoke, she looked at her own hands. They were covered in blood. Scrambling away from Bree's body, she pressed herself against the wall, breathing heavily, wiping her hands on the carpet in the small downstairs hallway of the maisonette.

In shock, Franny closed her eyes, but the image of Bree was still there in her mind. Hearing Mia begin to cry, she opened them, but going to stand up, a sense of nausea engulfed her. She swallowed hard, trying to steady herself, then took a deep breath before trying to get up again.

Mia's cry got louder before it turned into a scream. Forcing herself to get up, Franny unsteadily began to walk up the stairs. Speaking more to herself than Mia, she said, 'It's okay, it's okay, I'm here. It's going to be all right.'

Scooping Mia up, Franny gently bounced her up and down. She walked past the top of the stairs, looking down, hoping that somehow Bree's body wouldn't be there. Somehow the events of the last ten minutes hadn't happened.

She glanced around, her eyes darting wildly. She had to pull herself together. She would be no good to herself let alone Mia if she crumbled, and besides, she was a Doyle and being weak wasn't the way she'd been brought up. There was nothing she could do for Bree now, but she could still help Mia.

Quickly, Franny grabbed Mia's coat, putting it on her and placing her in the baby seat. Her heart raced as she worked out what she was going to do. There was money in the club, and her passport was there as well, and okay, she didn't have one for Mia, but she knew people who could sort that out, and she knew people who could get her out of the country safely. She just had to hurry. Time certainly wasn't on her side.

Rushing down the stairs as she carried Mia, and stepping over Bree's body, Franny raced for the front door. She opened it.

'What are you doing here?'

Vaughn stared at Franny as she began to push the door closed, but with the baby in one hand and with Vaughn's strength, she was no match for him as he pushed it easily open.

'I could ask you the same thing. I followed you because I wanted to know . . .' He stopped. Stared. Looked at Bree lying motionless on the floor before his gaze went to Franny, and to her jeans smeared with blood.

'Vaughn, it ain't how it looks.'

'I don't think even you can come up with a decent explanation. What the fuck have you done?'

'It was an accident.'

25

Pulling back from the memory, Franny stared at Alfie, who had been listening to the whole story intently. She glanced around the prison visitors' room, then smiled at Alfie, knowing it really was the truth.

'So there it is, Alfie, that's what happened. Afterwards I had to get rid of the body. I wrapped her up and took her to Epping Forest where I buried her. Vaughn must've followed me – there's no way the police would've found where she was otherwise.'

Alfie sat there in shocked silence. There was something in his gut that made him think Franny was telling the truth, but then she'd fooled him before. He didn't say anything; he just let her continue to talk.

'The fact is Vaughn knew it was an accident, but he's given a statement saying he saw me push her, and it's backed up by Shannon. I'm not going to let him get away with it.

I'm not going to rot in here for something I didn't do . . . Look, because of the situation I'm in, the people who run the trust fund that my father set up for me have agreed to release some money. You know, so I can pay for my legal team. It should come through in a day or so. I'll help you pay off Huang.'

'What?'

'Well that's what you want isn't it? You want to stay alive.'

Alfie glanced around at the prison officers, and seeing they were calling time, he spoke quickly. 'You would do that?'

'Of course I would . . . for a price.'

Alfie's expression hardened. 'There's always something in it for you, isn't there?'

'It doesn't mean I don't care about you, but I'm not going to pay off your debt and be left in this place to rot. You'd do the same in my position.'

'Go on then, Fran, tell me what price I have to pay this time,' Alfie said, as he stood up to go.

Franny, standing up herself, smiled. 'It's simple really. Two simple things. I want you to destroy Vaughn and bring down Balantyne with him.'

26

Two days later on Saturday afternoon, Charlie cackled as he hobbled along the busy streets of Soho. He smiled to himself at the plan he had up his sleeve. He was going to have some fun with Shannon. Just seeing her last week and how comfortable she'd got in Vaughn's flat, living the life of Riley, had made him think that she needed to be brought down a peg or two. Oh yes, he was going to bring down little Miss Hoity-Toity, all right, because if she thought that it was anywhere near okay to get up and go and live with Vaughn after everything he'd done for her, well he was going to make that selfish bitch think again . . .

Walking down the hallway of Vaughn's flat, Shannon hummed to herself happily. Vaughn was out with Mia, so it was nice just to be able to relax. Even though she'd moved in a while ago, each and every time she came into the plush apartment, she felt like the luckiest girl in the world, because finally she had somewhere that she could call home.

She'd never felt so safe in her entire life and now she couldn't imagine herself ever living anywhere else. But as Shannon opened her bedroom door, her whole body froze and she stared in horror, her blood running cold. There, lying completely naked on her bed, was Uncle Charlie.

She could hardly get out her words. 'What . . . what . . .'

Charlie grinned as he whispered, 'Surprise!'

Distraught, Shannon continued to stumble over her words. 'No. No, no. You were meant to have gone and not come back. Why . . . What . . .' She trailed off again.

'Spit it out, darlin', I ain't got all day. What am I doing here? Is that what you were going to say, Shan?'

Still in shock, Shannon began to tremble as she nodded her head. 'How . . . how?'

'I'm happy to tell you everything, but if I were you I'd shut that door – unless of course you want Vaughn to see me when he comes in.'

Quickly getting herself together, Shannon hurriedly closed the bedroom door, locking it from the inside.

She turned back to her uncle, her eyes full of fear. 'How did you get in?'

'Well if you will leave your house keys lying around, you're asking for someone to nick them, ain't you?'

Shannon stared at Charlie, suddenly remembering how she'd spent last night searching for her keys, only to end up using the spare set that Vaughn left in the desk bureau drawer. 'That was you? You took them?'

'I just said, didn't I? Now come on over here, and give me a kiss.'

A mixture of anger and worry rushed through Shannon. 'Vaughn could've been in. Did you think about that? What would've happened if he'd seen you?'

Charlie sniffed. 'If you must know I watched and waited to make sure he'd gone out. I was careful. I did you a favour, Shan.'

'You call that a favour?'

'I do actually. I could've just waltzed in here and not given a shit if Vaughnie was here or not, and I would've said it was *you* who gave me the keys. Next time maybe I'll do that.'

Shaking her head furiously, Shannon started to cry. 'There ain't going to be a next time. I want my keys back.'

'Not a chance.'

'Please . . . *please*, just give me them.'

Charlie glared at his niece. 'Oh it's please now, is it?'

Feeling desperate, Shannon said, 'Why are you doing this to me?'

'Because you owe me. I deserve to be looked after, Shan. I did everything for you and you just pick up and take off. So, then I thought if Shannon won't come to the mountain, the mountain shall come and see Shannon. And now I've got your keys, I can come anytime . . . Oh, and don't think about asking Vaughnie to change the locks because all I'll do is knock on the door and tell him what's been happening.'

'I told you he won't believe you.'

Charlie said nastily, 'And I've told *you*, if you want to risk it, then go ahead: change those locks and let's see what he says.'

'I hate you! I hate you!'

'Oh just stop the tears, will you? You know I can't stand you crying, gives me a fucking headache. Anyway, you ain't got that much to cry about, cos I'm a big ole softy really. I got a heart, you know, and I can see how much you want them keys back. So you can have them back, but you have to earn them.'

Eagerly Shannon said, 'How? What do I have to do?'

'Well, I ain't completely decided yet, but how about you start with giving me a long massage. Just the way I like it.'

Shannon shuddered as she stared at her uncle's bloated belly, falling to his side in waves of fat, his belly button filled with a mass of hair. His thighs were squashed together and a layer of sweat sat between them. His penis was retracted to the point where it reminded Shannon of a chestnut mushroom.

Her eyes filled with tears again. 'Please don't make me do this.'

Charlie smirked. 'Do what? All I'm doing is looking for a bit of TLC from my niece. It's about time, don't you think? You've been neglecting me for all these months. I'd be stupid not to get what's mine. After all, I've been the one who's put a roof over your head all these years so now it's time for you to put one over mine. I can use this as my second home with added extras.'

Tears began to roll down her cheeks. 'I ain't for sale and this ain't my house.'

Propping himself up on his elbow, Charlie stared at Shannon. 'No, but I know when we're on to a good thing. Look about you, Shan, this flat is like a palace and all paid for by that mug. We can milk Vaughn for all he's got. Think about it. If we play this right, he will never know that I'm here. *Ever*. This could last forever.'

She shook her head furiously. 'You *said* I could have me keys back.'

'I did, didn't I? But maybe, maybe I was a little bit hasty. I mean, I like it here. This place has got everything I need. It's got you, it's got all the creature comforts, like this iPad . . .'

Shannon interrupted. 'My iPad! Mine! The one that Vaughn bought me!'

'Calm down and stop splitting hairs. *Your* iPad then. Jesus, I never knew you were a grabby mare. You should be ashamed of yourself, Shan, I brought you up to share things.'

Shannon shook her head. Her voice was full of dismay. 'No, you brought me up to lie on me back and think of England whilst you took all the money. I never saw a penny of the money I earned.'

'I gave you food, I gave you drugs, I gave you work and I gave you a bed. You didn't need money in your pocket. Think of the Queen – she doesn't go around with a wad of notes and she seems happy enough. I bet she doesn't go around complaining.'

'Can you hear what you're saying? It's crazy. Uncle Charlie, you need to get out of here.'

Charlie's tone held a nasty threat. 'I'll go in my own time and don't try anything smart, otherwise I'll have to bring a close to your cosy world. I can't have you living here whilst I fend for meself. It's a harsh world out there on your own you know. I need to know I've got somewhere to come to for a little bit of love.'

Shaking and feeling sick, Shannon said, 'You make yourself sound like you're some vulnerable old man when all you are is a dirty parasite.'

Charlie chuckled again. 'Using big words aren't we, Shan? Do you even know what that means? If I were you I'd come down from that high fucking horse you're on because if you don't, you could have a nasty fall.'

'And what if he hears you?'

Charlie gave her a hard stare. 'He won't. As long as you keep your voice down and stop the hysterics. I had a little wander round when I came in. This apartment is hardly small is it? How many bedrooms has it got? Four? Five?'

Miserably Shannon muttered, 'Six. It's got six.'

'Exactly, it's hardly your regular council flat is it? And you could park three double-deckers along that hallway, plus you've got that top floor. Proper posh place, ain't it? Vaughnie's done well. Seems like a life of crime certainly pays. No wonder you want to keep your feet under the table. It's got it all. Solid marble floors, thick walls, high ceilings, two floors . . . and now it's got me! It's perfect, cos no one's going to hear anyone creeping about, so there's no need to worry on that account, Shan.' Seeing the look of distress on his niece's face, Charlie stopped and laughed.

'This is funny to you, isn't it?'

He winked. 'I can't deny, I am having somewhat of a good time . . . Now hurry up and come on over here and start my massage. I ain't looking to freeze me nuts off.'

Still trembling and with her face pale and drawn, Shannon her heart full of sadness said, 'I . . . I can't. I can't.'

'I think you can. Or do I need to start . . . *YELLING UNTIL VAUGHN COMES HOME!*'

Shannon darted across to her uncle. She dived on the bed, slamming her hands over his mouth. Her eyes were wide with fear as she whispered, 'Please, don't. Don't shout! Don't shout! Promise me you won't shout. I'll do what you say. I'll do anything but just don't spoil it for me. If he was to come home and hear you, it'd be over. It'd all be over.' And with that Shannon took away her hands from Charlie's mouth and began to weep into her uncle's chest.

With a smirk he smoothed down her mass of red hair, stroking it gently, which sent a chill down Shannon's body.

'That's it, Shan, you let it all out, darlin'. Uncle Charlie's here. I'll make it all better like I always have. There's no need to cry, and once you've calmed down, how about giving me that massage? It'll be a nice distraction from all them tears.'

Before Shannon could reply, she heard the front door open and Vaughn's footsteps come down the hallway. Her heart raced and she gazed up at her uncle in horror as she whispered, 'Don't say a word, just don't say a word.'

Charlie smiled and then whispered back just as quietly, 'Oh don't worry, I won't . . . as long as *you* do exactly as I say.'

27

In the day room across the hallway, Vaughn was exhausted, having spent the afternoon in the park with Mia who'd done nothing but cry. He started to pour himself a large drink, hoping that she'd sleep for the next few hours, but a sudden knocking on the front door had him jumping up and running down the long cream and gold painted hallway, frantically praying the noise wouldn't disturb her.

The knocking got louder. Vaughn grumbled to himself that the front porter, who was new to the job, kept letting people come into the block of flats without buzzing up first. He hissed out his words. 'All right, all right, I'm coming, for fuck's sake.'

In annoyance he swung open the door and standing there was Alfie, who stared at him with a look that Vaughn couldn't quite interpret. 'Everything all right, Alf?'

Alfie nodded slowly and when he spoke it was just as

slow. 'Oh I'm fine, I thought I'd pop in and see you. It's been a while since I've been here. Mind if I come in?'

Again, Vaughn looked at him oddly. 'Yeah sure but keep it down. Mia's just gone to sleep . . . Your face is looking a bit better by the way.'

Alfie said nothing as he followed Vaughn into his front room, which was tastefully decorated with Ralph Lauren furniture and expensive ornaments.

Still saying nothing, Alfie sat down and the two men stayed in silence until Vaughn, feeling the tension said, 'Look, Alf, I know why you're here.'

'You do?' Alfie was surprised. He had come here expecting to have to read between the lines, to grill Vaughn, to work out if Franny was telling the truth. Yet here he was, within minutes of arriving at the flat, with Vaughn ready to confess all about what he and Shannon had done.

'Yeah. I can see it in your face, and I know this ain't easy. It ain't easy for you to come here and ask me, but I knew you'd come . . . *eventually*.'

Alfie shook his head. 'How?'

Vaughn stood up, dropped some ice in a glass and made himself a drink before automatically pouring Alfie a glass of scotch. He passed it to him and gently said, 'Because I know what you're like, Alf, and it was only a matter of time before it ate away at you and you came to see me.'

In that moment, Alfie was surprised at how calm he felt; on the way over, he'd had visions of beating Vaughn to within an inch of his life, of teaching him a lesson for grassing Franny out and going against everything they lived and died by. And although Franny had told him not to

161

mention anything, to keep his mouth shut, he'd thought it was going to be hard because he wanted answers. Betrayal of any kind was hard, but from the ones closest to him, it was like a blade in his side.

He had come ready for his temper to get the better of him, for his emotions to send him spiralling when he watched Vaughn look uncomfortable when he spoke about Balantyne, though he had also half-expected his anger to boil over when he realised that it was actually *Franny* who'd played him once again and there was no truth in the accusations.

But it was clear that that wasn't the case: Vaughn knew the game was up. His openness and the fact that he was willing to confess without a fight, for whatever reason, soothed the betrayal slightly, although Alfie had to admit to himself that he was more sad than angry. 'I do want to know, and at the same time I don't want to. Does that make sense? Because it's going to change everything, ain't it? Nothing's going to be the same ever again.'

Vaughn took a gulp from the crystal glass; he swilled the ice at the bottom, clinking the cubes together. 'Yeah I know. Life ain't going to be the same again . . . Look, shall we just get on with it then? Shall I go and get her?'

'Okay. After all I need to see her too. It'll make it easier to sort this out sooner rather than later.'

Vaughn nodded before walking out of the room, leaving Alfie to stare at the flames in the large imitation fire on the wall and wait for the showdown.

'Here she is . . . Come on, Alf, say hello to her.' Vaughn stood in the doorway holding Mia in his arms.

Alfie blinked, then stared at Vaughn then Mia then back to Vaughn. 'What the fuck are you playing at?'

Vaughn tilted his head. 'What are you on about?'

Alfie's hand shook as he pointed at Mia, seeing not only Bree in her but also himself. 'Why have you brought her?'

Vaughn's puzzlement was shown in his face and voice. 'You said you wanted to see her.'

'I thought . . . I thought you were talking about Shannon.'

'Shannon? Why would you want me to go and get Shannon, Alf?'

'Well when you started saying about everything's going to change I just thought . . . I just thought . . .'

'You thought what? Go on, Alfie, what did you think?'

Alfie stared at Vaughn, suddenly wanting to play his cards close to his chest. 'Nothing, nothing. Just forget about it . . . I guess maybe I thought it would be nice to all have a sit-down chat.'

Vaughn shook his head as he placed Mia's dummy back into her mouth. 'A sit-down chat? Are you having a laugh? Only a few days ago you're snorting coke up your nose that hard I'm thinking you're going to hoover up the bleeding curtains . . . No, you're hiding something, Alf. I just know it.'

Turning back around, Alfie snapped, 'Well you were the one who said everything was going to change. So what the fuck were *you* talking about?'

'About the fact that you were going to embrace becoming a dad because it was eating you up knowing that you didn't have a relationship with your daughter.'

Angrily, Alfie jumped up. 'You can't just leave it can you? You got to keep pushing it.'

Vaughn's stare hardened as he jogged Mia gently in his arms. 'Well if you weren't talking about Mia, what were you talking about? Come on, and don't treat me like a mug either. I know you've got something else on your mind.'

A flash of anger raced around Alfie's body; the thought of Vaughn going against the code they lived by infuriated him so much the vein in his temples began to throb. 'I think I'm the mug here, don't you? I'm the one who's been proper mugged off.'

'How? Come on, spit it out. If you've got a beef, tell me, because otherwise I don't know what the fuck you're talking about,' Vaughn growled, shaking his head.

Everything in Alfie wanted to put his fist into Vaughn's mouth, but instead he shrugged, reining his temper back, knowing he wanted to play this right.

'Like I say, forget about it. I was just winding myself up. You know, about the police and about Franny. Can't get me head around it.'

Even though it was only the slightest of hesitations it didn't go unnoticed by Alfie.

'Why are you thinking about the Old Bill?'

Alfie gave Vaughn a tight smile. 'Just the fact you called them. It got to me. Still can't understand it.'

'Oh come on, Alf, not this again. We've gone over it. Okay, looking back it ain't what we usually do, it may not have been the cleverest of moves, but like I say, it was just a spur-of-the-moment thing. One call, that's all it was.'

Alfie chose his words carefully. 'And you haven't spoken to them since? You never said anything else? I mean you wouldn't be that stupid, would you? There's rules – and there's definitely punishments in our world for people who grass.'

Turning his back on Alfie, Vaughn said, 'What do you take me for? Look, I'm going to put her back in her cot.'

There was so much Alfie wanted to say but until he knew for certain he needed to keep his mouth shut. And if he did find out that Vaughn and Shannon had given statements, then both of them would be sorry. Very sorry indeed.

Then with a smile that didn't reach his eyes, Alfie said, 'Okay look, I'm going to get off now.'

'You've only just got here.'

Alfie shrugged again and answered drily. 'I'm sure we'll catch up very soon.'

28

Ten minutes later and certain that Alfie had gone, Vaughn picked up the phone. After two rings it was answered and Vaughn growled down the phone. 'It's me. Listen, have you been talking?'

'What?'

'Have you been shooting your mouth off that I've been speaking to you? Because if you have, I'm not the only one who's going to be a dead man around here – I'm going to kill you too.'

Over in the hospital Detective Balantyne seethed and stared at the phone as the call was cut off. He didn't know who the hell this man thought he was, speaking to him like that, but he wasn't going to have *anyone* threaten him, least of all some scumbag like Vaughn Sadler.

If it wasn't for the fact that he was caught up waiting to

find out what was happening with Claire, he'd go round and show Sadler what happened to people who thought they could threaten him – a detective and a highly regarded one at that. He hoped the trial was brought forward because the sooner he didn't have to deal with scum like Doyle and Sadler the better all round.

'Detective Balantyne, do you mind going over this again? I just need to get a few more details.'

Balantyne pushed the phone into his pocket and smiled at the dark-haired constable. 'Not at all . . . Shall we go and get a coffee? I could do with one.'

Without waiting for the officer to reply, Balantyne walked along the corridor of the hospital. There was an overpowering smell of bleach in the air and Balantyne did all he could to try to stop himself feeling sick. It wasn't helping either that his mind was focused on Claire.

She'd looked in a bad way when the ambulance had come for her. She hadn't moved, and her breathing had been short. As for Emma, she'd started to come around as they were carrying her on a stretcher into a separate ambulance. He hadn't got in with her, he'd travelled to the hospital with Claire – though he'd been careful not to hold her hand or to show any affection towards her. He hadn't wanted to give anything away.

'How is she, Detective? How's the Inspector?' The concern in the officer's voice was somehow comforting and he turned to smile as they made their way into the hospital canteen.

'I don't know. The nurse came to tell me about half an hour ago they found a bleed on her brain. They took her

167

into surgery, so it's now just a question of waiting . . . She's pregnant . . .'

The officer sounded as surprised as he looked. 'I didn't know that.'

Not quite sure why he'd told him, Balantyne answered in a weary tone. 'No, neither did I, until earlier . . . She mentioned it in passing.'

The officer raised his eyebrows. 'I didn't know she even had a partner. Every time there's a social do she never brings anyone. So, I presumed . . .'

This time Balantyne's tone was hard and it clearly didn't go unmissed by the young officer. 'First rule of policing, never presume anything, officer . . . Anyway, look, why don't you get the coffees and I'll get a seat.'

Again, without waiting for a reply, Balantyne turned and walked away from the officer, leaving him queuing up at the counter.

Pulling out the metal canteen chair, which scraped noisily along the floor, Balantyne took a deep breath. If he was going to pull this off, if he was going to walk away without anyone pointing the finger of blame at him, he needed to play it casually. Needed to play it cool.

If he played it right, if he was careful, this was a way of getting rid of Emma once and for all, and there was no way he could afford to mess this opportunity up.

'I'm sorry, I forgot to ask how your wife is?'

Balantyne's thoughts were interrupted by the officer bringing two large mugs of frothy coffee.

'She's fine, well she is physically. Mentally, I'm sure she's not very well. I haven't seen her yet.'

The officer's words rushed out. 'We can do this another time if you'd rather. I can speak to you later if you want to go and see her. They should let you.'

Balantyne snapped, 'No, I'd rather just get this over and done with.'

The officer nodded as he sat down and, pulling out a notebook, he spoke apologetically. 'I know this must be awkward but—'

Irritated by the officer's demeanour and losing all patience, Balantyne interrupted, and gave him a frosty stare. 'The only part of this that's awkward is you. Now why don't you just ask me the questions and then you can type up your report, and I can make sure my wife is okay.'

Licking the top of his biro pen out of habit, the officer nodded again. He cleared his throat and said, 'So why was Mrs Balantyne in Inspector Martin's car?'

Balantyne stared at the officer, trying to keep his voice as even as he could. 'Emma, as you now know, had been drinking and that's when she ran down Inspector Martin.'

'Yes, I understand that's what happened in the end, but that doesn't answer the question. *Why* was she in the car and in the driver's seat in the first place?'

Balantyne bit on his lip. He could feel a small vein beginning to throb behind his eye. 'Look, I can't tell you why a drunk person does something. They're not thinking rationally.'

'Yes but . . .'

'But what, *constable*?'

The officer looked at Balantyne seeing the challenge in his eyes, but he refused to back down. 'But why were you even there? Why was the car there? Why was she in the car? Detective, there's a part here that's missing and I just need to understand how this all came about.'

Knowing that he had to keep his cool, Balantyne gave a tight smile that didn't meet his eyes. 'All of us want to make our mark in the force, but you have to pick how you do it . . .'

'I don't follow, sir.'

'Officer, if I were you I'd stop treating me like I'm the criminal here. I don't appreciate being grilled. I'm *telling* you how it was, and I don't expect you to try to prove otherwise. Understand?'

For a moment it fell silent between the men before Balantyne continued, 'Inspector Martin had come to pick me up for a management training conference. We were parked on the high street working out the best route when she suddenly began to feel sick. She was embarrassed at the idea of throwing up in front of people, so I suggested we drive to a quiet lane I knew around the corner. I was concerned that she was ill and perhaps she shouldn't be going to the conference. And that's when she confessed to me she was pregnant. Like you I was surprised, but it was none of my business.'

Scribbling Balantyne's words down, the officer asked, 'And when did your wife turn up?'

'I suppose it was ten minutes after we'd parked. We were sitting there and Claire . . . I mean the Inspector, she was trying to gather herself together, when there was a huge crash and the back windscreen was smashed. Obviously afterwards we realised it was Emma putting a stone through the back of the car, but we both jumped out and there was Emma.'

The officer frowned. 'Why did she do that?'

The irritation came back into Balantyne's voice. 'I have no idea, I only can guess that she saw me and wanted to get her own back.'

'What do you mean, sir?'

Taking a sip of his coffee, Balantyne gazed at the officer who was young and clearly eager to make an impression, maybe too eager. Balantyne knew he had to be careful. He also knew that he was going to play the officer for a fool. He raised an eyebrow. 'Off the record?'

At first the officer looked dubious but then he put down his pen on the table and said, 'Yes, sir, off the record.'

'You see I feel like I'm betraying Emma by saying this, but she's a chronic alcoholic. The first thing she does in the morning is drink and she doesn't stop until she passes out at night.'

'We did find a couple of bottles of vodka in her bag. One was empty.'

'Exactly, and it's tragic, really. I've kept it a secret, of course, because I wanted to protect her, but many a night I've sat up worried sick about her. It's very difficult for me to leave her when I go to work, you can imagine how worried I am about her.'

The officer smiled, sympathetically. 'Yes, sir. It must be very difficult.'

Feigning gratitude, Balantyne reached across and touched the officer's arm. 'Thank you. Anyway . . . and you can write this next part down . . .'

The officer enthusiastically picked up his pen again as Balantyne continued to talk. 'We'd had a row; it was about her drinking. I was on edge because I had to go to the conference, and I was scared to leave her because by the time I'd got up she'd already started drinking. I'd thrown her hidden bottles of booze away, and maybe that was a mistake, but she was furious with me. She even hit me. That's not unusual either. Anyhow, I left and I guess she must have followed me and that when she saw me she was angry with me. Angry and drunk.'

'And that's when she threw the stone and when you and the Inspector got out of the car?'

'That's right, and then we saw it was Emma. She was beside herself. I was trying to coax her into the car. I wanted to drive her back home.'

'What about the Inspector?'

Balantyne sighed. 'I already told you, she wasn't well. I didn't think it was wise for her to take Emma home in the state she was. As I say she can be violent and I'm used to it.'

'So then what did Mrs Balantyne do?'

'Well it all happened so quickly. I walked across to tell the Inspector I was going to take Emma home or at least try, and then the next thing I hear the car start up behind me. Emma's in the driving seat revving the engine. I tell her to get out of the car, but she wouldn't. She had a wild look in her eyes. It was like she was in her own world. I was begging her but she ignored me. Then she suddenly screamed, *I'm going to kill her*, and the next thing I know she drives the car right into the Inspector.'

The officer stayed silent for a few seconds as his eyes glanced down his notes. Eventually he said, 'Why would she say that though, sir? Why would she say, *I'm going to kill her*?'

Balantyne narrowed his gaze. 'I don't know, officer, I mean, why do we say anything? And as I said before, we can hardly work out why an inebriated person says something, can we?'

'I suppose not.'

Taking a deep breath as he clenched his fists tightly under the table, Balantyne said, 'Now will that be all, officer?'

'But why didn't she want to kill you? Why did she want to kill the Inspector?'

The tight smile appeared again on Balantyne's face. 'Who knows? I don't suppose she knows herself. She's always had a thing about the Inspector. You might've heard that a couple of years ago she stormed into a party and accused me of all sorts, you know, that I was having an affair with Inspector Martin.'

'I had heard that and you're saying it wasn't true?'

A flash of anger came into Balantyne's eyes. 'I'm saying it's none of your business – but for the record, no, I wasn't having an affair. Emma was – and always will be – paranoid. She's jealous. So maybe there's your motive. Maybe Emma got into her head again that I was seeing the Inspector . . . Now if you don't mind, I need to go. There really isn't anything else to tell you.'

The officer stared at Balantyne and spoke slowly. 'Obviously it's not my decision, but you do know after what you've just told me, your wife will be charged? I understand she's already got history of drink driving?'

Balantyne nodded. 'That's how she got the scar on her face.'

'So you do realise it won't just be a slap on the wrist?'

Balantyne leant in. 'Constable, I've been in the force for a number of years, probably before you were even able to wipe the shit from your bum properly, so I do know exactly what's going to happen. And as much as I'd rather Emma be able to come home with me, I realise that the rules can't be bent just for my wife.'

The officer continued to stare at Balantyne. 'The problem is though, sir . . . Once we've got all the evidence it's likely your wife's going to be charged with attempted murder.'

Not wanting to show the officer his relief on hearing the news, Balantyne just nodded but a moment later something struck him. He looked directly at the officer. 'What do you mean by *all* the evidence . . . What other evidence?'

'Apparently Inspector Martin had a dashcam on her car, so we need to get that and check it. But it'll back up your story and the good thing is most of the dashcams record audio from inside of the car . . .'

29

It was midday Monday morning and Officer Brown stood in the doorway of Franny's cell. 'Got a new cell mate for you, Doyle.'

Emma Balantyne stood in a daze, staring at Franny, who glared back and said, 'I'm on remand so I shouldn't have to have a cell mate.'

Officer Brown smirked. 'And so is she. Perhaps you can swap stories over a bedtime cup of tea.'

Franny's face turned into a snarl. 'Piss off and get her out of here.'

Officer Brown's face mirrored Franny's snarl. 'Watch your mouth, Doyle; the fact is you've got no choice. This isn't the Holiday Inn, so like it or not you two are going to cosy up and you might as well get used to that fact.'

'Is that right?'

'Oh yeah, Doyle, so suck it up.'

Incensed, and with her emotions all churned up after the visit from Alfie, Franny stood and marched across to Emma. Then without warning she slapped her across the face before turning to Officer Brown.

'Now you *can't* have me in the same cell as her. So it's *you* who's got no choice. You know the rules, Officer Brown; any prisoner showing any signs of violence towards their cell mate *has* to be moved.' She stopped and turned back to Emma and smiled apologetically. 'No hard feelings, sweetheart, it's nothing personal.'

With Emma rubbing her cheek and in shock from what just happened, Officer Brown's face went red with anger. She pulled Emma out of the cell roughly before locking Franny in it. She spoke angrily through the flap. 'I'll be back soon to deal with you, Doyle, but consider your privileges well and truly stopped.'

As Officer Brown dragged Emma roughly down the corridor to another cell, Emma, humiliated and upset, yelled, 'Get your fucking hands off me. This place is full of animals and you're no better . . . I said, get your hands off me!'

'Just keep it shut.'

Emma, almost hysterical now, continued to yell and cry as the other women on the landing watched on. 'Or what? What are you going to do to me? Put me in a cell again with another crazy woman?'

Officer Brown – who was certainly not in the mood for any kind of trouble amongst the women – said, 'If you don't keep it down I'm going to place you in a seg cell; that way you can scream all you like and bother no one. Now come on.'

Trying to pull her arm free of the officer's grip, Emma snapped, 'I shouldn't be here! I didn't do it. I'm not like all these people here. I'm not a criminal. Do you hear me! I didn't do it! There's been some kind of mistake!'

Officer Brown stopped walking to turn and stare at Emma in contempt. Her voice dripped with sarcasm. 'Yeah, you and everyone else in here. The jail is full of innocent people.'

Emma's eyes blazed with anger. 'But it's true, I didn't do it!'

'Yeah, yeah, whatever. Save it for your solicitor. I've still got several hours to go before my shift ends, so I don't want to listen to your shit.'

'How dare you! How dare you speak to me like that? Who do you think you are? Do you know who my husband is?'

Officer Brown's eyes darted around, and she grabbed Emma even tighter around her arm before pulling her into a side room. She spoke firmly but quietly, her face inches away from Emma's. 'If I were you I'd keep the fact that your husband's a copper very quiet. As you can imagine the police aren't exactly the women's best friends, so if they hear even a whisper about you being married to one, I can't guarantee you'll walk out of here in one piece. Do I make myself clear?'

Emma paled as Officer Brown continued. 'It's for that reason you've got to go by your maiden name of *Walsh*. So don't mess this up by mouthing off. They've cocked up sending you here, and they'll probably soon transfer you to a prison up north, but until then, keep your head down.'

'I need a drink . . .'

'Will that be a piña colada or a double whiskey?'

Enraged, Emma growled, 'This isn't funny. Look at me, I'm shaking.'

Unsympathetically, Officer Brown said, 'You can see medical later for that. They'll give you something to stop the shakes. You should've asked them for something when they checked you in.'

'What, and have everybody talking about me? I don't want my private affairs broadcast.'

Officer Brown shook her head and chuckled. 'This is prison and the moment you came through those gates you gave up anything near private. You'll shit in front of the other women, you'll piss in front of them, you'll eat and shower in front of them and no doubt you'll cry in front of them, so whether they know you like your booze or not is really not such a big deal when you think about it.'

Not liking what Officer Brown had to say, Emma snapped, 'I want to see my husband.'

Officer Brown looked puzzled. 'Why? What's he going to do for you? There's nothing he can do for you in here. The police have no jurisdiction in prisons, and anyway, from what I hear, he was hardly trying to keep you out of this place was he?'

'What are you talking about?'

Officer Brown blinked a couple of times and then she smiled nastily. 'You don't know do you?'

Emma retorted, 'I don't know what?'

'I think you need to talk to your solicitor – he can fill you in.'

'Just tell me!'

Leading Emma out of the side room, Officer Brown said, 'From what I hear from the police officer who escorted you in, your husband gave a pretty damning witness statement. Apparently, he was adamant that you attempted to kill the woman he was with.'

Having put Emma in a cell further down the landing, ten minutes later Officer Brown stood in the open doorway of Franny's cell with two of her subordinate officers behind her. 'You think you're clever, don't you, Doyle?'

Sitting on her bed, Franny gazed up at her and sighed. 'I don't know what you're talking about, but I'm sure you're about to tell me.'

Officer Brown nodded to her officers who walked into the cell as she continued to talk. 'I think a search is needed, don't you?'

Franny shrugged, confident the phone she'd hidden wouldn't be found by the officers who only really gave a half-hearted search. 'I've got nothing to hide. Have a look. Search the cell for all I care – you ain't going to find anything.'

'You can't be too careful especially after a visit. We're cracking down. Too many prisons have drugs floating about. But that's not going to happen in my prison.'

Franny looked puzzled. 'You know I don't do drugs.'

'You could sell them though.'

Franny shook her head. 'Not my style, I'm afraid. So you're just wasting your time and mine,' she said, nodding in the direction of the officers.

Officer Brown smirked. 'We'll see. Come with me. And no, Doyle, it isn't a request, it's an order.'

The room Franny stood in was no more than twelve feet by twelve feet. In one corner there was a steel toilet and in the other corner Officer Brown stood with her arms crossed and her hands covered in latex gloves. 'Take your clothes off, Doyle.'

'You've got to be joking.'

'Nope, afraid not. You should've had this done before but sometimes my officers aren't as thorough as me.'

Franny stared at Officer Brown, her hatred for her oozing from her eyes. 'They already checked me. You know that.'

'Maybe not as thoroughly as they should. Like I say, I don't want my prison to be flooded with drugs.'

'This isn't about drugs. You're getting off on this, ain't you?'

'Just doing my job, Doyle. Now get your clothes off.'

Franny shook her head and then slowly unbuttoned her top before slipping it over her head. She undid the button and zipper on her trousers, dropped them to the floor and stepped out of them. 'Satisfied?'

Nastily, Officer Brown shook her head. 'You've only been here a short time and you're already causing trouble. I don't like women who think they can come into my prison and throw their weight about. Now take your bra off.'

Franny held Officer Brown's stare then slowly unclipped her bra.

'Don't be shy. Hands up in the air, Doyle.'

Again, Franny's movements were slow as she raised her

arms. She spat her words. 'Nothing, see. So your playtime's over.'

Officer Brown stepped into her space. She pushed her face into Franny's. 'I'll be the judge of that. Now take your knickers off.'

Franny felt the anger rush through her body. She breathed heavily, willing her temper to stay even, because she knew losing it was exactly what Officer Brown wanted. Keeping her voice steady she said, 'You know that's not how it goes. You're supposed to give me my top back first before I take my bottoms off.'

'Oh I know but it's more fun this way. It's more fun to see you squirm and let's face it there's nothing you can do about it: you're not leaving this room until you do what I say. It's about time you started listening, Doyle. So come on, I haven't got all day . . . though I guess you have.'

Knowing that Officer Brown wasn't going to budge on this, Franny slowly pulled her pants down, and stood in the middle of the room completely naked as Brown made her way behind her.

'Now squat.'

Quickly Franny swivelled around to face Officer Brown. 'What?'

'Don't pretend you didn't hear. Who knows what else you might be hiding up your arse, because I already know there's a lot of bullshit.'

It was Franny's turn to step forward. She was so close she could smell the toothpaste from Officer Brown's mouth. 'You're not worth what I want to do to you. Not now anyway. It can wait.'

Officer Brown smiled. 'The years you'll get, Doyle, when they find you guilty, I think I'll be waiting a long time, don't you? But in the meantime, you'll do as I say . . . unless you want more trouble . . .? No, I thought not. So come on then, squat, Doyle. Squat and cough.'

And as a naked Franny, slowly and full of humiliation began to squat, not for the first time that day she vowed to bring Vaughn down once and for all.

30

The next day on Tuesday afternoon, Vaughn stomped down the hallway.

'*Shannon! Shan! You're needed out here. I want to talk to you!*' He shouted through the thick, wooden door. His knock was full of irritation. 'For fuck's sake just come out here. I'm sick of having to talk to you through the door.'

Shouting back, Shannon – who leant on her bedroom door, shaking – stared at her uncle, who'd fallen asleep the night before, but when he had eventually woken up, had refused to leave. And although the place was huge, to make matters worse, her bedroom was the only bedroom without an en-suite bathroom.

When she'd first moved in Vaughn had given her the choice of bedrooms but instead of choosing the ones that not only had their own bathrooms but also their own walk-in wardrobes, she'd chosen the smallest room, because she'd fallen in love with the view that looked out across the rooftops towards Soho, reminding her of the life she'd left behind, knowing she never wanted to go back there.

But ultimately what it had meant was she'd had to bring Charlie a bucket to use as a toilet, which had not only been disgusting but for some reason it'd made her sad. Her happiness felt like it was dripping away and it was all getting too much for her.

And on top of the stress of being with Charlie, she'd also had to keep rushing between Vaughn asking her to help him with Mia and running back to her room to make sure her uncle wasn't about to blow their cover. 'I'm coming!'

'I don't get why you have to keep this door locked. You never did before!'

Still shaking as she yelled back, Shannon fought her tears. 'I just like a bit of privacy that's all.' She turned her attention back to her uncle, who was now sitting on the edge on the bed dressed in just his Y-fronts. 'Don't move, you hear me? Don't move a muscle. And later I want you gone.'

Charlie grinned. Talking in the smallest of whispers, he said, 'I can go now if you like. How about I do that? I can have a little chat to Vaughnie on the way out.'

As Charlie went to get up, Shannon grabbed hold of her uncle. 'Don't! Just stay there! *Please.*'

Mocking her, Charlie smiled. 'Make up your mind, Shan. One minute you want me to go and the next you're begging me to stay. I always knew you couldn't do without me.'

'Shannon!'

'Sorry, Vaughn, I'm coming!' Without answering her

uncle, Shannon ran for the door and stepped out of her room straight into Vaughn who was standing waiting for her. He stared suspiciously at her as she pulled the door shut behind her.

'Are you all right, Shan? You look jumpy.'

Wringing her hands and feeling the sweat run down her back, Shannon stared down at the floor. 'I'm fine, Mia was up in the night and I'm just tired.'

Vaughn frowned. 'I never heard her.'

Snapping, Shannon began to cry. 'I guess that's the good thing about having such thick walls, ain't it. And most of the time you forget to put the baby monitor on so it's me that gets up for her whilst you just snore your fucking head off . . . Sorry, sorry, I didn't mean that. Like I say I'm just tired.'

Vaughn, hating to see Shannon upset, put his arms around her. 'It's fine. Her cry can make a grown man weep. No wonder you're tired if she was at it all night. I'm useless, I'm sorry, I just ain't used to this baby lark.'

'It's okay, *really*. I shouldn't get angry just cos I'm tired.'

Feeling guilty for leaving a lot of Mia's care to Shannon, Vaughn smiled. 'I'm worried about you, that's all. Past few days you've been in that room a lot and you look like you've got something on your mind . . . I tell you what, how about you and Mia go out and get some fresh air? Get yourself something to eat. Take this.' He pulled out a fifty-pound note from his pocket and handed it to her. 'Treat yourself to something.'

Shannon shook her head. 'I'm fine. I'd rather stay in.'

Noticing the dark circles around her eyes, Vaughn gently

said, 'I can see how tired you are, Shan; you look like you've been keeping the vampire hours. Go on, a bit of sun will do you good.'

Shannon shrugged as she stared down at the floor, tears escaping once again. For the first time in forever she'd been happy. With Vaughn. With Mia. Just the three of them. Until her uncle had come and ruined everything. She didn't know what she was going to do because one thing she knew about her uncle was how much he enjoyed playing games.

It was too late to tell Vaughn now. Who would believe that she had nothing to do with Charlie staying and making himself at home? Especially as she knew her uncle would make it sound like it was her idea in the first place.

She was scared and she felt lost because she had no one to tell her secret to, no one to help her. So, the way it stood at the moment, it was down to her to try to get her uncle to leave – but for now she needed to try to act as normal as she could . . .

Looking up at Vaughn, Shannon tried a smile. 'Okay, I'll take her out.'

Only just noticing her tears, Vaughn said, 'Hey, Shan, why are you crying? Are you that unhappy here?'

Shannon shook her head furiously, bursting into tears again. 'No, no. I love it here. I love Mia, and I love . . .' She stopped before she said the words *'I love you too.'* But she did love him; she loved him so much it almost hurt – though she couldn't tell him. Not yet anyway. First things first: she needed to get rid of Charlie.

'I . . . what I mean is: it's great here and I don't want you to think that I'm being ungrateful.'

Vaughn gave her a hug as he said, 'I don't, sweetheart . . . Anyway, come on or the sun will have pissed off by the time you get out there.'

Smiling she turned and pulled out a key from her pocket and began to lock her bedroom door. Watching her curiously, Vaughn frowned. He didn't say anything; instead with various thoughts rushing through his mind, he went to get Mia ready.

Fifteen minutes later, having had to search the flat for Mia's favourite dummy, Vaughn waved to Shannon and Mia. The minute they had gone, he rushed back along the hallway to the kitchen.

Pulling open a drawer he pulled out a thin flathead screwdriver before running back out of the kitchen to Shannon's room.

Putting the screwdriver in the crack of the door, he hurriedly wiggled the lock, rattling the door handle. As much as he wanted to trust Shannon she was definitely hiding something and one way or another he was going to find out exactly what it was . . .

31

Detective Balantyne hadn't slept. All he could think of was the dashcam.

He'd spent the whole night in the hospital, partly to make sure that Claire's emergency surgery had gone all right – which it had, and although she was still unconscious, they'd told him the baby was all right. But the main reason he'd been awake was because he'd spent the night making discreet phone calls to find out where they'd taken Claire's car.

Then less than five minutes ago he'd found out and now the most important thing was to get there before they started checking it.

He was mad at himself – how could he have been so stupid as to forget to take the card out of the dashcam? In truth he hadn't even thought about it; everything had happened so quickly. But now there was no time to waste – if they saw the footage or listened to the recording it wouldn't be Emma banged up for life, it would be him.

And with that thought, Balantyne switched the blue light on and sped out of the hospital car park.

Across in Hartwood prison, Franny was marched down to the visitors' room by Officer Brown. 'You better make the most of these visits, Doyle. Don't get too used to them, will you? You might be able to get as many visits as you like when you're on remand but once you're convicted it won't be like this.'

'Then it's a good job I ain't going to get convicted, isn't it?'

Brown chuckled. 'Keep on telling yourself that, Doyle, if it makes it easier for you. But we both know the truth. We both know what's going to happen.'

Deciding not to answer Officer Brown anymore, Franny continued to walk down the long corridors. She passed Christine Lucas who she hadn't seen for a couple of days due to Christine being sent to seg for starting a fight in the library. As expected, Lucas chirped her greeting.

'Hello, Franny, good to see you. I've missed you. Why don't you come by and pay me a visit?' Along with the other group of women on the landing, Christine cackled, winking and licking her lips at Franny who ignored her and continued to follow Officer Brown.

As she walked through the various corridors, hearing the usual bangs and clatters and shouts of the prison, Franny stared at the back of the officer's head and breathed deeply, overcoming her temptation to give Brown a taste of her own medicine. Instead, she stayed silent and focused on her goal of getting out of there rather than adding any more charges to the ones she already had.

She hadn't heard from Alfie since he'd been to see her and when she'd tried to call him on his phone, he'd either not answered or rejected her call. She'd tried not to panic; after all she knew what Alfie was like – he'd go away and ruminate before deciding what to do. But hopefully she'd dangled enough of a carrot for him to be more than tempted to help her, and to be honest he really didn't have many other options. He knew that and she most certainly did.

Walking into the visitors' room, Franny froze. She'd been told it was her solicitor's paralegals wanting her to sign some papers, but looking at the man sitting at the table, he couldn't be less legal if he tried.

Throwing a quick glance at Officer Brown, who was now in the midst of gossip with one of the other officers, Franny walked over to the table and pulled out the chair. Sitting down she hissed, 'What the hell are you doing here?'

Franny stared at Mr Huang, who was as always dressed immaculately in a three-piece grey-striped suit. He pushed his glasses up his nose as he stared at Franny, a tiny smile dancing at the corners of his mouth. 'Ms Doyle, that's no way to greet me. After all I thought you and I were friends.'

'I'm not your friend, Huang, and it's not very clever to come in here and pretend you're one of my solicitors.'

Huang grinned. 'Why not? It worked; I'm here aren't I?'

'Did it ever occur to you that I don't want you here? What if you'd bumped into Alfie?'

'Ms Doyle, I can't work on what-ifs. I *don't* work on

what-ifs. He's not here so there's no issue, and besides, Mr Jennings seeing me isn't a problem to me, it's a problem to you.'

Seething Franny said, 'Whilst we're on the subject, why the hell did you do that to his face? He looked like he'd been hit by a car.'

'I have to make it look authentic. Don't you think it would be suspicious if I didn't do anything? After all I also have a reputation to keep up – I can't be seen to be soft. Anyway, what do you care?'

'Believe it or not, I care for Alfie.'

Huang stared at her for a moment before saying, 'You have a funny way of showing it, Ms Doyle. I wouldn't like to be your enemy if this is what you do to the people you care for. Maybe you and I are more alike than we thought.'

Franny's face darkened. 'I'm nothing like you. Now just leave him alone. Hurting him wasn't part of the deal.'

Huang leant over the prison table and clutched Franny's hand hard. Too hard. 'I beg to differ. The deal was you pay me the money Alfie owes me and I keep quiet about it. How I do that is down to me, and if I choose to go and give Mr Jennings a little warning to keep it real, as they say, then that's my call. If you don't like it, then why don't you confess all to him?'

'You know I can't do that.'

Huang examined his nails, which were beautifully mani-cured. 'I don't know why you bothered paying his debt in the first place. Surely Mr Jennings' death would be a loss to no one.'

'You know exactly why. How would Alfie being dead

help me get out of this place? I need to keep him alive, so you nearly battering him to death isn't on the table. You understand?' Franny said, spitting her words.

'Ms Doyle, I don't like your tone. I'd be careful if I were you; you've got a lot to lose. I take it he's agreed to your little plan?'

Franny's eyes were full of hatred. The only reason she'd told Huang of her plan was because he'd refused to help her otherwise. 'Not yet, but he will do. Once he realises that I'm his only option to get you off his back, then I'm sure he'll do what I want. He'll bring Vaughn down.'

Huang smiled. 'You really are ruthless, Ms Doyle, and it's a good job I'm a man of my word . . . otherwise you might be in trouble.'

'What are you talking about?'

'Well, Mr Jennings is running around terrified for no reason because you've *already* paid off his debt. When was it? Two months ago?'

'What's your point?'

'The point is, you've pretended you couldn't afford to pay me off when you always had the resources to do so. You pretended there was a trust fund set up by your father that you couldn't get your hands on, didn't you, Ms Doyle?'

Franny seethed. Her face was flushed red as she spoke. 'You know I did, but I want to know why you're bringing this up now?'

Huang smiled. 'All I'm saying, Ms Doyle, is that I don't think he'd be too happy to find out about all the lies you've been telling him, would he?'

'He's not going to find out though, is he?'

Huang stood up. 'That all depends.'

'Depends on what?'

'It depends if you see fit to pay me a little extra for my time and discretion.'

Infuriated, Franny banged her fist down on the table. 'You said that once I paid Alfie's debt and interest then that's it.'

Huang laughed, his beady eyes narrowing. 'I did say that but I think I've changed my mind.'

'You bastard!'

'You make a deal with the devil and you should expect to burn in hell, Ms Doyle.'

At which point Huang left Franny sitting at the table.

32

Inside Shannon's bedroom, Charlie, hearing something, suddenly sat up. He took off the headphones and listened. Shit, there was somebody trying to get in. Not bothering to wrap a towel around himself, Charlie stood up and waddled naked towards the built-in wardrobes, his prosthetic leg – stained and dirty from where he'd never cleaned it – making his body tilt slightly to the left.

Realising he wouldn't make it in time to the wardrobe, Charlie with his heart racing threw his obese body onto the floor, trying to fit his large, hairy, spotty buttocks under the wooden frame of Shannon's king-size bed.

As the door flew open Charlie only just managed to squeeze himself under, as Vaughn stalked around the room.

The minute Vaughn entered, he shook his head. The place was like a pigsty and stunk of sweat. He wasn't sure what had happened but something had changed. Only a few weeks ago, Shannon had taken pride in her room, taken pride in the small things, like arranging her make-up tidily and organising her clothes with pride, but now everything was strewn all over the place.

He looked around, sadly. He hadn't known what he was expecting to find but it wasn't this. Or maybe he had thought he'd find this and was just hoping he wouldn't.

He moved her clothes, which were piled up on the chest of drawers, not sure what he was even looking for. A crack pipe perhaps. A needle to prove she'd been jacking up? It certainly looked like a junkie's room.

Angry at the sense of betrayal, he pulled open the drawers, riffling through each and every one of them before he ran to the wardrobes, flinging open the doors. He pulled the clothes he'd bought her off their hangers, still not knowing what exactly he was going to find.

Swivelling around, his eyes darted across the room. He ran to where the photograph of the three of them sat on the bedside table. With his heart beating he ripped it out of its frame, praying he didn't find a rock of crack or a wrap of heroin.

He breathed out a sigh of relief as his eyes glanced on the floor and saw a sponge and an empty bowl discarded to the side. What was she hiding? He knew there was something but what?

He sat down on the bed heavily, unaware that his feet were inches away from Charlie's naked body, which was squashed and sweating underneath the bed frame.

Sitting and thinking, Vaughn twirled the screwdriver in his hand as he tried to work out what was going on.

Absentmindedly he dropped the screwdriver on the floor, it rolled under the bed, and bending over Vaughn went to retrieve it. As he did suddenly a shriek filled the air.

'Why are you in my room? Why are you snooping about?' Shannon rushed into her bedroom, charging at Vaughn, who stood back up. He watched as she flung herself towards him with wild eyes that were full of terror.

Shocked and partly ashamed for being caught, Vaughn turned to Shannon. 'I ain't snooping and anyway, what are you doing here?'

Her heart beat so fast, Shannon felt dizzy. She didn't have any idea what had happened to Charlie and where he was and she was too scared to glance around the room. Her voice trembled.

'It looks like you're snooping to me. And for your information, Mia was grizzly – she's teething – so I brought her back. She's in her cot . . . So if you don't mind, get out.'

Vaughn shook his head. He grabbed her arm. 'Just tell me, are you using again? Are you? Because I ain't fucking having it.'

Shannon shook and couldn't get her words out. Hurt rushed to her eyes.

'What's wrong with you, Shan? For fuck's sake just talk to me.'

'How can you say I'm using again? How can you think that?'

'Well look around you, it's a fucking pigsty in here. What am I supposed to think?'

Shannon shook her head furiously. 'Not that! You're supposed to trust me!'

Vaughn, losing his cool, yelled back at her. 'And you're supposed to trust me too! You're worrying me. I can't help you if you don't tell me.'

Shaking, Shannon raged, 'There ain't nothing to tell. The only thing I know is that I've come home and I've found you in my room.'

'I'm sorry, okay! I'm sorry. I'm just worried you're going to fuck up and that's the last thing I want, because I like you, Shan, and I want the best for you, but I can't have you around if you're using – you know that.'

Almost unable to get her words out from crying Shannon nodded. 'I know, I know and I promised you, didn't I?'

'Well if it's not that, what is it? What is it you can't tell me? Is it a boy? Has something happened with a boy? Has someone touched you?'

'No. No.'

Mystified, Vaughn shook his head. 'Then, is it me? Have I done something? Cos I ain't used to teenage girls and I know that I can be rough and insensitive sometimes and if I've hurt you, Shan, I'm sorry. But I wish you'd just talk to me.'

'Please, Vaughn, it ain't nothing . . . I just get like . . . I never had any nice things before, and I never had anyone to show me and sometimes . . . sometimes it just gets a bit much. You know, trying to make you happy. I'm scared I won't be good enough for you.'

Vaughn let out a long sigh. 'What are you talking about, Shan?'

'The pressure, it sometimes feels so much pressure.'

Sadness filled Vaughn's voice. 'I had no idea you felt like

197

that. You don't have to impress me. Is that why you kept the door shut – because it was a mess?'

Hating lying to Vaughn, Shannon shrugged. 'I guess, and also it's just nice to have a bit of privacy. This is the first place I've had where I could lock the door if I wanted to. Before, I wasn't allowed anything near privacy.'

'And here's me banging on your door, reminding you of what your life was like with that piece of shit uncle of yours.'

Shannon bristled, feeling uncomfortable. 'You weren't to know.'

'Don't let me off that easily. I've been a wanker. Thinking the worst of you. Look, I can see you're tired. Get some rest. I'm no Mr Sheen, but I'll help you tidy up if you like.'

Still not knowing exactly what had happened to Charlie, Shannon smiled. 'It's okay, I'll do it . . . but thanks all the same.'

Vaughn turned to go but then he stopped and began to walk towards the bed. 'I nearly forgot – I dropped my screwdriver.'

'I'll get it.' She smiled again and knelt down, but as she did her smile froze. There in the dark under the bed, grinning inanely was Charlie, who winked at her.

Beginning to shake again, she grabbed the screwdriver and stood up quickly, trembling so much she was almost unable to hold it in her hands.

'Shan, you all right?'

Terrified and incapable of speaking, Shannon just nodded.

'Are you sure?'

Again Shannon nodded her head.

'Look, we need to talk more, cos I ain't convinced that you're all right, so that's going to be the first thing I do when I get back.'

Shannon's face paled. 'Get back? You're going away? You can't!'

'What are you talking about?'

Fighting back the tears at the thought of being left alone with her uncle, Shannon raised her voice. 'What about Mia? You can't leave me here with her. You'll just have to cancel going.'

Looking at her strangely, Vaughn, hurt at Shannon's reaction, shrugged. 'Don't worry, I wasn't going to leave Mia with you, I wouldn't expect you to do it all on your own. It's just I've got a bit of business to sort out. Nothing much – I need to sign a few papers and I don't trust the toe rags I'm working with, so I like to do it face-to-face. I'll back in a couple of days though . . . Just think, you'll have the place all to yourself. You can just lie back and relax.' He kissed her gently on her head.

And as she shut the door behind him, Shannon promptly collapsed on the floor.

33

It had been over three hours he'd been waiting, but finally it was dark and Detective Balantyne carefully made his way along the wall, pressing himself against the bricks.

The large warehouse where a lot of the cars that were being held as part of ongoing investigations was based on the north side of Kent and luckily, he'd been here on a number of occasions, so he knew the place pretty well.

There were cameras on the left side of the building and at the back as well as the front but rather than police officers guarding the warehouse, the place was manned by a private security firm. From what he remembered the staff were more interested in watching their phones or having a crafty nap.

Keeping his ear out for any noise, Balantyne continued to creep along the side of the building, which stood next to a sloping bank that ran into a stream.

Not hearing anything apart from the rain that was

beginning to fall, he sprinted down the overgrown path, feeling the thorn bushes snag his trousers as he stumbled and tried to keep his footing.

Halfway along the wall, with his heart pounding, he came to the steel door he was looking for: a side door, which was always kept unlocked. Making sure that the coast was still clear, Balantyne put on a black pair of gloves and slipped into the warehouse.

Knowing there were no cameras inside, Balantyne made his way quickly along the rows of cars, keeping his eye out for Claire's grey Land Rover.

His gaze darted along the cars and each time he heard a noise he froze in his tracks. There were hundreds of cars and after ten minutes Balantyne was beginning to despair.

He stood in the shadows and suddenly his gaze came to rest on a car over on the far side of the warehouse . . . There was Claire's car, or he thought it was. He moved slightly to try to get a better view. And yes, yes there it was. He recognised the Reg number; a private number plate her parents had given her on her thirtieth birthday.

Looking around the dimly lit warehouse, Balantyne – feeling a surge of nervousness and excitement – rushed quietly towards the car.

He kept his body low and getting to Claire's car, he stopped, looking around again, listening for any noise. Certain there was nobody about, Balantyne tried the passenger-seat door, cursing as he found it locked. Then he made his way around to the other side and tried the driver's side . . . He smiled to himself. Bingo! The next moment Balantyne quietly opened the door.

He could feel the sweat dripping down his neck, and leaning over to the dashcam, he pulled back the cover of the card slot. Using the paper clip from out of his pocket, he gently popped it open allowing him to easily remove the SD card.

With trembling hands he let out a deep sigh, a rush of relief washing over him. Then ensuring everything looked exactly as it had before, Balantyne silently slipped back out of the car, placing the SD card in his pocket.

Suddenly his phone went off, echoing around the large chambered building . . . *Shit! Shit! Shit!* He silenced his mobile as quickly as he could but a moment later Balantyne heard a voice coming from the front of the warehouse.

'Hello? Hello? Anyone there?'

Crouching down, Balantyne scurried along the row of parked cars as quickly as he could, his heart racing. To the side of him he saw some tools. He snatched up a crowbar that was lying on one of the shelves as he listened to the person getting nearer.

'Hello? Hello?'

The voice called out again and Balantyne pushed himself into the shadows as he heard the footsteps getting ever closer. His whole body was shaking and his mouth was becoming dry as he inched himself further back, pushing himself along the wall, hoping whoever it was would eventually give up.

As he made it to the back of the building, passing dozens of cars, he froze again; it sounded as though his pursuer was right on top of him. He gripped on to the crowbar, holding it tightly in his hands, willing the person not to come any nearer.

'Hello? Is anybody there?'

The person was only inches away and deciding he had no other choice, Detective Balantyne lifted the crowbar into the air and with one heavy swing he brought it down, smashing it with a loud crunch onto the security guard's head.

Immediately blood and grey matter oozed out of the man's broken skull, and as he dropped into a pool of his own blood, Balantyne ran out of the warehouse and into the rain-filled night, without turning back and without a moment's hesitation.

34

Two days later on Thursday morning, Franny was pacing her cell. Her mind was rushing between Alfie and Mr Huang. She'd been desperate when she'd paid off Huang, desperate to be able to get Alfie to do what she wanted. Needing him without question to help her get out.

She'd paid almost three-quarters of a million pounds to Huang, which had been Alfie's original debt of half a million pounds plus the exorbitant amount of interest Huang charged. And as much as she hadn't believed him when he'd said there were no strings attached, at the time it had been her only option. But if he wanted more, she didn't have the sort of money he'd demand just lying about.

And the trouble was he was right; if Alfie realised that she'd paid Huang off a couple of months ago, and kept quiet about doing so for her own gain, she knew he would walk away without even a goodbye.

So the bottom line was: there was just no way Alfie *could* find out before he'd dealt with Vaughn and Balantyne, otherwise she'd be likely to rot in this place forever – and that thought kept her awake at night.

Rubbing her head and feeling more stressed than she had done in a while, Franny, unable to stay in the confined space any longer, marched straight out of her cell and right into the arms of Christine Lucas.

'Franny! Now this *is* a nice surprise.'

Not in the mood for Lucas at the best of times, Franny snarled, clenching her fists as she did so, 'What do you want, Lucas?'

'For a start not to be spoken to like that.'

Franny stepped forward and with her face inches away she shook her head, her eyes darkening. 'Lucas, I'm only going to talk to you any other way when I have some respect for you, and that's never going to happen.'

Christine's eyes flashed with anger but she stopped herself launching at Franny as a group of officers stood nearby. The tallest officer shouted across, 'Don't even bother starting trouble, ladies, otherwise the whole wing will be on lockdown until Monday morning. So think on, unless of course you want to spend forty-eight hours banged up.'

Christine Lucas spun around and faced the officer. She pulled up her top, exposing her large, saggy breasts. 'Trouble? Us? We're lovers not fighters, miss!' She cackled.

The officer, not impressed in the least, said, 'Well make sure it stays that way, Lucas.'

Under her breath, Lucas murmured, 'Fuck you, bitch.'

Then immediately she turned her attention back to Franny. 'We're going to pay a visit to one of your friends.'

Franny frowned. 'What are you talking about now?'

'Jessie. She and I need to finish off our conversation we were having in the showers . . . Why don't you come along for the show, pet?'

Without waiting for an answer, Lucas barged past Franny and marched along the corridor followed by four of her cronies. For a moment Franny thought better of it – she really didn't want to get involved in any agg – but thinking of how Christine had cut up the young girl in the shower, Franny found herself walking speedily down the corridor towards the others.

Getting to Jessie's cell, Christine nodded to two of the women who stood outside and kept guard. She stomped inside as Franny caught up just in time to see a surprised Jessie looking at Christine with her eyes filled with fear.

Seeing the terror in Jessie, Christine grinned, chuckling as she spoke. 'Howay, pet, why so nervous? You're amongst friends here.'

'I . . . I just wasn't expecting you, that's all.'

Christine frowned. 'Oh come on, you knew I'd be wanting what was mine.'

Jessie shook her head. The scars on her forehead and cheek were still red and angry from the last encounter she'd had with Christine and her voice trembled as she spoke. 'I haven't got it. I need more time.'

Plonking herself down on Jessie's bed, Christine ran her hands up and down Jessie's leg.

'Well that's the problem, pet, you haven't got any more

time. I think you've had more than enough, don't you? Howay, you were supposed to give it to me a couple of weeks ago.'

Jessie, unable to look at Christine, just shrugged. 'I'm sorry . . . I'm sorry.'

'It's too late for sorries, pet. The problem I have now, Jessie, is what are we going to do about it?' Taking a razor out of her sock, Christine smiled before licking the tip of it. 'Have you any ideas, Franny?'

Christine, who now had a drop of blood on her tongue, stared at Franny who was standing back watching.

Coolly, and not giving away any kind of emotion, Franny said, 'I don't even know what's going on.'

Christine winked. 'Well your friend here, she owes me money.'

Suddenly Franny remembered the piece of paper that had been stuffed inside Jessie's mouth. 'Oh, and shoving notes down her throat is the way to get your money, is it?'

Christine sniffed. 'If that's what it takes, then yeah. But unfortunately for Jessie she didn't take the hint.'

Franny nodded, as she recalled the numbers that she'd seen written on the paper. 'Not that it's any of my business, but why exactly does Jessie owe you?'

Christine, still holding the razor, got up from the bed and walked over to Franny, her body wobbling with fat. 'Does there have to be a reason?'

Franny frowned. She looked at Christine directly in the eye. Her voice was full of hostility.

'I reckon most people need one.'

Christine spread her arms out, gesturing around her.

207

'Have you not noticed where we are? In here, outside rules don't count unless I say they do. And I say, fuck the rules, I'll do what I like.' She stopped and turned to look at Jessie. 'So come on, I might as well ask you.'

Jessie felt the tension as her gaze darted from Christine to Franny then back to Christine. 'Ask . . . ask me what?'

'Ask you how you want to die.'

Immediately, Jessie scrambled up onto her knees, then bounded off the bed towards Franny, but before she got to her, one of Christine's cronies grabbed her by the waist, holding her back. She started to beg. 'Please, please, I swear my family are trying to get the money together for you. But it's hard, trying to get five thousand together isn't easy.'

Amused at the sheer terror in Jessie, Christine laughed. 'Then they should've tried harder because from where I'm standing it's clear they don't give a shit about what happens to you.'

'That's not true! That's not true!'

Christine turned her head to one side. 'Feisty little one, aren't we?' And with that Christine head-butted Jessie. Blood sprayed the walls as Christine's cronies, who'd been standing in the cell watching, began to beat down on Jessie, kicking and throwing punches as Jessie screamed in pain and terror.

As her scream sounded out, one of the women slammed her hand across Jessie's mouth. Franny, not being able to stand by and watch, leapt forward to try to protect Jessie but as she did her hair was grabbed and her head flicked backwards as the women tried to stop her.

From outside the cell Christine's other two followers

piled in before more women on the landing, hearing the commotion, came running in.

Punches were thrown and Christine drew back her foot and kicked Franny hard in the ribs, causing her to fall forwards into a woman she hadn't seen before. That woman turned around and pushed her onto the ground, where Christine launched another attack on her.

Scrambling up in the melee of women and with blood pouring from her head, Franny threw herself at two women punching Jessie.

'Get off her! Get off her!' she yelled as she pulled one of the women off Jessie, getting her in a headlock before throwing her hard against the wall. In the chaos and screaming, Franny charged at the other woman, throwing a hard uppercut punch to knock her sideward. Franny was vaguely aware of the wing alarm going off somewhere in the distance and as a tall Asian woman went to hit her, what seemed like a dozen officers came running into the tiny space.

Holding batons and riot shields the officers yelled and screamed instructions to the women, pushing them against the wall, forcing them to put their hands behind their backs as they fought to regain control.

As calmness descended on the cell, Officer Brown strolled in, staring at Franny and Christine and the rest of the women in total contempt. She looked around and spat out her words. 'Why doesn't this surprise me? Why doesn't it surprise me that it's always the same culprits, the same troublemakers? Lucas, it's always you, isn't it?'

Christine winked. 'Well I wouldn't want to disappoint you, miss, would I?'

Officer Brown's face turned red as she yelled, 'This isn't funny! You're animals the lot of you. Look at the state of all of you. You look like you've gone ten rounds with Tyson Fury. I've got a good mind to send you all down to seg.' She then stopped to stare at Franny.

'I'm shocked, Doyle, that you haven't learnt yet: there's only ever going to be one winner in this place and that's *me* . . . And, Jess, I'm surprised and disappointed in you, but then this is what happens when you hang around with troublemakers.'

Lucas wolf-whistled. 'I think Officer Brown's got a crush on Jessie. She never calls us by our first name. Teacher's pet!'

The other women roared with laughter as Brown scowled. 'Shut it, Lucas, and the same can go for the rest of you.'

'She didn't do anything!' Franny spoke up above the laughter.

Annoyed, Officer Brown strode towards Doyle. 'I beg your pardon?'

'Jess. She didn't do anything.'

'Oh, so now you're speaking for her as well, are you?'

Franny sighed. 'If I have to.'

For a moment Officer Brown fell silent before she said, 'Come with me, Doyle . . . And you, Jess.'

Furiously Officer Brown marched out of the cell with Franny following and Jessie running to catch up a few feet behind her.

At the end of the corridor Officer Brown unlocked the corner cell. She gave Franny a cold stare. 'As we're short-staffed and we haven't got time to play nursemaid, seeing as you like to babysit everyone so much, this can be your new cell.'

Franny glanced in and shook her head. 'I don't think so, and besides there's only supposed to be two women to a cell.'

'Then my suggestion is to snuggle up . . . Now get in there. I'll see you on Monday morning . . . Enjoy.' And with that, Officer Brown pushed Franny and Jessie inside, locking the door behind them and leaving them staring at Emma Balantyne who was shaking and vomiting in the corner of the cell.

35

Shannon stood in the pouring rain just a few feet from the front door of Vaughn's block of flats. Her hands were trembling as she smoked the cigarette, inhaling deeply as she fought the desire to go and look for some drugs.

For the past couple of days she'd spent most of her time sleeping on the couch whilst her uncle had either been watching and masturbating to porn on her iPad or mauling her or demanding food.

Worse still, Vaughn was due back any minute and her uncle *still* hadn't gone, although he'd kept promising her that he would.

Her nerves were now so frazzled, the only thing she could think of was smoking some crack and forgetting everything. That's all she wanted to do: to get high and forget.

Throwing the cigarette down on the ground, Shannon

suddenly made up her mind, and taking a deep breath made her way across to Gerrard Street. After all, how much harm could one rock of crack do? But as she hurried along the street, she didn't see Alfie beginning to follow her.

Gerrard Street in Chinatown was busy and milling with tourists, the restaurants buzzing with life as Shannon made her way down towards the basement of one of the Chinese restaurants. She could feel her heart racing as she looked around quickly. As she got to the bottom stair, she felt her phone vibrating in her pocket.

Pulling it out and seeing that the caller was Vaughn, Shannon sighed, not wanting to speak to him. But as it continued to ring she decided it was probably best to answer it. Trying to sound chirpy, Shannon spoke, her words tumbling out, 'Hey, Vaughn, is everything okay? How's Mia? How was your trip? What time are you back?'

'I'm good, and Mia's good, if you call crying most of the way back good. Remind me next time to take you with me. Anyway, I was just checking on you. I've just got back ten minutes ago. I knocked on your door and you weren't there. Don't worry, this time I haven't kicked the door in!' He laughed at his own joke as Shannon bristled, a cold sweat and apprehension pricking at her.

Unable to help her voice coming across as strained, Shannon said, 'Sorry, I was just having a cigarette then I suddenly fancied a Maccy D's. You want me to get you one?'

'Thanks, but I like my stomach the way it is. Anyway, as long as you're okay, that's all that matters. I'm going to catch an early night. I'm exhausted . . . so I'll see you tomorrow . . . Oh and, Shan, whilst I was away, it got me thinking and I realised that I don't say this often enough, but I'm really proud of you. You know, the way you've turned your life around. You're a superstar . . . Goodnight, babe.'

The call finished and the phone sat in Shannon's hand like a burning piece of coal. The guilt rushed over her and she closed her eyes but as she did, an image of Charlie came into her mind. An image of his fat, naked body on top of hers. Gasping, she quickly opened her eyes and shivered.

She was never going to be free of Charlie, no matter what she did. And the truth was she couldn't cope with it, she just couldn't cope, and as much as she loved Vaughn – and she did – even the thought of him couldn't make the misery of living with Charlie any easier.

She was afraid that he would never go until he'd either pushed her to the limits or Vaughn found out. Though at this point she feared it would probably be the former as her uncle seemed not only to be relishing tormenting her, but he was also comfortable in her room and no doubt he didn't want Vaughn to find out either. He was on to too much of a good thing.

Her anxiety was through the roof and her nerves shot to pieces. The only thing that *would* take the edge off, that *would* make it easier was what was being sold at the basement of this restaurant. And with that thought, Shannon took a deep breath and knocked on the steel door.

The basement of the restaurant was filled with smoke

and small tables were spread around with groups of men drinking and playing poker. The floor was sticky from spilt drinks that had never been wiped up and a group of young girls, who Shannon knew were prostitutes, sat on a broken-down couch waiting to be picked up by the various men in the room.

Pushing all thoughts of Vaughn and Mia out of her mind, Shannon squeezed her way through the room, feeling the heat of the place.

At the back there was a door, and taking a quick glance around, Shannon quickly knocked on it. A few seconds later she heard the bolts being unlocked before it was opened by a small, skinny man in his fifties.

As she stepped inside the room, she heard a familiar voice coming from the corner.

'We haven't seen you for a while. Couldn't keep away?'

Shannon stared at Mr Huang and his men, who sat playing a game of poker with thousands of pounds sitting in front of them.

Fighting back the tears, Shannon said, 'It ain't like that.'

Huang smiled as he reached for a bag full of wrapped crack cocaine in front of him. 'It never is . . . Your usual?' Huang held out a piece of crack, which Shannon stared at.

'What's the matter? It's not going to bite.'

Shannon snapped, 'I know that, I'm just . . .'

Huang got up and walked slowly towards Shannon. 'How's your uncle? I haven't seen him about either. He used to be a good customer of mine.'

Not wanting to think about Charlie and certainly not wanting to let Huang know anything about what was going on, Shannon shrugged. 'I dunno, I don't see him anymore.'

Huang smirked. 'I suppose that's not a bad thing; it just means that you don't have to share this with anyone.'

He pushed the piece of crack he held in his hands at Shannon. Suddenly she began to cry and shook her head. She ran for the door but as she did, the small, skinny man grabbed her, spinning her around so she was facing Huang.

Huang's voice was calm and velvety. 'What's the matter, Shannon?'

Streams of tears ran down her face as she suddenly realised what she was doing. She thought of Vaughn and how much he believed in her. 'I don't want it! I don't want it! I shouldn't have come here. I've made a mistake!'

'But you did, Shannon. You did come here.'

'Please, let me go home. I've changed my mind! I just want to go now.'

Huang cracked his knuckles before he walked over to her and stroked her face. 'The thing is, Shannon, you can say you don't want it, but the fact that you've come here in the first place speaks volumes. Perhaps you just need a little bit more encouragement.'

Huang nodded his head to one of his men who walked across to the side and picked up a glass pipe, dropping a small rock of crack in the end of the pipe. He lit it and begun to heat up the crack and holding it carefully in his hands, he walked across to Shannon as Huang said, 'There you go, it's all yours.'

Shannon shook her head, pursing her lips tightly closed.

Huang's tone was cold and menacing. 'Take some. *I said*

216

take some.' He pulled out a jagged knife from his pocket and placed it onto Shannon's cheek. 'Do I have to use this? Because I don't like people coming here and wasting my time.'

With her eyes wide with fear, Shannon trembled and slowly, slowly she opened her mouth as Huang grinned. 'That's it. Now take it, taste it . . . You know you want it.'

And with no other choice, Shannon let Huang put the pipe on her lips and she inhaled the vapours from the crack. Her eyes rolled backwards and an inane grin spread across her face as she felt like she was floating. She heard Huang's voice as she closed her eyes.

'That's it, Shannon – you see I knew you wanted it. And here's a piece for later; that's on the house. Enjoy . . .'

Then the next minute Shannon blacked out.

36

From the darkness Alfie watched two men carry out Shannon from the basement. He saw them dump her in a puddle of water at the corner of Wardour Street, where she lay in a haze on the dirty, rubbish-strewn pavement.

He ran over to her and crouched down, lifting her head up. Realising she was high on drugs, Alfie spoke quietly. All the suspicion towards her being wiped out by worry. 'Shan, Shan? It's me, Alfie. For fuck's sake what have you done to yourself, darlin'? I thought you were off that shit? I know I'm not one to talk but it ain't going to do you any good.'

Half opening her eyes, Shannon looked at Alfie, slurring her words as she said, 'Hello, Alf, it's good to see you.'

Alfie's voice was filled with sadness. 'It's good to see you as well, darlin', but I'd rather not see you in this state.'

Tears rolled down Shannon's cheeks. 'I'm sorry, I'm so sorry. I bet you hate me.'

He gave her a hug, smelling the sweet aroma of crack on her. 'Of course I don't hate you. Why would I? You're a good girl, Shan, look at the way you are with . . . with Mia.'

Shannon gave a stoned smile. 'You should give her a chance . . . You'd love her and you'd be a good daddy.'

Alfie bristled. 'Yeah well we can talk about that another time. I'm more concerned about you.'

'Everything would've been all right if it weren't for that cow, Franny. I only did it because of her.'

'Did what, Shan?' Alfie said frowning.

Almost incoherently, Shannon muttered, 'Vaughn told me not to tell you. He said you'd hate me and I don't want you to hate me . . . I don't want Vaughn to hate me either, cos I love him . . . I love him, Alfie, I'd do anything for him.'

Alfie raised his eyebrows not sure if it was the crack talking or it was what Shannon really felt. 'No one will hate you; but, sweetheart, I don't know what you're talking about. What did Vaughn tell you not to say?'

'About the statements we gave. He wanted me to do it, so I lied. Alfie, I lied. I said Franny had done it, I said she'd killed Bree. And I know that ain't true.'

As Alfie watched Shannon fall into a drug-fuelled sleep, he pulled his phone out of his pocket, leaving a message for the caller. 'It's me, we need to talk.'

Putting his mobile back into his pocket, Alfie stared at Shannon as it began to rain again. It was true, he didn't hate her. Not even close. She was just a kid who'd been used and abused by various people all through her life. No, the person he hated wasn't her. It was Vaughn, and now he knew the truth, now he knew that Franny hadn't been lying, he was going to take Vaughn down in a ball of flames.

At the same time as Alfie was trying to get some coffee down Shannon, Detective Balantyne sat by Claire's bedside thinking about the Doyle case. The CPS had been putting pressure on him to come up with some more evidence, but there was no one about to start talking. In situations like this, everyone closed ranks. But he would get her. If it was the last thing he did, Doyle was going to rot in prison.

Pushing the thought of Franny out of his mind, Balantyne held Claire's hand tightly, but he quickly dropped it when two officers he'd seen in passing down at the station came in.

They nodded to him respectfully, but it was the shorter Asian officer who spoke. 'How's she doing, sir?'

Trying to not feel panicked, Balantyne kept his cool. 'They don't know yet. She's stable, which is something I suppose, but now it's just a waiting game.' Then feeling obliged to make up a reason for being there again, he added: 'I just feel responsible. You know, with everything that happened with my wife. I couldn't bear it if anything happened to Inspector Martin because of Emma. I know being here won't change anything but it somehow makes me feel better.'

The officer nodded sympathetically. 'Everyone's keeping their fingers crossed down at the station.'

Balantyne smiled. 'Me too, but as you can imagine, I feel responsible . . . I know it was my wife who was driving but it's hard not to blame yourself. You end up saying, what if . . .' He trailed off and then cautiously he added, 'Anyway, how's the investigation going? I think it was Officer Gibbs who told me they were going to look at the dashcam recording. I'll tell you something, I'll be pleased when they do. I don't want it drawn out.'

The Asian officer looked at his colleague before saying sheepishly, 'That's what we came here to say. I'm afraid Inspector Martin didn't have an SD card in her dashcam, which means there is *no* recording of the incident.'

Balantyne feigned annoyance. 'You're joking?'

'No, sir, but I guess not everyone remembers to put one in there.'

Feeling relieved, Balantyne continued to play along. 'That's bloody stupid then . . . Sorry, it's just the recording would've been the evidence you needed to take this to trial.'

The officer nodded. 'I know, sir, though the way it stands the CPS are willing to still go ahead with the charges of attempted murder.'

Balantyne stayed silent though inside he was celebrating. After a few seconds he said calmly, 'Well thanks, officers, for coming to tell me.'

The officers turned to go but then the smallest one stopped and turned around. 'There is one more thing, sir. Strictly off the record . . . the warehouse where they keep the cars in Kent, and where Inspector Martin's car was, well one of the security guards was attacked. They took him to hospital.'

Balantyne felt the sweat prick on the back of his neck but he gave nothing away. 'Oh my God, that's terrible.'

'It is, sir. He had a wife and three kids.'

Balantyne frowned. 'Had?'

'Yes, sir, unfortunately he died in the early hours of this morning.'

37

'I can smell it on you, Shan. I can see it in your eyes!' Charlie, in the early hours of Friday morning, held his hands tightly around Shannon's neck. She spluttered her words as her face began to turn a deep red.

'I don't know what you're talking about!'

Charlie buried and nuzzled his head next to Shannon's ear before biting it hard. 'Don't try to bullshit me, Shan, I can smell that crack you've been smoking a mile away. It's in your hair; it's on your skin. When did you do it? How long have you been sneaking off to do it?'

He stopped speaking to inhale the aroma of the drug from Shannon who furiously shook her head.

'I haven't, I haven't!'

Releasing Shannon's neck, Charlie brought his hand up and struck her around the face before pushing her backwards onto the bed. He snarled as he straddled her, holding her down with his hefty body.

Kissing her neck and slobbering he rubbed himself all over her as she felt his erection against her thigh and although she kept her voice down for fear of disturbing Vaughn, she begged Charlie, 'Get off me, please get off me!'

Ignoring Shannon, Charlie cackled as he continued to grunt and groan on top of his niece, his sweat twisting and matting the thick hair on his chest and back. 'You know you want it, Shan, stop fucking messing me about. Why are you playing hard to get? It's not like you haven't had it thousands of times before.'

'I hate you! I hate you! You make me sick!' She struggled as she yelped, trying desperately to get away. She kicked out and wriggled but she was no match for Charlie's strength and weight. She hit at his face, clawing him, scraping her nails down his cheeks, which drew blood and fury from Charlie.

'You stupid bitch!' He wrestled her, and holding Shannon's arms down, he pushed himself inside her roughly.

'Stop, Uncle Charlie, *stop*!' Twisting her body, still trying to get away, Shannon pleaded with Charlie as he continued to cackle and push himself harder and harder inside her. She held on to the bed head, pulling herself away, frantically trying to escape her uncle's clutches.

As Shannon fought and flailed her arms around, her hand came to rest on her bedside lampshade and without thinking she grabbed it, bringing it down on Charlie's head, smashing into a thousand pieces.

Within seconds Shannon was covered in Charlie's blood

and he suddenly fell forward and stopped moving. His head lay on her chest and with her eyes wide open with fear, Shannon – to stop herself from screaming – slammed her hand across her mouth as she stared down at Charlie in horror.

Breathing hard and drenched in Charlie's blood, Shannon began to pull herself out from underneath him. He was heavy and motionless and it took everything she had to move herself from beneath him as his weight crushed down on top of her.

Eventually freeing herself, she stared at Charlie in shock, hugging her knees tightly. She closed her eyes, too scared to look.

Then after a few moments she forced herself to peek through her fingers and cautiously kicked him with her foot. 'Uncle Charlie? Uncle Charlie?'

There was no movement from him and panic surged around Shannon's body again. Her heart raced and tears rolled down her face. She shook so much she couldn't move.

'Uncle Charlie, *please* talk to me? I'm sorry! I'm sorry!' Again, there was nothing apart from an eerie silence. Her heart pounded as she stood up and went around the other side of the bed.

She reached out her hand and touched him but it felt like an electric shock and, trembling, she gazed at his face covered in a veil of his own blood and his obese bloated body lying motionless.

Terrified and holding her head, Shannon started to pace with her eyes constantly fixed on Charlie. What was she going to do . . . What was she going to do . . . What was she going to say? Panic hit her again and she ran across to Charlie, this time shaking him hard. 'Uncle Charlie? Uncle Charlie, I'm sorry . . . I'm sorry. You can do anything to me but please, please just wake up!'

She fell to the floor screaming silent tears, rocking back and forth as she buried her face in her hands. She jumped as she heard a voice.

'Shan? Shan, you fancy a coffee, sweetheart? I heard you awake – I can't sleep either. Could do with a bit of company. It'd be nice to catch up.'

Vaughn's voice boomed from the other side of the door and it made Shannon feel ill. She scrambled up from the floor and stared at Charlie as she spoke, her voice quivering with fear. 'I . . . I . . . I . . .' She trailed off and stared again. Her head felt fuzzy and she couldn't think properly, unable to comprehend what she'd just done.

'Shan? You okay?'

Knowing she needed somehow to answer Vaughn, Shannon just about managed to get the words 'I'm fine' out of her mouth.

'Then what do you say to a nice latte? I think I've got the hang of that fucking coffee machine! So, come on then, how about it?'

Feeling she was unable to breathe let alone chat with Vaughn, she was just about to say *no* but then she stared again at Charlie. Looking at him made her feel like the walls were closing in on her. She didn't want to be in the same room. She just couldn't.

Taking a deep breath, Shannon opened the door, and quickly shutting and locking it behind her, she stepped out of the room and twirled around to face Vaughn who stared at her in shock. 'Fucking hell, Shan. Fucking hell, what have you done?'

Shannon's legs went weak. She leant against the door as the hallway began to spin. 'I didn't mean to, it was an accident. I swear it just happened. I wasn't thinking straight. I'm sorry. I'm sorry and I just don't know what to do.'

Vaughn bent down to Shannon's eye level. She looked terrible. Her eyes looked full of fear and he held on to her shoulders very gently. 'Shan, show me where you've cut yourself. You're bleeding heavily.'

She blinked and then blinked again and suddenly it struck her. She realised that Vaughn *wasn't* talking about what she just did to Charlie but about her being covered in blood. *Charlie's* blood. In all the panic she'd forgotten.

Quickly trying to come up with something plausible, Shannon blurted. 'I . . . I was trying to clean up the mess and I broke the lampshade. It was an accident, I swear. I was stupid. I put it on the top of the wardrobe to clean the table and when I was polishing it fell on my head.'

'Oh Jesus, Shan, let me have a look.' He went to reach for her head but she moved away, ducking out of his grasp.

'Don't touch me!'

A mixture of confusion and hurt crossed Vaughn's face. He put his hands up in the air. 'Okay, okay, I'm sorry.'

Shannon's eyes filled with tears. 'No, I'm sorry, I never meant it how it sounded . . . It's just that it hurts . . .'

Sympathetically Vaughn gave a rueful smile. 'I told you I was rubbish with teenage girls. I didn't think. Do you want me to call the doc? Well he's not exactly a doc but he knows what he's doing. A guy called Davey – he sorted Alfie out good and proper. Yours might need stitches like Alfie's did, though he was a proper pussy.'

He smiled again but Shannon didn't smile back. She was beginning to panic at the thought of a doctor or *anyone* coming to see her. It would take less than a minute for them to realise that there was nothing actually wrong with her, or worse still, he might want to examine her in her room. 'Look, why . . . why don't I wash myself up and see how bad it is. Maybe it's nothing, sometimes these things look worse than they are.'

Vaughn shrugged and nodded. 'Okay, if you're sure. I'll leave you to it and try and go and make that coffee before Mia wakes up. I'll see you in a minute, babe . . . Oh, can you check in your room to see if you've got Mia's pink teddy? Or I can look if you like?'

'It's fine, I'll get it.' Feeling breathless she smiled, but waited until Vaughn had walked away to go back inside her room. And when she did, she immediately froze as she pressed herself against the door, hardly daring to move and almost unable to look at Charlie who still lay on the bed.

Quickly she looked around and saw Mia's teddy bear. Not wanting to be in the room longer than she had to she darted to get it but as she did, she saw the bed sheet that she'd taken off earlier to wash.

Picking up the bear as well as the sheet, with trepidation Shannon walked to the bed where she threw the sheet over Charlie to cover his face and body. A strange sense of relief and fear washed over her and she slid down the wall, rocking and holding on to the cuddly toy, whilst the tears streamed down her face, as they had done so much lately.

It was more than ten minutes before Shannon had calmed herself enough down to be able to get up and make her way to the bathroom to clean herself up, desperate for Vaughn not to become suspicious.

She had no idea what she was going to do, no idea whatsoever and although she'd experienced terror in her life before, the idea of Charlie lying dead, rotting in her room, terrified her more than she could even dare to think about.

As she walked trembling out of the darkened room, the rain began to beat down on the window and Charlie opened his eyes and sat up, throwing off the sheet that had been placed over him.

He smirked to himself. He was going to teach that bitch a lesson. If she wanted to play games then that's what he would do and if she wanted him dead, oh boy he would certainly play dead. And then, when he'd had his fun, he was going to destroy her and bring her happy world crashing down.

38

'Can you guys just stop? I've had it all night and I don't think I can take any more.' Franny sat on the bed with Jessie crying next to her and Emma alternating between hysterical sobbing and loud vomiting, which had been the case since Officer Brown had locked them up yesterday afternoon.

'It's not fair – I shouldn't be in here. I never did it! I never did it!'

Franny stared at Emma. 'Well that makes two of us don't it?'

Suddenly seeing some kind of allegiance with Franny, Emma scrambled towards her on her hands and knees. 'Then you know how I feel! You know how I feel!' She began to scream again but this time it was right in Franny's face. And without any sort of hesitation, Franny slapped her hard.

'Shut the fuck up!'

Shocked, Emma stared at her, rubbing her cheek, but she spoke calmly. 'That's the second time you've done that.'

'And it won't be the last time either if you continue to be a pain in the arse. Screaming and shouting ain't going to help get you out of here, and it's certainly not going to help my ears. You understand?'

Emma nodded but it was Franny who continued to talk. 'Anyway, what you in here for? What is it that you never did?'

Wiping her nose, which was running as much as her tears were, Emma muttered, looking up at Franny. 'Attempted murder.'

Giving a rueful smile, Franny whistled. 'I would not have thought that's why you were in here, Little Bo-Peep.'

Not enjoying being made fun of, Emma snapped, 'Like I say, I didn't do it!'

Leaning against the wall, Franny shrugged. 'Listen, you ain't got to convince me, I couldn't care less if you did it or not.'

With her face flushing red, Emma pouted. 'Well I didn't. I was set up . . . I knew he was a liar and I knew he was a bastard but I never thought he'd do this to me. My solicitor told me what he's been saying.'

With a mild bit of interest, Franny said, 'Who?'

'My husband.'

Franny shrugged again as she stared at the scars on Emma's face. 'Never trust a man. Come to think of it, never trust anyone.'

Emma's eyes darkened and Franny watched her with

interest as her whole demeanour changed. 'Yeah well if I ever get out of here, I'm going to make sure he pays.'

Laughing, Franny said, 'That's my girl, that's more like it. Tears ain't going to get you anywhere. It's the fighting talk that will get you through – even if we never get our revenge, believing we will is the main thing.'

Looking seriously at Franny, Emma shook her head. Her face turning into a snarl, she said, 'Oh no, believe me, he's got it coming. I may not have tried to kill anyone *this* time but that doesn't mean I'm not going to *next* time.'

For a moment Franny didn't say anything and then she winked. 'Word of advice, Em: when you go to court, keep that part to yourself, darlin.'

Smiling for the first time in longer than she could remember, Emma asked, 'And what about you, Franny, what are you in for?'

'Murder.'

Emma's eyes opened wide. 'Now why doesn't that surprise me?'

Franny laughed again. 'You have a way with words! If you want to make enemies in here carry on talking like that . . . and anyway, I already told you, I didn't do it.' She smiled ruefully.

Jessie, having not said a word until that point, snivelled, 'Well I did. I did what I'm in here for and wish I hadn't.'

Both Franny and Emma stared at her, but it was Franny who spoke. 'And what was that?'

Sheepishly Jessie said, 'I attacked the guy in the corner shop with a loaf of bread, and someone called the police. When they came I resisted arrest and threw a couple of jars of pickles at them . . . maybe there was even a can of soup, I dunno.'

The two other women burst into laughter, much to Jessie's annoyance. 'It isn't funny! I don't know why you're laughing. I thought I'd get community service at the most but because one of the jars hit and cut the policeman's face, I was done for Actual Bodily Harm and now I'm stuck in here.'

Franny sat down on the bed again. 'I ain't laughing at you, not really, but you've got to admit it's funny. But the real question is, *why*? Who attacks anyone with a loaf of bread?'

Shyly, Jessie shrugged. 'It was the first thing I grabbed. He was a friend of my dad's and every time I went in the shop he was always trying to touch me. He's been doing it since I was a kid . . . I dunno, I just snapped . . .' She trailed off and Franny and Emma no longer laughed.

Franny gave a warm smile. 'I'm sorry, Jess. You shouldn't be in here, he should be.'

Jessie smiled back. 'Thank you. It's been a nightmare in here. I've got another six months and I don't know if I can do it anymore. Not with Christine and her mates.'

'Listen, you've got me now. I'm here . . . and if it will help, I'll pay it.'

'What?'

Franny shook her head. 'Are you deaf? I said I'll pay for it. I'll pay Christine the money she wants and I'll make sure she keeps off your back from now on.'

'I . . . I . . . why? Why would you do that for me?'

Franny thought for a moment then she smiled, a small but genuine smile. 'Firstly, I know how much it will piss

Christine off if you *actually* pay her. And I'm not saying it's fair to have to pay her, but sometimes inside the rules are just shitty . . . And secondly . . . well, believe it or not, I ain't one to see someone bullied when they don't deserve it.'

Full of gratitude, Jessie shuffled up closer to Franny on the bed. Her green eyes were wide and concerned. 'But I can't pay you back. I mean, I probably can eventually, but I don't know when. My family haven't got a lot of money.'

'Listen, sweetheart, call it a gift. On the house. Anyway favours are sometimes worth more than money, and who knows when I might decide to call in a favour.'

39

As usual Detective Balantyne's head was filled with thoughts both about Emma and the Doyle case, though now, as he stared at the monitors around Claire's bed, he had something else to think about.

In between work he'd spent most of his time at the hospital, which had helped to take his mind off what had happened, though of course he'd still thought about it. Of course he had.

The guilt had sat on him; the guilt of Claire and the security guard, and he'd wondered how it could've all happened, and he'd blamed himself – well, at first he had . . . *at first*. But the more he thought about it, the more he realised that he couldn't quite bring himself to put the weight on his shoulders. How could he? How was he supposed to have sleepless nights over something Emma had done? Because that's where it all started. It had begun with *her*. Emma was the cause of everything.

He sighed and took a swig of cold coffee from the cardboard cup he'd got from the vending machine some twenty minutes ago. But it was true, no matter what he said to himself, everything started and ended with that woman.

If it hadn't been for Emma, none of this would be happening. Claire wouldn't be in hospital and he wouldn't have gone to Kent to get the SD card out of the car, and the security guard wouldn't be dead, leaving three children without a father.

So whilst at first he did *try* to blame himself, it turned out it wasn't possible. But of course that didn't mean he didn't care about the security guard, far from it. He cared so much that he was determined to make Emma pay, to make her *suffer* for the hurt she'd caused, and above all else to make her pay for that poor man's death.

A sudden groan stopped Balantyne's thoughts. He sat up and stared at Claire. He watched as her eyes began to flicker whilst another groan left her lips. Delighted, he sprang up and ran to the door.

'Nurse! Nurse! I think she's waking up . . . Nurse!' He gestured to the two nurses in the corridor, waving them in. They rushed across to Claire, checking the monitors, checking the read-outs, before standing back and smiling.

The shorter of the two nurses quietly said, 'Hello, Claire, it's good to see you. How're you feeling?'

'Not great.'

'Well I'm not surprised. You've had some major surgery

to stop the bleeding on your brain after the accident but the surgeon's really pleased with how it went. He'll be in to see you shortly.'

Claire's eyes flickered, focusing first on the nurses before her gaze came to rest on Balantyne. She gave what looked like a smile before she said, 'What happened?'

Balantyne stepped forward. He took her hand as he turned to the nurses. 'Would you mind leaving us alone for a moment?'

They nodded and left, leaving Balantyne clutching on to Claire's hand. Once they'd gone, Balantyne leant down and kissed Claire's head.

He felt free now that Emma was going to be out of his way once and for all, and it had been easier than he could've ever imagined.

'I've been so worried. I missed you.'

Claire blinked, touching his face gently. 'What's going on, Tony?'

'Can't you remember anything?'

She frowned and sounding fragile, said, 'I have only vague memories. I remember we were in the car talking about . . .' She trailed off almost immediately, uncertainty crossing her face.

'About the baby . . . We talked about the baby, Claire. You told me you were pregnant.'

A light suddenly came into her eyes before fear filled them. 'Oh my God. I haven't . . .'

Balantyne smiled. 'No, you haven't lost it. They told me it was fine. Everything's going to be fine, including you and me.'

237

Grateful, Claire squeezed Tony's hand but once again she frowned. 'But what about Emma? What about her? It's not fair. She needs you. We can't . . .'

Balantyne put his fingers on Claire's lips. 'Sshhhh. It's okay. It's all fine, it's all been sorted. You don't have to worry anymore.'

'What are you talking about?'

Having already worked out what he was going to say, Balantyne reeled off his words. 'You don't remember what I told you, do you?'

'No . . . Everything's such a blank.'

Wanting to lay the groundwork for the story he was going to feed her, Balantyne began to lie through his teeth. 'I told you that Emma and I had decided to go our separate ways. It was her decision as much as mine. So it was never a question of me just dumping her, which I know you've always been worried about.'

Claire looked at him in utter disbelief. 'But this is Emma we're talking about. After all this time why on earth would she just suddenly decide to make it easy for you? I don't understand.'

Balantyne shrugged, not particularly pleased that the conversation was going the way it was. He'd expected her to accept it, be pleased and move on, but instead she was questioning him and he felt irritated. 'She knew that her drinking was getting worse. Maybe she realised that it wasn't fair for anyone – even herself.'

'But—'

'Claire, *please*. You've had major surgery, don't try to work that head of yours too hard.'

238

She squeezed his hand again. 'Sorry, you're right.' She stopped then added, 'But how did I end up in here?'

Balantyne looked at her earnestly. 'It's hard to say this, but Emma tried to kill you.'

'What? What? Oh my God, but you've just said—'

He stroked Claire's hair, with the lies becoming easier and easier, he smiled. 'I know what I've just said and it's true. We'd decided to go our separate ways – that's why this is all the harder. Like I say she realised that it was over and that, to save her own life, you know from the drinking, it was the right thing to do. I'd even go so far as to say she was happy for us – well, as happy as Emma would ever be. She accepted it. But then she had a relapse and this is the result of that . . . She tried to run you over, Claire.'

Visibly upset, Claire didn't say anything for a moment. Her forehead creased into furrowed lines as she thought, desperately trying to dredge up the memory from what had happened, but it was all a blank. 'Emma *really* did this to me?'

'Yes, but don't hate her, Claire. She's unwell and she's finally going to get the help she needs. I'm sorry. I'm so sorry. Can you forgive me?' Balantyne buried his head into Claire's chest.

'Tony, you've got nothing to be sorry for. It's a shock – I mean, what you're saying is terrible – but it's not your fault, none of this is. How were you to know she was going to do something like this?'

Balantyne lifted his head and kissed Claire on her forehead. 'You're right but it's so hard. I was so scared I was going to lose you and I've been worried about Emma.'

'Because you're a good man, that's why,' Claire said.

He smiled. 'I'm just looking forward to getting you better and then us getting on with our lives.'

'And it's good to know that Emma's getting treatment. Hopefully some extended rehab will help her.'

Balantyne looked puzzled. 'Rehab? Emma's not in rehab – though she's getting the help she needs. She's somewhere where she'll no longer be a danger to others. They've locked her up, Claire. They're charging her with attempted murder. And hopefully they'll throw away the key.'

40

It was Saturday afternoon and hearing Shannon, Mia and Vaughn go out, Charlie stood up, stretched, broke wind and smiled to himself. Shannon hadn't come back into the room since yesterday; he suspected that she'd probably slept on the couch or in another room. Anything to avoid having to come into the room. She hadn't even put on the light before she'd left the room. Though that didn't surprise him. He knew his niece well enough to know that she tried to avoid anything difficult. Whether that was pretending something hadn't actually happened or getting off her head on drugs, she always escaped somehow.

He remembered a time when she was around about eleven years old and he'd brought a couple of friends back to have a bit of fun with her, do what they wanted with her. Though even he had been surprised at the things they *actually* did.

241

The next day, even though Shannon had been sore and unable to walk properly, it was almost like she'd blocked it out, pretending nothing had happened. There were hundreds of other times too, like the times he'd beat her, teaching her a lesson for being too cheeky or not listening to what he had told her to do. But her reaction was always the same: block it out or smoke some crack like it was going out of fashion.

He chuckled to himself at the thought. No doubt that's exactly what she was doing this time too: pretending it hadn't happened. Probably too afraid to see him, but that suited him all right, because then he wouldn't need to hold his breath, he wouldn't need to hold quite as still. All he had to do was lie there and play dead. At that thought Charlie roared with laughter, so much so that the laughter turned into a hoarse cough.

If she was so stupid as to believe she'd killed him then he would treat her like the dumb bitch she was. He smirked as he unlocked the bedroom door with the spare key before waddling out into the hallway naked.

He hadn't bothered dressing himself. There was hardly any point; he just wanted to have a nosy around properly. He'd seen most of the apartment: the plush rooms, the ornate bathrooms and luxury kitchen – as well as the office space that Vaughn had on the top floor – but what he hadn't actually seen were the details, the private stuff that was tucked away, so this was certainly going to be interesting.

Walking into Vaughn's extraordinarily large bedroom, which looked and felt expensive with the tastefully decor-ated grey and silver furniture along with the huge super-king-size bed in the centre of it, Charlie whistled but then immediately curled his nose up at the idea of Vaughn.

He'd never had any time for him and he didn't like the way he'd got his claws into Shannon. If he'd just left her instead of playing Soho's version of the archangel Gabriel, then Shannon would be exactly where she should be: on her knees and on her back, earning him money.

He sniffed in disgust at the thought of the money lost, and with that in mind he wandered over to the corner of the room and urinated in the corner with a huge smile on his face as it soaked the plush grey carpet.

Chuckling to himself, Charlie shuffled through the walk-in wardrobe, looking at Vaughn's expensive suits and shirts, his fat fingers touching and feeling the luxurious garments. He was certainly enjoying himself.

Then making his way across to the large dressers he smiled as he opened the drawers, riffling through them carefully: neatly folded silk handkerchiefs and socks, ties and underwear, perfectly arranged like a display in Harrods men's department.

Searching through the bottom drawer, Charlie stopped and stared. He raised his eyebrows and grinned. Tucked into Vaughn's Tom Ford underwear there was a bundle of money. Two bundles of money, in fact, and a gold and diamond watch.

He picked up the watch and flicked through the bundle of notes. By his reckoning there must be at least ten thousand pounds there, if not more. He spoke out loud. 'Thanks very much, Vaughnie, that will do nicely for now, son.'

He laughed as he wobbled out of the room, with the

bundles of money in his hand. Charlie headed to the room across the hallway. He pushed open a door and saw it was Mia's room. A nasty smile spread across his face and his eyes lit up as they rested on her tiny dresses and skirts, which were laundered and sitting on the wooden chest of drawers waiting to be put away.

Thinking of Mia he closed his eyes, his breath becoming deeper and louder. Suddenly he heard a noise. He could hear voices. It was Vaughn and Shannon coming back.

As quickly as he could, Charlie waddled along the corridor, back into Shannon's room, locking the door hurriedly, as he heard them come into the flat.

Scrambling on the bed, Charlie tucked the money and the watch down he side of the mattress before covering himself back up with the sheet and playing dead.

41

'I tried to call you.' Alfie leant across the visitors' table, staring in annoyance at Franny.

She hissed her reply, her eyes flickering quickly to the officers standing a few metres away. 'I've been banged up in my cell for the whole weekend, no privileges. And on top of that, I got moved and my phone's in the sole of my trainers, which are in the other cell.'

'Yeah, well, that's no good to me, is it? I've had to come here again, and you know I don't like being in this place.'

'And you think I do? You really know how to make me feel better.'

Alfie sat back and stared at Franny. The bruise on her face was fading and strangely she looked as good to him as ever. But that's what he *hated*. He hated how for some reason he was always drawn back to her when everything told him to run and never return.

Irritated further by those thoughts, Alfie snapped, 'I ain't here to make you feel better, Fran, I'm here because I've got no choice. I don't want to be pushing up daisies so I'll accept the offer. You pay off Huang and I do your dirty work.'

Inside Franny wanted to scream with relief, but instead she coolly said, 'That's great. Although I wouldn't call it dirty work, I'd call it necessary.'

Alfie stared at her for a moment then said, 'Whatever. Anyway, I'm here because I know you're telling the truth, which must be a new experience for you.'

Franny tilted her head. 'How do you know?'

'Shannon told me.'

Franny sat up in the chair. Her eyes darted around the room, making sure that no one was listening to them. 'What are you on about? Why would Shannon tell you? What did you do to her?'

Again, Alfie leant forward. 'In case you've forgotten, she's a kid. I didn't do anything to her.'

Franny narrowed her eyes. Her voice was hostile. 'That *kid* is a liar and she put me in here. Not to mention she's an ex-crackhead.'

Alfie shrugged. 'I wouldn't be so sure about her being an ex-addict.'

It was Franny's turn to be irritated. 'What are you on about? You know as well as I do she was on the pipe.'

'I'm not saying she wasn't. I'm saying I don't think she's an ex-anything. That's how I found out about her giving the statement to the police; she was bang off her head on crack.'

Franny stayed silent. Her thoughts rushed at a thousand

miles an hour. Then sounding genuinely shocked, she said, 'But what about Mia? I thought you said she was looking after Mia?'

'As far as I know she still is.'

Franny raised her voice, immediately regretting it when the officers looked over. 'Then you have to get Mia! Do you understand, Alf?'

'Like I already said to you, your days of telling me what to do are well and truly over.'

'I don't think so.'

Alfie's snarl mirrored Franny's. 'Oh I *do* think so, babe. I'll do what you want me to do to get Huang off my back but that's as far as it goes.'

'Then you'll go and get Mia, because I've just made that part of the deal. You take Mia or I'll be coming to water those daisies.'

Alfie squeezed Franny's knee hard under the table. She yelped and jumped, then booted him hard in the shin. He skidded back in his chair, rubbing his leg, but kept his voice to a quiet hiss, not wanting to attract the guard's attention. 'Fucking bitch – that hurt!'

'Oh grow up, Alfie. You've had worse – and Huang will definitely give you worse. He likes a painful ending.'

With the din of the noise of children playing and screaming in the visitors' area in the background, Alfie growled, 'You're enjoying this, ain't you?'

Franny shook her head. 'Are you kidding me? Do I look like I'm having a good time?'

'I'm not sure, I can't tell through that layer of ice around you.'

She gave a rueful smile before she relaxed slightly and said, 'I just want the best for Mia, that's all, and if you won't go and take her off your own bat, then you give me no choice but to force you to do it . . . Family's everything to you, and in time you'll thank me.'

Begrudgingly Alfie had to admit that Franny was right. Family, to him, was everything. But it started and stopped there. She wasn't right about Mia, and he hated the fact that she was forcing him into something he didn't want to do, the whole situation just felt wrong.

'Listen to me, darlin', I ain't going to thank you now or later, so you can put that idea to bed. Like I've said previously, it ain't healthy how you are always worrying about Mia when she's not even your daughter.'

Franny bristled. 'No? You like to keep telling me that whilst all the time you ain't doing anything for her. So whatever you think of me, even being banged up, I'm doing a hell of a lot more than you are for Mia. And for your information it isn't a crime to love and look out for someone – especially when they ain't got anyone else.'

'Yeah well you made sure of that, didn't you?'

'What happened to Bree was an accident, and you know that, Alf. I'm sorry that I kept everything from you – but you're choosing to stay away from her. You're choosing to snort the whole of Colombia up your nose. You're choosing to booze away your days. No one else. So don't use what I did as an excuse.'

Alfie sat back. There was something in what Franny had just said which resonated. Though it irked him to admit it even to himself. 'Fine, I'll go and get her. I'm not sure if they'll be too pleased about it, though, and I can't say I am.'

'Good and when you've done that let me know, Alf . . . and whilst you're getting Mia, tell Shannon I want to see her and tell her it's in her best interests to come.'

42

The next day, on Sunday afternoon a tap on the hospital door made Balantyne jump out of his sleep. He'd nodded off in the chair next to Claire's bed a few hours ago and the next thing he knew a police officer he recognised from down the station was putting his head around the door. 'The nurse said it was all right to come in.'

Balantyne stared at the officer. 'I think it's better if you came back another time. It's inappropriate to come in when the Chief's just had an operation.'

'Sorry, sir, of course.'

'No wait! Wait, it's fine.' Claire – who'd been asleep herself – spoke up.

Not keen on the officer coming in, Balantyne stiffened. 'Claire, you can do this another time. There's no need to do it now.'

'I appreciate you looking out for me, Tony, but I can do

this. Really I can . . . Come in.' She gestured to the police officer, who gave her a nod but looked slightly apprehensive.

Trying to put him at ease, Claire smiled and spoke warmly. 'I'll answer anything I can but I doubt that'll be much. Everything's a blank.'

Uncomfortable, Balantyne added, 'She can't remember anything, so it's a pretty pointless exercise.'

Turning to look at Balantyne, Claire remarked, 'Let him do his job, Tony.'

Balantyne said nothing, but gave a tight smile. This was the last thing he wanted. He could feel the sweat beginning to trickle down the back of his neck and the heat of the room felt cloying as he listened to the officer talk.

'This won't take long, ma'am, but the sooner we have it wrapped up the sooner the CPS solicitor will be happy to go forward with the case . . .' He stopped to clear his throat and then, looking very official with his notebook and pen, he said, 'Can you remember anything about what happened?'

Claire frowned. 'Something did come back to me earlier. I remember being in a lay-by. Why were we in a lay-by?' She looked at Balantyne who filled her in, aware of the constable's eyes on him.

'We were stopping because you weren't well.'

She nodded as if she was picturing it and she smiled. 'That's right, I remember now.'

Balantyne looked at Claire. It was one thing her remembering anything about that day when he was the only person around, but to remember it in front of other people – especially an officer of the law – was something else entirely.

And with that in mind and his heart pounding, Balantyne snapped and said, 'Look, this isn't what she needs as she wakes up. It's ridiculous.'

Taking Balantyne's warning look, the officer closed his notebook, slipping his pen into his pocket. 'Ma'am, he's right, I can do this later. The CPS will have to go ahead without your statement . . . It's just such a shame that you didn't have your SD card in the dashcam.'

Puzzled, Claire stared at the officer. 'What are you talking about? That's one thing I do remember – my car *did* have an SD card. I'm certain of it.'

'Oi, Lucas, I want a word with you.' Franny strode up to Christine, who was standing, pulling on her vape, in the busy, noisy courtyard of the prison, which was full of women milling about.

Squinting at Franny through the bright sunshine, Christine spoke, her tone as aggressive as Franny's. 'Don't get me wrong, pet, I like my women with balls but there's a difference between that and you being a mouthy bitch who gets on my nerves.'

Franny smirked. 'I don't care what you think, Lucas. And to tell you the truth, I've never met anyone whose opinion means less to me than yours – and believe you me I've met some scum in my lifetime. But I wanted to let you know that your money from Jessie will be in that account you gave her by the end of the day. And after that you stay away from her. If you go within a few metres of her, I'll slit your fucking throat.'

Franny turned to go but she stopped when she heard

Lucas say, 'I'm surprised at you. I'm surprised that you're hanging around with Jessie and some copper's wife. The other women don't like it either. They can't understand why you haven't sorted her out yet. I wouldn't trust her but then I don't trust you either, so howay, no matter. But I'd watch your back if I were you.'

Curiosity getting hold of her, Franny turned around. 'What kind of crap are you talking about now, Lucas?'

'Your new roomy, Emma. *Walsh*. Rumour has it that she's a copper's wife. If you ask me she's a plant. She's been placed in here so she can spy on the women.'

Franny laughed. 'You've been here long enough to know not to listen to rumours. They always end up to be bullshit.'

Still vaping and with it looking like smoke coming out of her mouth, Christine shrugged. 'Don't say I didn't warn you about Emma. I can sniff her out a mile away. She's a copper's wife if there ever was one, and mark my words, I'll be coming to pay her a visit, sooner rather than later.'

43

'Why don't you go into your room or something? You look tired. Have a kip or something.' Vaughn stared at Shannon over his paperwork, which he'd kept putting off. There was a pile of unpaid invoices and accounts that had needed sorting for the past couple of months, but he just hadn't got around to it. Before then it was Franny who did them . . . He stopped his thoughts as her name popped into his mind.

He rarely thought of her, or he tried not to, and when he did, he refused to allow his thoughts to go very far. The last thing he needed was her in his mind especially as last time he'd spoken to Alfie there was something odd, something strange about his demeanour. Of course it could've been all the coke that Alfie had been shoving up his nose; that would make anyone act differently. But there'd been something in his eyes that told him it wasn't just that.

He'd tried to get through to Balantyne, but when he'd called his mobile it'd been turned off, and when he'd tried the station, they'd told him he was on annual leave. He wasn't sure what was happening with the case, but the sooner Franny went to trial and was sent down, the better. To finally get her out of his life and Alfie's couldn't come soon enough.

'Vaughn! Vaughn!' Suddenly he looked up and saw Shannon standing in front of him.

'I've been talking to you for the last few minutes.'

'Sorry, Shan, I'm just tired, that's all, and I've got these poxy accounts to do. What were you saying?'

She sighed as she tried to push her uncle out of her mind. Even after everything, her heart melted when she was around Vaughn. Being near him was the only thing that mattered. She *lived* for him. He was the only thing that made sense in her life, and she'd make sure that no one took that away. 'I was saying I'd rather stay in here with you if you don't mind.'

Absentmindedly, he frowned. 'Why, what's up with your bedroom?'

Seeing the image of Charlie's bloated body in her mind, Shannon's fear and anxiety turned into anger. She'd been trying to avoid thinking about him, trying to pretend everything was all right, wishing and hoping that she'd wake up and it was all a bad dream. And now to make matters worse, it felt like Vaughn was pushing her away. Pushing her back into her nightmare. 'Well I can't do right for doing wrong with you, can I? Fucking hell, you was giving me an earbashing for staying in me room before and now you're complaining I ain't in it.'

Seeing that he'd upset her, and thinking that he needed to handle her with more care, Vaughn said, 'I never meant it like that, Shan, and yes I was worried about you before, and yes I'm worried about you now. I just want you to be happy and at the moment I never see you smile. I don't want to be a nag but I'm a bit lost with what to do with you, Shan.'

She gave a half smile, cravings for crack beginning to seep into her. Not physical ones, but mental ones. When Vaughn had helped her come off it the last time, she was surprised how easy she'd found it but then there'd been a sense of hope. Now? Now it felt like she was living on borrowed time and she was scared. Really scared. And as she'd done throughout her life when she was frightened, she turned to crack for support. Because it never judged her, never told her she was no good; all it did was make her forget. And that's what she needed right now. To forget. Because if she remembered what awaited her in her bedroom she just might start screaming and never stop.

Making an effort to smile, Shannon shrugged. 'It's not you, Vaughn. I'm just being a moody cow. Ignore me. I just thought it'd be nice to spend some time with you and talk.'

Grateful to have an excuse not to have to do his paper-work, Vaughn pushed it to one side and grinned. 'Well that sounds like a lovely idea. Okay, what do you want to talk about?'

Shannon took a deep breath and now that she'd opened the box in her mind, shyly, *cautiously* she said, 'You know if you die or, I mean, when someone dies, how long does it take for their body to start smelling?'

256

Vaughn did a double take. He blinked once, then twice before bursting into laughter. 'Why, who've you killed?'

With her eyes filling up with tears, Shannon jumped up and shouted, 'I ain't killed no one! I ain't! Why are you always thinking bad of me!'

'Fucking hell, Shan, I'm only joking.'

Shannon shook her head furiously. 'No, no you're making fun of me! You're always making fun of me. And yeah okay, maybe I ain't very clever cos I never went to school, and maybe I ain't ever going to know big words like you but that don't mean I don't want to learn. I just saw something on the telly, that's all. Made me curious, but sorry for asking! I'll know not to bother next time. *I'm sorry for fucking asking!*'

Shannon screamed the end part of her sentence then the room fell silent and Vaughn stared at her: looking at her properly, looking at the dark circles around her eyes, looking at the amount of weight she'd lost, looking at the paleness of her skin, looking at the fact she was just a kid who'd had the worst of bad starts. And then he looked at himself and he realised he'd been letting her down.

He'd been letting her fend too much for herself when she needed much more support. He couldn't imagine what kind of issues she was dealing with in her head. Her childhood had been an abusive nightmare, though at least she was now well shot of Charlie. When he'd been in Soho last week he'd been talking to one of the other club owners and they'd mentioned Charlie had gone AWOL – which was no loss to anyone. Hopefully it meant that he'd packed up and gone, never to be seen again.

'Shan, Shan, come here. I'm so sorry, I'm so sorry, baby.' He walked up to her, taking her in his arms. He held her tightly, feeling her whole body racking with tears and he just kept holding her. 'It's okay, Shan, it's okay. I'll keep you safe. I'll make sure nothing ever hurts you again.'

He listened for her reply but the only thing he heard was the sound of her crying.

'Sshhhh, Shan, it's okay, baby. It's okay.'

As Vaughn spoke, Shannon held on to him tighter than she'd ever held on to anyone in her life before. She could smell his aftershave, she could feel his strong body against hers and she never wanted this moment to end. She never thought it was possible to feel the way she did now.

'Shan, wait here, baby. I've got something for you. I was meaning to give it to you before.' Much to Shannon's disappointment, Vaughn suddenly broke away from her and ran to his bedroom. He rushed across to the dresser and excitedly pulled open the drawer. But immediately he frowned, though he continued rummaging through it before trying the other drawers.

After a minute or so he stood back and stared. A heavy feeling sat in his stomach. There was no mistake; he knew he'd left it there. The money – over ten grand in cash – had been there, and most importantly the gold and diamond watch he'd bought Shannon as a thank you gift had been there. And now it'd gone. But the problem was – the problem that made him feel sick to his stomach, the thought that he didn't want to enter his head – there was only one possible person who could've taken it. But just as he was working out quite what to do, quite what he felt, Vaughn was startled to hear a loud banging.

'*Open the fucking door! It's me, Alfie! Open this fucking door, now!*'

44

At the same time as Alfie was banging down Vaughn's door, in the side room of the hospital on the other side of London, Balantyne stood and smiled, looking down at Claire. The police had come and gone a few hours ago.

He spoke softly to her, his voice full of conviction and his words seemingly caring.

'Sweetheart, listen to me. I didn't want to say anything in front of that police officer but what you said wasn't true.'

Sounding puzzled, Claire asked, 'What do you mean?'

'Well about the dashcam – you know, about the SD card. You said that there was definitely one in the car.'

'That's right – because there was. I can remember that.'

Balantyne gave a sickly smile. 'That part is right. There was one, but when the accident happened there wasn't.'

'*Yes*, there was. I know that as a fact, Tony.'

'Claire, there's nothing wrong with *my* memory. I mean who had the accident, you or me?'

'Well, me, of course.'

Balantyne nodded. 'Exactly, and we're not talking about a broken leg are we? I think what's happening to you is you *think* you're remembering everything but you aren't. Can't you recall what you asked me?'

'No, so much of it's a blank,' Claire said, shaking her head.

He took her hand and squeezed it. 'And that's my point, darling. You want to remember so much that what you're doing is having false memories. In fact, the reason why I know you didn't have an SD in the car is because we had a long discussion about it.'

'Did we?'

'Yes, there was a problem with your card. You said it wasn't recoding properly and you thought it might've been damaged and therefore it was pointless putting it in the dashcam. You wondered if we could stop off on the way and get one. Do you remember now?'

Claire squeezed her eyes shut and kept them closed for a few moments, desperately trying to recall the conversation. She eventually opened them and said, 'No I don't, it's almost like the conversation never happened . . . It's so embarrassing; how can I not remember? I don't want people thinking I can't do my job. I don't want them talking down at the station about this. There were a whole group of people who didn't want me to have the job in the first place, so I'm going to play right into their hands, aren't I? Inspector Martin who can't remember a thing!'

261

Balantyne stroked her face. 'Don't get upset. How well you do your job has *nothing* to do with how well you can remember events surrounding the accident.'

'I know that but they'll use it as an excuse.'

Balantyne looked at her, feigning concern. 'How about when they ask you *anything* about the accident or anything surrounding it, you just tell them you can't remember and then you can check with me? I can fill you in on everything. That way you'll feel secure about what you're saying and when you speak to them again, they'll think you're getting your memory back so the rumour mill will stop before it's started.'

'I don't know, Tony, it feels dishonest somehow. Like I'm lying.'

Balantyne gave her a small kiss on the head. 'How can it be lying, Claire, when in fact what you're doing is making sure your information is correct? Instead of giving them some half-cooked-up memory, you're going to give them the concrete truth.'

Claire thought for a moment. It was true that the last thing she wanted to do was to give a statement or answers based on a memory that wasn't there, and she certainly didn't want anyone gossiping about her, wondering if she was still capable of doing the job. 'If you're sure?'

'Totally. It's the least I can do.'

'Thank you, Tony. I really am lucky to have you, aren't I?'

And with those words Balantyne kissed Claire again on the head, letting out a huge sigh of relief. Life was looking up.

* * *

262

With recreation time over, Franny sat on the bed in the cell, watching Emma. As much as she didn't want to believe what Lucas had said, there was a possibility it was true whether she liked the idea of it or not.

She'd heard of crazy stuff like that before – moles and grasses being planted in a jail – but no matter how much the authorities wanted to keep it quiet, eventually it always came out. *Always.*

'You all right, Fran?'

Franny shrugged at Emma. 'Why wouldn't I be?'

'No reason, you've just been sitting there staring for a long time.'

Coldly, Franny said, 'Problem?'

Starting to become uneasy, Emma shook her head. 'No, none. I . . . I . . .'

She trailed off as Franny said, 'You seem a bit better today.'

'Yeah, they've given me some medicine to help with the alcohol cravings. It sounds odd but I haven't felt this good for a long time.'

Tightly and sarcastically Franny said, 'Well ain't that great for you, darlin'. I'm glad *you* are, at least that makes one of us.'

Emma looked at Franny nervously before going to the doorway of the cell. 'Listen, I'm supposed to meet Officer Brown by the library. I've got to go and meet the deputy. They're talking about me being transferred.'

Still holding Emma's stare Franny said, 'And why would that be?'

Looking even more uncomfortable, Emma – remembering what Officer Brown had said about not telling the women about being a policeman's wife – shrugged. 'I couldn't tell you . . . Look I better go, you know what Brown's like.'

Franny didn't reply as Emma walked out of the cell.

Jessie, having listened to the conversation, sat down on the bed next to Franny. 'What was that about, Fran? You seemed angry with her?'

Franny gave a warm smile to Jessie. Her heart went out to the girl. There was no way she should be in a place like this and the idea of Jessie serving time because she stood up to some rotten pervert made her sick to her stomach. 'Don't you worry about it, Jess, but do yourself a favour and steer clear of Emma, cos I don't think she's all that she seems.'

45

'That took you a fucking long time!' Alfie stood at the door staring at Vaughn. Everything about him made Alfie want to smash him in the face. The last time he was here, he'd been unsure if Franny had been telling the truth, but now he knew for certain that Vaughn was a lowlife grass – a dirty no-good snake – and it was taking all his willpower not to put him through the wall. But he had to wait. Wait until the time was right.

Furious about not only Alfie's attitude but also about Shannon's huge betrayal, Vaughn gave as good as Alfie. 'Well it's my fucking door, I'll take as long as I like. And what is it with you lately, what's with the calling around for a visit crap?'

Not waiting to be invited in, Alfie strode into the long hallway. He was just about to say what he was there for when Vaughn – hurt and not knowing what to do – blurted out the words, 'I think Shan's robbing from me. In fact I know she has, cos unless Mia's been thieving from me, the only person it could be is Shan. Not only that, she took the watch I'd got her as a present. I know I was going to give it to her anyway but that ain't the fucking point. I'm gutted.'

An image of Shannon high on crack came into Alfie's mind. It was obvious she'd taken the money to feed her crack habit; perhaps she'd given it to some scumbag who was involved in the whole scene and fed off vulnerable druggie kids. 'It don't surprise me.'

'Why would you say that? Come on, Alf – if you know something, tell me.'

There was a part of Alfie that wanted to grass Shannon up like she had done him, but for everything that had happened he still liked the kid. Okay, he was pissed off with her – well pissed off was putting it mildly, in fact he was fucking fuming – but it was *Vaughn* who'd been the driving force behind it. He'd taken advantage of her like everyone had taken advantage of her all her life.

And besides, anyone who was expecting her *not* to fall off the wagon, now and then, was expecting too much from her. It wasn't realistic – *especially* taking into account her background. He only had to look at himself to know how hard it was to knock the drugs on the head, and he wasn't even an addict. He just had an occasional taste for coke, and when things went wrong in life for him, his occasional taste for coke turned into a real hunger. So thinking about it, who the hell was he to put a bomb under her life by telling Vaughn?

Growling at Vaughn, Alfie shrugged. 'What is there to

say? She's an ex-junkie, sometimes thieving becomes a natural part of their life.'

'What, ten grand?'

Alfie raised his eyebrows. 'Fuck me, that's some dipping. Who fucking knows but maybe she's feeling insecure.'

'What the hell is that supposed to mean?'

Wanting so much to let Vaughn know that he'd found out about the statements they'd given to the police, Alfie glared at him, fighting the temptation as he spoke. 'It means maybe she don't trust you, maybe she thinks that when you're done with her and got what you want out of her, you'll just dash her aside.'

'Look, Alf, I don't want anything from that kid.'

Alfie stepped closer to Vaughn. 'Really? Are you sure about that?'

Not liking his tone or the ongoing attitude, Vaughn poked Alfie in the chest. 'Yeah I'm fucking sure, so for her to think like that or not to trust me—'

Alfie pushed back at Vaughn, causing him to stumble towards the wall. 'Shut up, Vaughn! Have you heard yourself? She's just a damaged kid; she ain't going to think like other people. Maybe she *is* terrified that she's going to be out on the street, so she's making a plan B by taking your cash so that when you're done with her she don't have to go back to the life she had . . . Like I say, even though she thinks the sun shines out of your arse maybe she don't trust you. Maybe deep down she knows what you're really like.'

'Don't talk shit!'

'Come on, Vaughn, you've only got to see the way she

looks at you to know she's smitten. She'd do *anything* for you, but maybe she knows you wouldn't do anything for her.'

Vaughn shook his head. He wasn't going to let Alfie wind him up but he was going to think about what he'd said about Shannon. Maybe he shouldn't pull her up about the money, maybe she was genuinely worried she was going to be out on the street. Shit, once again he felt like he'd let her down. Angry with himself he snarled, 'What do you want, Alf?'

Before Vaughn had finished his sentence, Alfie marched down the hallway towards Shannon's room. 'I've come for my . . . I've come for Mia. So you best get her clothes packed, cos I'm taking her now.'

From behind Alfie, Vaughn shouted, puzzlement in his voice, 'What the hell did you say?'

Finding Mia's room, Alfie walked in. 'I said, I'm taking her.'

A second later Vaughn appeared in the doorway. 'What do you mean you're taking her? You mean for the evening, right?'

'No, Vaughn. I mean forever.'

Shocked, Vaughn walked up to Alfie, a bemused look on his face. 'You're having a laugh?'

In the quiet and warmth of Mia's bedroom, Alfie stepped forward. 'This is what you wanted didn't you? You kept going on about me taking her and now I'm here.'

Vaughn's gaze went from Alfie then to Mia who was just waking up in her cot. 'I never said take her. I said *see* her. And yeah, yeah, you two should be together and eventually you should be in the same place, but not like this. She doesn't even know you. It takes time. And look at the state of you. You're all over the place.'

'Not that it's anything to do with you but I ain't. I'm getting my head straight, and the clearer it becomes the less I like what I'm seeing.'

Vaughn clenched his jaw. 'Then what about Huang? What if he turns up?'

Alfie stared at Vaughn. For the past few days he'd actually been expecting Huang to turn up. Franny had promised she'd pay a standoff fee to Huang, making him back off until the whole amount was paid, but he didn't trust Huang to agree to it. Nor did he necessarily trust Franny – but then he had to face it, Franny was his best – his *only* – option. And, annoyed by Vaughn pretending he gave anything less than a fuck, Alfie scowled. 'Listen, don't you worry about that. And anyway, I'm not here for conversation. I'm here for Mia.'

'Look, I ain't saying you can't take her . . .'

Alfie interrupted. 'I'm glad to hear it because there's fuck all you can do.'

Vaughn's face twisted. 'Is that right?'

'Yeah it is.'

With his stare still locked on Alfie, Vaughn shouted, 'Shannon! Shannon, get here now!' Within a few minutes, Shannon appeared at the entrance to Mia's bedroom, and, seeing Alfie, she shrunk back as Vaughn continued to rant. 'Have you heard this, Shan? Have you heard what this fucking joker is saying?'

Unable to look at Alfie, Shannon shook her head. 'No. I've been watching TV.'

269

Red-faced, Vaughn turned to Shannon as Alfie walked towards Mia's cot. 'He wants to take her. For good.'

Panic crossed Shannon's face. 'You can't. Please don't. You can't take her, she's happy here.'

Vaughn gave a small smile. 'Oh don't worry, he ain't going to take her anywhere . . . Look after Mia and stay inside this room.'

And with that, Vaughn clenched his fist and threw a punch before kicking Alfie out of the room.

46

Taken by surprise, Alfie stumbled backwards into the hallway, giving Vaughn an opportunity to slam his fist into Alfie's stomach, which sent him sprawling on the floor and allowed Vaughn to follow up with a boot in the ribs.

'Who the fuck do you think you are, Alfie? Don't think you can come in here and fuck up people's lives. Your life might be a mess but that don't mean everyone else's is.'

Spitting out blood from his mouth, Alfie snarled as he felt the pain rush through his body – which hadn't yet healed from Huang's beating. 'I'm going to kill you, you piece of shit!'

'If anyone's going to kill anyone, Alf, then it's going to be me killing you.'

But as Vaughn finished his sentence, Alfie dived for Vaughn's ankles. He grabbed them and pulled hard, causing Vaughn to clatter against the wall.

With a heavy thud, Vaughn dropped to his knees, giving Alfie a chance to scramble up and swing back his foot to kick Vaughn hard in the side of the head. Immediately, Alfie followed it up with his fist as he jumped on top of Vaughn, pummelling his knuckles into Vaughn's face, drawing blood as Vaughn's lip split in two.

Enraged, Alfie continued to bring his fists down as Vaughn struggled underneath him. Eventually, Alfie exhausted himself and got up. Panting, he stared icily. 'That's it now, you hear me? I ain't going to fight you no more . . . not over Mia. So this is what's going to happen. I'm going to go inside that room and take her, and you're not going to move. You're going to stay there. And after that, I'm going to walk out of the door, you hear me?'

But as Alfie turned towards Mia's bedroom door, Vaughn struggled up with a mighty effort and grabbed the small hallway table, picking it up and swinging it at Alfie, slamming it against the back of his neck.

Alfie fell forward, sprawling along the hallway carpet, and a moment later he felt Vaughn's foot on his back. Although in agony, Alfie managed to roll over with enough strength to cause Vaughn to become off balance; Alfie took his chance and brought up his leg, kicking Vaughn hard in the testicles.

As Vaughn bellowed out in pain and dropped to his knees again, Alfie stood up with beads of sweat and streaks of blood mixed together on his face. He bent down and grabbed Vaughn around his neck, pushing him hard and driving him against the wall.

Then with one hand, Alfie went into his pocket and

pulled out a gun and, without another thought, he smashed the butt of the gun against the side of Vaughn's skull, knocking him clean out.

Still breathing hard, Alfie stormed into Mia's bedroom where Shannon stood shaking. He glanced at her. 'Don't worry, babe, I ain't going to hurt you. And don't worry about Vaughn either – I ain't killed him . . . not yet. He'll be fine.'

Shannon stared at Alfie then she reached out and grabbed his arm, tears streaking down her face. 'Please don't do this. Don't do this. Don't take her . . . Not like this. Look she's frightened.'

With blood flowing down his face, Alfie shook Shannon off his arm. 'She'll be okay, I'll take good care of her.'

Panicked, Shannon watched Alfie grab a bag and throw Mia's clothes into it.

'Is this because of me, Alf? Is it?'

He turned to look at her as he put the bag over his shoulder and picked up a crying Mia.

'You mean is this about you taking that shit?'

'Well is it?'

Ignoring her, Alfie walked out of the bedroom. Shannon grabbed at him, but he pushed her off again as he opened the front door and began to walk away.

She raced after him, her eyes full of desperation. 'It is because of me, ain't it? It's because of the other day. I swear, I *swear*, I won't do it again. You just don't understand, you don't know what's going on. I was just feeling so shit . . . I wish I could tell you why but I can't . . . I . .'

Continuing to walk down the corridor towards the stairs,

Alfie said, 'Look, I don't blame you, I can't imagine what you've been through, Shan, but let's have it straight; no one wants a crackhead around a baby do they? You were in a right state the other day.'

Shannon's eyes pooled with sadness, and she darted in front of Alfie, trying to block his way.

'Then it *is* me. Oh my God, I'm so sorry. Please, don't tell Vaughn why you're taking her, please don't.'

Hating seeing Shannon in pain, Alfie stopped walking and looked at her directly.

He sighed. 'Look, it ain't all you, there's other stuff as well.' He stopped a moment and thought about the money Vaughn had told him she'd taken. 'And as for Vaughn, I think he'll be sniffing a rat very soon, Shan. Did you think he wouldn't notice? Are you that fucking stupid?'

'What are you talking about?'

Winding himself up at the mess he was in, Alfie leant into Shannon, inches away from her face, but he held back his anger, seeing how vulnerable and young she looked. After all, like he told Franny, she really was just a kid. 'I'm saying you're a fool to yourself. You had it all Shan, you had Vaughn who don't usually give a fuck about anyone but himself, looking out for you, and what did you go and do? What were you thinking?'

In tears Shannon said, 'I don't know what you're talking about? Please, Alfie, you're frightening me.'

Alfie shook his head. 'Stop, Shan, you've turned us all over ain't you? I'm not saying that it's your fault . . . Fucking hell, if I had an uncle like Charlie, I'd be more bang on it than you. But my problem is I was your mate and you still

274

betrayed me. In my world we don't do that, we sort it ourselves.'

Shannon stepped back slightly, her heart beginning to race. 'What are you saying?'

'I'm saying I know that you wrote a statement. I know you lied.'

'I . . . I . . .'

'Don't try to deny it, Shan. You told me yourself when you were high on that shit. Like I say, you're your own worst enemy.'

'But you're angry with her so why do you care?'

Alfie stared in bemusement at Shannon. 'For all the shit me and Franny had, all the crap that was going down, it wasn't your place to do that. We don't have snakes in the world I live and besides she was my woman and I would've dealt with her. *Me*, not you, not Vaughn, *me*. And if I wanted her punished, I would've dished it out . . . Which reminds me, Franny wants to see you.'

Shannon's face was a picture of shock and fear. 'Franny? What about? Why does she want to see me?'

Readjusting Mia on his shoulder, Alfie began to walk again, heading for the stairs. 'I don't know, Shan – I ain't her calling boy – but if I were you, I'd go and see her. And if you don't want Vaughn to think any worse of you than he does already, I'd keep that mouth of yours shut.'

Once she was back inside the apartment, Shannon bent down to Vaughn, who was still unconscious and slumped on the floor. She kissed his head and then she kissed him gently and quickly on his mouth. She looked at him and a sad smile appeared on her face. 'I know you can't hear me but I'm so sorry, Vaughn, I never meant to bring all this trouble . . . I love you so much.' And with that Shannon curled up against Vaughn on the floor.

On the other side of Shannon's door, Charlie smiled. He'd heard everything: the fight, the screams – and Shannon professing her love. Being here was turning out to be more fun than he could've ever imagined.

47

It was late on Sunday night and Alfie breathed a sigh of relief as he stared at Mia in the cot he'd bought earlier from Mothercare. Finally, she was asleep, though he reckoned most people would be asleep if they'd given out that amount of screaming. From the moment he'd brought her home, which he guessed was a good few hours ago, the only thing she'd done was cry at the top of her voice.

'Alfie, you want me to stay the night?'

Alfie looked up and immediately put his finger over his lips and frowned. He whispered, 'I'm telling you, if you wake her up, I'm going to bleedin' well kill you!'

He said this firmly but he winked with warmth at Julie, a girl who'd once worked for him at the club he used to own on Old Compton Street.

Julie was a good girl – or rather woman, she was probably well into her sixties – but she was old-school and he'd met her children on many occasions. Although Julie had spent her life as a prostitute and had worked on the streets as well as in the clubs, her kids were well mannered, well looked after and they clearly loved their mother.

It was credit to Julie that none of them had been in trouble, far from it in fact. The eldest two had just finished college and her youngest one had just gone off to work at a kids' camp in America. So who else better was there to look after Mia than Julie?

Creeping out of the room, terrified that any noise would disturb Mia, Alfie smiled wearily at Julie. 'Fuck me, are kids always this exhausting?'

Julie grinned, showing off the large gap between her front teeth. 'It's been less than a day, Alf, and you already look like shit. The fun ain't even started yet!'

Taking a couple of fifty-pound notes out of his pocket, Alfie gave them to Julie before saying, 'Well that's why I got you, Mary Poppins.'

Julie giggled. 'I'm not sure if Mary Poppins was an old whore.'

Alfie kissed Julie gently on the cheek. 'Yeah she was, that's what she was singing about when she said, *supercalifragilisticexpialidocious*.'

Playfully, Julie slapped Alfie on his chest and laughed. 'You silly bastard! Now are you sure that you don't want me to stay? I can sleep in your spare room seeing as you're not offering me a night tucked up in your bed.'

Alfie looked across to a sleeping Mia; this was certainly not what he wanted, but Franny had given him no choice. A huge part of him wanted to just tell Julie to move into the guest room full time, that way he could pretend this wasn't happening, that way he could tell himself he didn't feel anything at all.

But when Mia had been crying and he'd been walking around the room struggling to get her to calm down, he'd felt something he never thought he would. He'd looked into her big eyes and from nowhere he'd begun to care.

And it'd taken him by surprise; he wasn't sure how to feel about that fact. He thought he'd be angry for a long time. And yes, he was pissed with Franny – in truth he was raging – and he was definitely still hurt by Bree's actions, but the anger, the burning fury that he had linked to Mia, had subsided and he needed a few hours on his own with her to get his head around it.

'Thanks for the offer but you go home. I'll see you tomorrow . . . Oh and, Julie, make sure you're here fucking early! I'm not sure how I'm going to cope with a whole night on me own so keep your phone on because I might have to send out for reinforcements.'

Laughing as she made her way out of Alfie's flat, Julie left him alone. He smiled to himself as he heard her singing *supercalifragilisticexpialidocious* at the top of her voice as she walked down the corridor.

Turning to go back to where Mia was sleeping, Alfie crept into the room again. He sat down by her cot, watching her sleeping. It was the first time he'd looked at her properly. Really properly.

Her hair was a mass of soft bouncing curls and her complexion was rosy. Her face was round and chubby-cheeked, and her cute button nose reminded him of Bree.

279

The thought made him draw a sharp intake of breath and he rubbed his head, trying to push out the pain it caused him.

He'd loved Bree and although that had been complicated because he'd also loved Franny, it didn't make the fact any less true. And it'd hurt him when she'd left, hurt him when he'd found that she'd hidden her pregnancy and Mia from him, and it'd hurt him to find out that she was dead.

But the more he looked at Mia, the more he could see what a spitting image of Bree she was and it certainly felt like there was a part of Bree still here . . . He breathed out feeling like a weight was being crushed down on his chest as he continued to stare at the sleeping baby.

Looking back, he realised he hadn't let himself grieve for Bree, hell he hadn't even said goodbye. What he'd done was push her out of his mind and find comfort in a line of coke and a bottle of whiskey. But he couldn't do that anymore, so now he was feeling it.

He could feel the pain; it was almost physical, holding him and knocking him sideward, emotions rushing through and over him. And slowly, very slowly, Alfie reached out and touched Mia gently on her tiny hands. Immediately, she stirred and wriggled before her eyes fluttered open.

She stared at Alfie and gave him a big, gummy smile and for Alfie it was like a shockwave, an arrow straight through his heart. He smiled back with tears in his eyes. 'Hello, darlin'. You all right, girl?'

Mia gurgled with delight and held her toes.

'You ain't going to cry again, are you? Not that it matters, cos darlin', you can cry, you can laugh, you can do whatever you like because from now on I'm here. I'll always be here for you and I ain't ever going to let you go . . . That's right, Mia, I'm here . . . Always and forever, *Daddy's* here.'

48

On Monday afternoon, Shannon sat shaking in the visitors'
room of the prison, squirming and feeling uncomfortable.
She'd even go so far as scared. She had no idea what Franny
wanted and the way she felt certainly wasn't helped by the
fact she hadn't slept properly for the past couple of days.
She'd spent the night on the couch again not wanting to
go anywhere near her bedroom. Not for anything.

She hadn't even gone in to get her clothes. She was
wearing the same ones she'd worn for the past few days.
Yes, she'd washed them – but she didn't know how long
she could go on wearing them before Vaughn started asking
questions, *especially* as he'd gone out of his way to buy her
a new wardrobe of clothes. But that was the least of her
worries. She was terrified her uncle's body would start
smelling and then it would all be over for her. But she
had no idea how to get rid of her uncle's body; she had no

idea who to turn to. What was she going to do? In truth she'd be happy to smoke herself into oblivion and never wake up.

The last thing that she could do now was to bring trouble to Vaughn's door. He'd never forgive her especially since the visit from Alfie – who they hadn't heard from since he'd taken Mia. Vaughn had been edgy, angry and she would even go so far as saying he was being paranoid.

She'd listened to him on the phone, and although she hadn't heard him say his name, she suspected that he'd been talking to Balantyne – or at least he'd left a stream of messages for him. And the words that stuck in her mind, the one sentence that stayed with her since she'd heard it, was: *'If Alfie finds out what I've done, he'll kill me. I'm a walking dead man.'* She'd felt sick and even though it'd been part of the reason why Alfie had come to get Mia, her desire to smoke some crack was almost unbearable.

'Shannon. I can't say it's good to see you, but you've done the right thing by coming here.'

Shannon jumped as Franny's voice boomed over her. She looked up and, seeming larger than life, there was Franny. Beautiful. Powerful. Strong. And a cold-hearted bitch.

Shannon mumbled, 'You didn't give me any choice.'

Franny gave a hostile smile, and as she went to sit down, she brushed her hand against the back of Shannon's neck before leaning down to whisper into her ear, 'We've always got a choice, Shannon. The issue isn't about choice, it's about what we do with that choice.'

She sat down at the table opposite Shannon, watching her play nervously with the cheap silver rings on her fingers.

Continuing to observe her, Franny noticed the dark circles around her eyes, the breakout of spots, and how thin she was compared to last time she'd seen her. And if she cared, if she cared at all, she might be worried about the kid. But instead she said, 'I know you made a statement, Shannon. I know that you're part of the reason why I'm here, and I'm sure that you know it would be stupid to start denying it.'

Shannon continued to shake. She looked around the room, from the prison officers standing in the corner to the other prisoners and their visitors, before turning back to Franny. All she wanted to do was run, and for what seemed to be the thousandth time that day, she asked herself how the happy life she thought she was getting had suddenly come to an end.

Shannon dropped her gaze down to her lap. She spoke quietly. 'I wasn't going to . . . I wasn't going to . . .'

Before Shannon had finished the sentence, Franny banged on the table. 'Did you think you were going to get away with it? Did you? Did you think that I wasn't going to find out what a lying bitch you are? You *know* that I didn't kill her. You weren't even there when Bree fell down the stairs, and yet that's what you're putting in your statement. Why, Shannon? Why did you do that?'

Crying, Shannon shook her head. 'You were horrible to me.'

Franny reached across the table and gripped Shannon's hand. '*I was horrible to you*? Have you heard yourself, Shannon? I was horrible to you, so you set me up for a murder I didn't commit? That is fucked up beyond belief.'

Wiping her running nose with her sleeve, Shannon shrugged, looking even younger than her sixteen years. 'I hated you though.'

Still holding Shannon's hand, Franny pulled her nearer to her. 'You didn't even know me, and if you thought that you hated me then, just wait until I finish with you . . . But I have to say, thank you, Shannon, because I was sitting in this place trying to work out how to bring down Vaughn and that excuse for a copper, Balantyne, and you played right into my hands.'

'What are you talking about?'

Franny stared at her. 'I want you to retract your statement. I want you to go and tell them you made a mistake. Take it back.'

Shannon shook her head frantically. 'I can't! I can't! Vaughn will find out and then . . . and then he won't want me anymore.'

'Want you? What are you talking about? He doesn't want you anyway; he's just using you. That's what Vaughn does. He got you to make the statement because he knew that you would. He knows that he could make you do anything.'

'That's not true. He's kind to me. He looks after me.'

'Oh, Shannon, you're so easy to play. And someone like Vaughn will've spotted that a mile off. If this case went to trial, once it was over he'd throw you away. Even you must be able to see that. He's made you feel important and that's part of his game.'

'No, that ain't how it is. You don't see the way he is with me.'

Franny said nothing as she studied Shannon's face. After

285

a minute or so, she said, 'Oh my God, you love him, don't you? You've fallen for him? You really are more stupid than you look, but it makes it all the easier for me. The stakes have just gone up.'

With fear crossing her face, Shannon asked, 'What do you mean?'

'I mean it sounds like you've got almost as much to lose as me. Vaughn's your life and this is mine. So what you're going to do is help me get my life back, and in return I'll let you keep yours.'

Shannon began to stand up, clutching her bag tightly against her body. 'I can't do it, I can't do what you're asking.'

Franny pulled her chestnut hair up into a ponytail as she stared at Shannon. 'You'll do as I say, otherwise I'll be telling Vaughn about you and that crack you like so much . . . That's right, Alfie told me.'

Shannon's face was a picture of shock. 'He . . . he . . . he told you?'

'That's right, darlin', he told me *everything*. Did you really think that Alfie would've kept that from me? He and I have a bond that nothing will break. We're a team. Who do you think told him to come and get Mia?'

'It was you? I thought—'

Franny cut off Shannon again. 'There was no way I was going to let Mia be around you if you're back on that stuff, no way . . . So you see, Shan, Alfie will do anything for me, just like you'll do anything for Vaughn – and if I decide to get Alfie to tell Vaughn all about your nasty little habit, he will.'

'He can't ever know.'

Franny shrugged, getting up herself. 'If you do as I ask, he'll never need to know, and now Mia's safe away from you, I don't care how you live your life. After what you've done to me, I don't care if you smoke that crack to oblivion. As long as I get out of here and have my day with Vaughn, I couldn't care less.'

Shaking with tears, Shannon muttered, 'But if I take back the statement, he'll be angry. He'll never forgive me.'

'Then make something up, make up a reason why you've done it – you might stand half a chance that way. But if he finds out you were back on that crack when you were looking after Mia, he'll throw you out and turn his back on you forever. So you've got a choice, Shannon, and now is your time to decide what to do with that choice. I'll be in touch.'

Standing on the corner of Meard Street, Shannon, overwhelmed and feeling like her world was beginning to crash in on her, pulled out her phone. Her hand shook as she dialled the number. 'Hello, can you put me through to Detective Balantyne please?'

'Who's calling?'

Not wanting to give her name, Shannon said, 'I just want to speak to him. Put me through, it's important.'

'I really need to get your name, caller.'

Panicked, Shannon spun round, watching the tourists walk by as she gripped her mobile phone. She shouted down the phone, 'Put me fucking through! I need to speak to him – you don't understand!'

The operator on the other end of the line fell silent for

a moment before she said, 'Okay, caller, I'm putting you through.'

'Hello, this is Detective Balantyne. I'm away from my desk but if you'd like to leave a message, I'll get back to you soon. In an emergency, please contact the duty officer on . . .'

Breathless and frustrated that she had to speak to his voicemail, Shannon spoke quickly after the beep. 'Hello, this is Shannon Mulligan. Please, you've got to help me. I've given you a statement but I need to talk to you about it . . . Look, I don't want to say any more on the phone, you just need to call me. Please, please, please . . . It's *urgent.'*

49

For some reason, the showers were unusually busy and Franny could feel a strange atmosphere in the air. She watched Lucas and a group of women milling about at the far end of the shower room, looking like they were planning something.

Franny, sensing any minute now it was about to kick off, turned to Jessie, who'd become like her shadow. Not that she minded; it certainly seemed necessary with Lucas about. She knew that given an opportunity Lucas would take as much from Jessie as she could.

'Listen, Jess, why don't you go back to the cell? Keep yourself in there – I have a feeling that Lucas is up to no good.'

Worried, Jessie gave a quick glance to Lucas, who saw her looking and blew a kiss, causing Jessie to turn away quickly. 'Do you think it's about me?'

Franny shook her head. 'No, I think she's got another iron in the fire. But you don't want to be caught up in anything if it does kick off, so get gone.'

Tucking her hair behind her ears, Jessie asked, 'What about you? Will you be all right?'

Franny smiled, touched by the concern. 'I'm still standing, ain't I? I've looked after myself this long, so I'm sure I'll be fine. Now go.'

Without saying another word, Jessie turned to leave, and as she disappeared out of the shower rooms, Lucas called over to Franny, 'I see your bitch has walked out on you.'

Franny's eyes darkened and she smirked. 'No, I don't think so; you're still here ain't you?'

Although Lucas didn't make a move, she drew her finger threateningly across her own throat. 'I've already warned you, that mouth will get the better of you.'

'And I've already told you, come at me anytime, Lucas, and I'll be waiting.'

Lucas snorted in disgust. 'Another day, pet, I've got a different fish to fry today.'

As Lucas finished her sentence, Emma, oblivious to the conversation, stepped out of the shower. She looked from Christine to Franny, and walked towards her, giving her a small smile.

'Hey, Fran, you okay?'

As coldly as she'd spoken to Lucas, Franny answered, 'Why do you ask? You think I should have a problem?'

Taken aback, Emma muttered, 'I . . . I . . . I was just asking . . . Franny, have I done something to offend you?'

Franny, who stood taller than Emma, looked down on

290

her. 'I don't know, have you? Which reminds me, how was your meeting with the deputy governor?'

Before Emma could answer, Christine Lucas and her cronies charged forward, grabbing hold of Emma, dragging her backwards.

Jeering, they pushed her about, shoving her against the wall, kicking her to the floor as Emma slipped on the wet tiles and screamed in fright.

Scrambling away, Emma – to the shouts of the other women – desperately tried to make her way towards Franny, who stood and watched as a tall black woman got to Emma first.

Putting her in a headlock the woman dragged her back to Lucas who proceeded to grab a handful of Emma's hair and pull her head up, making Emma look her directly in the eye.

'A little birdie has told me something. They've told me what you've been up to.'

Terrified, Emma's voice was almost inaudible. 'I haven't done anything, I haven't done anything.' Lucas's fist came flying at Emma's face. She screamed in pain and a huge, angry welt rose up on her cheek. As Lucas was about to hit Emma again, Franny stepped in.

'That's enough. Leave her now.'

Christine did a double take. 'Howay, you seem to like taking on other people's fights. This isn't anything to do with you, Doyle.'

Franny stared, her gaze not wavering as Emma began to cry. 'Maybe not, but let's at least hear what she's got to say.'

Christine looked around then nodded, more to herself than to anyone else. She then turned her attention to the woman who was holding Emma down and said, 'Let her go.'

The woman released Emma and pushed her down on the ground, leaving her to curl up on the wet tiles with the other women circling her.

'I'll do the talking,' said Franny looking at Lucas.

Lucas sneered but didn't answer and moved slightly away with her cronies as Franny knelt down to Emma. 'I guess you know why we've got a problem with you. We're all a bit worried about what we've heard . . . I'm not siding with Lucas, I just need to know for myself if it's true.' Franny reached for Emma and she put her hand on her chin, lifting up Emma's head to force her to look up.

'I don't know what you're talking about.'

Franny gazed at Emma, staring at the angry scar that took up half her face. She saw the fear in her eyes and for some reason it stopped her from going in hard. 'Come on, Emma. Look around you – the game's up, darlin'. It'll be easier if you tell *me* the truth rather than have me hand you over to Lucas for her to get it out of you.'

Emma gasped, her eyes quickly glancing at Lucas. 'Please, don't. I'm not sure what I've done, but I thought we were friends.'

Franny put her face almost close enough to touch Emma's. She whispered, a bemused tone coating her words. 'Friends? I'm banged up in a cell with you, that's all. No more, no less. I don't do friends, least of all people like you.' Franny stopped speaking and she was surprised to see a look of hurt in Emma's eyes.

'People like me?'

'Oh come on, Em, you're trying my patience here. You know exactly what I'm talking about. Like I say, you're better to tell me than Lucas getting hold of you . . . Didn't you see what she did to Jessie?'

Lucas, overhearing what Franny was saying, cackled. 'I'll be glad to show you if you want, pet.'

Franny snarled at Lucas before dropping her hold on Emma's face. 'Shut it, Lucas. I said I'm dealing with this.'

'Well from where I'm standing you don't look like you're doing a good job. Howay, just get it over with and slash her face – that will make her start talking and you'll be doing her a favour. It'll match the scar she's already got.'

Franny stood up and walked across to Lucas. 'Listen, nobody's going to touch her. Not now anyway.'

'Not sure if we can agree to that, can we, girls?' Lucas looked across at her cronies who grinned, waiting for the nod to attack.

Glancing back across at Emma, who still sat frightened on the floor, Franny – not understanding why she felt sorry for her – said, 'Give me ten minutes and if I haven't got anything out of her, then I'll throw her to your dogs. How about that?'

With her mouth open, Lucas coughed then absentmindedly wiped the phlegm off her chin as Franny turned her face away in disgust. 'Why would I do that when I can just get my girls here to sort her out?'

Hating having to negotiate with Lucas, Franny chewed on her lip a moment, getting her temper into check before coolly saying, 'Because, if you beat her senseless, Christine, she's likely to tell you anything you want to hear and it won't necessarily be the truth. But it's down to you of course. I want to get to the bottom of this just as much as you do but I'm interested in the truth, nothing else. Don't forget I've spent a few days locked up with her – she's more likely to talk to me than you.'

Franny kept her gaze steady, watching Lucas weigh up what she'd just said. 'Fine, but you've got ten minutes, Doyle, and then it's my turn.' Christine winked and licked her lips and walked away, gesturing to her cronies to follow.

At the door, Christine turned and looked at Franny. 'I'll be just outside . . . waiting . . .'

50

The door closed and immediately Emma scrambled up and rushed to Franny. Desperate, she clung to her, holding and gripping her top as she trembled. 'Don't let her touch me! Please, don't let her touch me. *Please.*'

Franny held Emma's hands. 'Calm down. Calm the fuck down, Em!'

'I can't! I can't!'

'Stop, Emma! This ain't going to do you any good.'

But unable to stop, Emma continued to shake, and, knowing that Lucas was outside the door counting down the minutes, Franny grabbed Emma and dragged her towards the shower causing Emma to scream even more.

Holding on to a struggling Emma, Franny lifted her leg and used her foot to flick on the shower. The next minute, she threw Emma under the cold water and as Emma spluttered and gasped, Franny spoke to her firmly. 'Now listen to me, Emma, you need to calm down, as you know Christine is right outside waiting for me to go and give her answers. If you value your life, you'll start talking.'

'*Why* are you doing this to me? *Why* are you doing this?'

Emma tried to run out of the shower cubicle but, blocking her escape, Franny pushed Emma back under the cold water.

She tilted her head as she looked at Emma, who was now shivering and trembling but had finally stopped crying. 'I ain't doing anything, Emma – it's you who's come in here trying to find out what's going on. I have to admit, you were good; not many people can scam me, but you did, Em. And for some strange reason, even though you've tried to turn us over, I ain't looking for you to get hurt – but if you don't tell me, I can't protect you from Lucas.'

The look of genuine confusion and shock on Emma's face surprised Franny so much she flicked the shower off and listened closely to what Emma had to say.

'I don't know what you're talking about. I swear. I came in here because my husband set me up. I told you that before – and anything else I can't help you with.'

As Emma said the last part of the sentence, she looked away causing Franny to say, 'You ain't telling me the full truth are you? There's something else, I just know it.'

Dripping wet and still not looking at Franny, Emma shook her head. 'There isn't.'

'I don't believe you and if I don't believe you, Em, Lucas certainly won't.'

'I can't tell you what I don't know, and I really don't understand what you want me to say.'

Franny stared at the top of Emma's head. 'It's simple; I want to *understand* why there's a rumour going around that not only are you a copper's wife but you're also a plant.'

Emma's head shot up. She stared at Franny. 'That's not true, that's not true! That's crazy.'

'Problem is, these rumours don't just come from nowhere.'

Remembering what Officer Brown said about keeping her background a secret, Emma continued to deny all knowledge. 'Well, this one does.'

Franny stared at Emma sadly and then glanced pointedly at her watch. 'Em, I know you're lying – or at least I know you're not telling me everything. I'm not the bad guy here, but in less than five minutes, Lucas and her cronies are going to walk through that door. Is that what you want?'

With the look of a startled rabbit, Emma shook her head. 'Of course, I don't but I—'

Cutting in again, Franny said, 'Yeah, yeah, yeah, I've already heard it, you don't know anything about the rumours . . . Fine, Em, if that's the way you want it, but don't say I didn't warn you, babe.'

As Franny got up and started to walk towards the door, Emma shouted after her in a panic. 'Wait, no! Please, no! I'll tell you. But it's not what you think.'

Franny gazed at her coldly. 'Well that all depends what I'm thinking, doesn't it?'

Emma began to cry. 'Please, Franny, don't make this harder . . .'

'Just say it. Your tears won't help, and they certainly won't make me feel sorry for you. I've never liked a snake and I ain't going to start now.'

'But that's the point. You've got it all wrong. It's nothing like that. He did the dirty on me. He set me up; I'm only here because of that. Though I wasn't even supposed to come to this prison in the first place – or that's what they tell me. It's only because of overcrowding in Eastwood Park and Drake Hall, as well as someone messing up on the paperwork. But the point is they were waiting for the admin to come through to move me to Hi—'

Franny cut her off. 'I ain't looking for an A to Z of her Majesty's prisons, I just want answers, Em . . . *Is* your husband the Old Bill?'

Wringing her hands in her lap and keeping her eyes on the shower room door, Emma nodded. 'Yes . . . yes he is, but I hate him, you've no idea how much I hate him . . . He's an abusive cheat and a liar – and okay, yes, my drinking got out of control but it's only because of him and *her*. And I never, ever did what they say I did. I never tried to kill anyone. It wasn't even me driving.'

Franny pushed her against the wall. 'But you're still married to the Old Bill.'

Emma screamed and beat her fists against Franny's chest. 'And I wish I wasn't! Look at me, look at my face. You have no idea how much he hurt me! He hurt me, Franny, and I just want him dead! I just want him dead! And if I ever get out of here, I'm going to kill him. You hear me? Do you understand what I'm saying? I want him dead.'

Franny didn't move as Emma fell weeping against her shoulder. For a moment Franny stayed frozen – rigid and emotionless – then slowly, unexpectedly, she found herself putting her arms around Emma and holding her tightly. 'It's okay, Em. It's okay. Look, don't cry . . . I'm sorry okay; I don't want you to be upset. This place is hard enough already without us turning on each other.'

Emma looked up. 'But what about Lucas?'

Franny glanced at her watch. 'Look, I'll sort her, but you have to trust me on this.'

'I don't understand.'

Franny smiled warmly. 'You will.' And with that, Franny raised her fist and smashed Emma in the face with lightning speed, blacking her eye before bringing back her fist to strike Emma in the mouth.

Emma shrieked and held her face, crying so much she couldn't speak.

Moving Emma's hands away from her face, Franny gave her another smile and quickly gave Emma a hug. 'I'm sorry, Em, I had to do that. I've got to make it look realistic. I don't want them to go after you. Trust me, okay? I've got to make sure Lucas believes—'

Before Franny could finish her sentence, Lucas walked in followed by her cronies. She had a huge smirk on her face. 'Have we got our answer yet?' She stopped in her tracks as she saw Emma's bloody lip and her swollen and bruised black eye. 'I'm impressed, Doyle, I see you meant business. I wasn't sure for a minute; I thought you were all talk.'

Franny stood back and shrugged. 'Well it's not just you who can raise your fist. Difference is I don't need a band of bitches behind me.'

Lucas's cronies lurched forward towards Franny but Lucas held them back. 'Leave her, we're all on the same side.'

Franny shook her head. 'We're not, but I don't like snakes any more than you.'

Lucas chuckled, her Geordie accent dancing with amusement. 'You're a brazen bird, Franny Doyle. It's a shame we'll never be friends. Howay, you want us to take over?' Lucas nodded her head towards Emma.

'No. Turns out your source was wrong.'

'In what way?' Lucas frowned.

'Turns out Little Bo-Peep here ain't married to the Old Bill, she's married to some fucking watchdog. A security guard from over at Poplar. That's the problem with rumours; one minute you're married to a dustbin man, next thing you know people are saying you're with the getaway driver.'

'How do we know it's true?'

Franny shrugged casually. 'I'm going to get someone to check it out. She's given me the name of the place he works. If it turns out she's lying, then I'll be the first to let you know, because I don't like being made a mug of. So sorry to disappoint you, but there's no drama to be had here, Christine.'

Lucas stared at Emma and then at Franny before she shrugged and, without saying anything more, she sauntered out the showers, followed by her crew. Emma and Franny left a few minutes later.

In the corridor of the prison, Emma whispered in Franny's ear. 'Thank you, Franny. I owe you – and I tell you, if it's the last thing I do, I'm going to make sure my husband pays. I'm going to make sure the mighty *Detective Balantyne* gets what's coming to him.'

Suddenly, Franny pulled Emma into the nearest empty cell. She stared at her. 'What did you say?'

'I said I owe you and—'

Agitated, Franny urged, 'Not that, the name. The name of your husband. What did you say his name was?'

'Balantyne. Detective Tony Balantyne.'

51

Later on that Monday evening, Charlie opened the door. It was dark and he couldn't hear anything as he walked along the corridor of Vaughn's flat. He'd heard Shannon go out but he wasn't so sure about Vaughn, and yes, it was a risk, but what else was he supposed to do? He was hungry. Before she'd decided to try to kill him, Shannon had brought in a shopping bag of food, but he'd got through that, so the only option left to him was to find the kitchen and make his own food.

He chuckled at the thought of Shannon's face if she caught him naked in the kitchen. He had a good mind to take a bath as well, because even he could smell he needed one. And what was the point of making this place his home if he didn't treat it like one?

Scratching his large, sagging testicles, Charlie shuffled along the lengthy hallway, turning a corner to head towards the kitchen, which was situated on the far side of the sprawling apartment, but he stopped as he heard a noise coming from Vaughn's bedroom.

He listened again, then taking another step closer, he leant towards the door, which was slightly ajar. He smiled . . . Snoring. He could hear Vaughn snoring.

Still smiling to himself, an idea came to him and he crept very carefully into Vaughn's room, making his way towards the en suite. At the doorway, he glanced back over his shoulder quickly before heading into the bathroom.

Looking around, Charlie saw what he was after. He reached for the tube of toothpaste and popped off the top. Then with a huge grin on his face, he drew a love heart on the mirror with the words, *I love you*, written in the middle of it.

He laughed so much he broke wind and had to hold on to the sink to stop himself from stumbling about with laughter. But suddenly he heard the front door and he crept behind the black shower curtain as he heard Vaughn stir and call out very loudly, 'Where've you been, Shan? Shan? Shan?'

Having missed the bus from the prison, an exhausted Shannon walked into the darkened room. 'Hey, sorry I'm late.'

'I was worried. Where've you been?'

Shannon, seeing Vaughn resting on his bed, his broken face lit up by the moonlight, smiled, and lying she said, 'I . . . I just feel terrible about Mia. I just needed to go for a walk.'

Vaughn flinched as he smiled sadly. 'I've tried to get in

contact with Alfie again but it just keeps going to voicemail. I've got a good mind to go around and finish off what we started.'

'No! No!' Shannon sprang towards Vaughn on the bed and he looked at her strangely. 'I mean . . . what I mean is look at you. You're hurt. You could've been killed . . .'

'He's the one who's going to be dead, not me. Mark my words.'

Shannon looked at him wide-eyed. 'But it may not be him. What if it is you? I don't know what I'd do if . . . if anything happened to you.'

'Shan, you don't have to worry about me, I can look after myself.'

'But I do worry, cos I know you're worried. I heard you on the phone to Balantyne . . . I heard you say if Alfie found out he'd kill you.'

Annoyed, Vaughn pushed Shannon to the side as he got out of bed and walked across to the crystal decanters he kept on the bedside dresser. He poured himself a large whiskey, trying once again to push the fact that Shannon had robbed him out of his mind. 'Why are you listening to my conversations? Ain't anybody told you how fucking rude that is?'

'I didn't mean to, but it wasn't like you were keeping your voice down. I was upstairs in the games room watching TV when you were in the office. You had your door open.'

Knocking back the drink, Vaughn stared at her. 'Maybe if you didn't hang about out here all the time, instead of going into your room, then you wouldn't hear anything, would you? I wanted to say something before but I think it's odd. I mean if you don't like your bedroom just tell me. If you want to swap to one of the bigger ones, that's fine as well. Or we can even decorate and change the dining room into a bedroom. Just let me know, cos I don't know what's wrong and why you're hanging around like a lost dog.'

Feeling uneasy not for the first time that day, Shannon looked pained. She wanted to tell him everything. She wanted to tell him about Franny and about Charlie lying dead a few feet away, but she just didn't know how, and with the image of Charlie in her mind, she began to shake. 'I thought you didn't mind me being about. You said to treat this place like my own.'

'That's right, I did. And I mean it. But I can't understand why you're sleeping on the couch or even the other rooms when you've got a bedroom and a bit of privacy. Come on, Shan, help me out and tell me what's going on.'

'I just don't like sleeping in there . . . cos I'm getting nightmares, that's all.'

'Nightmares?'

She nodded and Vaughn's shoulders slumped. He hated to say it but Alfie had been right; the kid had come from the sort of background that he couldn't even imagine.

The abuse she had been through was horrific to think about, let alone live through. When it came down to it, she'd been amazing; she'd broken the cycle. When so many people he knew were still caught up in it, she'd escaped – from her past and from Charlie, and if she needed to sleep on the sofa, or disappear on walks, or even squirrel some money away to make her feel secure, so be it.

'Shan, I never knew. Why didn't you tell me?'

Hating lying to him even more than she was already and wishing she could just tell him the truth, Shannon shrugged. 'I dunno, I just feel better on the couch or crashing in the games room. I don't know why, but I do, and I thought you might think it's silly if I told you about the dreams. Like I was a baby.'

'Of course I don't. Fuck me, girl, I told you already, I'm proud of what you've achieved . . .' He trailed off, deciding not to add that he was disappointed in her for robbing from him because, whilst it did piss him off no end, it wasn't the end of the world – after all she certainly was a messed-up kid. 'Look, how about we go and get something to eat? We could go to that nice Italian on Greek Street, take our mind off what a shitty couple of days it's been.'

For the first time that day, Shannon felt safe, but it was short-lived as she felt her phone buzz in her pocket and saw a text from Franny, which read:

Change of plan, don't go and talk to Balantyne until
I speak to you. Come and see me on Wednesday.
Make sure you do, otherwise I'll get Alfie to pay a
visit to Vaughn and we'll see how much Vaughn
wants you then, once he knows about your secret
little habit.

Shannon's face paled and her hands shook, and she pushed the phone back into her pocket.

'Who was that from, Shan?'

She shrugged. 'No one . . . No one. It's a delivery message. I . . . I just texted Alfie earlier to ask how Mia was.'

Vaughn looked at Shannon sympathetically. 'You're not the only one who misses her . . . Look, let me just jump in the shower, and we'll hit the town, shall we?'

As Vaughn walked into his en-suite bathroom, Charlie stood naked, keeping very still behind the shower curtain. He peeked with interest through the small crack between the curtain and the grey-tiled wall and suddenly realised Vaughn was heading towards him.

Charlie breathed deeply, psyching himself up, waiting for the big showdown, excitement filling his body as he imagined what Vaughn would do when he found him there. Holding his breath he waited as Vaughn put his hand on the shower curtain, but suddenly he saw Vaughn catch sight of the mirror and freeze. Charlie watched with curiosity.

Shock crossed Vaughn's face as he saw the toothpaste heart on the mirror with the words, *I love you*, scrawled on it. He frowned and then shook his head, remembering what Alfie had said about Shannon having a crush on him.

He hadn't believed it but the evidence was right in front of him, and not only that, he had to admit it gave him a weird feeling, knowing that Shannon had come into his bathroom and written a message to him . . . It made him feel uncomfortable because, besides anything else, the last thing he wanted was to lead a kid like that on . . . *Fuck*.

Quickly, and angry with himself for being so stupid, Vaughn rubbed the toothpaste off the mirror before stomping back through to the bedroom. Maybe having

Shannon stay wasn't the cleverest thing he'd done. He thought he'd been helping her but perhaps all he'd done was put ideas into her head. Well, he was going to put a stop to it. Draw the line . . . Fuck, he had no idea what he was supposed to do in this situation. He wasn't sure if he was meant to be angry? Understanding? Cold towards her? Who knew?

Feeling completely out of his depth, he grabbed his jacket and headed for the door with Shannon following a few feet behind.

'That was quick, you ain't going to have a shower?'

With his embarrassment over the situation turning to anger, Vaughn decided acting uncaringly would be the way forward, because at least then she would soon go off him and think he was just an idiot. He snapped, putting his plan into action, 'No I ain't. I'm going out.'

'I thought we were going to the Italian?'

'Sorry, darlin', I've gone off the idea now . . . so I'll see you later.'

Like she had done with Alfie, Shannon ran after Vaughn. She grabbed him by his arm, wanting Vaughn to see how much she needed him to make her feel safe. 'Have I done something wrong?'

He turned to look at her, trying to figure out why he hadn't seen this coming. He hated being hard towards her, but he was certain being this way would snap her out of it and in the long run it would be doing her a favour. 'You haven't done anything, Shan, I just changed my mind . . . after all you're just a kid and I'm a grown man. I'm sure you can think of better ways to spend your Monday night. I know I can.'

Tears came to Shannon's eyes and Vaughn had to turn away to stop himself giving her a hug.

'But that's the thing, I couldn't think of anything better. I like your company, Vaughn.'

'Oh well, c'est la vie, as they say. I'm sure you'll find another way to spend your evening.'

At which point Vaughn, thinking he was doing the right thing, walked away, leaving Shannon fighting back tears, knowing exactly how she was going to spend her Monday night.

52

It was late as a scared and troubled Shannon made her way down the concrete stairs, and the busy streets of Chinatown had mostly become deserted, save for the few late clubbers and the old, drunken man at the corner of Gerrard Street, shouting at the top of his voice to no one in particular.

Still upset from earlier, Shannon knocked on the basement door but it was a few minutes until one of Huang's men opened it.

'Hello, Shannon, I knew we'd see you again. Couldn't keep away. Come on in . . . Don't look so hesitant, Mr Huang will be delighted to see you.'

Shannon hurried inside and followed the man to where Huang sat, playing, as he always did, a game of poker.

Putting down his handful of cards, he nodded, peering at her over his rimless glasses. 'This is a nice surprise.'

Sounding distressed, Shannon shook as she blurted out the words she never thought she'd have to say again. 'I ain't got any money, but if you want me to work for you I will. I'll do anything. I just need a hit.'

Huang nodded and observed her for a moment before gesturing to a large man in his early seventies, who had a rotund, red nose, a huge stomach bulging over his ill-fitted jeans and was sweating profusely.

'That gentleman over there has been waiting for one of the other girls to finish with their client. But seeing as you're here and so willing – and from what I remember you were good at your job – why don't you go over and pleasure him?'

'And you'll give me what I want?'

Again, Huang nodded. He went into his pocket and placed a rock of crack cocaine on the table. 'Yours for the taking, like it always was when Charlie left you without money.'

Shannon reached out for it but Huang slammed his hand across it and smiled a sickly smile.

'Yours for the taking *after* you've done what you need to do . . . He's waiting.'

Slowly Shannon turned and, feeling numb and like everything was beginning to spin out of control, she walked towards the man who began to fumble with his belt.

As she knelt down in front of him, as she'd done with thousands of men before, she watched him unzip his trousers pulling out his swollen penis and she shuddered, choking back her tears as she opened her mouth in anticipation. And, not for the first time in her life, she wanted to forget who she was and the feeling that no one could ever love her.

It was nearing midnight and Balantyne stood in the hospital room and shook his head as he stared down at Claire coldly. 'That's ridiculous, Claire, nothing like that happened.'

'But I *remember* there was an argument, and you said you were going to take Emma home.'

Balantyne's face turned red. 'No, you *think* you remember, that's a different thing entirely.'

Claire stared at Balantyne. 'But I'm so sure about it. I can remember—'

Balantyne interrupted, grabbing Claire's hand hard. A little too hard for comfort. 'Do you know what's going to happen if you carry on saying things like that? I'll tell you, shall I? People are going to start believing you, and then where will that leave me?'

Claire looked down at her hand. She eyed him strangely. 'Tony, you're hurting me.'

Balantyne gave a tight smile as he let go. 'Am I? I didn't realise. You must be feeling sensitive . . . I obviously don't know my own strength.'

Rubbing her hand, Claire gave Balantyne a small smile back but there was a flash of doubt in her eyes. 'It's fine, don't worry about it . . . Look, are you sure that you didn't say anything to Emma about driving her home? It's just so clear in my head.'

Balantyne slammed down his hand on the table, knocking the jug of water onto the floor. He raised his voice, his whole body shaking as he pointed at her. 'I don't know if it's your bloody hormones or you're just deliberately trying to be difficult, but you need to stop this talk, Claire. I told you what happened and that's all there is to it. Continue like this and you'll be sorry.'

Shocked by Balantyne's outburst, Claire turned her head away from him, staring out of the hospital window, which looked out over the field of the nearby cricket ground. Uneasily she said, 'What's going on, Tony?'

Suddenly realising what he was doing, Balantyne rushed around to the other side of the hospital bed. 'Nothing, nothing. I didn't mean it the way it sounded. What I meant was, you don't want people to start questioning either mine or your judgement. Think of your job. You need to look like you're still as sharp as you were before.'

'I know, but if—'

'If nothing, Claire. What I told you about the accident is how it happened. I don't know why you keep on thinking about it.'

'I just keep having these flashbacks.'

Trying to keep his temper in check, Balantyne rubbed his temples before clenching his fists together. He hissed through his teeth, 'There you go again. I don't need this. I'm under enough pressure already without you making up stories in your head . . . I've got Emma to worry about and you, and then there's work. I even had a call from that Mulligan girl – you know, the one who gave the statement against Doyle. She left a message telling me to call her back, but she's got her phone turned off. I can't get through . . .' He suddenly stopped and gave an apologetic smile. 'Sorry, you don't want to hear my rant do you? The point is, it's all getting a bit much – but of course I've got no right to take any of this out on you.'

The room fell into a strained silence, save for the monitors, which beeped rhythmically in the background. Eventually, Claire nodded. 'I understand, and you've been so good to me. You've been here day and night. Look, why don't you go home and rest? Go on, it'll be fine.'

Feeling uneasy and agitated, Tony tried to keep his voice light. 'If you're sure? Maybe I could do with some sleep.'

'I am, now go . . . and, Tony? You're right, I can't trust my memory.'

Ten minutes later and certain that Balantyne had left the hospital, Claire reached for her phone and called a number. It rang twice before it was answered.

'Hello, is that Officer Gibbs? This is Inspector Claire Martin. I was wondering if you could come over and talk to me . . . I wanted to have a chat to you about the accident again; I think I remember something else. I'd appreciate it if you didn't say anything – especially not to Detective Balantyne . . . For the time being I want to keep this between ourselves.'

53

It was Tuesday morning and Alfie sat staring at Franny across the prison table. He didn't want to be there and his mood was only made worse by the fact he hadn't had a good night's sleep. In truth, he hadn't had one for the past couple of days.

Mia had been grizzly and although Julie had offered to stay, he wanted to be the one who was there for her when she went to sleep and when she woke up – and boy didn't she just constantly wake up.

It was strange though – even after this short space of time, he wouldn't have it any other way. He wouldn't have Mia with anyone else now.

Though that hadn't stopped every single box in his head opening up. All he could do was think of Bree and everything that had happened to get them all where they now found themselves. And, yes, it was tempting to hand the reins over to Julie for the night and take a bottle of whiskey to bed along with a couple of grams of coke and a hooker too. But he couldn't. He wouldn't. And the anger he felt today towards both Franny and Bree sat on his shoulders like a raging monster.

'Tell me how Mia is. I know you said on the phone Vaughn kicked off when you went to get her, but how is she?' Franny smiled at Alfie, her face lighting up as she thought about Mia.

Unlike Franny's face, Alfie's certainly didn't light up; only a scowl appeared. 'You really are something else. How the fuck do you think she is? She's been pulled from the place and people she knows . . .' Then sounding like a worried parent he added, 'And on top of that I think she's teething.'

'But you're coping?'

Incredulously, Alfie said, 'It's a bit late to worry about that now, ain't it? And let's say I wasn't coping. What then? You want me to take her back? What string are you going to pull now? Cos I'm only the fucking puppet, ain't I?'

Franny's eyes narrowed. 'You're lucky I'm helping you.' Then lying through her teeth she continued to say, 'I paid Huang to back off, but he'll only do that for so long because he wants what you owe him. So yes, Alfie, I am pulling the strings – because I'm helping you and don't you forget that.'

Alfie slammed down his plastic cup of water. 'Let's have it right, Fran, I'm the one helping you because if I walk away, you're going to rot in here.'

'If you walk away, you're a dead man.'

Alfie clenched his jaw. He wanted to throttle her; he

wanted to wring the smugness out of her. 'You'd like that wouldn't you?'

'Grow up, Alf, this will help both of us. I'm innocent and you're desperate for three quarters of a million quid and counting.'

Alfie stared at her for a moment. 'Oh I'm desperate, all right, but let me tell you something: you ain't innocent. Far from it. It's like you're playing a game of chess with us all. One day, Fran, you'll really get yours. Be careful.'

Franny leant towards Alfie and sensually stroked his face. She smiled as she whispered, 'I hope that's not a threat, Alfie, because if it is, that would be very silly of you.'

Wanting to but unable to hate the fact that Franny was touching him, Alfie sneered. 'Now who's threatening?'

'Oh I am, Alfie, and I'm warning you that I have another player in the game now and I've got big plans for them.'

As Franny's fingers caressed his neck, Alfie stopped her, grabbing hold of her hand. 'Who are you talking about?'

'Work it out.'

Seeing one of the prison officers looking across, Alfie brought his voice down even lower than it already was – though he kept it firm. 'I hope you're not talking about Shannon.'

'Who else?'

'I ain't saying I'm her biggest fan after her giving that statement, but we both know that Vaughn was behind it. So, once she retracts it, keep away, Fran. You hear me?'

'Oh I've got bigger plans than that for her.'

Alfie shook his head. 'For fuck's sake, she's a kid. She's sixteen, and she's been used enough in her life without you

317

doing the same. You know as well as I do the kind of life she led with Charlie. I'm just pleased he's gone AWOL – means he can't hurt her anymore, which doesn't mean that *you* need to step into his shoes.'

'Then she should've thought about that when she decided to go up against me.'

'Fran, have you heard yourself? What happened to you?'

Franny sat back in her chair, taking a sip of her coffee. 'You sound like a broken record, Alf. Ain't nothing happened to me. This is who I am, especially if I'm cornered. What do you expect me to do?'

'I expect you to leave Shannon alone. I won't let you hurt her.'

Ignoring him, Franny changed the subject. 'Tell me more about Mia.'

'I *said*, leave her alone.'

Franny's eyes darkened. 'Keep out of it, Alfie. You really think I'm just going to sit back in this place when I've done nothing wrong? I'll do what I have to and if you're wise, *you'll* do what *you* have to.'

Everything in Alfie told him to get up and leave, but how could he? How could he just tell Franny to go to hell? If he backed out, Huang would have him buried alive before the end of the day. That wasn't even an option, because now he had someone apart from himself to think of . . . Mia . . . His daughter.

'I hate you, you know that, Fran?'

Franny gazed at Alfie. Even though his face was battered and bruised, he was still so strikingly handsome. She smirked. 'But that's the thing, Alf, you don't hate me. You

318

want to, but I'm in your head and your heart, so you might as well stop fighting it.'

Incensed not only by Franny's arrogance but by the fact that what she was saying was true, Alfie growled, 'Just tell me what you want me to do now because the sooner this is over with, the quicker I can get on with my life.'

Taking another sip of her coffee, Franny continued to stare at Alfie, her big brown eyes gazing intently at him. 'There's a safe deposit box in a jeweller's, the diamond shop on the corner of Hatton Garden. As long as you've got the pass card – which you'll find at my house in the bedroom safe – and the PIN, you'll be able to access the room and deposit box. The deposit box has a PIN code itself; that one is your date of birth.'

Alfie shook his head at the irony as he listened to Franny.

'Anyway, you'll find what you need in the box. You'll know what to do with it. Let me know when it's done.'

'What's done? For fuck's sake, Fran, you're speaking in riddles.'

Franny began to stand up but she stopped and leant over, kissing Alfie gently on his lips. 'You'll know what I mean when you see it.' Smiling she paused and knowing she had already paid Huang but needing to keep Alfie thinking she hadn't, Franny added, 'I'll make sure that Huang gets his money once you've done this. Then you're a free man and hopefully, I will be free as well . . . But don't mess up, Alf, otherwise we're all in big, big trouble.'

54

Having been to Franny's to pick up the pass card, Alfie walked through Leather Lane Market, pushing his way through the crowds of city workers and tourists who were lining up outside the various cafés and stalls to get their lunch. He barged past the market traders who were chatting and laughing with each other as he made his way to Hatton Garden.

Nearing the corner he felt his phone buzz. Sighing, Alfie pulled out his mobile and saw that it was Vaughn *again*. He had no wish to speak to him and had only half listened to the dozens of angry voicemails he'd left, which veered between asking about Mia and threatening to come around to shoot him.

Tucking his phone back in his pocket, Alfie arrived at the diamond shop. The place reminded Alfie of the old-fashioned porn shops that had once taken centre stage in

Soho; a black shop awning with blacked-out windows and a black door with a camera and buzzer entrance.

Not knowing quite why he was feeling so uneasy, Alfie straightened his clothes and took a deep breath before pressing the buzzer.

The door clicked open, allowing Alfie into the store. There were four – no, five – security guards standing around the empty room and Alfie suspected the diamonds were all kept in the vault or various safes throughout the building.

He shivered slightly; the air conditioning had been turned up slightly higher than it needed to be, causing a chill to sit in the air.

As Alfie walked further into the room, he could hear his footsteps tapping on the marble floor and echoing around the silent chamber.

'Can I help you, sir?' A small Jewish man, dressed in an expensive suit, appeared at the entrance of a door on the far side of the room. He smiled, but Alfie could see it wasn't reaching his eyes.

'Yeah, mate, I've come to get something out of a safe deposit box.'

The man looked Alfie up and down. 'Certainly, sir, if you'll come this way.'

Without waiting for Alfie to say anything else, the man turned and went back the way he'd come, and Alfie found himself having to jog down a long white corridor to catch up.

At the end of the corridor the man gestured to an electronic entrance door. 'If you swipe your pass card and put in your PIN code, it will give you access to the safe deposit room. Once you're in there, there's another swipe machine. If you swipe or touch your card again, your safety box locker will ping open.'

'A bit like the Amazon pick-up lockers then.' Alfie winked.

The man, clearly not amused, simply said, 'Quite.' And with that he left Alfie to enter the room.

The safe deposit box room was even chillier than the shop had been. It was tiled floor to ceiling with large, cream marble slabs, along with row upon row of variously sized silver lockers. The only thing that stood in the room was a small table in the centre.

Not wanting to wind himself up, Alfie tried not to think of Franny coming here along with all the secrets and lies she'd hidden from him, but feeling the familiar rush of anger, Alfie slammed the pass card against the swipe machine on the wall.

Immediately one of the silver lockers popped open, revealing a safe deposit box. He walked across to it and pulled it out, placing it on the table, not knowing what to expect.

The box itself had a PIN pad and Alfie, with his heart racing and feeling suddenly hot despite the chill in the room, punched in, as Franny had said, his own date of birth.

The box sprung open and Alfie's face turned into a picture of horror as he pulled out a pair of gloves from his pocket, not wanting to touch the items he recognised only too well.

There was a phone.

There was a wallet.

There was a necklace with an engraving on the back. All

322

items he'd bought for Bree. All items covered in blood – and Alfie knew it was Bree's blood.

A wave of nausea overcame him and he swallowed down the bile as he held on to the table. He squeezed his eyes shut, incensed with rage, before he dragged out his phone, and seeing he still had signal, he dialled a familiar number.

On the tenth ring it was answered and speaking in a loud whisper, Alfie snarled down the phone, 'You sick bitch, what the hell do you think you're playing at?'

'I take it you found it all right.'

'What the fuck is this all about? You're warped.'

From inside her prison cell, Franny spoke quietly, aware the prison officers were milling along the corridor. 'No, Alfie, I'm sensible.'

'Sensible? What the fuck is wrong with you? These are Bree's things.'

Drily, Franny answered, 'That's very astute of you, but what's your point, Alf?'

Not knowing if he was hurt, upset, angry or a mixture of all three, Alfie rubbed his face, sweat dripping down his neck. 'Doesn't it bother you? Doesn't it bother you that these are her things?'

'No, Alfie, she's dead. She won't be needing them . . . however, I will.'

'Oh my God! Oh my God, it's like these are trophies to you. Kill Bree and keep the memorabilia.'

Shutting down any kind of emotion, Franny said, 'Alf, I didn't kill her.'

'You may as well have done. She'd be alive if you hadn't hidden her away.'

'Well we'll never know, will we? And as for trophies, you need to remember who we are and the world we live in. This is just part of it, so put away any kind of sentimentality, Alfie. I don't have to tell you what needs to be done . . .'

And with that Franny put down the phone leaving Alfie alone in the room with the blood-covered necklace, the necklace *he'd* given Bree on the day he first told her he loved her.

55

On the other side of London, Officer Gibbs sat by Claire, taking notes and asking dozens of questions. 'So you're saying that there was an argument and Detective Balantyne put Mrs Balantyne in the car?'

'Yes, I'm sure of it.'

Officer Gibbs frowned. 'But Detective Balantyne didn't mention any kind of argument like that. In fact he said once Mrs Balantyne had thrown the stone through the back of the car, almost straight away she jumped into the driver's seat and . . .'

Claire, now able to move about, sat up. She put her hand up in the air. 'Stop, stop, something else is coming back to me. Just before Tony – I mean Detective Balantyne – said that, he asked me to stay and wait for him in the lay-by and . . . oh my God, oh my God . . . I . . . I remember now, it was . . .'

'Hi, you all right?' Balantyne put his head around the door of the hospital room and smiled, but his smile faded when he saw Officer Gibbs. 'What's going on, Claire?'

Shocked to see Balantyne, Claire glanced quickly at Gibbs.

'Claire, I said what's going on?' Not getting any answers, Balantyne then turned to Gibbs. 'Officer, would you mind telling me what's going on?'

'We're just going over the accident.'

Balantyne pulled a face. 'I've already told you she's not up to questioning. So I'd appreciate it if you left.'

'She asked me to come, sir.'

Balantyne turned back to Claire, a puzzled look on his face. 'Is that true?'

'Yes but, it was . . . it was only . . .' She trailed off as Balantyne glared at her. Then, turning once again to Officer Gibbs, Balantyne spoke in a cloying manner. 'Why don't I see you out? I think it's best you came back another day.'

Officer Gibbs, unsure quite what to do, looked across at Claire, who nodded. 'It's fine, I'll call you . . .'

Balantyne followed the officer into the busy corridor of the hospital and proceeded to walk with him. 'I'll see you out.'

Gibbs frowned, uneasy. 'It's fine, sir, I know my way out.'

Balantyne patted Gibbs on his back. 'It's no problem at all. After all it's good to have a chat. You know how it is, you see people around the office and you never get a chance to talk to them properly. We could even call this our bonding session.' Balantyne laughed, a laugh that sounded forced and unnatural to Gibbs.

Now even more uncomfortable, the officer nodded. 'Yes, sir, we could call it that.'

They walked on in silence.

At the end of the long corridor, Balantyne pressed the button for the ground floor, watching the lift's lights sequence down towards their floor. Eventually and without looking at Gibbs, Balantyne spoke. 'So, what did she say?'

'I'm sorry, sir, you know I can't disclose that.'

'So she did say *something*?'

Gibbs looked at Balantyne, though Balantyne still didn't turn his head. 'I never said that, sir, I never said anything.'

'You might as well have done.'

Gibbs started stuttering. 'I . . . I . . .'

Playing to the officer's ego, Balantyne said, 'Look, Gibbs. Can I trust you?'

'Of course, sir.'

It was at this point that Balantyne faced him and smiled. 'What I say is totally off record, you understand?'

Eagerly, Gibbs said, 'Yes, sir, absolutely.'

'Good. Because if this went any further . . . well, it's her job. No one wants to think this accident has affected her ability to do it.'

Puzzled, Gibbs said, 'I'm not following you, sir.'

'The fact is, Gibbs, Inspector Martin's memory isn't what it seems to be. You can't rely on what she says. Her moods are all over the place, probably because of the brain injury, and she's angry and frustrated by it and . . . Gosh, how do I put this without it sounding like I'm betraying her . . .?'

'Sir, it's fine. This won't go any further.'

Nodding as his eyes followed a group of doctors about

to go about their ward round, Balantyne brought down his voice. 'She asked me to fill in the blanks. As in, she didn't want people to think she can't remember things, so she asked me to help her.'

'Sir?'

'When you asked her questions about the accident, she was going to wait to answer them until she checked the details with me. Once she knew them, she was going to come back to you and make it seem like *she'd* actually remembered the details. Obviously, I said I wouldn't be part of anything like that . . . It somehow seemed dishonest.'

Gullible, Gibbs nodded. 'Absolutely . . . But if that's the case, if the truth is she can't really remember, then why did she call me?'

Balantyne feigned a sad smile. 'You know how stubborn the Inspector can be. I guess, seeing as I wouldn't help her, she thought she'd try to remember on her own. It must be frustrating for her, you know, not having a memory, but at the same time she's desperate to help and show due diligence . . . Please don't hold it against her, will you? I hope she hasn't said anything to compromise her integrity?'

Gibbs looked around before he pulled out his notebook. Flicking through it, he shrugged. 'She didn't say anything really, sir. Nothing new . . . apart from she did mention something about how she remembers you volunteering to drive Mrs Balantyne home. It was a bit vague really.'

Balantyne nodded. 'Well that's ridiculous – it never happened. As I told you before, sadly it was my wife driving. In some ways I wish it had been me . . . Look, I think perhaps it would be best if you could leave your questioning

328

for a few weeks, let her mind settle. Perhaps her memory will be back by then. Otherwise the whole situation becomes awkward and ultimately she looks rather foolish. I wouldn't want that. I don't think any of us would.'

As the lift finally arrived, Gibbs stepped back to let people out and said, 'I'm sure Inspector Martin will appreciate your loyalty, sir, and of course, I'll make sure that her position won't be compromised.'

'Thank you, Gibbs.'

As Officer Gibbs stepped into the lift he smiled. 'Inspector Martin's lucky to have you on her side, sir.'

Balantyne raised his hand and kept it raised long after the lift had closed. A sneer appeared on his face and he smiled to himself at the idea that finally he had something in common with Franny Doyle . . . He had been betrayed.

He hated betrayal, especially when it came from those closest to him. How many times had he warned her? How many times had he said to her to keep her mouth shut? But no, Claire had to play good cop, bad fucking cop, thinking that she had to go around interfering. Whatever happened to loyalty? Why the obsession to remember things that could put a bomb under their new life? Well, if she didn't care about their future why should he?

As he stood by the lift he suddenly realised the only person he should think about was himself. And of course, what he had to do now was stop Claire talking anymore . . .

56

As Officer Gibbs was leaving the hospital, Charlie lay back naked on the bed in Shannon's bedroom, enjoying the salami and bottle of cola he'd found in the fridge. He grinned at the teenage girl on girl action he was watching on Shannon's iPad, suspecting the girls were no older than fourteen, fifteen at the most. Almost too old for him.

Suddenly, Charlie sat up, breaking his thoughts. He was sure he'd heard something . . . He paused the video and listened again, straining to hear, but this time there was only silence. Maybe it was just the cleaners outside in the main hallway.

Frowning, he pressed play and began to settle back down to continue to watch the porn from the illegal site one of his friends ran. But within a few seconds, Charlie paused the movie again, certain this time he *really* had heard something . . . Yes, there was definitely someone in the hallway.

Shit, Vaughn must've come back earlier than he usually did on a Tuesday night.

He looked at the door, realising he hadn't locked it, and he glanced around quickly before scuttling off the bed, waddling as fast as he could towards the large inbuilt wardrobes.

Wanting to hide, he tried to step inside them but the sheer amount of clothes hanging up and shoeboxes stacked neatly at the back made it impossible to tuck himself inside and close the doors.

A mixture of excitement and panic rushed through him as he looked around for another hiding spot. He hurried to the far side of the room, ruling out trying to get under the bed frame again, it having collapsed when he'd been lying on the bed yesterday evening.

Hearing the footsteps coming nearer, Charlie rushed behind the silver and gold hand-painted bedroom screen, but standing almost as tall, Charlie was forced to sit down. He began to listen and watch.

Seeing a shadow in the hallway through the crack of the door, Charlie kept still, intrigued to see Vaughn walking into Shannon's room and looking around. Charlie held his breath and his heart beat faster, and suddenly he realised it wasn't Vaughn at all . . . it was Alfie.

What the hell was Alfie doing in the flat? Perhaps he'd come to take the rest of Mia's things when Vaughn was out; he couldn't imagine after the fight Vaughn and Alfie had gotten into the other night, that Alfie would be welcome. Or perhaps he'd come to . . . The thought froze in Charlie's mind as he watched Alfie begin to open wardrobes and drawers. What *was* he doing? Charlie had no idea and, still breathing as quietly as he could, he stayed absolutely still as he continued to watch.

Alfie scrunched up his face as he searched the room. The place was a pigsty and it stunk, but if Shannon was back on the crack then the mess didn't surprise him. She wouldn't be caring about anything other than getting high. This was something else, though. It was filthy and . . . 'Jesus . . .' Alfie spoke out loud and jumped back, putting his arm over his nose and mouth. He stared in horror at the bucket in the corner: it was full of what looked – and certainly smelt – like shit. He shook his head unable to believe that anyone would want to live like this.

He doubted that Vaughn had been inside her room and seen this mess, so it surprised him that she'd left her bedroom door unlocked. But then, perhaps she was beyond caring, beyond noticing even. He screwed up his face again as he looked at the bed sheet covered in dried blood.

The whole place was depressing and a sadness filled him when he thought of how loved Mia had been in her few short months of life compared to how little Shannon had been loved in her entire life.

Deciding he didn't want to be in her room any longer, Alfie made for the door, but something caught his eye. He walked to the bed and saw that tucked down by the side of the mattress was a watch and a bundle of money. No, two bundles of money. Vaughn's money.

He stared at it and, for a split second, he thought about taking it just to piss Vaughn off. But then he realised he wouldn't be hurting Vaughn, it'd be Shannon. He had no doubt if Shannon continued the way she was, she'd be out on her ear before long and then she'd certainly need a few notes in her pocket.

And with that thought, choosing to leave it for her, Alfie began to move away, but he frowned as he noticed the iPad and the kind of movie it was paused on. He picked it up and for a moment he continued to stare at it before, confused and not knowing why Shannon would watch that kind of stuff, he threw it back down on the bed.

As he moved into the hallway again, he checked his watch. He still had time. It was Thursday and he knew Vaughn would be at the club he co-owned until late. As for Shannon, he'd had someone follow her to make sure that they could keep tabs on where she was; the last thing he needed was her coming back unexpectedly.

He walked towards the room opposite, noticing how silent the whole place was and that in the air there held the heavy scent of lilies from the vase of flowers on the table.

Standing in the entrance of one of the two lounges of the apartment, not seeing Charlie who was now watching him through the crack of Shannon's bedroom door, Alfie made his way into the room.

From where Charlie was, he could just see Alfie pulling something out of his pocket before he moved near the large leather couch, turning the whole thing on its back and staying there for a couple of minutes before righting it and walking out of the lounge.

Losing sight of him, Charlie heard nothing for a long

while. Eventually, the sound of the front door opening and closing signalled to him that Alfie was gone. Breathing out a sigh of relief, Charlie frowned. He had no idea what Alfie had been doing, but there was only one way to find out.

Still completely naked, Charlie rushed out of Shannon's room and across to the lounge. He looked around the minimally decorated room before making his way across to the sofa where Alfie had stood only minutes before.

What was it that Alfie had come for? What did he want from Vaughn?

Absentmindedly, Charlie scratched his head. What was it that Vaughn would've hidden here for Alfie to want to break in? People like Vaughn didn't keep things in their flat, not stuff that might incriminate them or be of interest to others.

Charlie put his hand down the back of the sofa, feeling along the cushions. He scowled but then carefully he pushed the sofa backwards as he'd seen Alfie do.

He gazed at the bottom of the couch, looking at the stapled-down black fabric, and at the top corner, Charlie saw what he was looking for.

The corner fabric had been tampered with and Charlie carefully peeled it back. He put his hand in the hollow of the couch and immediately felt something there. Carefully pulling, Charlie dragged it out of the settee. He quickly glanced at the package and saw it had been what Alfie had pulled out from his pocket. Then, without stopping to scrutinise the contents, Charlie quickly placed the couch back down and hurried back to Shannon's bedroom, locking the door behind him.

334

He sat on the bed and stared at the white plastic bag, quickly looking inside it. 'Well, well, well . . .' He smiled as he pulled out the contents of the bag. A phone, a wallet and a necklace – and they were all covered in dried blood.

He picked up the heart-shaped necklace and turned it around, looking at the engraving on the back. It simply read, *To Bree with love. Alfie.*

57

On Wednesday morning, trying to stop herself from throwing up, Shannon sat at the table opposite Franny and a woman she'd never seen before in her life. Not that who the woman was concerned her right at that moment; the only thing that bothered her was how she was feeling, and that was ill.

She'd gone in heavy last night; off the top of her head she couldn't remember how many rocks of crack she'd actually had. The night was a blur, which she was thankful for – it being a mixture of trying to chase the high of the first hit to giving countless blow jobs and having rough sex with men who were old enough to be her grandfather.

But now she was paying for it. She felt ill and shaky and sore. She hadn't bothered going home; she didn't see the point. Mia wasn't there and Vaughn hadn't seemed to want her about and besides her uncle's body was probably beginning to smell by now, so it was basically all over for her anyway.

'You look a fucking mess. I see that you've been on that shit again.'

Shannon wanted to cry as she stared at Franny, but instead she bit down on her lip to stop herself and simply shrugged. 'My life, I can do what I like.'

'No, you can't, because I've got something that I need you to do and I don't want that crap you like to take messing up any of my plans. Do you understand?'

Shannon didn't say anything, causing Franny to lean forward on her chair and grasp hold of Shannon's hand. 'I said, *do you understand*? This ain't a joke, I don't want any mistakes.'

Sullenly, Shannon sniffed. 'I'm here ain't I?'

Staring coldly at Shannon, Franny shook her head. 'No that ain't good enough, because if you do mess this up, Shan, I'll know why. I'll know that you were smoking that crap instead of doing what I asked you. And that means not only will I tell Vaughn what you've been up to, I'll be sending someone after you, Shan, because if my life's going to end then so will yours.'

Feeling the hatred brew up inside her, Shannon gazed at the woman sitting next to Franny.

'What's she got to do with it?'

Slowly, Franny said, 'This is Emma and she's going to help us with Balantyne. Let's just say she knows him rather well.'

Puzzled, Shannon said, 'What happened to just retracting my statement?'

'Like I said on my text, change of plan. You'll have more fun with this one.'

Emma glanced at Franny, keeping her head down in the busy visitors' room so prison staff wouldn't notice she'd slipped across to join the conversation, leaving her solicitor on his own. As she turned her head, Shannon noticed the scar on her face.

'What's in it for you?' Shannon asked her.

Emma gave a half smile. 'He's had this coming for a long time.'

Still not sure what was going on, Shannon turned back to Franny. 'What do you want me to do then?'

'I want you to listen very carefully to what Emma is going to say. Can you do that?'

As Shannon was about to answer, the wave of nausea suddenly got the better of her, and she vomited the contents of her stomach all over the floor.

Half an hour and several glasses of water later, Shannon had been told what she was expected to do. She looked at Franny and shook her head. 'I can't do what you want, I can't.'

'Shannon, you can because, simply put, you've got no choice.'

'But . . .'

Franny stared at her as Shannon trailed off. She spoke over the noise of the visitors' room, which was filled with young children playing and screaming, letting off steam. 'But nothing. Save it, I ain't interested. When it's done, then you get in contact straight away. No delays.'

'Why are you doing this to me?'

Franny leant across the table. 'Shan, stop whining, stop feeling sorry for yourself. You're free, you're not the one in prison.'

Shannon burst into tears. 'You have no idea what I am. You have no idea how sometimes it feels exactly like that.'

Franny stared at her strangely. 'What are you talking about?'

Thinking of Uncle Charlie, Shannon shook her head. 'It doesn't matter. I don't want to do this. I just want to be left alone.'

Glancing at Emma, Franny pulled a face. She spoke in a softer tone. 'You love Vaughn, right? Well just do it for him.'

Shannon raised her eyebrows, but she didn't say anything, choosing to let Franny continue to talk.

'That's all you have to do: think of Vaughn. It'll make it easier for you and, at the end of the day, Shan, you've been doing this most of your life.'

Rubbing her eyes and looking young and vulnerable, Shannon whimpered. 'But I never wanted this life, and this isn't fair.'

Losing patience, Franny shook her head. 'Fair doesn't come into it. Do you think that it's fair I'm stuck in this frigging place? Do you think it's fair that I'm looking at life inside if this ain't sorted? So, don't play the fucking victim, Shan. We've all got our problems and you did this to yourself.'

Wringing her hands in her lap, Shannon shrugged. 'I only did what I thought was right.'

'Right for you and right for Vaughn. Let's be honest, you wanted to get me out of the way from the beginning. You were jealous, and you were happy to go along with Vaughn's plan, so now you're going to go along with mine.'

Emma nodded. 'Just make sure that you follow everything I've told you. That way you can't go wrong.'

Almost in unison Franny and Emma stood up and as Franny stared down at Shannon she said, 'And keep your mouth shut, Shan. I don't want anyone knowing what we're going to do. This is between us . . . Remember: mess this up and you'll be very, very sorry.'

58

That same morning Detective Balantyne walked into the hospital room and looked around. He pulled a face at the empty bed before he went across to the locker to check for Claire's things. They were gone. All of them.

He was surprised that she hadn't called him to let him know that she was changing rooms. Sighing he walked into the corridor and gestured to one of the nurses who'd been looking after Claire. He smiled. 'Hi, could you tell me what room Claire Martin has been transferred to?'

'Oh, didn't you know? She's gone home. She discharged herself.'

Breathing hard, Balantyne's stare was full of hostility. Angrily he spoke through his teeth. 'If I'd fucking known then I wouldn't have had to ask, would I?' And with that, Balantyne turned on his heel and headed for the exit.

* * *

'Claire? Claire?' Balantyne walked into Claire's flat using the key he'd never given back. As usual it smelt of fresh laundry and lavender.

He wandered through the flat, poking his head around the door of the bedroom and then, not finding her there, the kitchen.

'Claire? Claire, it's me. Where are you?'

He walked into the bathroom and saw that Claire was in the bath, fast asleep. He sat on the edge of the bath and looked at her as she lay motionless, apart from her chest, which silently rose and fell.

Putting his hand into the water, he spoke. 'Claire?'

Claire jumped up with fright, splashing the bath water all over the sparkly floor tiles. She put her hand on her chest and closed her eyes for a moment, breathing out slowly. Then she opened them and, in an irritated tone, said, 'Jesus Tony, you gave me a fright . . . Anyway, how did you get in?'

'You gave me a key, remember?'

Claire frowned. 'That was four years ago, and a lot has changed since then.'

Balantyne shrugged. 'Well, it came in handy anyway.'

Not feeling fully comfortable, Claire hugged her knees. 'What do you want, Tony?'

'What do I want? Now that isn't very nice, is it?'

Claire smiled but for some reason she started to feel frightened. 'I'm sorry, I didn't mean it like that . . . Look, could we do this tomorrow? I'm a bit tired.'

It was Tony's turn to smile. He stroked her head, staring at the long operation scar. 'They told me that you'd discharged yourself. Was that sensible?'

'It's only a couple of days early. They said that they were going to release me by the end of the week anyway. They said I was doing well. Of course, I won't be going back to work for a while, but what's the point in taking up a hospital bed when I don't need one?'

Balantyne spoke tightly. 'Why indeed . . .' The room stayed silent until Balantyne spoke again. 'You seem tense, Claire.'

Claire stared at Balantyne. 'Do you mind passing me a towel? I want to get out now.'

Balantyne turned to look at the towel hanging on the rail but he didn't move.

'Tony, *please*, the towel.'

Ignoring her request Balantyne placed his hand in the water. 'Why did you call Officer Gibbs to come and see you?'

'I . . . I just wanted to talk to him.'

A dark look came into Balantyne's eyes. 'But what I don't understand is why. Why would you want to mess everything up when it was all going to plan?'

'That's not what I was doing.'

Breathing heavily as his anger surged around his body, Balantyne growled, his face turning red. 'But that's exactly what you were doing. You betrayed me, Claire, and I don't take that lightly.'

'Tony, please, how can you say that?'

'Why didn't you tell me you were discharging yourself? Were you trying to get away from me? Were you trying to avoid me?'

Beginning to shiver, Claire shook her head. 'Don't be

silly, of course not,' she said, not sounding or looking very sincere.

Balantyne narrowed his eyes. 'What are you hiding?'

Claire shook her head. 'Nothing.'

'Claire, I know you too well. I can always tell when you're keeping something from me.'

Without saying anything, Claire stared at Balantyne. She put her head down and then eventually she quietly said, 'I know.'

Puzzled, Balantyne asked, 'You know what?'

'I know that it was you who was driving the car. It wasn't Emma at all, was it? I remembered everything; it all came back to me.'

Like Claire had done, Balantyne stayed silent for a moment until he said, 'And I suppose you're going to report this? Or have you done that already?'

Claire's voice was gentle. 'No, I haven't but I will. You know I have to.'

Balantyne nodded sadly. 'It was good whilst it lasted, you and me. We didn't really have a chance, did we? But I suppose you have to do what you have to do, like I do.' And with that Balantyne grabbed Claire and pushed her under the water.

She splashed about, her legs and arms flailing, struggling as she fought for her life. She tried to scream but each time she managed to come up for air, Balantyne pushed her down under again.

Managing a few words, Claire, panicked and terrified, yelled, 'Stop, I'm pregnant, you know I'm pregnant. What about the baby, Tony, what about the baby?'

But Balantyne continued to push Claire under the water and as Claire began to run out of strength, he gently placed his hands on her face and pushed; watching her slip further down into the bath. Then he pushed again, only this time a little bit harder, watching her mouth fill with water and staring fixedly into her eyes, which were wide open with panic and fear.

After a couple of minutes, Claire's body had stopped fighting and Balantyne sat with her in the quiet of the bathroom for a minute, before dragging her limp body towards him and kissing her gently on her lips. Wanting to make it look like an accident, he then pulled her completely out of the water and threw her back as hard as he could against the tiles behind the bath, hearing the crack of her skull as he watched her slip back down under the water.

He stood back and studied the scene, nodding in satisfaction. Anyone who saw this would imagine that Claire had slipped against the tiles and fallen back into the water when she'd been trying to get out.

Suddenly his phone rang, and he jumped. Pulling it out of his pocket, Balantyne saw it was caller withheld. 'Hello?'

'Is that Detective Balantyne?'

Watching the blood mix with the bath water, Balantyne tried to sound as neutral as possible. 'Yes, who's this?'

'It's Shannon. I need to speak to you.'

'How did you get my number?'

Hesitating for a moment, Shannon said, 'They . . . they gave me it when I called your office.'

Thinking that he'd have to have a word with his office about that, Balantyne asked, 'What's going on?'

345

'I just need to talk.'

'Where are you now, Shannon?'

'I'm at your house.'

Confused, Balantyne snapped, 'What the hell are you doing there and . . . and how do you know where I live?'

Lying again, Shannon said, 'I followed you here the other night. I'm afraid to come to the station in case anyone sees me.'

'You do realise that this is highly inappropriate?'

'I know, but I've been needing to speak to you for a while and I didn't know what else to do. You see, I've changed my mind. I'm afraid of what Franny will do to me if she finds out I've been helping you. I ain't Vaughn. He'll be all right, he can look after himself, but I can't . . . I'm sorry, Detective, I can't go through with it. I need to retract my statement.'

With his heart beating faster, Balantyne gave one more emotionless glance to Claire before he stormed out of the bathroom. There was no way he was going to let Doyle slip through the net, no way was he going to let her get away with it this time. He was going to bring Doyle down if it was the last thing he did. 'Listen to me, Shannon, stay where you are. I'm coming. I'll be there in just under an hour.'

And as Balantyne clicked off the phone, on the other side of London, Shannon closed her eyes, letting out a long sigh at what she was about to do.

59

It was over an hour before Balantyne showed up at his house, having been caught up in traffic on the North Circular, and, annoyed, he pulled up into his drive and turned the engine off. He squinted into the darkness looking to see if he could spot Shannon, hoping that she hadn't got fed up of waiting.

He needed to stop her doing anything stupid. The whole case was based on circumstantial evidence apart from her and Vaughn's statements and if he didn't have that he doubted he had a case.

A loud banging on the back window of his car made him jump for the second time that night. 'Fuck! Fuck! Fuck!' He turned around to see Shannon peering through the window and he furiously opened the driver's door.

'Did you have to do that?'

'I'm sorry, it's just that I've been waiting around for you for ages, and I'm cold and desperate for a wee.'

Sighing, Balantyne nodded and headed for his front door. Unlocking it and gesturing to Shannon to come inside, he pointed. 'First door on the right.'

Without saying a word, Shannon went to the bathroom. Balantyne threw down his coat and walked through to the dining room, pouring himself a large drink and refusing to think about Claire, knowing that if he did he'd be angry with her for what she had done; for her betrayal, for her pushing him to do something he hadn't wanted to do.

By her actions she'd made him not only lose her, but also lose his baby. His child, she was pregnant with his child, and her selfish actions had caused him to lose them both.

With that thought he slammed his drink down on the table just as Shannon came in.

'Are you all right, Detective?'

Balantyne rubbed his temples. 'I'm fine. Look, this talk about you not going ahead with your evidence needs to stop. I mean why now, Shannon? Why back out now? You knew what Ms Doyle was like when you gave your original statement . . . Talk to me, let's see if we can get this sorted.'

Shannon nodded. 'Do you mind if I have a drink first?'

Balantyne shrugged. 'Yeah, of course. Whiskey? Gin? Brandy?'

'Can I just have some water please?'

'Sure, no problem.' He gave a tense smile as he walked out of the dining room into the kitchen, giving Shannon the opportunity she was waiting for. She ran across to the glass that Balantyne was using and out of her pocket she undid the wrap of crushed Rohypnol, which Franny had arranged for her to pick up from one of her contacts.

'Do you want ice, Shannon?' Balantyne called from the kitchen whilst Shannon quickly dipped her finger into the whiskey, stirring it around and making sure the powdered tablet was dissolved.

'That would be nice, thanks.'

With her heart racing, Shannon placed the glass back on the table and back ran across to her chair. She called to Balantyne, hoping to slow him down as she watched his drink gradually stop swirling around after she'd stirred it. 'Actually, scrap that. No ice, thanks.'

Calling again from the kitchen, Balantyne said, 'Okay, no problem!'

A couple of minutes later he appeared at the door with the glass of water and Shannon reached out for it.

'You're shaking, Shannon.'

'I know, I think it's cos I got cold, I'm not feeling too great.'

Balantyne went across to his glass of whiskey and Shannon stared, holding her breath as he began to drink it. As long as the Rohypnol was dissolved properly then she knew he wouldn't be able to taste it.

She could almost hear her own breathing as she sat tense and anxious as he finished it off and then stared at the bottom of his glass. Terrified there was still some remaining powder that he'd be able to spot, Shannon tried to distract him. 'Maybe this is a bad idea. I shouldn't have come. I'm going to get off.'

Balantyne looked up at her. 'No, please, wait. Sorry, I've got my mind on other things . . .' He put the empty glass on the side and then smiled. 'Look, I'm all yours now. So come on, talk to me. Tell how I can make things better for you. How can I reassure you that everything's going to be fine?'

Shannon gave a weak smile back then began to talk, waiting and watching for the drug to kick in.

Twenty minutes later Shannon was still talking to Balantyne. 'So, of course Vaughn says he'll look after me, but what if he doesn't? What if he decides to ditch me? What then? Franny will be able to come after me.'

Feeling woozy and not understanding why, Balantyne rubbed his eyes. He spoke but his words were becoming slurred. 'Sorry, Shannon, what did you say?'

'I said, I'm worried about Franny.'

'What? Sorry, I'm not following you.'

Shannon stared at Balantyne intensely. She could see the Rohypnol was beginning to kick in: his eyes were starting to roll and he could hardly respond to what she was saying. Cautiously she got up and walked towards him. 'Are you all right, Detective?'

Balantyne tried to answer but the room was spinning and he couldn't quite remember why he was there. He couldn't remember what he was talking about. Where was he?

'You look tired, shall I help you upstairs?'

There was no real reply from Balantyne – only a grunt – and Shannon quickly helped him to his feet. She didn't want him to black out completely before she got him upstairs. Putting his arm over her shoulder, Shannon stood him up and led him towards the stairs, remembering where Emma had told her their bedroom was.

60

Shannon stared at Balantyne as he lay on the bed in his room. Occasionally he let out a grunt and his eyes kept flickering open, but his breathing was heavy and she could see he was well and truly out of it.

Letting out a sigh and loathing every moment, Shannon began to undress him with shaking hands; first taking off his shirt, then his trousers before finally she took off his pants.

She shuddered at his nakedness and in the cream and peach bedroom she walked over to the dressing table, which was opposite, and placed her phone on the side, pointing it at the bed as she set up the self-timer camera.

Slowly and hating Franny and hating Charlie and hating herself and hating having to do it, Shannon unbuttoned her top and began undressing herself out of the camera's viewpoint. Then, closing her eyes for a moment, she let out another long sigh and walked across and got up on the bed.

Following Franny's instructions she bent down and kissed Balantyne on his lips, making it look real, making it look like Balantyne was participating in the whole affair, getting the photos that Franny had told her to.

And as Shannon continued to do what Franny had told her to, she turned her face from the camera, not wanting it to capture her tears.

The early morning sun was just beginning to rise and Franny lay on her bed staring at the photos that had just beeped in on her phone. 'Hey, wake up, sleepy head . . . look at this.'

Yawning and seeing Jessie gently snoring on the top bunk, Emma got up and walked across to where Franny was lying.

Getting on the bed to lie next to Franny, Emma stared at the phone screen at the photographs. 'Oh my God, you're a genius.'

Franny turned her head to look at Emma and nodded. 'They're pretty good, aren't they? Really clear. It looks real; you'd think they were a proper couple. And when he wakes up, he won't even know it happened. The Rohypnol will wipe away his memory and he won't remember a thing. He might not even recall Shannon arranging to meet him, so he'll get a shock when they see these photos. The shit will hit the fan. He won't be able to wriggle out of it . . . There's no escaping from the fact that that's Detective Balantyne's dick!'

Emma burst into laughter, but then her face became serious. 'I hate him and he had this coming – I want to see him punished – but I'm worried about Shannon. Will she be all right? I mean, they're pretty explicit, aren't they, and well my husband is hardly a catch for a young girl.'

Franny's tone hardened. 'She'll be fine. It's what she does, and let's face it, I ain't going to start feeling sorry for her seeing it was her who put me in here in the first place, am I? She had a choice.'

Emma sounded doubtful. 'Did she? From what you've told me about her, it doesn't sound like she's ever had one in her life.'

Franny shrugged, knowing that she couldn't start being sentimental and not even sure if she was capable of it anymore in any case. 'Don't pity her too much, Em. She gets what she wants now.'

'What's that?'

Franny yawned. 'Well, I ain't going to say anything to Vaughn. Mia's safe so I don't need to mess with her life anymore. She's done what I told her to, so she can do her happy ever after with him, for now anyway . . . For all I am, Em, I keep my word.'

Emma gave a small smile. 'So what's going to happen now?'

Franny let out a long sigh of relief and for the first time since being locked up, she allowed herself to have a bit of hope. 'Now? Well I'm going to send these to my solicitor and hopefully I'll be walking out of here pretty soon. Your husband sleeping with one of the people who gave evidence against me compromises the whole case. Once my solicitor gets these in front of the CPS, I'm bound to be able to get bail sooner rather than later, and more than likely the whole case will collapse.'

'I'll miss you.'

Franny lay on her side as she looked at Emma. 'What do you mean?'

'When you leave here. I know you said that we're not friends, but you're the nearest person to a friend I've had in a long time.'

Suddenly embarrassed, Franny smiled. 'Thank you, Em, and you know I couldn't have done this without your help. Not like this anyway. And I'm sure that it won't be too long before you get out. These photos will help you too.'

'I doubt it, Fran. It won't change the fact that he says it was me driving.' She fell silent as she watched Franny ping the photos through to her solicitor.

'Is that it then? Is it all done?'

Surprising herself, Franny placed a gentle kiss on Emma's lips, and then she shook her head. 'Oh no, Em, it's only just begun.'

61

Exhausted, Shannon made her way into Vaughn's flat. She was tired and worried because it was only a matter of time before Balantyne realised what she'd done. She knew the Rohypnol would stop him remembering anything but – although she wasn't sure *how* Franny was going to use the photographs – she knew that he would see them eventually. And when he did, she was scared what he might do.

And if Vaughn saw them, which she knew in her heart he would, she was afraid that he might think that she didn't care about him anymore and that she was just some cheap tart. But perhaps, if she stuck to the story Franny had told her to – that Balantyne forced her, gave her no choice, took advantage of her – Vaughn wouldn't think the worst of her.

And then there was her uncle to think of. She was sure that the smell of his body would be beginning to creep into the flat, and terrified and taking a deep breath, she opened the door but was surprised to be greeted by Vaughn.

Vaughn smiled at her; in truth he was relieved to see her after the other night. He'd felt bad and he'd talked over the situation with one of the women in the club, explaining about the feelings that Shannon had for him and how uncomfortable that had made him.

And boy, she'd put him straight. Told him that he was being an idiot, a fool, and that he should treat her with kindness, be himself and not try to push her away, because the last thing she needed in her life was somebody else rejecting her and being cruel.

'Hey, Shan, how are you, baby?'

Shannon looked at Vaughn strangely. He'd been so cold with her the other night yet here he was smiling at her and being so friendly. It just made her feel worse about everything she'd done: about the crack, about Charlie, about Franny, about Balantyne. Before she could say anything, she burst into tears.

'Oh fuck, Shan, come here, darlin'. I've been a right wanker, ain't I? Will you ever forgive me? Shan, I'm so sorry.'

Crying hysterically, Shannon sobbed as Vaughn held her in a tight embrace. 'I hate my life, I hate it.'

'Oh Jesus, don't say that, girl. I can't bear it. I've let you down, ain't I?'

Shannon shook her head. 'It's me who's let you down. If only you knew.'

'Knew what, baby?'

Again, Shannon just shook her head. 'I wish I could say.'

Vaughn pulled away from Shannon and gently lifted her head up towards him. Gazing at her now he was shocked to see how terrible she looked. Maybe she was feeling guilty over the money she'd taken. Not that he gave a damn about that anymore – all that mattered was that she was safe and cared for, something he didn't think he was doing very well of late.

'Whatever it is, you can tell me. But there ain't any rush . . . Anyway, I had an idea when you were out. How about you and I get away for a bit? Go on a little holiday. There's a lovely hotel in Scotland I know; top notch, it's up by Loch Ness. Who knows, maybe we'll spot a monster. What do you say?'

Shannon was not sure what to say because she never could've imagined that she'd ever have a moment in her life like this. She never could've imagined that she would go on holiday, let alone have anyone ask her, let alone it be the person she loved. And then she smiled, a huge wide smile, displaying the few teeth that Charlie hadn't knocked out or the crack hadn't caused to drop out.

Vaughn laughed, delighted at the happiness in her face. 'I take that as a yes then. So go on, pack your bags, get all your gear together.'

Shannon's face dropped. 'I have to pack a bag?'

Vaughn looked at her oddly. 'Yes, you've got to take some clothes. Shan, what's wrong?'

'I just don't think I need any.'

Vaughn frowned. 'Shan, everyone needs a change of clothes. I don't understand. Do you want me to help you pack, is that it?'

Shannon walked down the hallway and turned and stared at her bedroom door. She began to shake. Fear rushed through her body. She didn't want to go in there. She couldn't go in there. She couldn't go and see Charlie lying there, rotting, smelling, decomposing. She'd tried to push it out of her head; she'd tried to pretend to herself it hadn't happened. That's why she'd hit the crack so hard, but who was she kidding? Everything was falling apart.

'Do you not want to go? You don't have to. If you'd rather stay here, we can go on holiday another time.'

Shannon shook her head. Her voice was breathless. 'No, no I want to go . . . I'm just so shocked you'd do this for me. Sorry . . . Of course, I need clothes.'

Vaughn grinned. 'Well go on then, go and pack! Oh and, Shan, we're only going for a week so you don't have to pack the kitchen sink. I know what you girls are like!'

And at that point Vaughn walked to his bedroom, leaving Shannon to walk down the hallway to her room.

At the door, she pulled out the key, which she always kept in the back of her mobile phone case. Shaking she put it into the lock and slowly, slowly, she opened the door and, trembling so much her legs were weak, Shannon took a deep breath, preparing herself for what she was going to find.

As she stepped inside her room, she was surprised that the smell of Charlie's body hadn't hit her yet, but even more surprised to find his body not there.

She stared, puzzled, *afraid*, and she tiptoed forward. Suddenly she felt a hand slamming over her mouth. 'Boo! Hello, Shannon, have you missed me?'

She screamed but no noise came out as Charlie held her mouth shut. He cackled, biting at her ear and whispering, 'Oh yeah, you thought I was dead didn't you? Well, hate to disappoint you because I'm still here. Now I'm going to take my hand off your mouth and if you want to scream, go ahead, but then Vaughn's going to hear you and it's over.'

As Charlie released his hand, Shannon, hurt and shocked, shook her head. Her eyes were wide open in pain. 'How could you do this to me? How could you do this, Uncle Charlie? Why do you hate me so much, what did I ever do to you? You're sick. I was so scared. I thought I'd killed you, and now I wish I had! I wish you were dead.'

He grabbed hold of her hair, yanking it as hard as he could and pulling her towards the bed, throwing her on it. 'You really thought you could get away from me, didn't you?'

She moved up the bed away from him. 'Please don't do this! Please!'

Charlie's eyes darkened. 'Then scream, bitch. Go on, scream – I dare you!'

Shannon looked at the door and then opened her mouth but nothing came out and Charlie laughed, climbing up on the bed towards her. He pushed her down, ripping off her clothes. 'You can't do it, can you, Shan? You can't even call for help, and you know why? It's because you want me really, don't you? This is what you want.'

Being crushed by Charlie's weight Shannon shook her head as Charlie's face nuzzled into her neck. 'I don't want it! I hate you, I hate you!'

He ripped off her knickers and threw them to the side,

360

and she lay naked underneath his own naked body. 'This is all you're good for, Shan, you know that? Come on, give me a kiss.'

But before Shannon could say another word she heard a loud banging on the front door. *'Open up! Police! Open up!'*

The next thing she heard was the front door being kicked open.

62

The police charged along the corridor, running into every room, knocking Vaughn out of the way, racing into his bedroom and kitchen and lounge as they tore up the apartment, searching.

Stunned, Vaughn yelled at the top of his voice. 'What the fuck are you doing?'

A tall officer raced into the flat, flashing the search warrant at Vaughn as he stormed past him. 'We've had information that there's an illegal weapon in the house, as well as items that are linked to a crime.'

As Vaughn went to speak to him, dozens more police started searching the flat, and Vaughn watched on as two officers with dogs suddenly smashed down Shannon's door. They froze, and, unsure what they were looking at, Vaughn ran along the hallway to see for himself.

Horrified, he stared in disgust at the sight in front of

him. Charlie and Shannon naked in bed together. He could hardly get out the words. 'What the *fuck* is going on?'

With Charlie getting off her, Shannon was able to scramble off the bed. 'I can explain, I can explain. Please let me explain.'

As the police officers stood back, Vaughn stepped into the room. He stared at her. 'Put some fucking clothes on.'

Grabbing a pair of jeans and top from the floor, Shannon pulled them on as her words tumbled out. 'It's not what it looks like. It's not. It's not.'

With his face twisted, Vaughn snarled, 'What it looks like is you're fucking your uncle in my bedroom, in my flat!'

With a smirk on his face, Charlie shrugged. 'He's got a point, Shan.'

Vaughn charged at Charlie, pushing him back, knocking him over. 'If it wasn't for the fact there's a dozen or more coppers next door I'd kill you. Now get the fuck out of my house and if I do ever see you again, I will kill you . . . And that goes for you too, Shannon, get the fuck out!'

Vaughn screamed his words as Shannon ran up to Vaughn clinging on to him. 'Please, please don't do this, I wanted to tell you, I swear I did.'

'Tell me what, Shan? That you two have been shacked up right underneath my nose? It all makes sense now. It all fucking makes sense. That's why you wanted the door shut wasn't it? And like a mug I believed it was because you wanted your privacy, when all you really wanted to do was fuck your uncle. Get out! Get out before I do you some damage.'

As Vaughn raged, Charlie took advantage of the distraction and furtively picked up the bag of Bree's items, slipping them through the slightly opened window down to the gardens below. He smiled to himself. Who knew when they may come in handy? Who knew when somebody or other might pay good money to get them back? And, pleased with himself, he smirked as he watched the tears stream down Shannon's face as she pleaded with Vaughn.

'Please, you've got to listen to me, I didn't know how to tell you. I thought if I told you I'd lose you.'

'Well you've done a good job of losing me on your own.'

Shannon held her head, putting her hands across her ears. She screamed, 'Don't say that, please don't say that! He wouldn't go, he wouldn't go. I tried everything to make him go and he wouldn't.'

Charlie chipped in. 'She's lying. She invited me to stay. She's fed me, bathed me . . . pleasured me. It's been like home from home.'

Vaughn, raging with anger and disgust, spun around to look at Shannon. 'What is this, Shan? Is it fucking true?'

'No, not really, I mean, no . . . I mean . . . He wouldn't go and I had to look after him, I had to otherwise he said he'd tell you. He said he'd ruin everything. I had to look after him.'

'NO, YOU DIDN'T!' Vaughn's bellow seemed to fill the whole room.

'I was so scared of losing you. I was so scared you wouldn't believe me.'

Watched by the officers still, Vaughn laughed scornfully. 'Well you're right about that – I don't believe you . . . because you know what I think? I think that this was one sick game; you and him.'

Racked with sobs, Shannon shook her head furiously. 'It wasn't! It wasn't.'

Before Vaughn could answer, Charlie, having finally put some clothes on, headed for the door, chuckling to himself. 'Well it was nice whilst it lasted. Thanks for the hospitality, Vaughn. I'll make sure I give you a good review on Airbnb.'

Out of the sight of the officers, an enraged Vaughn pushed Charlie into the wall, twisting his arm behind his back. 'Say one more word, Charlie, and I'm going to snap this arm out of your shoulder, do you understand?'

Knowing at this point, it wasn't worth *literally* chancing his arm, Charlie nodded. Vaughn released him and he slunk out of the room, leaving Shannon and Vaughn alone.

'Now you get out as well.'

Again, Shannon shook her head. 'I can't. I can't leave you.'

'Then let me help you.' And with that Vaughn began to drag a screaming Shannon along the corridor, not caring that there was a roomful of police watching on.

He opened the front door to where Charlie was being detained and talking to a police officer. 'Now get out. Go! Go on, Shannon, get out of my fucking sight.'

'I'm sorry.'

'Out.'

'I'm so sorry.'

'I said out.'

'I love you.'

He ran at her. A mixture of rage and disgust and hurt

rushed through him. 'You don't know what love is! You're sick; you're twisted. Now go! I said *go*!'

Shannon dropped to her knees. 'Please, please, please, don't make me go, don't! Please, you're the only person I've ever loved . . . I lied for you, I lied for you and I did it because I loved you. Don't you understand?'

Vaughn dragged her up from the floor. 'No, I don't understand. I don't understand how you've done what you've done.'

'I've got nowhere to go! I've got nowhere to go!'

A flicker of empathy ran through Vaughn's eyes but it was soon replaced by more seething anger. 'I don't care, you hear me, Shannon? As long as I never see you again, I don't fucking care.'

And with that, Vaughn grabbed her, throwing her into the corridor to join Charlie before slamming the front door in her face.

63

'What do you mean they didn't find anything?' That same evening Franny spoke on her phone in her cell to Alfie.

'I just told you, they couldn't find anything in the flat.'

Franny paced about as Jessie and Emma looked on. 'Then what went fucking wrong?'

'I don't know. I spoke to my source and he said that they searched the place, every inch of the place and they went away with nothing.'

Franny kicked the wall, staring out of her cell window. 'Then you must have hidden it too well . . . if you hid the stuff at all, that is.'

Fuming, Alfie growled down the phone, 'I did *exactly* what you said. I tipped the police off that he had a gun and that there was stuff they'd be interested in.'

'You mean Bree's stuff.'

'Yes, Fran, that's exactly what I mean and you know it

is. I put them in the bottom of the couch and apparently they looked there but like I say they found nothing. I don't understand it, but then I also don't understand how calling the coppers makes me any better than what Vaughn did to you.'

Trying to hold herself together, Franny snarled, 'How can you even compare the two? It's totally different. He had this coming or he would've done if you hadn't fucked up.'

Standing in his kitchen, Alfie gazed out of his window. 'How many times do I have to tell you I didn't fuck up? Maybe Shannon found it.'

'And why would Shannon be looking under a fucking couch? And besides, she's been busy doing something for me.'

'I told you to leave her alone. She's just a kid. If I find out you've been making her part of your game, I'll—'

Franny interrupted. 'You'll what? You'll sacrifice your own life for her? You'll be happy for Huang to kill you for Shannon? Because don't forget I still need to pay him, and the way this is going, that ain't going to happen – and if you threaten me, Alfie, it's definitely not going to happen. So go on, is it what you want? Are you going to sacrifice yourself for her?'

Alfie walked through and stared at a sleeping Mia, and he knew it wasn't an option. It pained him that he couldn't tell Franny yes, and it hurt him more to know that Shannon didn't have anybody in her life who would sacrifice anything for her.

Feeling emotional, Alfie whispered his reply. 'No, I'm not.'

'I thought as much . . . Look, I can hear someone coming. I'll speak to you later.'

As Franny hid the phone in her shoe, Officer Brown sauntered into the cell. 'Doyle.'

Franny looked up and stared at her in contempt. 'What the fuck do you want?'

Officer Brown walked up to Franny and stared at her. 'It's lucky for you that you're getting out today, otherwise you and me would have a problem.'

Franny blinked and a surge of emotion rushed through her. 'I'm getting out?'

Officer Brown pulled a face. 'Has this place made you deaf as well? I said you're going. Apparently your solicitor got an emergency bail hearing this morning. You've certainly got friends in the right places.'

A smile spread across Franny's face. Her solicitor must've got the photos of Balantyne and Shannon in front of the CPS quicker than she'd thought he would. More to the point it'd worked. And, smiling, she said, 'I bet it really bothers you, doesn't it? I bet it eats you up that I'm getting out.'

'If I knew you wouldn't be back, perhaps it would. But I'll see you again, Doyle. People like you always come back.'

'Not me.'

Officer Brown turned away and headed out. 'That's what they all say, Doyle. Now hurry up, we need to check you out.'

Franny turned to look at Jessie and Emma. Her excitement was palpable. 'It worked. It bloody worked! I can't believe the photos worked. It actually frigging worked.'

369

Jessie looked at Franny but there was sadness in her eyes. 'I'm pleased for you, Fran, I really am.'

Franny went to give her a hug. 'You'll be all right and if you're not, call me and let me know. Plus you've got Emma to look after you. You ain't alone now . . . Make sure when you get out you look me up. You hear me?'

Jessie nodded. 'Thank you, Fran, thank you for everything.'

Turning to Emma, Franny smiled. 'And as for you, I'm sure it won't be long till you get out of here. I've just got a feeling . . . Stay in touch, won't you? Good friends are hard to find and when I find one, I know how lucky I am.' She smiled again then gave Emma her hidden phone. 'Here, you might want this. I'll call you. Take care, babe, I'll see you on the other side.'

She began to walk away but Emma called her back.

'So what's the first thing you're going to do, Fran? You going to treat yourself?'

Franny turned and winked at Emma. 'Oh yes I'm going to treat myself all right. I'm going to buy myself a big, sweet box of revenge.'

64

'Why? Why did you do it?' The next morning Shannon stood at the door of Charlie's flat staring at him as he lay on his black leather couch eating a large packet of Maltesers.

He broke wind and stared at Shannon. 'What are you talking about?'

She ran up to him and standing above him she said, 'What am I talking about? Are you serious? Vaughn's thrown me out; it's over. The best thing that ever happened to me in my life is over. Do you hear that, Uncle Charlie?'

Charlie tutted. 'Well it's hard not to, seeing as you're shouting. Go and get me a tea will you?'

Shannon kicked the coffee table, knocking it spinning across the wooden floor. 'Get it your fucking self.'

Charlie's eyes narrowed. 'Oh that's how it's going to be is it?' He stood up and Shannon slightly backed off as he stepped forward. 'You're lucky I don't beat the shit out of you.'

'Well it wouldn't make any difference would it? I couldn't hurt more than I do already.'

'Stop the melodrama, Shan. You're back home now, where you belong. I knew you'd come crawling back.'

Shannon shook her head. Her eyes were tired from crying. 'This ain't my home. Any place where you are ain't home.'

Charlie leant into her face. 'It's the only home you've got, so I'd be grateful if I were you. Now go and make that fucking tea before I put my fist through your face . . . Oh, and seeing as you've been on a break for the past few months, I thought you could get straight back to work. I've arranged for some of your old punters to come and visit you tonight. It can be one big celebration, one happy family.'

Shannon began to shake. 'I ain't doing it.'

'Oh, Shan, you are. You ain't got any choice, darlin'.'

Screaming at him and backing towards the wall, Shannon pointed. 'I'm sick of people saying I ain't got a choice, because I wanted one. I wanted a choice. And my choice was to be happy. That's all. I didn't want money; I didn't want clothes. I only wanted to be happy. Ain't that supposed to be free? Cos it feels like I paid a price trying to get what other people have . . . Why couldn't you let me be happy? Why didn't you want to see me happy, Uncle Charlie?'

Charlie stared at her then slapped her hard across the face. 'I told you already, stop the dramatics.'

Shannon rubbed her face. 'Don't do that! I ain't your punching bag!'

Roaring with laughter, Charlie said, 'You're anything I want you to be.'

Choking back the pain and her words full of sadness, Shannon spoke quietly. 'Not anymore. I ain't doing this anymore. None of this had to happen, none of it . . . It never had to come to this . . . Now please, just let me go.'

He slammed her against the wall, putting his hand around her throat. 'You're not going anywhere. You're mine, Shan, mine to do what I want with. When will you understand that?'

Continuing to shake, Shannon looked at him as her tears blurred her vision. 'And when will *you* understand that's not how it's meant to be, Uncle Charlie? You've made your choice that this is how you want it to be and how you want to live your life, well now I'm going to tell you my choice . . . My choice is: it's over . . . It's over, Uncle Charlie.'

And with those words Shannon slipped the scissors out of her pocket and stabbed her uncle in his back, over and over again.

65

'Hello, Alfie.'

Alfie stood and gazed in shock at Franny standing at his front door.

'How . . . when . . . how the fuck did you get out?'

Franny smiled. 'Oh it's a long story.'

He grabbed her arm. 'A story I probably won't like. What have you done, Fran?'

Franny stared at him coolly. For all she was and for all she protected herself from being hurt, she could feel the disappointment of Alfie not being pleased to see her. But as she always did, as she was brought up to do, she turned her hurt into a cold, hard front.

'I want to see Mia.'

Alfie shook his head. 'No.'

Franny looked at him. 'Get out of the way, I want to see her.'

'You've done enough damage and I decide who she sees. After all, she is *my* daughter.'

Even though Franny thought she was protected from words, they hit her and for a moment they took her breath away. Recovering slightly she said, 'I . . . I'm pleased you finally feel like that. That's good. Well, another time . . . I'll see her another time. And, Alfie, you know all this – all I've been doing – it's business, that's all it is, but when it comes to you and me . . . well, what I said about still being in love with you, it's true. I do. I still love you and I want to find a way back.'

Alfie stared at Franny, refusing to be drawn in. He knew her well enough to know she was hurting right now, and damn it, as much as he fought it and as much as she was more ruthless than he ever wanted her to be, he couldn't stop loving her either. But, as much as he also knew how much she loved Mia, he wasn't convinced Franny's kind of love was what he wanted around his daughter – or him.

He had a lot to think about, though with Huang still hanging over his head, now wasn't the best of times to work out what he wanted to do and what was right and what was wrong.

Sighing he said, 'What do you want, Fran? How many pounds of flesh do you need from me now?'

'This is the last thing I want.'

Alfie shrugged. 'And that is?'

'I'll pay your debt, but before I do, I want you to bring Vaughn to me on a plate. And this time you're not going to mess up.'

* * *

375

It was a couple of hours later and Franny had detoured along Kennington Road, near Elephant and Castle. She took a right turn and pulled up. Checking the time, she looked at her phone. She needed to be quick, but there was something she had to do.

Getting out of the car she hurried along the street, enjoying every moment of her freedom. Ducking into a shop, she picked up a packet of gum and walked to the counter. She smiled.

'I'll have that please . . . Oh yeah and I nearly forgot.' Out of her pocket she pulled a gun and pointed it at the man. She drew back the trigger and she watched the man's face pale as beads of sweat trickled down his face. As he put his hands up in the air, Franny saw that he had wet himself in fear.

She smiled again, getting the money out of her jeans to pay for the gum. 'So here's the thing: I came here to tell you, if you ever, ever touch, look at or speak to Jessie again, I will come back and blow your fucking head off.'

66

Shaking, Shannon stood opposite the police station in Agar Street in Covent Garden. It was a tall, cream building and she watched the police and pedestrians milling in and out. She didn't know how long she'd been standing there, and she didn't know how she'd got there in the first place. All she remembered was the blood on her hands – Charlie's blood. And unlike last time, this time she knew he was really dead.

She'd showered and changed and then the rest was all a blank. Everything seemed to be a blank, no matter how hard she tried to remember. She couldn't even recall walking out of the flat, but somehow she'd found herself standing here.

She blinked and then, trembling, Shannon began to cross the road towards the police station. She had to talk; she had to explain. Maybe if they understood why she'd done it they wouldn't make her go to prison.

* * *

'Shan? Shan, are you all right? Shannon, it's raining, you'll catch your death.' Alfie, who was having to take a detour because of the amount of traffic in Holborn, called over from his car as he suddenly spotted Shannon.

'Shannon! Hey, Shannon!'

Frowning, he watched her walk, looking like she was in a trance. Quickly he pulled up at the side of the road, unbuckling the seat belt of his Range Rover before running over to her.

'Shan! Shan, didn't you hear me?'

Shannon blinked and then looked at Alfie.

'Shannon, what's going on, didn't you hear me calling you? What are you doing here? Why're you going in there? Why are you going into a police station?' Alfie bombarded her with questions but she still didn't answer, and frustrated he grabbed her gently by the shoulders, bending down to look in her face. 'Shan, have you taken something? Are you on that shit again? Tell me. I can't help you if you don't tell me . . . Is this about Franny? Or is it about Vaughn?'

'I didn't mean to hurt him. I just wanted him to stop.'

Puzzled and worried about her, Alfie asked, 'Who, baby? Who did you hurt? Vaughn?'

She shook her head and Alfie, trying to put the pieces together, said, 'Is that why you're here? Because you hurt someone?'

Again Shannon didn't answer and again Alfie tried to figure out what was going on. 'Shan, please tell me, whatever it is, you can tell me.'

'It's Charlie.'

'Charlie? You hurt Charlie?'

'Yeah, and I need to tell someone.' She moved forward towards the station but Alfie grabbed her, pulling her to the side near the black railings.

'Listen, sweetheart, I don't know what exactly has happened, but I do know whatever it is, going to tell the Old Bill what you've done maybe isn't the best way to go.'

'But I need to explain. Maybe they'll understand.'

With his mind racing at all the possibilities of what she might have done, Alfie said, 'You're a good kid and a lot of bad things have happened to you, and I know the way you looked after Mia was loving and kind and I know that you've got a good heart. And I reckon that you'd only hurt someone if they hurt you, and I know that Charlie hurt you over and over again. I won't let you ruin your life for Charlie. He's done enough damage already. It should be him here, not you.'

Shannon suddenly burst into tears. 'But he can't, that's the point. He can't do anything anymore . . .'

And as Alfie was about to say something else, Shannon panicked and ran off into the rainy night.

67

Stumbling along and banging into all the passers-by, a scared and bewildered Shannon made her way through the familiar streets of Soho. The rain was getting heavier and she didn't know how long she'd been walking around – nothing felt real anymore and it seemed like she had a constant screaming in her head. She didn't know where to turn and she had nowhere to go.

She slowed down, then she found herself heading towards Gerrard Street – making her way, almost in a trance, down into the basement of Mr Huang's Chinese restaurant. She supposed it was where she belonged; turning tricks and smoking crack. Why she'd thought that she deserved a better, happier life, she didn't know. Why she'd thought that Vaughn could've loved her was a complete joke. Uncle Charlie had always told her she was nothing but a piece of trash, and at that moment Shannon Mulligan believed he'd been right.

It was late as Franny pulled up a few streets away from Balantyne's house. As she made her way along the road she could see his car parked on the driveway and, quickly checking behind her, she headed for the pink, wooden side gate, looking for the tall potted plant where Emma had told her that she kept a spare key.

Finding it exactly where it was supposed to be, Franny grabbed it and made her way to the front door. Then, as carefully and as quietly as she could, she unlocked it, stepping around the shoes and straight into the hallway of Balantyne's house.

Creeping along, Franny made her way up the stairs and as Emma had instructed her she took a right at the top of them and headed for the first door.

Opening it quietly, Franny tiptoed into the room with her gun at the ready. 'Hello, Tony. Going somewhere?'

Balantyne jumped, turning around from the suitcase he'd been packing. His face twisted in shock and then into rage at the sight of Franny. 'What the hell are you doing here?'

'I've come for you, Tony. Surely you were expecting me? You must've heard that they let me out. How did that feel, Tone? How did it feel to hear that I was out? I mean all that effort you went to in trying to nail me, for it to come to nothing.'

Balantyne's fury bubbled into his words. 'Get out of my house! Get out!'

Franny laughed as she continued to point the gun at

Balantyne. Then her voice dropped to a menacing tone. 'Is that the best you can do? Is that the only thing you can say to me? I ain't going anywhere, and neither are you, because we're going to have a little chat. I don't like people messing with my life and thinking they can get away with it.'

Not backing down from Franny, Balantyne stared at her. 'So what are you going to do, kill me?'

'I could, but what fun would that be? Cos once I put a bullet in your head, it's over, and I wouldn't be able to see you suffering. And that's what I want. I want to see you squirm.'

Balantyne stared at her. He hadn't known for certain that they were going to let her out – in fact they'd told him very little. But he knew that something was going on when he'd got an off-record call from a good friend, one of his colleagues at the station, giving him the heads up that they were going to bring him in for questioning.

His first thought was that they'd found Claire and made the connection, or even linked him with the killing of the security guard, but then his friend had gone on to tell him it was to do with a compromise in the Doyle case.

He hadn't known what it was, and his friend had been unwilling to share any more information, but the call had still made him feel uneasy. Made him feel paranoid, making him feel like it was only a matter of time before they did link him to the killings. And he wanted to get a head start, get out of the country, before they came looking for him.

'The thing is, Tone, I wanted to come and tell you myself,

or rather *show* you myself, how you helped me get out of prison.'

'What are you talking about?'

Franny walked across the room to where Balantyne was standing. She grinned and blew him a kiss. Her tone was dark and nasty. 'Thank you, Tony, I couldn't have done it without you. I mean, if I didn't think you were a lowlife piece of scum that I absolutely hate, I'd give you a hug. But hey, we can't have it all, can we?'

Anger surged through him. 'What the fuck are you talking about, you stupid bitch?'

Franny winked, pulling out of her pocket some printed photos before slamming them on the table. 'These . . . Take a look.'

In horror, Balantyne stared at the naked photo of himself with Shannon. For a moment he couldn't get his breath, his chest felt tight and his mouth went dry, making it hard for him to get out any words.

Franny narrowed her eyes as she glared at him. 'Shocked? You don't remember a thing, do you? It's amazing what Rohypnol can do.'

Balantyne's face screwed up. He trembled with rage. 'You bitch! You fucking bitch! You set me up.'

'That's what happens when you try to play games with me, Tony. You'll always lose, so what this is, is my big, sweet box of revenge.'

Unable to hold back any longer, Balantyne suddenly lunged at Franny, taking her by surprise and knocking her back into the wall. She stumbled and lost her grip on the gun, dropping it onto the floor.

Then scrambling for it at the same time as Balantyne, Franny reached forward but was dragged back by him grabbing hold of her hair.

He pulled her neck backwards before slamming her face into the floor. The pain rushed through her but she managed to twist her body around enough to send her elbow crunching into Balantyne's face. The cracking of his broken nose filled the air.

'Bitch!' Balantyne rolled over, clutching his bleeding nose, and, taking the opportunity, Franny crawled along the floor, clasping her fingers around the gun. But, as she did so, Balantyne, having now got himself together, jumped up and stamped down on her fingers, causing Franny to let go. She yelled out in pain but pushing on, she threw herself at his legs, knocking Balantyne down onto the ground where they began to grapple.

Then in the distance, Franny heard the sirens and as they became louder Balantyne, not wanting to wait to see if they were coming for him or not, suddenly let go of Franny and scrambled up, running for the door. In the doorway, he turned to look at her as he wiped the blood from his nose. 'This isn't over; it's far from over. I'm going to come after you. I'll be back, make no bones about that, Doyle, and when I come, you better start running.'

As she watched him race down the stairs and out of the house, she started making her own way out. But as she got up she noticed Balantyne had dropped something out of his pocket when they'd been fighting.

Quickly she bent down and picked it up and saw it was

an SD card. Frowning she slipped it into her pocket as she heard the sirens getting closer. The last thing she could afford was to be spotted here. The next moment, Franny began to run.

It was the early hours of the morning and, unable to sleep, Franny switched on her computer. She put the SD card in the slot and waited for the window to open, feeling curious. A moment later she found herself listening to two familiar voices. Tony and Emma Balantyne . . .

'I hate you! I hate you! How could you do this to me?'

'I said get off me! For fuck's sake, you crazy bitch!'

'Well if I am, it's you who's made me like this!'

'Oh yeah, it's so easy to blame isn't it, Em? Because if you do that then you don't have to look at yourself – and let me tell you it isn't a pretty sight. You're nothing but a drunk. Do you wonder why I ended up in bed with her? Do you wonder why I thought it was such a joke you wanted to start a family? Who wants a drunk for a mother?'

'Stop the car, Tony, stop the car! I want to get out. Let me out!'

At that point Franny pressed pause and she rewound the clip slightly to listen to Emma's last words again. *'Stop the car, Tony, stop the car! I want to get out. Let me out!'*

Franny smiled to herself. So Emma was telling the truth

after all. With that thought, Franny picked up the phone and dialled a number.

'Hey, Em, it's me. Guess what, I think I've just got your get out of jail free card.'

68

It was still early on Friday morning and Franny stood in the basement of the Chinese restaurant on the corner of Gerrard Street, speaking to Huang. 'This is the final piece in the jigsaw. I want this finished; I want it over. Alfie's arranged to meet Vaughn later at the warehouse in East Tilbury – it's the disused shipping site, you know the old motor factory by the river? And I want you to end it. Today.'

Huang nodded and stared over his glasses at Franny. 'Ms Doyle, have you forgotten the last conversation we had? You didn't want to pay what you owe me, but now you want me to do something for you.'

Franny stared hard at Huang. 'I paid you everything already. Two months ago, I paid you what Alfie owes you, plus the exorbitant interest you charge. So, I'd say I had a clean slate. I don't owe you *anything* else – you know that, and the fact that I didn't pay you for something that was never in the contract can't be held against me. In actual fact it's to my credit I didn't pay you any more money, otherwise you might see me as a pushover, and I'm far from that.'

A smile slowly appeared on Huang's face. 'It's true what they say about you, Ms Doyle. You really do have balls of steel, and for that I respect you.'

Franny continued to stand tall. Her voice was firm. 'I don't need your respect, I just need to know that you'll do what I'm asking you to.'

Huang tilted his head as he looked at Franny. 'As someone who has balls, why don't you do it yourself?'

'Because I'll be the obvious suspect. I need to keep my hands clean.'

'Ms Doyle, your hands are dirtier than mine.'

'Like I say, I can't be involved, so I need to know you'll do it.'

Huang looked up at the clock on the wall. 'What time did you say Mr Jennings was meeting him?'

'Not until much later. They're meeting at 5pm.'

Huang asked, 'Why at the warehouse?'

'Because Vaughn thinks it's neutral ground. They've met there before over the years – it's the perfect place to do business away from prying eyes and ears. And it's the perfect place for us to do what we need to.'

Huang went to sit down on the chair in front of a large table. 'Have you got the money?'

Franny pulled out a large envelope from her bag. 'Of course.'

She tipped the money onto the table. 'There's five

hundred thousand pounds there. I think I'd call it enough, wouldn't you?'

Huang stared at the money and then up at Franny. 'You certainly want him dead, Ms Doyle . . . But I don't see the rest of the money. What about the money you owe me for keeping my mouth shut with Mr Jennings?'

'We've just been over this. I paid you all that you're going to get.'

Huang smiled. He didn't say anything for a while and then he said, 'Okay, Ms Doyle, message heard loud and clear . . . Yes, we have a deal. I'll do your job, and there'll be no mistakes. And as of this moment, you can begin the countdown of the hours Mr Sadler has left on this earth.'

Ten minutes after Franny and Huang had left, Shannon sat up from behind the couch in Huang's basement. Having fallen asleep on the floor last night after smoking the crack she'd gotten from Huang in exchange for having sex with his poker-playing clients, she'd been disturbed by the sound of Franny and Huang's voices. And she'd heard everything.

A chill of fear ran through her. She'd thought she was frightened before, but this was different. She'd never felt this scared in her life and her fear wasn't for herself – it was for Vaughn.

She glanced around for a moment, peeking around the sofa, to check that no one was about. Then standing up, Shannon bolted for the door.

At the entrance of Vaughn's flats, Shannon pressed the buzzer. She held her finger down on it, and then, not getting a reply, she pressed the buzzers of the other flats, but again she wasn't let in. About to give up, Shannon saw one of Vaughn's neighbours coming out of the building and as they opened the door she rushed through.

Speeding along the corridor and not bothering to wait for the lift, Shannon raced up the stairs, running harder than she'd ever done in her life.

On Vaughn's landing she charged along to his front door, hammering on it loudly.

'Vaughn! Vaughn! Vaughn! Please, I need to speak to you! Vaughn!' There was no answer and Shannon, panicked, looked around.

From her jeans pocket she brought out the front door key that she still had. But putting it in the door, Shannon realised that Vaughn had changed the locks.

She pulled out her phone and dialled Vaughn's number, but it went straight to voicemail, and with that, Shannon started to run back out of the block of flats. Whatever she did, she needed to find Vaughn before it was too late . . .

69

Alfie sat in the car, heading towards the warehouse. It was still raining and his thoughts were bouncing between Shannon and Vaughn.

He was worried about Shannon and he couldn't help thinking that Franny was behind some of what had happened – but perhaps that was just him not trusting Franny. He didn't know what to think and, as usual, his head was a mess.

He'd really wanted to phone Shannon, but he wasn't sure what Franny had been saying to her or what was going on with the retraction of the statement. Jesus, he didn't even know how Franny had been allowed out of prison.

He was in the dark about the whole situation and it pissed him off. It felt like he was being played. But what choice did he have? If anything happened to him – if Franny didn't pay his debt – then Mia would have no one.

He'd tried to get in touch with Franny to ask her what exactly was happening with Vaughn, but his call had just gone to voicemail. The only thing he knew was he'd arranged to meet him at 5pm. But the problem was he didn't know for certain if Vaughn would show up or not.

He wasn't sure if Vaughn would be suspicious that they were going to meet at the warehouse. Not that they hadn't met there before; they had, on many occasions, when they'd needed to sort things out on neutral territory. But, knowing Vaughn as well as he did, he hadn't wanted to leave it to chance, so he'd left another message in addition to the original one about Shannon being in trouble.

He just hoped it would be enough to entice him to come. Because if it was, after that – after doing what Franny had ordered him to do – she would pay off Huang and he'd finally be a free man.

But, although it was cause for celebration, although being free of Huang was something he didn't think was possible, he couldn't help wondering why he had the sense something wasn't quite right.

With a sigh and a sinking feeling in his stomach, Alfie looked at the car clock and accelerated, heading towards the docks.

Twenty minutes later, Alfie turned left, driving along the uneven track that took him across the wasteland to the derelict warehouses. It was five to five and in the far distance he could just make out Vaughn's black Range Rover.

He parked up behind some old rusting oil drums, then

pulled out his phone, dialling Franny's number. Again it went to voicemail.

'Franny, for fuck's sake it's me. Where are you? I'm here already, up by the old moorings. I can see Vaughn's here, but I don't know what you want me to do. Do you want me to speak to him first, or do you want me to wait for you? Just call.'

Needing to stretch his legs, Alfie lit a cigarette and got out of the car, but he was surprised to see three more black Range Rovers heading his way. Apprehensively, he looked around, wondering what the hell was about to happen.

The cars pulled up in front of him, blocking his path, and he spun round and stepped backwards, cursing the fact he'd left his gun in the car.

The blacked-out window of the first car opened. 'Hello, Mr Jennings, it's good to see you again.'

Alfie's heart raced and he could feel the sweat beginning to run down his back. There was nowhere to run. There was nowhere to go.

Huang laughed. 'Don't look like that, we're not here for you . . . well, not really.'

Refusing to let panic overwhelm him, Alfie asked, 'Then why *are* you here? What game are you playing?'

'Not me, Mr Jennings, Ms Doyle. I'm here because of Ms Doyle.'

Alfie's gaze darted from Huang to his men. 'What are you talking about?'

Huang stepped out of the car as he spoke. 'Ms Doyle feels you can't be relied on, so she's recruited me to carry out my services.'

Alfie shook his head. 'No . . . no, you're lying.'

Laughing again Huang spoke quietly. 'Mr Jennings, ask yourself why I would lie. I mean, I'm here, aren't I? Ms Doyle wanted us to finish off a job. Extinguish the problem.'

'That wasn't the deal. No one said anything about killing Vaughn.'

Yawning, Huang stared at Alfie. 'No, Mr Jennings, no one said anything to *you*, which is an entirely different thing. Now, if you'll excuse us.'

Huang gestured to three of his men who came over. 'Make sure Mr Jennings is looked after.'

The tallest of the men grabbed hold of Alfie's arms and the other two held on to his body as he struggled. 'What the fuck are you doing? Get your fucking hands off me.'

He tried to fight but he was no match for the three of them as they began to tie his hands behind his back and his legs together. Alfie, panicking and afraid that any moment they were going to throw him into the river, glowered at Huang. 'Tell your dogs to get off me. You'll get your money, it's all been arranged. Franny's going to pay you; call her if you don't believe me.'

'Mr Jennings, I've already been paid. Two months ago in fact. Ms Doyle made sure of that. She wanted to keep you alive.'

The fight fell out of Alfie. His face dropped. 'What?'

'Oh yes, she needed you alive to make sure that you'd do her bidding. Rather clever I think, but sadly Ms Doyle neglected to pay me for keeping my mouth shut. But then that was her choice. I did give her every chance to rectify that situation.'

'I don't believe you,' Alfie growled, still in shock.

Huang shook his head. 'Not this again, Mr Jennings. I have no reason to lie, no reason whatsoever. Why do you think you're not dead? Did you think it was because I liked you?' He chuckled as he gazed at Alfie's shocked expression.

'But then if she'd paid you, why did you come and—'

'Give you a warning? Well, I had to make it look authentic, didn't I? Though I must say she was very cross with me when I did that to you. She wondered why I had to hurt you so much.'

To himself Alfie muttered, 'Fucking bitch.'

Huang smiled and said drily, 'My sentiments entirely.'

Alfie stared at Huang; hurt and angry by Franny, but most of all wanting payback. He would get payback. Oh God, he was going to get her all right. But this time there'd be no let-off, no second chances; this time Franny Doyle had dug her own grave.

As Alfie considered everything, Huang turned to his men and nodded and they proceeded to bundle Alfie into his own car, tying him tightly to the steering wheel.

'Don't worry, Mr Jennings, you won't be here long. Ms Doyle just wanted you out of the way. She wanted to make sure you didn't do anything stupid like warn Mr Sadler what we were going to do to him.'

Watching Huang's men get a briefcase and a huge rectangular bag out of his car, Alfie asked, 'And what's that? What are you going to do to him?'

Huang smiled as he put on a pair of black leather gloves. 'Oh, Mr Jennings, we're going to have fun . . . Lots of fun.'

70

Along the riverfront, the harsh chill of the air cut through Vaughn's clothing as he walked down the path of the warehouse, hearing the crunch of his feet on the stony gravel. Looking at his watch, he saw it was just gone five and he hurried through the long grass, making his way into the crumbling, derelict warehouse.

He pulled up his jacket, feeling the rain getting heavier, and wandered into the darkened warehouse he knew well. Over the years, he'd had meetings here, done drug deals here, got into fights here, bought and sold guns here, so it was the perfect place to get the mess with Alfie sorted or at least call a truce.

He walked along the abandoned corridors, which were strewn with rubbish; cans of beer and bottles discarded on the floor and broken glass and rusting metal sat along the floor. At the end of the corridor, which was pooled with water, Vaughn turned into the main area of the warehouse.

He shivered and pulled his jacket tighter around him. Behind him he heard a noise.

'Alfie? Alfie?' He walked forward, peering into the darkness but he heard no reply. 'Alfie?'

'Hello, Mr Sadler.' Huang stepped out of the darkness and Vaughn swivelled around to run, but as he turned, he saw a group of Huang's men blocking the entrance. He looked to the side and again, it was blocked by one of Huang's men.

With his heart racing he began to back away towards the wall as Huang walked closer to him, his footsteps echoing around the warehouse.

Vaughn screwed up his face. 'You fucking bastard, I've been set up.'

He turned to run again but he knew it was pointless, even before Huang said, 'There's nowhere to go, Mr Sadler, you're surrounded. There's no way out of here for you. This is it, Mr Sadler, this is your goodbye.'

As Huang talked, he walked towards the concrete stairs and a couple of Huang's men grabbed Vaughn, dragging him along behind.

On the next floor up, Huang strode towards the far end of another passageway and entered a large room. The wind had got up and was driving the rain through the smashed-out windows. Huang pointed to one of his men carrying the large rectangular bag.

'Put it over there.'

Vaughn, with his heart pounding, watched wide-eyed as

the man unzipped a collapsible, portable table from the bag and it took only a matter of seconds for Huang's henchman to unfold the aluminium legs and place it by the far end of the room.

Huang smiled, watching his men tie Vaughn to the table and, panicking, Vaughn blurted out his words. 'What are you going to do? What the fuck are you going to do?'

Before replying, Huang turned to his men. 'You can leave us now . . .' He then walked across to where Vaughn was tied and looked down on him. 'What am I going to do? Like I told Mr Jennings just now, I'm going to have lots of fun.'

Vaughn lay tied up on the bed with the ropes cutting into his wrists, making it hard for him to adjust himself and causing searing pain to shoot through his body every time he moved. He watched Huang open a black briefcase and take out a scalpel.

Vaughn could hear his own breathing as he watched Huang walk over to him holding the sharp, pointed blade in the air.

At the table, Huang held the ends of Vaughn's hair in between his fingers. 'I should warn you, Mr Sadler, this isn't going to be a swift execution. That's not what I was paid to do and I'm a man of my word.'

Huang smiled and placed the scalpel against Vaughn's face and with a swift movement, Huang slashed the blade up, cutting from the inner corner of Vaughn's mouth right into his cheekbone, the scalpel slicing the flesh with delicate aggression.

Vaughn screamed in agony as the pain stabbed through

him and Huang brought the scalpel down onto Vaughn's chest, dragging it along the skin, laughing as he did so. But suddenly Huang stopped and his eyes started to roll into the back of his head; he swayed on the spot before falling forward onto Vaughn and then sliding onto the hard concrete ground.

Vaughn, his face covered in blood, looked up and saw Shannon standing there. He glanced down at Huang and saw a knife stuck in the back of his head. Despite the excruciating pain, he spoke.

'Shannon! Shannon! What the fuck are you doing here?'

As she shook with fear, she whispered her words quickly and began to untie Vaughn. 'I heard Franny planning it, and I tried to warn you. But I couldn't find you and then . . .'

Vaughn glanced across to the door as he sat up, swinging his legs onto the floor. 'So you came to save me? You made your way here all by yourself?'

Shannon nodded.

'Oh Jesus Christ, Shan, I don't deserve you.'

'I've been so scared.'

'And so brave, but I always knew that, Shan . . . Look, we can't talk here. We've got to get out.'

'All of Huang's men are down by the front. I thought they were going to see me, so I ran around the back and came in that way. I found an entrance; there's a door just by the corner of this corridor. It leads out to the back. We can go back the way I came in.'

Vaughn nodded. 'I owe you, darlin' . . . and I'm sorry, I'm sorry for throwing you out. I fucked up, I let you down . . . Look, we'll talk later, but I did try to come and find you afterwards, I swear . . . Come on, we can't hang about.'

Shannon pulled back as she said, 'I need to tell you something first . . . I . . . I killed Charlie.'

Vaughn stopped in his tracks. 'What?'

Crying and staring at Huang's body, Shannon whispered, 'I killed Charlie. He just wouldn't leave me alone, I couldn't take it anymore.'

With his eyes still half on the door, Vaughn pulled Shannon into an embrace, covering her with blood. 'It should've been me who did that. I should've done that a long time ago.'

'What's going to happen to me?'

'Nothing, because I'm going to look after you. Nobody's going to hurt you or take you away, you hear me? But it's going to be a hard road – they'll be after us: Huang's men, the police, Franny, Alfie. They'll be looking for us. Can you handle that?'

Shannon nodded. 'I can face anything as long as it's with you.'

Spitting out a mouthful of blood, he kissed her on her head as he pulled her gently towards the door. 'Well let's hope you still think that when the walls come tumbling down and we have to lay low. But we'll be back, Shan, once we get ourselves sorted, we're coming back for payback from them all, because this is war . . .'

Acknowledgements

A big thank you to Avon books for your continual support, but especially to the fabulous two-band gang, Katie and Molly, who helped put this book together. Great thanks as well goes to Helena Newton, a fantastic copyeditor who keeps it all sharp. A great big shout out to Darley and his team who always have my back. And of course, to friends, family and readers alike: thank you so much.

Betrayal and lies come with consequences, and
old sins cast long shadows . . .

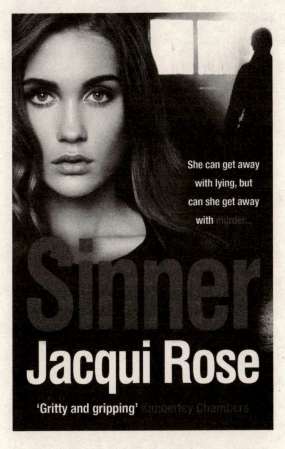

She can get away
with lying, but
can she get away
with murder...

Sinner
Jacqui Rose

'Gritty and gripping' Kimberley Chambers

Available in paperback and ebook.

An eye for an eye.
A tooth for a tooth.
A daughter for a daughter . . .

Available in paperback and ebook.

Bree Dwyer is desperate to escape her husband,
take the children and run. But he's always
watching. And she always gets caught.
Until now . . .

Available in paperback and ebook.